"The words of the Foolish and those of the Wise
Are not far apart in Discordian Eyes."
(HBT; The Book of Advice, 2:1)

WARNING

First of all, what you are about to read is a role-playing game. It's not real. You aren't going to be able to cast a fireball without the assistance of dangerous chemicals no matter how hard you try. So don't even bother. It's a waste of time and will only make you even more of a social outcast than you already are. Believe me.

Second, while some of the content of this book may have been influenced by real world events and some of the people may bear a striking resemblance to people you have heard about, read about, otherwise know, or whose campaigns you may have donated to… everything contained in this book is purely fictional. Despite how it may appear, this is not a socio-political commentary on the state of world affairs. Quite frankly, I can't think of anything less interesting right now than world affairs. The only major correlation between this world, which is a fantasy setting, and the world you live in, which is the real world, is the fact that both of them are messed up in a major way.

Third, the myths contained in this book are myths. Though they may have been inspired by consultations with Eris via pineal gland, I have no reason to believe that they are true regardless of how convenient an explanation they provide. Too often in the history of the world people have fallen prey to the idea that a convenient explanation must be a correct explanation. This mistake has led to countless wars, undesirable tax rates, and terrible television programming. Please, learn for the past. Don't believe everything you read…and, in the name of all that does not suck, put Firefly® back on the air you fascist program-directing jackasses!

Fourth, as the person who wrote this monstrosity, I can guarantee you that there are no hidden messages contained in this text. The conspiracies detailed herein are either complete bullshit or so good at covering their tracks that I couldn't find any evidence of their existence. The races and their histories are a bunch of crap. The people, places, and most of the things depicted don't exist in the real world. Chances are they never have and probably never will. So don't waste your time looking for them. Instead use that time to get a job and move out of your parents' house. Believe me, they'll thank me for it, and some day you will too. Ok, maybe you won't, but your parents definitely will.

Fifth, I'm an adult, though my level of maturity has often been questioned. I wrote this book for people like me. I put a warning on the cover so that you wouldn't buy this for your 8 year old grandson and then have the gall to sue me because you don't like the content. I didn't make you buy it. I didn't make you read it. And I sure as hell do not take responsibility for what you do while you have it in your possession. As you will probably come to realize as you read this, I have enough of my own problems without you adding yours to the mix. Be courteous and blame your hang-ups and psychological ailments on some one that truly deserves it…like that moron who thinks that homosexuality is a disease caused by SpongeBob SquarePants©.

Last but most certainly not least, have some fun. For the love of Eris, life is much too short to be taken seriously all the time. Grab a few pizzas, get some beverages, maybe a couple of bags of chips, invite some other social outcasts over to your house, and enjoy life for a few hours. Chances are you'll be worm food at some point within the next 7 to 10 decades. Enjoy being able to breathe while you still can.

The Lady's Rock Campaign Setting

Created By:	Ben Schultz & Matt Fezatte
Primary Text & Development:	Some figment of Ben's imagination
Other Text & Editing:	Another figment of Ben's imagination & Michelle Schultz
Good-looking Illustrations:	Matt Fezatte
Illustrations that Suck:	Ben Schultz
Some art copyright:	Larry Elmore, used with permission
	Other World Creations, used with permission
	Louis Porter, Jr. Design, used with permission
	Bradley K McDevitt, used with permission
	Reality deviant Publications, used with permission
	Joseph J. Calkins & Cerberus Illustrations, used with permission
	Michael Davis, used with permission
Significantly Influenced by:	The Principia Discordia - Malaclypse, the Younger & Lord Omar

Special Thanks To:

Michelle Schultz	for putting up with my bullshit for all these years.
Keri Fezatte	for putting up with Matt & letting him hang out in my kitchen until odd hours of the morning working on this project.
My Parents	for conceiving me in the first place and letting me live this long.
My brothers	for providing the proper mix of companionship and ridicule to make this all possible
My children	for giving me an excuse to continue to watch cartoons & buy toys
St. Gulik	for acting as a liaison & relaying all of those important messages for me when my pineal gland was decidedly out of order.
Erich Brungraber	for all of the technical support
Kevin Luebke	for reminding me that life isn't always what it seems
Kyle Kroening	for helping me always maintain my love of the game.
Ralph Gadbois	for opening the doorway to Chaos in your own special way
Peter Bamke	for providing a voice that was willing to disagree…even if you were usually wrong.

All content of this book, regardless of designation, is copyright 2007 by Erisian Entertainment. All rights reserved. Reproduction of use without the expressed written permission of Erisian Entertainment is expressly forbidden.

Author's notes

I know what you're thinking. Releasing another role-playing game into an already saturated market is completely absurd. It'll never work, and you'll never make a dime.

You're probably right. The truly funny thing is that I don't really care. Role-playing games aren't supposed to be about making money. They aren't supposed to be about realism. Role-playing games are supposed to be about escape. About living your fantasy and doing things you could never even dare to dream of doing in real life.

When I was younger, I was picked on in school mercilessly. I was fat, had glasses, usually did my homework, and maintained a solid B average even if I didn't. My father always had guns in the house and a ready supply of ammunition. There weren't any trigger locks in those days, so these things were easily within my grasp. So why didn't I snap like so many children today have?

The answer, I suspect, is two fold. First, I had parents who took an active role in my life. There was absolutely no way I could have made a duffle bag full of pipe bombs in the garage without them finding out. Second, I role-played.

That may not seem like an important factor, but think about it, really think about it, for just a minute. After a difficult day of ridicule I could go home and kill hundreds of imaginary goblins. I could rescue the princess. I could be the hero. I could vent my anger and my frustration in such a way that not a single person was hurt. Can you really discount the effect that can have on the fragile psyche of a growing child?

Role-playing provided me with other, more useful skills as well. I quickly learned my multiplication tables and addition and subtraction were a breeze. Spending your free time trying to calculate what you need to role on a 20-sided die in order to hit someone wearing full plate armor and carrying a shield has that effect on people.

Algebra wasn't difficult to master once I realized I had been solving for X for years. Alright, if I he has a dexterity of 10, I should hit him on a 16. I missed on the 16, but hit on an 18, so either his Dexterity has to be somewhere between 12 and 14 or he has a magical item. At any rate, at this level his armor class has to be somewhere between -2 and -3.

My role-playing skills didn't just help me in math. I learned about ancient history, medieval political structures, and even a little actual history. Soon I was reading books that my parents wouldn't have touched. How many 6th graders do you know who've read Homer?

Running role-playing games for others opens you up to a whole new set of skills. Creating new worlds to play on taught me cartography, topography, and basic climatology. I had to consider what impact available resources would have on a growing population. The effects of the population on the local ecology would also have to be considered.

Not only was I receiving a well rounded education, I was doing it on my own - for fun! What more could a parent ask for? Luckily my parents were smart enough to recognize this… and too intelligent to let on that they had.

Of course, not all the knowledge I gleaned from role-playing was academic in nature. I learned how to interact with other people. Girls didn't frighten me the way they did some of the others in my class. I had sweet talked princesses, what danger was there in talking to a mere prom queen?

I learned to think on my feet. Few things can prepare you for have to think quickly like the impending doom of the King's guard approaching the room of his only daughter. Of course, this particular skill I didn't get to use nearly as often as I would have liked to.

I also learned to be creative and think outside "the box." Supplies in role-playing, like life, are often limited. The difference is that, in the real world, your home or job may depend on your ability to adapt, in the role-playing world the fate of whole kingdoms may hang in the balance.

In short, role-playing and Scooby-Doo ® did infinitely more to prepare me for the real world than the public school system ever did. And despite facing some of the same problems that other children face, I never lashed out at my fellow students. Role-playing, though not the only factor, played a significant role in that single simple fact.

Now that I am older, though my reasons have changed, I still role-play as often as possible. My adult life is no less stressful than my childhood and the same catharsis is necessary every once in a while to help me cope. Sometimes when the rent, phone bill, and utilities bills come due you need to just let loose and take on a rampaging goblin horde. Sometimes putting a bastard sword through an arch-villain that you imagine looks like your boss is enough to let you suffer his stupidity for a few more weeks.

At any rate, this pastime is something to be enjoyed by children of all ages. This game embodies my most sincere desire that you take a moment and enjoy the catharsis for yourself.

- Ben

Table of Contents

PREFACE	1
THE CREATION OF THE WORLD	5
HISTORY OF THE WORLD, PART 1	6
HISTORY OF THE WORLD, PART II	10
THE LADY'S ROCK	12
MAGIC	13
GOVERNMENT	13
CALENDAR	14
HOLIDAYS & FESTIVALS	14
TRANSPORTATION	14
ARTS & ENTERTAINMENT	15
ARCHITECTURE	15
SOCIAL HIERARCHY	15
NOBILITY	16
ROYALTY	16
THE ERISTOCRACY	16
THE ORTHODOX CHURCH OF ERIS	17
SOCIAL CUSTOMS	17
EDUCATION	18
MONEY	18
TAXATION	18
Sales tax	*18*
Luxury tax	*18*
Inheritance tax	*18*
Market tax	*18*
Tolls	*19*
Dwelling tax	*19*
Landed Tax	*19*
Arms tax	*19*
Tithes	*19*
Income tax	*19*
Poll tax	*19*
Magic tax	*19*
Weapons tax	*19*
Miscellaneous taxes	*19*
TECHNOLOGY	19
FLORA	20
FAMILIES OF NOBLE PEERAGE	25
HOUSE BELIOR	25
HOUSE CALYDON	26
HOUSE CAMAYSAR	27
HOUSE CHASMALI	28
HOUSE CHAPARRAN	29
HOUSE DANNAN	30
HOUSE DE VECI	31
HOUSE ELGION	32
HOUSE HONBLAS	33
HOUSE KADOCH	34
HOUSE KEROON	35
HOUSE KHEMBRYL	36
HOUSE KREYES	38
HOUSE LECABEL	39
HOUSE MALGRIN	40
HOUSE MARKUNE	41
HOUSE MERELAN	42
HOUSE MILLIKAN	43
HOUSE MOLIKROTH	43
HOUSE MYTHERIE	44
HOUSE NASREDIN	45
HOUSE NEFAR	45
HOUSE NERILKA	46
HOUSE NEZATHAR	47
HOUSE PETIRON	47
HOUSE TELDEVAR	48
HOUSE TESSADYL	49
HOUSE VALERMOS	49
HOUSE VALTURIS	50
HOUSE VASSAGO	50
HOUSE VATHEK	51
HOUSE VON ROHM	51
THE IMPERIAL GOVERNMENT	53
THE IMPERIAL COURT	53
IMPERIAL DEMOGRAPHICS	53
LAW & ORDER	54
GRIEVANCES OF THE FIRST ORDER	55
GRIEVANCES OF THE SECOND ORDER	55
GRIEVANCES OF THE THIRD ORDER	56
GRIEVANCES OF THE FOURTH & FIFTH ORDERS	56
ORGANIZATIONS	57
IMPERIAL MILITARY	57
THE KNIGHTS OF THE TEMPLE OF ERIS	59
WATCHMEN	60
THE DOVES	61
THE GADBIANS	62
TEKSARIAN RANGERS	63
TEKSARIAN RANGERS	63
DOLUS MERETRICIS	65
THE WATCHFUL ORDER OF MAGES	67
GLOSSARY OF ERISIAN SLANG	68
PLAYER'S	71
SECTIONCREATING A CHARACTER	71
CREATING A CHARACTER	73
GETTING STARTED	73
CHARACTER CONCEPTS	73
Character History	*74*
Character History Questionnaires	*74*
RACES	76
AILURE	77
Fellen (Subspecies)	*79*
DWARF	81
Grey Dwarves (Subspecies)	*83*
Mountain Dwarves (Subspecies)	*84*
Dorcs (Half-Breeds)	*85*
ELVES	86

Aquatic Elves (Subspecies) 88
Drow (Subspecies) 89
Eburnae (Subspecies) 91
Grey Elves (Subspecies) 93
Grey Elves (Subspecies) 93
Wood Elves (Subspecies) 94
Elfling (Half-Breed) 96
Racial Traits 96
Size: Small 96
Gelf (Half-Breed) 97
Half-Elves (Half-breed) 98
GNOMES 99
GOBLINS 100
Hobgoblins (Subspecies) 101
HALFLINGS 102
Quarterlings (Half-Breed) 103
Quarterlings (Half-Breed) 103
HUMANS 104
Laham (Subspecies) 105
Tiefling (Subspecies / Half-Breed) 106
Decani (Subspecies) 108
MEPHISTI 109
MINOTAURS 111
Baphan (Half-Breed) 112
Morc (Half-Breed) 113
ORC 114
Half-Orcs (Half-Breed) 116
TEG 117
Racial Traits 118
Size: Tiny 118
Crimbils (Half-Breed) 119
Racial Traits 120
Size: Medium 120

BUILD POINTS 121
RACE 121
ATTRIBUTES 121
DICE POOLS 121
HIT POINTS 121
ACTIVE SKILLS 121
KNOWLEDGE SKILLS 121
ADVANTAGES 121
DISADVANTAGES 122
WEALTH 122
PURCHASE EQUIPMENT, WEAPONS, AND APPAREL 122

ATTRIBUTE SCORE 123
PHYSICAL ATTRIBUTES 123
Strength 123
Coordination 123
Quickness 123
Constitution 123
MENTAL ATTRIBUTES 123
Reason 123
Insight 123
Psyche 123
DICE POOLS 123
Action Pool: 124
Vigor Pool: 124
Willpower Pool: 124

SKILLS 125
SKILL TESTS 125
UNSKILLED TESTS 125
CRITICAL SUCCESSES 126
CRITICAL FAILURE 126
RULE OF ZERO 126
RULE OF FIVES 126
RULE OF NINES 126
CONCENTRATION 126
PULLING YOUR PUNCHES 126
ACTIVE SKILLS 126
KNOWLEDGE SKILLS 129
SKILL SPECIALIZATION 132

ADVANTAGES & DISADVANTAGES 133
ADVANTAGES 133
DISADVANTAGES 137

EQUIPMENT 143
WEAPONS 143
Weapon Qualities 143
ARMOR & SHIELD 151
Defining Armor 151
Armor Descriptions 151
Defining Shields 152
Shield Descriptions 152
ADVENTURING EQUIPMENT 153
TECHNOMAGICAL EQUIPMENT 153

COMBAT 161
HOW COMBAT WORKS 161
Time Keeping 161
Initiative: 161
Action: 162
Attack Test: 162
Damage: 162
Defense Test: 163
Gaffing Test: 164
MICELLANEOUS COMBAT MODIFIERS 164
VISIBILITY MODIFIERS 164
ILLUMINATION 165
A Brief Note on Magic and Light 165
COVER 168
FIRING BLIND 168
KNOCKDOWN 168
CHARGING 168
BASIC WEAPONS 168
FIGHTING WITH TWO WEAPONS 168
SIZES AND COMBAT 169
OVER-SIZED WEAPONS 170
UNARMED COMBAT 170
OBJECT RATING 170
OBJECT DAMAGE 170
DODGING A BULLET 171

MOVEMENT 172
NORMAL MOVEMENT 172
RUNNING 172
SPRINTING 172
OVERLAND MOVEMENT 172

Speed & Size	172
Quadrupeds & Other Multi-pedal Creatures	172

HEALTH AND HEALING 173

Healing	173
Treat Injury Skill	*173*
Death and Dying	173
Fatigue & Rest	174
Sleep	175

MAGIC 177

Laws of Magic	177
Types of Casters	178
Hedge Wizards & Witches	*178*
Mages	*178*
Clerics	*178*

ELEMENTAL ASPECTS 180

Boom	180
Sweet	180
Pungent	180
Orange	180

RELIGIONS & DEITIES 181

Ahbendon	181
Aren	181
Barak	182
Cetari	182
Chalysse	183
Chuck	183
Dumathan	184
Durian	184
Dynah	185
Eris	185
Jhaemaryl	185
Kyerhan	186
Laeroth	186
Makath	187
Manak	187
Myra	188
Narsin	188
Semis	188
Solvarus	189
Steve	189
Tchoren	189
Valderon	190
Vastra	190

SPELLS 191

Defining Spells	191
Casting Spells	191
Defending Against Spells	191
Dispelling	192
Spell Signatures	192
Sustained Spells	192
Spell Ranges	192
Schools of Magic	192
Abjuration	*192*
Biomancy	*192*
Conjuration	*193*
Divination	*193*
Enchantment	*193*
Evocation	*193*
Illusion	*193*
Transmutation	*193*
Necromancy	*193*

CREATING SPELLS 194

Determining the Effects of the Spells	194
Designing the Spell	194
Learning Spells	194

MAGIC IN THE MAKING 196

Verbal Components	196
Somatic Components	196
Material Components	196
Abjuration	197
Healing Spells	*197*
Body Modification Spells	*197*
Conjuration	198
Conjurations	*198*
Creations	*199*
Divination	200
Enchantment	201
Evocation	202
Illusions	203
Transmutation	204

REFINING ESSENCES 205

Gathering Raw Materials	205
Refining the Material	205

RITUAL MAGIC 206

SUMMONING SPIRITS 208

Types of Spirits	208
Summoning a Spirit	208
Summoning Components	*208*
Services	209
Errands	*209*
Magical Aid	*209*
Nourish a Spell	*209*
Physical Service	*209*
Binding a Spirit	209
Banishing a Spirit	209

COSMOLOGY 211

The Outer Planes	*212*

SPIRITS 218

Ancestor Spirits	218
Elementals	220
Common Elemental Powers	*220*
Boom Elementals	221
Orange Elementals	221
Pungent Elemental	222
Sweet Elementals	222
Familiar Spirits	224
Summoning a Familiar Spirit	*224*
Attributes	*224*
Special Powers	*224*

vii

IMPROVING YOUR CHARACTER ... 226
IMPROVING ATTRIBUTES ... 226
LEARNING A NEW SKILL ... 226
IMPROVING SKILLS ... 226
TRAINING ... 226

THE DIRECTOR'S CUT ... 227
ASSIGNING TARGET NUMBERS ... 230

REWARDING THE CHARACTERS ... 231
Treasure ... 231
Social Rewards ... 231
Issuing Mana Points ... 231

MANA AWARDS TABLEMAGICAL ITEMS ... 232

MAGICAL ITEMS ... 233
MYSTICAL SUBSTANCES ... 233
Mystic Woods ... 233
Mystic Metals ... 233
MAGIC ARMORS ... 233
MAGICAL HELMS ... 234
MAGICAL WEAPONS ... 236
MAGICAL RINGS ... 238
MAGICAL STAVES ... 239
MAGICAL MEDALLIONS ... 240
MAGICAL AMULETS ... 242
MAGICAL APPAREL ... 243
MAGICAL APPAREL ... 244
MISCELLANEOUS MAGICAL ITEMS ... 246

ATTUNEMENT AND BONDING ... 247
BONDING RITUAL ... 247
CLEANSING RITUAL ... 247
ATTUNEMENT ... 247

ARTIFACTS & RELICS ... 248
Armor of the Warrior Queen (Artifact) ... 248
The Maiden's Kiss (Artifact) ... 250
The Shield of Rayuk, the Bold (Artifact) ... 252
Robe of the Arch-Magi (Relic) ... 253
Spagenhelm of Vulnerability (Relic) ... 253
Staff of the Magi (Relic) ... 254
BONDING TO AN ARTIFACT OR RELIC ... 254

MINUTIAE ... 255
AGING ... 255
DRINKING ... 256
Racial Beverages ... 257
FALLING DAMAGE ... 257
FEATS OF STRENGTH ... 257

APPENDIX 1: CRIMINAL INDICTMENT ... 258

APPENDIX II: LIABILITY WAIVER ... 259

Preface

It was a night much like tonight. So much like tonight, in fact, that it may have been tonight. Of course, it could have been another night. Last night or a week ago Tuesday would work just as well. The truth of the matter was that it could very well have been the middle of the day, the middle of tomorrow even, and that would be perfectly fine. It could have occurred a month from next Thursday and this information would still be as relevant then as it is right now.

Come to think of it, it wasn't a month from next Thursday. That would be ridiculous. A month from next Thursday I'll be on vacation. And with two young children, that means I'll be entirely too busy to have anything even remotely resembling a thought, profound or otherwise.

No. It was five months from next Friday. I remember it clear as a bell, or at least I will after it happens. I was sitting in the kitchen partaking of a hot dog produced by the descendants of Saint Oscar of Meyer when it hit me…or will hit me as the case may be.

My pineal gland was, or will be, particularly active that day. I attribute this bout of hyper activity to an acute overdose of nicotine and caffeine enhanced by yellow dye number 5 and carbon monoxide. The yellow dye is an important catalyst. If you are consuming beverages containing caffeine but lacking yellow dye number 5 or that contains either Blue dye number 1 or red dye number 40, true enlightenment can only be achieved if you add some from of alcohol to the mixture.

But we're not here to discuss my pineal gland, not yet anyway. We may talk about it later, though, so don't be shocked if the topic comes up again.

At any rate, I was sitting in my kitchen alone in the dark eating a hot dog as I said earlier. I could almost hear Freud talking about the latent homosexual implications of the act. Then I realized I was hearing Freud clear as a bell, as if he was standing right beside me. I even turned and looked, but it was dark and I couldn't see a thing.

It probably wasn't Freud. After all, Freud was dead. What were the chances of a dead Austrian psychologist hanging out in my kitchen on a Friday night? But it didn't have to be Freud. I had never met the man. It could have very well been any psychoanalyst with an Austrian accent who was preoccupied with sexuality. It wouldn't have even had to be Austrian for that matter. My idea of European accents was completely formulated in my early youth by the wizards of Hollywood.

As far as I knew, based strictly on accents the British would one day rise up and form a galactic Empire whose technological superiority would one day be defeated by primitive teddy bears wielding sticks and stones. Apparently in the hands of a teddy bear, sticks and stone break more than bones. They also decimate heavily armed and armored Imperial walkers.

As a matter of fact, I knew without a doubt they were the same just as I knew that Luke and Simba shared the same father. I had heard it for myself. And that always brought the role of the uncle into question for me. If he had killed the Emperor's personal executioner, didn't that make him a hero, not a villain, even if it was death by stampeding wildebeest? No wonder kids today were so confused.

But far away from wildebeests and artificial moons capable of destroying planets, I sat in my kitchen being psychoanalyzed by some dead guy. The more I thought about it the more that the very idea that Sigmund Freud would be in my kitchen at eleven o'clock at night on a Friday and interrupting my consumption of hot dogs seemed patently absurd. Didn't he have something better to do on a Friday night? That was why I had no choice but to turn on the lights and investigate further. Someone was there. They had to be. Either that or I was crazy. Of course, crazy would explain why I was alone eating hot dogs on a Friday night, wouldn't it?

"Zo how longk haf joo hed dees feelinks?" the voice said as I fumbled for the light switch.

"Zer es nogthink to be eshamed ov. Ve boess know dat you haf been feelink dis vay for a longk time, hafent joo?" the voice continued.

I flipped the switch without warning hoping to catch my uninvited guest unaware. For some reason I did not suspect my bumbling ambulation would alert him to my intentions. It was late. That's my excuse. As my eyes adjusted to the change in light, I began to look around the room for the source of the voice. I found no one. I was still alone in my kitchen. It was still the middle of the night, and I still had not had a chance to finish my hot dog. But I decided that eating in the dark was no longer in my best interests. Anything that makes Sigmund Freud hang out in my kitchen could not be good.

It's not that I'm afraid of Freud or my own sexuality. The fact that he was supposed to be dead didn't bother me. Why should it? A few thousand years ago we had carpenters rising from the grave, and people accepted that without question. Why couldn't one of the most brilliant minds of the last century do it too?

But rumor has it the man did heroine by injecting it directly into his left testicle. That just doesn't sit well with me for some reason. I don't really know why. It wasn't the idea of the drug. I couldn't care less what people choose to do with their bodies. Maybe I thought it was unfair to favor one of the boys over the other.

At any rate, I didn't need Sigmund Freud interrupting my Friday night hot dog consumption. I'm sure there were other people on this floating ball of dirt who could really benefit from his expertise. And I didn't see a reason that I should monopolize his time.

So I, again, took my seat at the table and prepared to finally eat the now room temperature hot dog only to find that the dog had beat me to it. This was turning out to be a wonderful night. Maybe Freud should spend some time with him discussing the psychological implications of stealing other people's phallic shaped food.

I went to the stove and turned on the burner to bring the water to a boil. I know I could have put it in the microwave, but that just didn't seem right. Taking the easy route somehow seemed wrong… like drinking beer out of a can. Sure you can do it, but why? Beer tastes better out of the bottle for some unknown, and probably also psychological, reason.

I'm sure Freud, if he was still around, would say it had something to do with the shape of the bottle. Thankfully, he wasn't which was a good thing, as relatively speaking as anyone is when they describe something as good. I was running out of patience and time. If I wanted to get this hot dog in my stomach before the end of Friday, I was going to have to get moving.

Why would I have a need to eat the hot dog while the clock still said it was Friday? That's an interesting question, and I suppose it deserves some semblance of an explanation. The truth is simply that I wanted to. It was a ritual, like any other. It was my own personal communion.

"A Discordian is Required during his early Illumination to Go Off Alone & Partake Joyously of a Hot Dog on a Friday; this Devotive Ceremony to Remonstrate against the popular Paganisms of the Day: of Catholic Christendom (no meat on Friday), of Judaism (no meat of Pork), of Hindic Peoples (no meat of Beef), of Buddhists (no meat of animal), and of Discordians (no Hot Dog Buns)."

Those were the words of the *Principia Discordia*. Of course, I understood that there were no requirements in Discordianism. The very idea of Discordian Commandments was funny. That's why they referred to their commandments as the "Pentabarf." But that didn't change the fact that I chose to eat a hot dog on Friday night.

That's not really what some would consider a good explanation, and, truth be told, I don't have a better one, nor did I need one. The fact that I wanted to eat the hot dog was enough for me. Besides, what did it matter to the world if I did eat the damn hot dog? Was Armageddon going to occur because I decided to eat a hot dog? I doubt it. So, in reality, whether I ate the hot dog or not was of no concern to anyone other than me. That being the case, the reasons don't really matter, and I try not to dwell on things that don't really matter. Of course, I don't always succeed, but I try nonetheless.

I went to the refrigerator to get another hot dog and begin the process again. No sooner had I opened the door than I heard the voice again. Freud was back, but this time he had lost his Austrian accent in favor of a dialect I more readily understood – Spanglish.

"See mang, 'at's the prollem with all a yous," the voice started. I didn't move. Instead I concentrated on the sound trying to ascertain its point of origin.

"Lights mang. Everythin' is lights. Are you all afraid a the dark or sumsing?" the voice asked.

Quickly I turned and focused my gaze on the part of the room that I thought the voice was coming from, and there it was - the source of Freud and the spanglish speaking stranger. On the cupboard sat a lone creature about 2 inches long. Out of the corner of my eye I saw my cat approaching this creature as if he was a majestic lion and it was a drinking gazelle. A quick look of reproach sent the king of beast fleeing into the living room.

"Gulik!" I exclaimed. "You know better than to visit unannounced. The cat could have torn you to shreds."

"Really?" said the roach. "Have you learned nothing in the past few years? And it would please my greatly if you would use my correct title. "

"Your pleasure is really no concern of mine," I stated and dropped the first of two hot dogs into the pot of now boiling water.

"Double, double toil and trouble; Fire burn and cauldron bubble," Gulik said as the second hot dog hit the water.

"Very funny, Gulik," I replied more annoyed now than before.

"Eye of newt, and toe of frog, Wool of bat, and tongue of dog, Adder's fork, and blind-worm's sting, Lizard's leg, and owlet's wing, For a charm of powerful trouble, Like a hell-broth boil and bubble," he continued obviously he had either just left the theater or was, for some otherwise unknown reason, obsessed with the bard tonight...that night.

"Macbeth shall never vanquish'd be until Great Birnam wood to high Dunsinane hill shall come against him," I replied. "So are the trees moving? Does Macbeth need fear?"

"More than you know, child," was his reply. "That's precisely why I'm here."

Many people would be bothered by the presence of a roach in their kitchen much less the presence of a talking roach. I, however, was not most people. Saint Gulik being here talking to me was no different than that talking cat on that TV show about the teenaged witch. Except that the show, like every other show based on witches, was clearly bullshit. Just a few years before that show aired that same woman was trying to explain it all to us on a different show on another channel. One of those *had* to be bullshit. Besides, every one knows that a witch wiggles her nose to work magic.

Well, I admit I've seen witches who don't, in fact, wiggle their noses, when casting spells but some type of wiggling is going on. The fact remains that the show wasn't real. Saint Gulik, however, was. At the very least, he was a delusion of such incredible depth that I was not able to distinguish it from reality, and that was really the most important point.

"Ben," he began. He often called me Ben because…well…it's my name and I respond to it quite well after all these years of conditioning. He sometimes liked to use my Holy name – "Lord High Emperorator Skippy the twenty-third, Admiral of the Evil Balloon Animal Navy, Sovereign of the Really Spooky Legions, Master-at-Arms of the 173rd Demonic Care Bear Battalion, Keeper of the Sacred Book of Scary Names, Borrower of the Sacred Chao," but that seemed a bit too formal for this casual visit.

"A long time ago, in a galaxy far, far away," he continued. "…there is unrest in the General Assembly. Under the leadership of Grigori II, the 43rd Emperor, Eristonia has conspired to set the delicate balance that is their world a skew and immanentize the eschaton."

"Wait just one damn minute," I interrupted. "You're sitting here at damn near midnight to tell me the story of the end of the world and it's taking place in a galaxy far from here?"

"You do not understand the delicate balance that is the multiverse I fear," Saint Gulik replied.

"Fear leads to Anger. Anger leads to Hate. Hate leads to suffering," I replied quoting yet another piece of popular culture.

"Why don't you sit your ass down and shut the fuck up?" he remonstrated.

"You're the one who started with the random quotations," I retorted.

"If you spent half as much energy trying to comprehend the world around you as you do being a smart ass," he replied, "then maybe, just maybe, you wouldn't be such a fuck up."

That hit close to home – a little too close. The man…umm…roach just did not know when to quit… He had gone from Sigmund Freud to a Spanglish-speaking Stranger, to my father in less time than it took a fat kid to devour a Twinkie. And having been a member of the Fat Kids' union local 313 since I was in third grade, I was keenly aware of exactly how fast that was.

I sat back in my chair and tried to feign interest as the roach regaled me with his tale of impending doom. Luckily he was too engrossed in his own story to notice that I couldn't give a shit less about anything that he had to say. Of course, this wasn't unusual for a meeting with Saint Gulik either.

So now, having nothing better to do myself, I will relate the roach's tale to you, as it was told to me in my kitchen five months from next Friday as I wait for my hot dogs to boil. Hopefully you will find it half as entertaining as Saint Gulik had hoped I would. And if not, it doesn't really matter to me. At least I won't be the only one bored off my ass by that obnoxious roach.

You know, now that I'm a pope and all, maybe I should think about revoking his sainthood. Popes can do that, right? I'll have to consult my pineal gland…

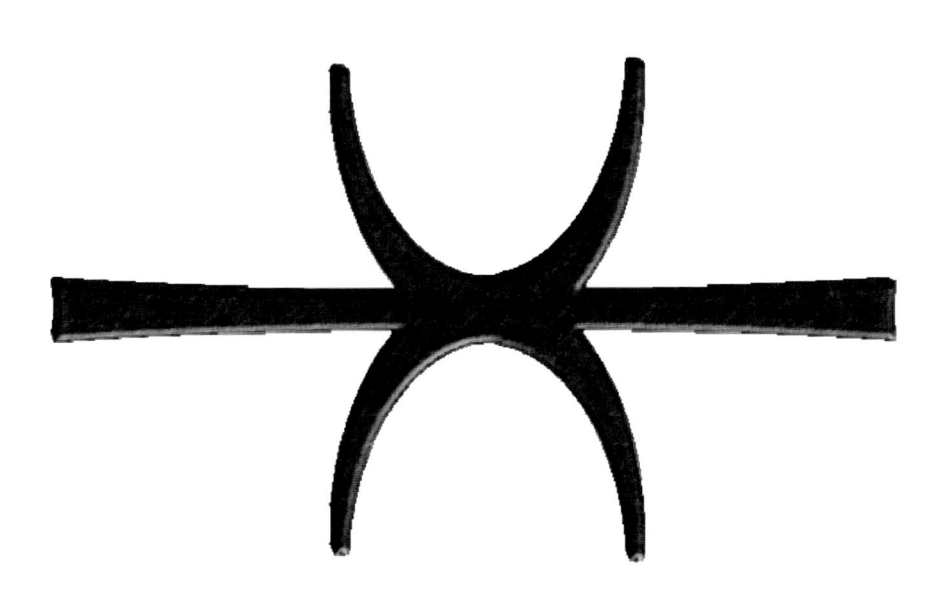

The Creation of the World
(Or…why things are the way that they are)

The *Principia Discordia* explains the creation of the universe thusly:

In the beginning there was VOID, who had two daughters; one (the smaller) was that of BEING, named ERIS, and one (the larger) was of NON- BEING, named ANERIS. (To this day, the fundamental truth that Aneris is the larger is apparent to all who compare the great number of things that do not exist with the comparatively small number of things that do exist.)

Eris had been born pregnant, and after 55 years (Goddesses have an unusually long gestation period-- longer even than elephants), Her pregnancy bore the fruits of many things. These things were composed of the Five Basic Elements, SWEET, BOOM, PUNGENT, PRICKLE, and ORANGE. Aneris, however, had been created sterile. When she saw Eris enjoying Herself so greatly with all of the existent things She had borne, Aneris became jealous and finally one day she stole some existent things and changed them into non- existent things and claimed them as her own children. This deeply hurt Eris, who felt that Her sister was unjust (being so much larger anyway) to deny Her her small joy. And so She made herself swell again to bear more things. And She swore that no matter how many of her begotten that Aneris would steal,

She would beget more. And, in return, Aneris swore that no matter how many existent things Eris brought forth, she would eventually find them and turn them into non-existent things for her own. (And to this day, things appear and disappear in this very manner.)

At first, the things brought forth by Eris were in a state of chaos and went in every which way, but by the by She began playing with them and ordered some of them just to see what would happen. Some pretty things arose from this play and for the next five zillion years She amused Herself by creating order. And so She grouped some things with others and some groups with others, and big groups with little groups, and all combinations until She had many grand schemes which delighted Her.

Engrossed in establishing order, She finally one day noticed disorder (previously not apparent because everything was chaos). There were many ways in which chaos was ordered and many ways in which it was not.

"Hah," She thought, "Here shall be a new game."
And She taught order and disorder to play with each other in contest games, and to take turns amusing each other. She named the side of disorder after Herself, "ERISTIC" because Being is anarchic. And then, in a mood of sympathy for Her lonely sister, She named the other side "ANERISTIC" which flattered Aneris and smoothed the friction a little that was between them.

Now all of this time, Void was somewhat disturbed. He felt unsatisfied for he had created only physical existence and physical non- existence, and had neglected the spiritual. As he contemplated this, a great Quiet was caused and he went into a state of Deep Sleep which lasted for 5 eras. At the end of this ordeal, he begat a brother to Eris and Aneris, that of SPIRITUALITY, who had no name at all.

When the sisters heard this, they both confronted Void and pleaded that he not forget them, his First Born. And so Void decreed thus:

That this brother, having no form, was to reside with Aneris in Non-Being and then to leave her and, so that he might play with order and disorder, reside with Eris in Being. But Eris became filled with sorrow when She heard this and then began to weep.

"Why are you despondent?" demanded Void, "Your new brother will have his share with you." "But Father, Aneris and I have been arguing, and she will take him from me when she discovers him, and cause him to return to Non- Being." "I see," replied Void, "Then I decree the following:
"When your brother leaves the residence of Being, he shall not reside again in Non-Being, but shall return to Me, Void, from whence he came. You girls may bicker as you wish, but My son is your Brother and We are all of Myself."

And so it is that we, as men, do not exist until we do; and then it is that we play with our world of existent things, and order and disorder them, and so it shall be that non-existence shall take us back from existence and that nameless spirituality shall return to Void, like a tired child home from a very wild circus.

"Everything is true - Everything is permissible!"
-Hassan i Sabbah

History of the World, Part 1

Eris had given birth to a great number of things. One of those things was a lifeless chunk of rock. Eris was fond of the rock. She liked its shape. She liked its form. Of all the things she had brought into existence, this one thing was special to her for reasons that cannot be explained.

As much as she liked her pet rock, Eris knew in her heart that it could be better. Better than what, exactly, is yet another mystery. So Eris set out to make her pet rock the best pet rock the universe had ever seen. This was a fairly easy task since it was the only pet rock in existence at the time.

The rock was dark and difficult for her to view at any distance, so Eris took another one of her children, a star she named Malaclypse, and set it in the area above the rock. Malaclypse sucked the darkness right out of the sky making the rock shine and the Goddess was pleased.

Soon, however, the brightness caused by Malaclypse and the rock began to annoy Eris. She had other things to do and the bright light given off by the rock once the darkness was gone distracted her. So she set Malaclypse in motion around the rock. For a portion of time Malaclypse would suck the darkness off of the rock so that she could enjoy it. For an equal amount of time the light of Malaclypse would be hidden by the rock, and the rock would be dark.

Again all was well, good, and right with the world…or at least with Eris and that's all that matters. Of course, as the universe is prone to do, things began to get more complicated and Eris' attentions again turned to her rock for comfort. She decided to plant a garden and thought her rock would be the perfect place.

Soon the rock was covered with all sorts of fauna. Flowers and trees bloomed in abundance. It truly was beautiful. Then Eris' attention again wavered. Goddesses can be fickle creatures. When she finally returned to the rock all of the plants had died. What did she expect? After all, she had not watered them in millennia?

So Eris began her garden anew. This time she placed a ready supply of water on the rock in the hopes that the plants would drink whenever they were thirsty. Unfortunately plants are stupid and they did not drink of the water that the Goddess had provided. So Eris, in a divine blot of inspiration, placed puffs of water vapor in the air above her garden and instructed those puffs, which she called clouds, to collect water and disburse it among all the plants that she had made.

This too only worked for a period of time. Over time the plants continued to slowly die. The goddess was perplexed. For several years she pondered the predicament of her little rock until the answer came to her. She created creature to tend her garden for her. She made bugs that crawled and flew. She made worms to dig into the soil and aerate the roots of her garden.

For several thousand years the little rock garden floated blissfully and self-sufficiently as Eris fluttered about doing whatever it is that deities do when they aren't meddling in the affairs of man. Her attention had been elsewhere when she saw the flash of lightning. She was curious as to what the lightning was and so she stared intently at her garden trying to ascertain the origins of that brilliant flash of light. Then she saw two of the cloud puffs, heavily laden with water vapor, collide in mid-air. The noise of the impact was almost deafening and the flash nearly blinded her. That's what happens when you fly through a thunderstorm without an airplane to protect you.

The lightning bolt struck a tree severing a branch which then landed on her favorite rose bush destroying all of the beautiful purple flowers.

The insects she had created were ill-equipped to deal with this calamity. So Eris created another creature to tend her garden, but she knew no base creature driven by instinct alone would be capable of understanding the beauty of the garden. No. In order to be able to accomplish the task she was going to entrust to them these creatures would need to be intelligent. Along with the creation of sentient creatures came the long and winding spiral that would ultimately descend into civilization.

The first race created by Eris was created in her own image to be graceful, delicate, and beautiful. They had high pointed ears to allow them to hear all the beautiful music created by the wind and the trees of her pet rock. In order to give them the intelligence they needed, she instilled them with a bit of her own chaotic essence. She called this race the fey.

The fey lived peacefully for about 21 days before they became bored with existence. They grew despondent, depressed, and extremely bitchy for no apparent reason. This continued for five to seven days before the bitchiness wore off enough that their elders could meet and discuss the problem.

"Oh, Eris, great mother of us all," the elders cried. "We are bored with existence. What shall we do?"

"What seems to be the problem?" Eris asked.

"We are troubled because we know not what to do. We had been entertaining ourselves with games of the mind, but we all seem to have mastered them already and they are no longer fun."

Eris pondered this for a minute and then she spoke.

"I will create a variation of the species," she declared. "It will be slightly larger than the current fey so that it can be used for manual labor. It will be pleasing to look at, but would have two head, one much larger than the other."

"But how will this help us great mother?" the fey questions.

"Simple," Eris replied with a mischievous grin. "Though I shall give them two heads each will have a separate function. One will be used for rational thought and the other will fill them with desire for you. Of course, I only intend to give them enough blood to use one head at a time."

Thus the male fey came into existence and all was again good on the little rock. Males proved no match for their female counterparts in games of the mind, but thanks to Eris they were hopeless attracted to the females – hypnotized into subservience by their mammary glands.

But being born of chaos and instilled with the essence of the goddess herself, the fey were flighty at best. They often neglected their duties in favor of frolicking mindlessly in the woods and toying with each other's affections. Eventually, the rock began to suffer from their whims.

Though she truly enjoyed watching the fey dance and sing, it was soon apparent to Eris that she would need a more trustworthy group of caretakers for her rock. So she went about creating a more suitable custodian.

This new race she made strong and stocky, capable of moving a dead tree trunk from the forest with ease and stable enough to carry it without fear of falling into another rose bush. Because they were intended strictly for labor and had no other meaningful purpose, she also made them male. She did not name this new race, instead leaving that task to her children the fey.

But this new race bothered the fey. They were orderly to a fault. They lacked a sense of humor and were rarely know to play at all. To ensure the harmony of her creation, Eris caused this new race to band together in clans. She told the clans to inhabit the highest points of her rock and venture forth only to maintain the rock. She had hoped that they would leave the fey alone and that peace would ensue. To ensure that these custodians would do no more harm to the fey, she gave them a distinctive scent that the fey could smell to warn them when custodians were approaching. And all was good… for about a week.

The custodians, who the fey had named "stinky little vermin," were uncomfortable in the cold upper altitudes of the rock and they did not like their smell. To appease the stinky little vermin, Eris caused them to grow long breads to shield them from the cold and taught them how to ferment grains to make ale. They still smelled terrible but now they were too drunk to notice.

But the alcohol made the stinky little vermin, who had begun to call themselves "dwarves" for some strange reason, unable to think rationally. Soon fights erupted among the dwarves. Chaos threatened to engulf the entire rock. Eris contemplated destroying the lot of them, but then, remembering the pain she had felt when her sister had stolen some of her other children, she decided just to "ground" them. Eris ordered the dwarves to dig homes for themselves out of the very mountains they inhabited. She intended to banish them there until they could learn to behave themselves. (I bet you were wondering where the term "grounded" came from weren't you.)

But inside the mountains the dwarves found deposits of shiny rock they called metal. They separated this metal from the rock and began to horde it in vast underground caverns. But the process of removing the metal was arduous because tools had yet to be invented.

The fey and dwarves both discovered fire about the same time. It was shortly after another lightning strike. While the fey viewed fire as evil because it destroyed the trees, the dwarves cherished the fire and the warmth it provided. The dwarf responsible for keeping a clan's fire was a very important position. He led the clan in all things and his word was law. In later years, "the man who kept the fire" would be shortened to "the man" and then finally to "thane," but that won't happen for a few generations.

A very charismatic dwarf, at least as charismatic as a short hairy man that smelled like badly rotting fish could be, realized, while under the influence of fermented grain, that the current Dwarven living conditions were a direct result of the fact that Eris favored the fey. He began to identify the larger fey as evil. It was the first recorded use of that word.

Around the same time another drunken dwarf learned that by heating metal and beating it with another piece of metal you could shape it into useful tools. This was infinitely more efficient than the previously common practice of banging your head into the metal until your head hurt, decided you didn't really need a tool that badly anyway, and gave up.

Now armed with tools the Dwarven mining operations increased in efficiency that it could not be measured. So another dwarf, who would grow to be despised by school children everywhere, decided that they needed a way to measure their progress quickly and easily. He called this method geometry from the Greek words geo, meaning earth, and metron, meaning measure, both of which they had learned from Eris who was, after all, Greek.

As more mining was done so too was more alcohol consumed as tired dwarves flocked into taverns through out the Dwarven holdings. The hatred of the "evil ones," now called "elves" due largely to the slurring effects of alcohol, became louder and louder. Soon the dwarves, armed with pick axes and shovels, were prepared to march on the elves and remove this blight from their planet.

The Dwarven army found their elven victims in a cluster of rose bushes playing their favorite game. The dwarves saw this as the opportune moment and struck ruthlessly. Luckily, as the first blow was struck, Eris noticed what was going on and intervened immediately.

The game that had so engrossed the elves is one still enjoyed today, though the pieces have changed slightly over the years, the basic concepts and strategies remain the same. The females ask the males if the fig leaf they are holding makes them appear to be composed of more cellulous than they actually were. The male then attempts to discover an answer that will not place him in a position of disfavor with the female. Of course, no right answer exists and the males always lose. Nevertheless they continue to play trapped by the hypnotizing power of mammary glands.

"What are you doing to my beautiful roses?" Eris demanded of the dwarves.

"Oh great lady," the dwarf began.

"Don't 'great lady' me!" Eris retorted cutting him off in mind sentence. "These flowers have taken me many millennia to grow. You better have a good explanation and you better have it fast."

"Forgive us," the dwarf cried. "We were merely jealous of the attention you paid to the elves and sought to destroy them as a means to seek your favor."

"Men!" Eris snorted. "When will you ever learn?"

And it was at that moment she realized that she, and not the dwarves, was to blame for this predicament. After all, she had made the entire race male so they were incapable of reason. She took half of the dwarves aside and changed their sex immediately. Though she left the beards on to ensure that no other creature would possibly find them attractive. She did not want to rock full of stinky half-breeds.

"So that you will remember the folly of crossing me, "she decreed, "these roses shall forever more bloom red to remind you of the blood you have spilled and black so you will know without a doubt what will happen should you try this again."

Then she created a new race, because that had worked so well in the past, to be a pacifying factor on the rock. She took some primordial clay and crafted her new race. This race was neither as chaotic as the elves nor as orderly as the dwarves. They were not overly attractive nor did they smell like fermenting feces. She called this new race "humans" and instructed them to keep peace on her world.

When she was finished, she realized that she still had some clay left over, though it was not nearly enough to make another human, it seemed like such a waste to just discard it. So Eris crafted one final race. This one without any real purpose other than to use up the remaining clay. They appeared human though only half as tall. These creatures made from the wasted flesh of creating humans became known as "halflings" and the world still wonders what their purpose might be.

The humans had only been on the rock for a few hours when Malaclypse made its descent. Immediately they were distraught for they could not see without the sun to draw the darkness away as could the other races living on the Lady's Rock. So they called to Eris and begged for her aid.

So Eris broke a small piece off of the star Malaclypse and set it in orbit opposite the first so that it could illuminate the night when Malaclypse was not in the sky. The humans rejoiced, danced, and sang. And Eris left for the humans were neither as pleasant to listen to as the elves had been nor half as graceful. It was many weeks before the humans called to Eris again.

"Oh, Eris, please help us we beg you," they cried.

"What is it this time?" was her reply.

"We have grown tired of eating the plants, roots, and berries as the elves have done. We want something else to eat."

"Like what?"

"I don't know…something red that tastes good flame broiled with a side of mushrooms, onions and a tall mug of Dwarven ale."

Eris heard this request and it troubled her. But she was pleased with the fact that the humans had managed to bring peace to both the elves and the dwarves, so she conceded. She produced all manner of animal for the humans to consume and again they were pleased.

History of the World, Part II

Eris had created the world and populated it with sentient races. She watched her creation for several minutes before her attention was drawn to something completely different. Then she left.

In another portion of the universe other children of Eris were starting to play together for the first time. Eris watched intently, but was determined not to interfere. Soon Cronus had slain his father Uranus creating a new world. Then Zeus slew his father Cronus and allowed humanity to leave the caves they had been previously trapped in. A titan named Prometheus gave these men fire and was condemned for it.

Chaos, glorious chaos, reigned supreme and Eris was content just watching this fascinating new world. Eventually she made herself known to Zeus and his children, but they were uncomfortable around her partly because she dwarfed even their considerable power and partly because she was an extremely attractive goddess & Zeus' wife Hera, in particular, was jealous of her. This didn't bother the goddess. She reveled in the play of order and chaos on this new world.

Soon it came to pass that there was to be a great wedding. All the best gods and goddesses were invited, all except Eris that is. The Olympians, in their short-sightedness, thought that Eris would ruin the party. They were a stuffy lot and didn't understand the value of an attractive goddess who could dance, sing, and would readily do body shots.

Eris was hurt by this slight, which we now know as the "Original Snub." She decided it was high time she put these self-righteous would-be deities in their place, so she crept into the wedding unannounced (and uninvited) and tossed a single apple made of pure gold into the mix. On the apple was written a single word – "Kallisti."

Depending on whom you talk to, "Kallisti" means a variety of things; it may mean "to the fairest" or "to the prettiest" as some scholars have indicated. Of course, it may also mean "take that you self-righteous assholes" or simply "kiss my divine ass." Whatever its true meaning, the end result was a war the engulfed the whole miserable planet.

Believing the word to mean "to the prettiest" the various goddesses vied for the apple. Eventually, Zeus decided that a mortal, who happened to be in attendance for reasons yet unknown, should decide who to give the apple to. That mortal was Legolas Turner, blacksmith extraordinaire and Prince of something or other. He naturally chose Aphrodite, the goddess with the largest breasts, and she, in turn, gave him permission to kidnap someone else's wife. (Apparently no kidnappings took place on this planet without the permission of the buxom goddess.)

The woman he kidnapped was named Helen by her parents, Mr. & Mrs. "of Troy." She was the wife of Hamish, King of Sparta, and a doctor working at the Spartan National Archives. Because of this, Mickey Bishop, underground street fighter and spy extraordinaire, led an army of monkeys to get her back. Actually, it wasn't much of an army because they were only 12 of them, but they thought of themselves as an army nonetheless.

It was during this war that General Thade, only a private third class at the time, learned the skills he would later use to conquer the world and attempt to save us from the evils of Marky Mark and Moses. But that has little to do with our current tale. By the time all that happens, Eris has long since grown bored and left this little planet to fend for itself.

After the original snub, Eris ate a hot dog, but she ate not a bun. As she consumed the hot dog, she began to reminisce about the pleasure she had gained from watching her own pet rock. As she contemplated what had transpired there in her absence, it dawned on her that she could simply "pop" back over to that part of the universe and see for herself. So she did just that.

Eris returned to her pet rock to find a world very different from the one she had left. The humans she had created to keep the peace on the rock had done their job…a little too well. In their attempts to quell the mounting hostility between the elves and dwarves the humans had created an empire that encompassed all of the populated regions of the rock. Even more irritating to the goddess was that they had done this in her name.

She was filled with rage at the blasphemy they had committed. She was the goddess of chaos and discord after all, not the goddess of slavery and oppression. Her children were meant to be free, not prisoners in their own lives. This would never do.

As she approached her rock to set things right, she was surprised to hear music, laughter, and cheers. Intrigued, she went to investigate. In a lonely corner of her floating rock garden people were celebrating. Disguising herself as an extremely attractive peasant with large breasts, she entered the festivities to find out what was going on.

It was rebellion. Not a big rebellion, but a rebellion nonetheless. The leader of this motley crew of revolutionaries was not a peasant. He was a noble by birth and was showing himself to be a noble by action as well. He told the people that Eris did not wish them beholden to each other. He said that the goddess wanted her children to live free according to their abilities and not the dictates of a monarch or church…even if it was her own.

Eris flushed with pride as she heard the man speak. Someone understood. Someone had been born with the ability to see through the bullshit and find the truth. They did not pray to her for success though they did honor her in name and deed. Against all odds, this mere human was showing his fellows that they deserved a better life if only they were willing to do for themselves.

From that minute forward, she decided that this was a new breed of man, not a mere human, but something more. She dubbed them "latent humans" because of their underlying potential and to differentiate them from "mere humans." It was the Sweetmorn of the 19th of the Aftermath in 3083 YOLD.

Of course, because she was in disguise at the time, these latent humans had no real idea what kind of compliment they were really being paid. As time went on, the terms latent human and mere human found their way into colloquial speech. Eventually, as often happens with words we use everyday, they were shortened to "laham" and "mehum" respectively.

Rather than intervene again, Eris was content to sit back and watch this revolution take hold among the people. Vicious battles were waged. Despite harrowing defeats at the hands of the seasoned Imperial armies, the spirit of rebellion lived on. Eris was pleased indeed.

In 3125 YOLD the leader of the rebellion, a man who called himself Malaclypse after the star the lady had given them to light their way, died from multiple gunshot wounds. Eris was at his side when he breathed his last breath. Malaclypse's own son took up his father's mantle, and the rebellion lived on. Eris, however, was deeply troubled by his passing.

Eris again left the rock, this time to spread Malaclypse's wisdom to other rocks floating aimlessly through space and time. Because she was a goddess and goddesses can do that.

Eventually she would return to earth and share her knowledge with two men who would bring it to the whole of humanity. One would call himself Lord Omar. The other would mistakenly take the name Malaclypse the younger in reverence for the man who had touched the goddess so deeply.

The Lady's Rock

Geographical Overview

According to legend and confirmed by the discoveries of science, the Lady's Rock consists of several land masses, called "continere," floating in a semi-tangible mass known as the Erisian Sea. This strange body consists of a substance known as aether. It is colorless, odorless, slightly warm to the touch, and contains a slight, almost electrical, charge. It is possible for someone to breathe in the aether, though it is not the most comfortable of feelings. This has led some individuals to refer to aether as heavy air. This is not correct despite its wide use among the more uneducated portions of society. It is possible to "swim" through the aether, but creatures seem to lose buoyancy once they've traveled further than 12 miles from shore.

Scientists theorize that beneath the aether lies a second mass of land. This has never been proven because the aether is too deep to see to the bottom and any person who has fallen into the aether has not returned to tell the scientific community what they had discovered.

Water is readily available on the Lady's Rock in the form of many fresh water lakes, rivers, and streams. This system of interconnected water ways then flow over the side of the various land masses and plummet into the aether. What happens to it from there is anyone's guess.

Legend holds that these deposits of water were placed here by Eris herself, though the more skeptically minded scientists hold that there must be some source for the water otherwise it would have ran out by now. They are usually decried for not having faith in the Lady.

Slight variations in the orbit of Malaclypse, the planet's star, cause seasons on the surface of the Lady's Rock. The Lady's Rock goes through five such seasons each year (See the section on the Erisian Calendar on page 17).

The orbit of the Lady's Rock's moon does cause minor changes in the elevation of the various bodies of water. Both the moon and prevalent winds cause conditions on the aether to vary as well.

Magic

The creation of the Lady's Rock took a considerable amount of deific power. Some of this energy remains unseen in the background of every day life. Some people are born with the ability to wield this magical energy. These people tend to have a strong connection to one of the five basic elements that make up the universe – Sweet, Boom, Pungent, Prickle, and Orange. Depending on which element infuses a child identifies exactly what powers they will be able to wield.

This elemental connection is referred to as the child's aspect. The child's personality tends to reflect their connected element. "Sweet" children tend to be passive and pleasant while "Boom" children tend to be aggressive and abrasive. Children aspected toward Orange tend to be optimistic and caring. And children with a Pungent aspect tend to be cynical trouble-makers. No child has been born aspected to Prickle since the time when the great undead armies of the Necromancer Vandal Nefar marched through the empire. Prickle is an element of hatred, suffering, and loathing and all of these traits were manifest in Vandal.

The ministry of Magic keeps a close watch for children with a Prickle bend. Rumors abound about what would happen to such a child if they were to be born. Suffice to say, none of them are particularly pleasant.

Government

The government of Empire of Eristonia is a theocratically-elected imperial dynasty. The current Emperor is able to appoint his own heir. This heir does not have to be related to the Emperor in any way though tradition dictates that children are usually selected as heirs. However, his ascension to the throne is not guaranteed. Emperors rule by the will of the Lady alone, as determined by her Orthodox Church of course.

The hierarchy of the Orthodox Church of Eris, known as the Eristocracy, grants their blessing to any ruler they approve of. While this support is not required in order to ascend to the throne, no monarch in the history of the Empire has been able to hold on to power without this divine blessing. In this way the Eristocracy is able to exert considerable control over the affairs of state.

In the event that an Emperor dies without appointing an heir, a new Emperor is selected by the Eristocracy from among the noble families. This means that several of the Noble families have had the rank of "royal" in the past and several more will probably hold it during the course of life on the Lady's Rock.

To help with the governance of the realm, the Emperor appoints a number of ministers to aid him. Traditionally these offices include the Ministries of War, Finance, the Art, Science, Transportation, Agriculture, Labor, Commerce, Health, Urban Development, the Interior, Education, and Justice. This cabinet is led by a Prime Minister who reports directly to the Emperor himself. Some monarchs choose to appoint other non-traditional posts and others have chosen to leave some posts empty or consolidate positions. He, of course, has the ability to remove any of these individuals at any time for any reason. He is the emperor after all.

The Emperor also appoints a regent who will act in his stead should he ever be unfit to fulfill his duties. This regent is not the next in line for the kingdom should the Emperor die, but often serves as the Prime Minister making this a position of considerable power.

The Ministry of War is responsible for the readiness of the realms military. Since the Empire lays claim to the entire known world, this department is often used more as a peacekeeping entity than an actual military force.

The Ministry of Finance is responsible for the condition of the Empire's coffers. Agents of this office collect taxes, which are payable several times each year. They are also responsible for minting coins and prosecuting counterfeiters.

The Ministry of the Art concerns itself with all things of a magical nature. This Ministry maintains the Imperial schools of magic including the very prestigious Suidae Verruca School of Wiz-craft and Witchery.

The Ministry of Science monitors the activities of scientists throughout the realm. It is their job to make sure that these researchers adhere to Imperial levels of ethics and Morality in their research.

The Ministry of Transportation is responsible for maintaining the Empire's public transportation systems and roadways. They also monitor safety trends and create arbitrary legislation that they feel may decrease the number of deaths thus increasing the money generated for the Imperial coffers.

The Ministry of Agriculture is tasked with monitoring the Empire's agricultural production and doing whatever is in their power to increase that production.

The Ministry of Labor handles all Imperial dealings with the various guilds throughout the realm. They also investigate claim of the mistreatment of workers and ensure that everyone is treated fairly. Keep in mind that "fair" does not necessarily mean "good," or, as one minister was accidentally quoted as saying, "If everyone feels screwed then the treatment must be equal."

The Ministry of Commerce this ministry was originally created to handle the imports and exports of the Empire. Since every part of the known world is, nominally at least, part of the Empire, this task has fallen to the way side. Subsequent ministers, in a bid to keep what little power they had, quickly shifted to regulating businesses. Any aspect of business that is not directly related to labor is the province of this ministry.

The Ministry of Health is responsible for the well-being of the Empire's citizens. It is their responsibility to health standards and ensures that they are met.

The Ministry of Urban Development is tasked with monitoring the urban expansion of the Empire. It ensures that adequate sewer systems and roadways are installed and that each city has the proper infrastructure.

The Ministry of the Interior is responsible for the overall development of the Empire. It maintains any Imperial park lands as well as monitoring environmental concerns.

The Ministry of Education is tasked to oversee the education of Imperial citizens. It provides all curriculums that schools are to use, sets goals for the schools, and licenses teachers.

The Ministry of Justice has the arduous duty of enforcing the laws of the Empire. They also maintain the Imperial court and prison systems.

Calendar

By tradition, time on the Lady's Rock is measured starting at the moment that Eris intervened in the war between elves and dwarves. This moment in history is known as the beginning of the first year of our Lady of Discord, or "1 YOLD." That fatefully day was 3172 years ago, so the current year for those of you who are mathematically challenged is 3172. Think about it for a bit, it'll make sense.

A year is divided into 5 seasons of 73 days each. These seasons are named Chaos, Discord, Confusion, Bureaucracy, and The Aftermath. The seasons are further divided into weeks consisting of 5 days each. These days are named Sweetmorn, Boomtime, Pungenday, Prickle, and Setting Orange after the five elements that make up the world.

Holidays & Festivals

On the fifth day of each season the denizens of the Lady's Rock celebrate the Apostle Holidays honoring the patron apostle of each month.

The fifth of Chaos is Mungday honoring Saint Hung Mung who first developed the Sacred Chao.

The fifth of Discord is Mojoday honoring Saint Doctor Van Van Mojo a maker of fine dolls.

The fifth of Confusion is Syaday honoring Saint Sri Syadasti whose full name, by some freak happenstance, translates into a very long, but entirely accurate, Erisian truth.

The fifth of Bureaucracy is Zaraday honoring Saint Zarathud who first recorded the Pentabarf, the five Erisian Commandments.

The fifth of the Aftermath is Maladay after Malaclypse the Elder who, though not a prophet, was a pretty nice guy.

Additionally, the 50th day of each month is a holiday honoring the spirit of the season. These holidays are a time of great merriment and much alcohol consumption. They are named Chaoflux, Discoflux, Confuflux, Bureflux, and Afflux respectively.

Transportation

Transportation on the Lady's Rock can occur in a number of ways. The most popular being horse back. The Imperial Road System, or IRS, is not known for being user friendly or for its reliability and other modes of transportation are usually too costly for the average citizen to afford. Wagons are often used to transport goods from one place to another with traditional wheeled wooden wagons being more common folk and more reliable metal lev-wagons being used by more affluent members of society.

Travel by water way is notable swifter and more dependable than travel over land. But water borne travel is not without its share of hazards. A water craft swept into the aether will plummet like a stone… or, more precisely, like a man made device constructed out of wood or metal carrying goods and / or passengers. Regardless of the analogy you use, the boat is gone. The people on the boat remain buoyant and able to swim as long as they are within 12 miles of shore.

Travel between contineres cannot be accomplished by using traditional water bound vessels instead it is done by using special aether-ships. These ships are similar in appearance to their water bound brethren, but bear some striking differences that allow them to navigate the heavy air as easily as a great galleon cut through waves.
It is important to note for those travels that may not have crossed the aether before that it is not thick enough to serve as a base for lev-vehicles. Your lev-wagon will sink if it goes over the edge.

Despite having mastered levitation (hover) technology, air travel on the Lady's Rock is very limited. Airships exist and some of them use propellers to assist their forward motion. Yet to this day no one has been able to construct a craft that relies on its forward motion to produce lift. Many have tried. Every attempt has met with disaster.

The last and most famous of these attempts at flight was made by a human named Hugh Howards. His plane, the "Glorious Gift of the Lady" made its maiden voyage on the 14th of the Aftermath, 3113 YOLD. The plane flew about 70 feet off the ground at around 90 miles per hour before landing in a river and being swept over the edge into the aether despite all the efforts of Mr. Howards to save her.

Most have given up on the idea of producing a positive lift aircraft. They feel that their efforts would be better spent elsewhere and that the Lady just doesn't want them to fly.

Arts & Entertainment

The Lady's Rock has undergone periods of both artistic repression and rebirth depending mostly on who sat on the throne at the time. Despite the views of the Imperial Court, the arts have always found a place to flourish on the rock. After all, the Empire is simply too vast of an area to completely stamp out any practice, especially if it's one that the people enjoy.

The 40th Emperor of Eristonia, a brilliant orator known as Renaldo, the Impressive Commentator, realized that the people derived some pleasure from viewing works of art. Since happy people caused significantly less problems than unhappy people, he started an Imperial endowment to ensure that the people would always be pacified by the art they enjoyed.

While Eristonia is home to some very talented artists, the people living on the Lady's Rock have an appreciation for any product of individual talent and effort. To them a well crafted shovel is just as impressive, and slightly move useful than a painting or sculpture. That is not to say that they don't appreciate art, only that they appreciate all the fruits of a freeman's labor.

Architecture

Architecture on the Lady's Rock is a strange blend of functionality and beauty. The extravagance of these buildings is limited only by the taste and pocket book of their owners.

Military structures tend to be built out of steel reinforced stone. Crenulated wall and high towers are very common and draw bridges never seem to go out of style though more modern buildings use telescoping steel instead of the more traditional wood.

Palaces, like military structures, are built to last. The main difference being that palaces are almost always ornately decorated, some, like the Imperial Palace in Erisia, are even gilded. Of course, apples tend to be a favorite motif for obvious reasons.

Dwellings in the city tend to be narrow and tall. The wealthier freemen own homes of brick while the average person lives in a home made of predominantly of wood. This wood is often sided with paneling or covered in plaster. Some tenement buildings are metal framed buildings with walls made of either wood or a crushed stone and iron mixture known as ferrocrete.

Dwellings in rural areas tend to be built low with only one or two stories. Their roofs tend to have a steep pitch and they generally lack any exterior ornamentation. Other builds tend to be built exclusively for functionality. Outdoor toilets and cisterns are still common though promising developments in waste treatment are starting phase out these outdoor latrines in favor of new "tank and leach" systems.

Home interiors tend to be as well appointed as the inhabitants can afford. Though the Ministry of Urban Development does their best to insure adequate sewage and water systems in every city, some of the more rural areas are lacking these functions still today.

Social Hierarchy

Eristonia considers itself an enlightened society. Only approximately 5% of its population is involuntarily in service to someone else. The vast majority of these thralls are criminals making restitution for their past crimes. Thralls do receive minimal compensation for their time in servitude though the cost of this compensation is added to the term of their service.

The vast majority, 73%, of the denizens of Eristonia are freemen. These people are usually tenant farmers, unskilled workers, and soldiers. Freemen have the privilege of carrying arms to protect themselves and traveling within the Empire without needing papers. They are legally able to own property, though few do. If they are able to purchase land, they earn the lofty title of "landed freemen."

Of the freeman, just under a third of them are landed freemen (about 24% of the total population). Landed freemen enjoy all the rights that freemen enjoy, plus they own land. This class is made up of people that own establishments that cater to the needs of others, taverns, inns, etc...

Soldiers also make up a significant portion of this class of citizens. They often save their salaries for a few years and purchase businesses or country homes with the intent to retire to them one day. Some of them never do make it, but their children then inherit the land.

Just above the freemen on the social ladder are the artisans composing approximately 15% of the people living in the Empire. These are skilled craftsman and often belong to a guild or other professional society. Many mages & members of the clergy fall into this category though magic is neither a prerequisite nor a guarantee of status.

After the Artisan come the Noble Peers. Noble Peers are granted titles and land in exchange for fealty to the Emperor. They make up approximately 4% of the population. In addition to living in palatial estates, nobles are able to keep a standing group of soldiers in their realm with the understanding that these soldiers are at the Emperor's disposal should he need them. Nobles are also responsible for collecting taxes on their lands and turning the Empire's share of those taxes over to the Ministry of Finance (see taxation on page 23).

Some Noble Peers are granted the ability to bestow noble status upon others in order to help them better administer their realms. These nobles, regardless of title, are referred to as the lesser nobility. This can lead to some confusing social situations when, for example, a Baron appointed by the Emperor encounters a Count appointed by a Duke. Technically, the count out ranks the baron, but the baron's authority comes from the Emperor while the count's comes from a duke. Who, exactly, out ranks who is a matter for debate. Usually the answer depends on whether the baron or the duke has a stronger relationship with the Emperor. Of course, if the count has fallen out of favor with the duke for some reason, the baron wins hands down.

The next level of societal elite is the Eristocracy itself. Arguably either equal to or more powerful than the Imperial families, the Eristocracy consists of the most important members of the Orthodox Church of Eris. They comprise approximately 1% of the entire population. Though there is quite a bit of power held in that 1%.

On the topmost rung of the social ladder sit the Royals. This segment makes up almost 2% of the population. It consists of the extended imperial family and those who formerly graced the imperial throne. The Royals have almost free reign throughout the Empire.

Nobility

Officially, the Empire recognizes 5 different levels of nobility. Each noble has a different level of responsibility, but they all share the common bond of fealty to the Emperor.

Some nobles are granted the ability to appoint other nobles of lesser rank. These provincial nobles hold less power than their counter-parts in the imperial peerage.

The lowliest title of nobility is **Baron**. Barons are charged with maintaining order in a single domain called a barony. Dwarves who hold this rank often prefer the title of Thane. This is because the ranking baron is often a descendant of "the man who keeps the fire."

The **Viscount** (pronounced: vie count) is the next highest ranking. A viscount manages 2 or more baronies.

A **Count** is a noble in charge of at least three baronies. The greater domain is called a county. Dwarves who hold this rank generally prefer the title of Earl. This is because the first dwarf to earn this title happened to be named Earl. Despite his rank, he refused to be called by his title often telling his people, "My name is Earl."

A **Marquis** rules over 4 or more separate domains. They are granted the ability to entitle barons to oversee portions of their realm which is called a March.

Dukes are the final rank in the Imperial peerage. A duke controls at least five lesser realms. Dukes are able to entitle any lesser noble ranking provided that noble meets the land governance requirements outlined by the Ministry of the Interior.

Females are also able to hold any of these positions of authority. A female noble has all the same rights and privileges that her male counterpart enjoys. Their titles are Baroness, Viscountess, Countess, Marquesa, and Duchess respectively.

Royalty

Royalty is divided into two distinct groups. The first is the royals themselves this group consists of the Emperor and his immediate family. The next group is made up of families who, in the past, had served as royals. The patriarch (or matriarch) of these families are granted the title of either Marquis or Duke. They are called **Grand Marquis & Archduke** respectively and their realms are Grand Marches or Grand Duchies.

The Emperor may also appoint **Kings** to rule over portions of the Empire thought this is an exceedingly rare occurrence and no kings have been seen in the Empire since Vandal Nefar (the origin of the words vandalism and nefarious) led his rebellion against the Empire on the 67th of Bureaucracy, 2473 YOLD leading to seven of the darkest years in Imperial History. Were a king to be appointed, his realm would be called a kingdom. Kings are usually granted the ability to entitle lesser nobles.

A **Prince** is the son of either a King or an Emperor. A prince who is destined to inherit the throne of a kingdom is known as the Crown Prince. A prince who has been acknowledged as the heir to the Empire is known as an Imperial Prince. Princes do not have any inherent authority unless they are also a titled noble, in which case they have all the rights and privileges of that title and their realm is known as a principality.

The highest ranking royal in all of Eristonia is the **Emperor** himself. His realm is known as the Empire. The Emperor can pretty much do whatever he wants because he is, after all, the Emperor. To date, only humans have ascended to the Imperial throne.

Again, females are able to hold these titles as well. A female King is called a queen and a female Emperor would be called an Empress… though no female has ever been listed as heir to the Empire and, since no kings have been appointed for almost 700 years, queens are unheard of. The female children of royalty are known as princesses.

The Eristocracy

The Orthodox Church of Eris is led by the **Polyfather**. He is the highest ranking member of the Eristocratic clergy on the Lady's Rock. The general population considers his words to be those of the Lady of Discord.

Below the Polyfather are the **Priests** of Eris. These priests serve to direct worship and guide the faithful. The vast majority of priests serve the Lady in cities across the Empire.

Chaplains are roughly equivalent to priests except that a chaplain serves in more rural areas. Because of this, chaplains do not possess nearly the clout of priests.

Below the priest and chaplains are the deacons. **Deacons** assist priest and chaplains in their duties and fill in for them by leading rituals and ceremonies if the affairs of the lady call the priest or chaplain away for their respective places of worship.

Below the deacons are the **Disciples**. They are the novices of the Eristocratic faith. They serve in a variety of menial tasks while they continue their studies.

The Orthodox Church of Eris

The Orthodox Church of Eris, or OCE, is divided into 5 houses. Each house is led by a priest appointed by the Polyfather and this individual holds the title of High Priest within the church.

The first house is the **House of Obedience**. The purpose of this branch of the church is to ensure that all members of the clergy know the will of Eris, as decreed by the Polyfather, and follow that will. The Orthodox Church of Eris does not tolerate deviance.

The **House of Sovereignty** serves as a liaison between the royals, the nobility, and the church. It is their duty to ensure that Eris' will is done throughout the Empire of course it goes without saying that they receive the will of Eris from the Polyfather.

The House of Sovereignty also maintains and operates the Eristocratic Coalition, a "grass roots" organization whose purpose it to make the people believe that the Eristocracy's desires are in the best interests of the Empire as a whole. The EC's propaganda machine conducts numerous rallies, fundraisers; other politically orientated functions designed to "remind" the people what's best for them and show the government that the people support the Eristocracy.

The **House of Thralls** was created by the Church when Grigori I, the 41st Emperor and father to Grigori II the current Emperor, asked the OCE to help in monitoring the thrall population. This house ensures that thralls are not mistreated… at least not horribly… and by that we mean visibly…

The **House of Purity** works closely with the Ministry of Education to provide high quality Eristocratic learning materials for the public school system. This house is also responsible for maintaining the Eristocratic schools.

The **House of Arms** is the militant branch of the OCE. It is the province of this house to provide security for all Eristocratic facilities throughout the empire. The personal guard of the Emperor also draws its numbers from the Paladins of Eris.

Social Customs

When meeting another person, especially in public, your station in life dictates you behavior. Among warriors and freemen it is customary to shake hands high on the arm. This evolved as a custom among warriors. It was a polite way to check and see if the other person was armed without offending their honor. Freemen adopted this tradition as well.

Knights and officers simply give a two-fingered salute to signify opening the visor on their helms, even if they do not wear one. This too is a deep seeded warrior tradition harkening back to the jousting fields.

It is considered proper to bow before someone of higher station than yourself though women may curtsy if they would prefer. More romantically inclined courtiers often kissed the hand of the person they are greeting as a sign of deference. This is largely considered an archaic custom and is rarely seen outside of the noble & royal courts.

When two mages greet each other it is customary that they cross their hands in front of their chests with their wrists touching. This is to show that they have no intention of casting spells against the person they are greeting. This is thought to represent a symbolic tying of the hands to stop

17

them from reaching their material components or performing the somatic gestures necessary to cast some arcane spells. This practice has fallen out of favor with younger mages who view it as a sign of weakness and subservience. These up and coming mages prefer a more flashy approach, a deep bow as flowers pour from the hat, a phantom fanfare and fireworks show, or other illusory magic is often seen.

In the Empire, men and women share equal rights under the law. For as long as anyone can remember there have not been any significant social differences between the various civilized races.

Despite these official proclamations, Imperial power has never been transferred to a female heir nor has it been held by a non-human. This is done by tradition or so it is said. Likewise, the Eristocracy is almost entirely males though other races have been elevated to this rank in the past.

Education

Thanks to the 17th Emperor of the Empire, the Ministry of Education was established in 3033 YOLD. And with the birth of the MoE came the public schools system.

Every child regardless of class is able to receive an education. The children of thralls are entitled to education through grade 5. The children of freemen are able to continue schooling until grade 10. An artisan's children are entitled to an education through grade 15. Children are allowed to continue on in school after their state education has been completed, but this additional schooling is done at the expense of the parents or guardian.

Noble, royal, and Eristocratic children do not receive any state funded education. This is both to make a show for the general populous and because state education is paid for by taxes, this is the same money that lines the pockets of the nobles & royals, so they would essentially be paying for the education anyway.

The Eristocracy simply prefer to teach their own children in Eristocratic schools. These schools are among some of the best in the Empire and many noble, royal, and artisan children from wealthy families attend Eristocratic schools & universities. This program was further bolstered when Emperor Grigori II, a staunch proponent of the Orthodox Church of Eris, made his now famous Chaos Based Initiative decree in the 3167 YOLD as Imperial funds now became available to assist in maintaining and operating the Eristocratic schools.

Money

Imperial money is minted by the Ministry of Finance and comes in 5 denominations. The smallest of these is the Sec (plural: secs). The next is the Lance (plural: Lances). Then the Lut (pronounced "loot;" plural: Luts; pronounced "loots" or "lutes" but never "luts"). Luts fell out of use right around the beginning of the third age though some diehard remnants that remember the second age and long to continue in its rich history still cling to this outdated coinage even though we're currently half way through the third age. The most common denomination and the next largest, is the Brig (plural: brigs). And finally is the Star (plural: stars, but that's only important if you have entirely too much money).

1 Sec
1 Lance = 10 Secs
1 Lut = 5 Lances (or 50 Secs)
1 Brig = 2 Luts   (or 10 Lances or 100 Secs)
1 Star = 5 brigs (or 10 Luts or 50 Lances or 500 Secs)

Most citizens do not carry coinage on their persons, instead they carry script, small documents noting how much coin they should have been paid, but weren't. Theoretically this script can be traded in at any bank in exchange for actual coin. Unfortunately, some provinces of the realm refuse to recognize the script issued by other provinces. This is especially true when the issuing province is at odds with the state itself. This leads to devalued money and really poor peasants.

Sec   Lance   Lut   Brig   Star

Script from various realms carries with it different names. These names usually have something to do with one of the province's major products. One province, renowned for its strong ale, might issue Alescript. Another province, known for its superior brewed coffees might issue Javascript. The net result is a myriad of different currencies which may, or may not, be accepted elsewhere in the Empire.

Taxation

Running an Empire is costly business and the Empire of Eristonia is no different. Each year the citizens of the Empire are subjected to a variety of taxes.

Sales tax is 5% of the value of any goods sold within the confines of the Empire.

Luxury tax is an additional 5% charged for the purchase of luxury items such as furs, lev-wagons, and attractive mail order brides.

Inheritance tax is charged any time a deceased person gives his possessions posthumously (after they're already dead) to someone else who is not yet dead. It is 10% of the value of the item or items so transferred.

Market tax is collected each time the market is open in the city. It is a flat rate of 1 Sec charged to anyone entering the city that day.

Tolls are charged at every bridge and major crossroads in the Empire. The fee in nominal, 1 Sec per person or animal & 2 Secs per vehicle, but it can add up quickly, especially if you're a merchant on your way to market with a caravan of goods to sell.

Dwelling tax is charged to every dwelling in the Empire and payable by the person who resides in that dwelling. The rate varies based upon location and size of the dwelling. A simple rural dwelling is charged 1 Sec if it is not in a city, 2 Secs if it is, and 5 Secs if that city is fortified. Larger dwellings are charged 10 times those amounts. Inns, hostels, and hotels are charged a rate of 5 Lances per room available to rent. Manors are charged a flat rate of 1 Brig and castles and other fortifications are charged a flat rate of 1 Star. Dwelling taxes are due on or before the 23rd of Bureaucracy each year.

Landed Tax is charged at a flat rate per acre based on functionality. (For those of you who are not familiar with the term, an acre is 43,560 square feet. It's an odd measurement I know, but that's what you get for living on the Lady of Discord's pet rock.) Barren, unusable land is charged at 1 Sec. Water (i.e. ponds, lakes, rivers, & streams) is charged 2 Secs. Unused but usable land & woodlands are also charged at 2 Secs. Farm land is charged at 4 Secs. Land in an unfortified city is charged at 1 Lance 5 Secs while land in a fortified tow is charged at 2 Lances. This tax is payable on or before the 32nd of Bureaucracy each year.

Arms tax is charged to every noble house for the privilege of having a coat of arms. This tax is always 5 Brigs each year and is due on or before the 32nd of Confusion.

Tithes are the Empire's percentage of the money nobles earned during the year. On or before the 32nd of the Aftermath, each noble must send 10% of all taxes collected to the Ministry of Finance.

Income tax is due on or before the 32nd of Discord each year. All persons earning a wage, which includes damn near everyone, must send 1% of their earnings to the MoF.

Poll tax is due every Aftermath the Empire does a census. Each person and any marketable animals they own are taxed. The rate varies depending on you age and perceived income. Children cost 1 Sec each. Adults are charged 2 Secs each. Paying for thralls is the responsibility of the person who owns them. Livestock is charged 1 Sec each as are beasts of burden. Horses, on the other hand, are charged 2 Secs each.

Magic tax is charged on the sale or transfer of any magical item within the confines of the empire. This tax amount to 10% of the value of the item and this tax is charged in addition to sales and luxury taxes.

Weapons tax is a fee you pay for the privilege of being able to own a weapon. The fee is 1 Lance per year and it is payable each year on or before the 23rd of Confusion. This is not only a way to increase the Imperial coffers, but also a convenient way to keep track of who is and is not armed.

Miscellaneous taxes are charged by provincial and tributarial governments as they see fit. It would be impossible to list them all of the different things that various rulers feel it necessary to tax. Some of these taxes even change from day to day depending on the whim of the nobility in question.

Technology

Despite the trappings of feudal government and medieval living, the Lady's Rock is a fairly technologically advanced society.

While their technology may bear little resemblance to anything someone from our own world would recognize, the human's quest for dominance over their new world led to numerous technological advancements. Aqueducts were developed to move water from the lush lands inhabited by elves to the desolate areas to which humans were originally confined. The quickly learned to harness both wind and water to do menial labor. From there it was a short jump to steam powered devices.

The accidental discovery of electricity by a group of Dwarven long spearmen during a raid on a human village heralded a new age of technological development. Soon things thought possible only through feats of arcane skill were accessible to the common man. Artificial light sources, instantaneous communication over great distances, and interconnected electronic repositories of pornographic images were all just a few years off. Of course, some technologically inept members of the establishment felt the ERP could better serve society as a repository for all knowledge and defiled it for such a purpose much to the appreciation of the Eristocratic Coalition.

Telcom units are quite common. Almost every Imperial citizen has access to one of these devices and many carry a portable telcom with them wherever they go. Likewise, vidcasters are also common place. Originally only capable of broadcasting a two dimensional monochromatic image, modern vidcasters are capable of so much more. Some of the more advanced models even allow for three dimensional images.

The latest video game console, the Adventure Terminal 360, even includes a sensor array that detects the physical location of the player within its optical field and projects a three dimensional reality overlay superimposing the game world over the real world for the most intense game experience ever.

Of course, there were a few minor problems. Like the grandmother who, after spilling scalding java on her genitalia went and picked up a copy of Grand Theft Carriage for her 8 year old grandson despite the warning clearly listed on the package saying it was only suitable for "Humans 17 and up, Elves 125 and up, and Dwarves 75 and up. Under no circumstances should this game be purchased for children under the recommended ages or Halflings of any kind."

Her grandson had difficulty distinguishing the game from reality, both because he was still too young and because he was an idiot...mostly because he was an idiot. He was not, however, nearly as much of a moron as his grandmother who bought the game for him in the first place. Apparently the title of the selection wasn't a clue that it may be of questionable content... assuming, of course, that you believed that the warning was intended for someone else. Luckily, the accident happened in such a way that grandma walked with a severe limp and the boy will never be able to breed.

Grandma sued the manufacturer, Dominant Stone Entertainment. The judge assigned to the case had the grandmother summarily executed for sheer stupidity. And those of us who had previously lost faith in the justice system had it suddenly restored in spades.

An accident at the famed Suidae Verruca School of Wiz-craft and Witchery's new Techno-Arcana program led to the development of levitative technology as one group of promising young graduate students attempted to permanently imbue a carriage with the effects of a levitation spell.

This atmosphere of technology and magic creates a truly unique environment. In the beginning technology was used mainly to replicate magical feats and allow the common man access to things that were formerly only possible for those of substantial means. Lately however technology has been used to supplement and augment magical effects. This blending of magic and technology is known as "technomancy" and has become the standard throughout the Empire.

Flora

Several unique species of plant make their homes on the Lady's Rock that have yet to be found elsewhere in the multi-verse.

Acus Labruscae: More commonly known as "blood vine" or "Needle Bush," Acus Labruscae is among the hardiest plants known to exist on the Lady's Rock. Specimens have been found growing in a wide variety of climate ranging from the tropical to the sub arctic. It ranges in color from deep crimson to pale bluish purple. Its leaves are broad shaped like rounded arrowheads.

The plant can be found in both creeping and climbing varieties. Some specimens have even been known to form small shrub-like bushes when there was no suitable structure to climb and no where to creep. Marbled red and pink flowers appear in late Bureaucracy or early Aftermath. Around mid Aftermath reddish black berries begin to ripen in early Chaos.

The Acus Labruscae does not sustain itself through photosynthesis. Instead it feeds on the blood of small to medium sized mammals. This is accomplished by way of tiny hair-like needles along the vine of the plant. These tiny hairs are rigid and easily puncture skin allowing the plant to feed off the resulting wounds. Usually the injured creature struggles to free itself as a result of the wound. This has the effect of further entangling the creature in the vine. A creature trapped by an Acus Labruscae in this manner may live for days while being drained of precious fluid. The corpses of this prey are then eaten by carrion birds and the presence of crows and vultures perched near-by an empty field is a telltale sign of the presence of this plant.

The fruit of Acus Labruscae has a slightly meaty taste. Because it blows during the coldest months of the year, it is a welcome source of food for bears that might awaken early from their hibernation. These animals are often too large to be seriously harmed by the plant and have little difficulty harvesting this meal. The plants resilient seeds than pass through the animal's digestive tract and are deposited when the animal defecates. The animal's waste then attracts flies that lay their eggs and these eggs hatch at approximately the same time as the fledgling vine begins to bud. This provides an available and abundant supply of food for the plant allowing it to grow large enough to capture larger prey.

Some tribes of goblins and uncivilized orcs use this plant as a defensive measure. They go to great pains to cultivate and grow the plant to hang over cavern entrances. Since the plant does not require light in order to grow, it can even be found growing deep in their subterranean lairs.

Carbonis Tree: The Carbonis is a large deciduous tree. The bark of the Carbonis is black in color with some streaks of gray appearing almost as if the tree had managed to survive a great fire. This is not far from the truth as the sap of the Carbonis is highly flammable and used in the production of gun powder and elven fire wine.

The fruit of the Carbonis tree, firecorns, are nuts containing a single gray & black marbled seed, rarely two, encased in a leathery shell. Firecorns mature in about three seasons after which time they drop to the ground. The impact usually causes the shell to crack resulting in a small explosion and spreading the seeds of the plant. Rodents will sometimes take firecorns for food. This is an error they are rarely able to make twice.

Firecorns can be dried out and used as fuel for both heating and cooking. The process for drying these plants is exacting. Too much heat causes the firecorns to explode, while too little heat will not dry the seed thoroughly enough for this use resulting in a subsequent explosion when used as fuel. Properly drying firecorns is a lucrative, if dangerous, business. Many of the homes on the Lady's Rock are heated using this fuel.

The Imperial Military soaks firecorns in the sap of the carbonis tree to preserve their explosive qualities. They are then used as sling stones and miniature grenades during combat operations.

Due to its resistance to heat and fire, the wood of the Carbonis tree is often used to make spoons, ladles, and bowls. It is also used to make handles for pot and pans. However, it is never used to make the pots or pans themselves. This is because the properties of the wood stop the food inside from heating.

Fumi Ficus: The Fumi Ficus, or smoke tree, is a tall semi-deciduous tree that can be found in any tropical or temperate climate. The tree can grow as high as 100 feet tall and it unique among trees in that leaf bearing branches extend from the top of the tree to the very bottom. In warmer climes, the tree remains green and produces fruit roughly once every season. In cooler temperate areas, the Fumi Ficus sheds its leaves in the final days of Bureaucracy and springs to life anew in the early days of Discord. In these climates the tree bears fruit in the three "green" seasons.

The bark of this tree is ground into a fine black powder and, when mixed with the sap of the carbonis tree, makes the "smoke powder" used in ballistic weapons. This black powder also forms the basis of many modern explosives.

The leaves of the Fumi Ficus grow in clusters of five and have a noted golden sheen to them. In earlier times these clusters were called the hands of Eris and the Fumi Ficus was considered sacred. These leaves are harvested for use in a number of ways. Primitive cultures chew on the leaves of the Fumi Ficus while in more civilized cultures the leaves are often dried, fermented, and ground and rolled to make smoking sticks of various sizes. These dried leaves take on a reddish tint and smoking stick are known as "reds" for that vary reason.

The leaves contain a powerful neurotoxin causing mild euphoria and eventual addiction in those who consume it. Eating just one leaf is enough to kill an average sized human, but the exposure to the neurotoxin is significantly reduced by smoking or chewing. In recent times, the wide spread use of the leaves of this tree by those who oppose the rule of the Orthodox Church of Eris has led to that organizations determination to end use of this plant.

The Ministry of Health has released several studies that attribute a large number of diseases to the smoking of the crushed leaves of the Fumi Ficus tree. They have even gone so far as to say that even minute quantities of smoke can be enough to cause serious and dire consequences stating that each smoke stick takes 8 minutes off of your life. As a result, many provinces have outlawed the use of the Fumi Ficus for anything other than producing explosives and ballistic powder.

The fruit of the smoke tree is shaped much like a normal apple. When it first begins to bud, this fruit has a bright red colored outer skin. That skin changes as the fruit ripens to a slightly metallic golden yellow. The "meat of the fruit can vary widely in color but is always some shade of pink. The fruit is safe to eat at anytime during its lifespan though most people prefer the sweetness of the ripe fruit to the decidedly sour taste of the young red specimens.

The fruit of this tree is also harvested for its juice. In addition to being consumed fresh from the press the juice of the fruit is used to make a variety of wines, ciders, and beers.

Ghost Wood Tree: The ghost wood is a large deciduous tree that survives by way of an active form of photosynthesis. The tree actively absorbs light in its immediate vicinity, but unlike other trees, this process takes place in the bark of the tree instead of the leaves. This rapid absorption of light gives the ghost wood its inky black bark. A forest of ghost woods is blanketed in almost impenetrable darkness even in the middle of the brightest days. The bark retains this light absorbing property even if removed from the tree.

The immediate vicinity of a ghost wood tree is several degrees cooler than the air around it. This disparity in temperature causes a slight breeze to blow as the air attempts to equalize the temperature. This breeze stirs the leaves and smaller branches of the tree and creates and eerie howling sound.

Because photosynthesis takes place in the bark rather than the leaves, the leaves of the ghost wood tree are translucent almost to the point of transparency. Once they fall from the branches of the ghost wood tree, the leaves darken to shades of silver with a slightly metallic sheen.

The wood inside of the tree is pale, almost white in color. When it burns, ghost wood gives off a bright and even pale green flame. The heat produced by this fire is considerably less than would be expected. It has been surmised by some botanists that the black bark of the ghost wood actually converts light into heat and that the tree somehow uses this heat to sustain itself.

By far the strangest property of the ghost wood trees is the fact that it is semi-intangible. Organic material, even that which is no longer alive, passes through the plant as if it wasn't really there. This is also a property that wood from the tree retains even after death. Strangely enough, undead creatures do not pass through ghost wood despite previously being alive. Scholars believe this has to do with the negative energy that sustains the undead.

Ghost wood trees are difficult to harvest and work with. Nonetheless, the more wealthy people of the Empire still find a variety of uses for this strange wood. Ghost wood bark is used to make privacy screens, curtains and to line the inside of treasure chests and vaults. The wood is used to construct said chests because the intangible properties make it difficult for thieves to abscond with the treasure. This same property makes it ideal for constructing trap doors.

Sugar Stalk: The sugar stalk is a plant that can be found in the wetlands throughout the empire. Typical plants grow from 3 to 6 feet tall. They bear starchy, strap-like leaves that alternate up the stalk of the plant.

The thick stalk of this plant stores energy in the form of a thick sweet syrup. This syrup is refined and dried to become the crystallized sugar that people of the empire use in their daily lives.

The sugar stalk is a wind pollinated plant that bears unisexual flowers in dense, complex spikes much like a cattail which this plant resembles greatly. The male spike develops directly over the larger female spike. The male stamen consists of a pair of thin, hair-like structures that wither once the pollen is released. The female flower is a cylindrical structure that ranges in height from 3 inches to a foot and a half.

The pollen comes in contact with the outer membrane of the female flower and is absorbed, fertilizing the plant. Approximately five weeks later, the female flower bursts open revealing strands of sticky pink fibers that are caught up by the wind and spread to the surrounding area.

These fibers are sometimes collected and eaten by children as a form of candy. The high sugar content gives them a very sweet taste and their delicate structure causes them to melt when in contact with saliva.

Because it grows in wetlands, water is readily abundant. The root structure of young plants forms fibrous webs of vegetation just inches below the surface of the soil. This web helps protect the delicate soil of the wetlands from erosion. The appearance of sugar stalks is one of the first steps in reclaiming wetlands and they are often planted as a retaining wall providing a natural barrier between usable land and the ever encroaching water.

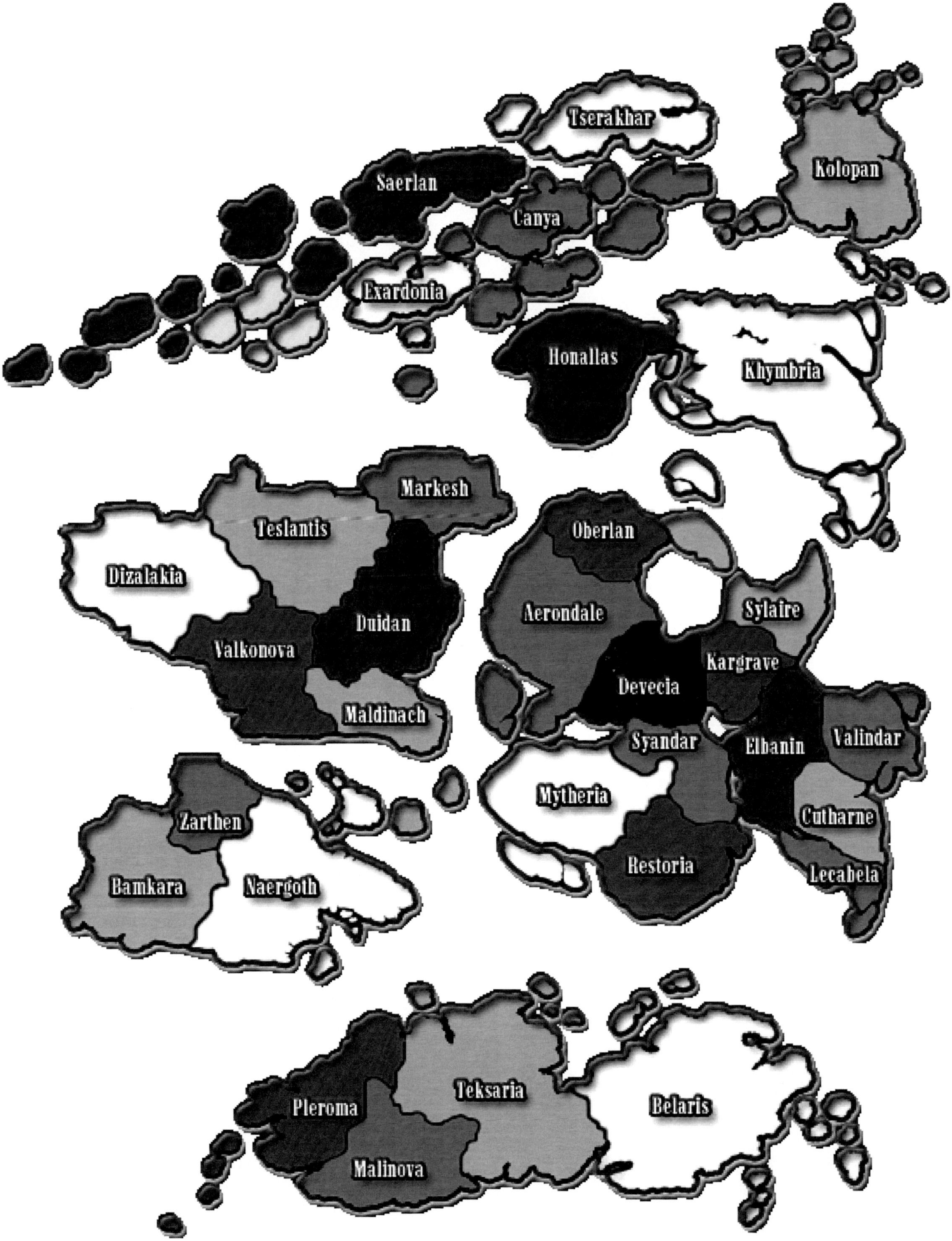
Tserakhar
Kolopan
Saerlan
Canya
Exardonia
Honallas
Khymbria
Markesh
Teslantis
Dizalakia
Oberlan
Duidan
Aerondale
Sylaire
Valkonova
Kargrave
Devecia
Maldinach
Syandar
Elbanin
Valindar
Mytheria
Zarthen
Cutharne
Restoria
Bamkara
Naergoth
Lecabela
Teksaria
Pleroma
Belaris
Malinova

Families of Noble Peerage

House Belior

Prominent Members
    Patriarch: Vintos Belior
    Consort: Lucera Belior
    Heir: Gedeon Belior

Coat of Arms:

Notes: On of the oldest houses of nobility in the Empire, House Belior would probably hold considerable clout and may have even ascended to the gilded throne before if it were not for the "Taint of Belior."

This taint is not a curse, but rather a continuing trend among the nobles of this house. Several times in their history the scions of Belior have "tainted their blood" by mixing it with that of other races. Some rulers of Belaris have taken elven or even the occasional halfling mistress. A few, including Duke Vintos himself, have even gone so far as to take elven brides.

By tradition and decree of the Eristocracy, this "mixing of the blood" has effectively removed any claims House Belaris might have had to the Imperial throne. Instead the members of House Belior must be content with seeing to the affairs of their duchy. This is a task that they seem to approach with as much passion and compassion as any subject would ever hope for. Of all the houses of nobility, House Belior is one of the most beloved by those whom they hold power over. If it was not for they undying loyalty to the crown, they would easily be a threat to Imperial sovereignty.

- **Duchy of Belaris**

Population: 297,000
    Human: 46%
    Elf: 37%
    Dwarf: 13%
    Halflings: 4%

Demographics
    Thralls: 1%
    Freemen: 53%
    Landed Freemen: 26%
    Artisans: 18%
    Other: 2%

Per Capita Income: 350 Brigs

Description: The Duchy of Belaris is composed of rolling hills and old growth forests. Several large lakes and numerous clear streams provide the duchy with an ample supply of water.

The soil is extremely fertile and therefore produces from Belaris' numerous farms are sought after among those wealthy enough to import it. The ruling house maintains a group of scientific advisors tasked specifically with monitoring the soil and assisting the agricultural sector. Belarians are so good at this, in fact, that the Imperial Ministry of Agriculture regularly sends their own experts to Belaris to learn.

Belaris, either by chance of by design, maintains a provincial feel despite its age and size. Most people live in sprawling rural villages. As a matter of fact, the only population center that even resembles a city by Imperial standards is the Belarian capital itself. Partly because of this, the duchy also has a burgeoning tourists industry as wealthy persons from all over the realm flock to enjoy its idyllic landscape and plentiful woodlands.

The Lords of Belaris have always ruled their people with a fair and even hand. They do not share in the excesses enjoyed by so many other noble families that come to plague their people. They treat all their people with compassion and kindness. This temperate province appears to be a veritable utopia - the promised land of freedom, opportunity, and clean country living. At least it is to those outside of it looking in.

The truth, as is often the case in situations such as this, is a bit darker that the citizens of the duchy would ever care to admit. The people of the duchy sacrifice much to maintain the appearance of the provincial paradise. Many of the conveniences that other Imperial citizens take for granted are all but unknown in Belaris' rural communities. While citizens of other provinces use the latest in agricultural technology to help them go about their daily tasks, Belarians do things the way that they always done them. This isn't, as some suspect out of some sense of pride or heritage, instead it is the price that they pay in order to maintain the appearance of the "simple life" that has made Belaris a much sought after destination for tourists.

In most Belarian villages only the town hall & local constabulary are equipped with such modern devices as a telcom unit or vidcaster. Lev-wagons are only seen in the service of wealthy merchants & travelers. Even something as common as equestrian enhancement is also unheard of. Life in the duchy may be good, but the price for that good life is more than most people would be willing to pay.

House Calydon

Prominent Members
    Patriarch: Kinthas Calydon
    Consort: Talina Calydon
    Heir: Arissa Calydon
Coat of Arms:

Notes: The youngest of the non-human noble house, House Calydon is ruled by a family of elves who broke away from the much older Dannan family. Few people outside the houses of Calydon and Dannan know the reason for this separation and the families still appear to have an amicable relationship.

Count Kinthas of Aerondale, patriarch of the Calydon family, is an elf of high moral integrity. He prides himself on the firm, yet fair, manner in which he runs the county. Being somewhat of a traditionalist, it took the rest of the Empire completely by surprise when he announced his heir. The Count by-passed all four of his sons in favor of his youngest child Lady Arissa Calydon, a young elf maiden who, though 25 years old, is still a child in the eyes of the elves.

Count Kinthas staunchly maintains that Lady Arissa is the best choice to govern his realm and that she will mature into a wise ruler. That is, of course, assuming that Kinthas lives long enough to give her the opportunity. Shortly after making his decree, one of the Counts sons went missing. Coincidentally, within a week civil unrest began to brew in the county including one assassination attempt.

The assassin failed, but something about the attempt seems to have struck a cord with the Count. Since that fateful night he has become even more withdrawn and has rarely been seen outside of the palace. Lady Arissa also remains under constant guard and her studies now include a much heavier dose of tactics & strategies.

- **County of Aerondale**

Population: 180,000
    Human: 30%
    Elf: 51%
    Dwarf: 14%
    Halflings: 5%
Demographics
    Thralls: 1%
    Freemen: 63%
    Landed Freemen: 15%
    Artisans: 20%
    Other: 1%
Per Capita Income: 375 Brigs

Description: The County of Aerondale was probably one of the best defended provinces even before the Count withdrew into his shell. Build in the traditional elven style, most buildings are either built into the tops of trees or inside the trees themselves. Wide balconies and high walkways provide ample cover for skilled even marksmen making it nearly impossible for an opposing army to successfully lay siege to an Aerondalite city.

Skilled artisans make up a large percentage of the population of this province. They specialize in woodwork of various kinds. Most of these works seek to enhance nature rather than twist it into some other form.

Besides their beautiful works of art, the people of Aerondale are also renowned for the rare herbs and flowers that are gathered from their forest home. These botanical treasures are sought by scientists and alchemists alike and are a staple of the Aerondalite economy.

House Camaysar

Prominent Members
    Patriarch: Briziac Camaysar
    Consort: Daelia Camaysar
    Heir: Jherek Camaysar

Coat of Arms:

Notes: House Camaysar embodies every bad stereotype of humans and their relationships with other races & with each other. They treat their subjects as things to be used and discarded rather than as other sentient beings.

The progeny of this noble house rule the land with an iron fist. Their rule is fair only in that all of their subjects are mistreated the same. Cruelty and abuse mark the lives of the members of this house. Even the family's coat of arms is said to be a representation of hand prints left by an escaped thrall after his beating at the hands of the House's founder Pretas Camaysar.

Jherek, heir to the Syandarian throne, is rumored to be even crueler than his father. Tales abound of the numerous slaves who have met the Lady by his hand. It is said that he claims a tower in the family's palace as his personal abode and that screams can be heard issuing forth from it throughout the night. He is said to have a thing for elves.

Jherek personally commands "the hand," the Syandarian secret police force. He wields this group like a butcher wields a cleaver separating the unwanted portions of society from the remainder.

- **Barony of Syandar**

Population: 221,000
    Human: 73%
    Elf: 18%
    Dwarf: 7%
    Halflings: 2%

Demographics
    Thralls: 41%
    Freemen: 33%
    Landed Freemen: 12%
    Artisans: 12%
    Other: 2%

Per Capita Income: 225 Brigs

Description: The Barony of Syandar is a dismal realm of gloom. The general attitude of this Barony can be summed up in three words "waiting to die."

The poor people who remain in this oppressive land do so only because they lack the means to escape. The Baron doesn't take too kindly to emigrants. Anyone caught trying to leave the Barony is tortured, killed, or worse. Yes, there are worse fates than death. Don't believe me? Visit Syandar and see for yourself.

Approximately 41% of the population of the Barony of Syandar is composed of indentured persons. Many of these slaves are born into there role. Others are being punished for various offenses, both real and imagined. This reliance on slave labor makes it difficult for the barony to compete with its more enlightened neighbors.

As a general rule, buildings in Syandar reflect the gloom outlook of those who inhabit them. Most dwellings are little more than rickety boxes that have yet to be knocked down. Other more stable buildings tend to be build of dark stone and adorned with all manner of spikes and blades.

Even the landscape reflects the pain of the people who call the barony home. Trees appear diseased and twisted. Grass grows a brownish gray. Even the waters of this province appear brackish despite being perfectly fine both before entering this land and after leaving it.

House Chasmali

Prominent Members
    Patriarch: Telos Chasmali
    Consort: Micea Cereth
    Heir: None
Coat of Arms:

Notes: Though currently enjoying a moment of prosperity, House Chasmali is no stranger to tragedy. Three years ago the heir to the Viscounty, Telos' eldest son Marik, died during a tournament held in his honor. Distraught by the loss of her son, the Viscountess took her own life.

Overwhelmed by grief and guilt, Viscount Telos of Malinova refrained from politics leaving the running of the viscounty to his trusted advisors. His subjects began to fear that he too might end his life and leave them to the mercy of neighboring lords. That all changed a little less than a year ago when Telos reemerged from the palace with Micea Cereth on his arm, a human woman some 30 years his junior.

Born to a blacksmith and a seamstress, Micea is a down to earth beauty. Her calm demeanor and level head not only have helped the Viscount regain his zest for life, but have made her well loved by the population as a whole despite her young age. Many of the Viscount's subjects hope to some day see the two married, but Telos does not seem to be ready to take that step just yet.

Despite this fact, rumors abound that Telos is preparing to name Micea as heir to the throne of Malinova. If the two are not wed before power is transferred, this would mark the end of the Chasmali line.

- **Viscounty of Malinova**

Population: 238,000
    Human: 63%
    Elf: 10%
    Dwarf: 24%
    Halflings: 3%
Demographics
    Thralls: 2%
    Freemen: 59%
    Landed Freemen: 14%
    Artisans: 23%
    Other: 2%
Per Capita Income: 380 Brigs

Description: With the return of their lord, the people of Malinova seem rejuvenated as well. They are enjoying prosperity the likes of which they had scarcely dreamed of in the past. The air seems sweeter, the land seems richer, and the water tastes wetter than it ever did before. This general optimism is almost palpable to those traveling through Malinova.

The viscounty itself is a center of learning for the entire Empire boasting no fewer than 3 different universities, only one of which is controlled by the Eristocracy. Malinovar scientists continue to research a variety of new innovations with the help of hefty governmental subsidies.

Though it is improbable that the province will be able to sustain its current level of growth, its future remains bright. If the Malinovar have one short coming it's the amount of sway that their lords personal well-being has on the lives of his subjects. Of course, other nobles flock to the province in hopes of learning Telos' secret.

House Chaparran

Prominent Members
- Patriarch: Jebulon Chaparran
- Consort: Collia Chaparran
- Heir: Grigori Chaparran III

Coat of Arms:

Notes: The House of Chaparran has more influence in Imperial politics than any other house. This is because Emperor Grigori II, the 43rd Emperor of Eristonia, and the three Emperors who preceded him were all members of this bloodline.

Grigori II is not the most articulate or well-loved emperor to ever sit on the gilded throne, but he has secured his position by maintaining closer ties with the Eristocracy than any other emperor in the history of the Empire.

Despite having two children of his own, Grigori has yet to name his heir. Many speculate that this is due to the fact that, though both his children have shown themselves to be at least as capable as their father, both are female. OF course, the Eristocracy has never given it's blessing to a female heir and has, in the past, even orchestrated the deposition of a royal family because of the appointment of a female heir as was the case with the now vanquished house of Sheylar.

Grand Marquis Jebulon has his work cut out for him. He's torn between vying for his brother's favor so that one of his own children may one day be emperor and standing with his people against his brother's slow erosion of the few freedoms that Imperial citizens still possess.

- **Grand March of Teksaria**

Population: 221,000
- Human: 73%
- Elf: 18%
- Dwarf: 7%
- Halflings: 2%

Demographics
- Thralls: 2%
- Freemen: 78%
- Landed Freemen: 9%
- Artisans: 7%
- Other: 4%

Per Capita Income: 245 Brigs

Description: The Grand March of Teksaria is a rich province populated by poor people. Most citizens of this province struggle merely to survive.

The economy of Teksaria is based on fuel. Logging, mining, and drilling operations employ over three quarters of the population. While these industries bring in a considerable number of Brigs every year, the people see little of that money.

Those who are not engaged in producing fuel for the rest of the Empire serve as hands on the numerous ranches that the Chaparran family keeps for rest and relaxation.

Most of the buildings in the province are simple structures constructed out of plaster covered wooden frames. Lower class families tend to live several families to a single structure. Middle class families tend to live in modest structures. While members of the upper class, those who manage the Chaparran's various economic concerns, generally live in lavish accommodations.

The Law in Teksaria is maintained by the Chaparran family's personal secret police, the Teksarian Rangers. In addition to maintaining the peace, this group of trained thugs serves as the "active arm" of the Chaparran dynasty. They have been used for tasks including the elimination of political dissenters, interrogating citizens, and, in the case of Emperor Vasyl the Unchaste, to pick up women. While they are the law in Teksaria, their ties to the Imperial throne make it possible to find one of these "peace officers" in any one of the Imperial provinces doing the work of their masters.

House Dannan

Prominent Members
    Matriarch: Kildara Dannan
    Consort: Kheloran Veladorn
    Heir: Talina Dannan

Coat of Arms:

Notes: House Dannan is the oldest house of elven nobility tracing its heritage back to before the coming of man. Since that time, tradition holds that leadership of the house is passed through the mother's blood with the mantle of leadership passing to the eldest female of the family. This succession has remained uninterrupted since the founding of the house by Lady Aria Dannan.

Today the Dannans appear to be a happy go lucky and devil may care bunch of hedonists. Their legendary parties are the talk of noble courts across the Empire. They do not maintain a standing army for defense. Nor do they impose any restrictions on trade.

As I said, to the casual observer, the Dannans appear to be little more than privileged hedonists, but that is all part of a carefully orchestrated illusion. In truth, the Dannans are some of the shrewdest politicians the Empire has ever seen. The back room politics of a single Dannan gathering have been enough to stop wars and even, on an occasion or two, crown an Emperor.

- **March of Duidan**

Population: 282,000
    Human: 32%
    Elf: 65%
    Dwarf: 1%
    Halflings: 2%

Demographics
    Thralls: 2%
    Freemen: 33%
    Landed Freemen: 33%
    Artisans: 31%
    Other: 1%

Per Capita Income: 365 Brigs

Description: Like most elven communities, the March of Duidan is largely built in, around, and above their primeval forested home. Though all races are welcome in Duidan, many, especially those of Dwarven blood, are uncomfortable living in such a free and unbridled society.

Duidan has relatively little agriculture. The thick canopies of the many large trees that make up the province let in little light making farming almost impossible. Duidan is, however, the focal point for environmental studies in the Empire. Many members of society work either directly or indirectly on ways to minimize the environmental impact that Imperial civilization has on the Lady's Rock. This technology is then traded or sold to help meet the agricultural needs of the people.

The architecture of Duidan stresses beauty over functionality. Many races find the buildings of this march breath-taking, but impractical. Most residences and shops are constructed inside a living tree. One giant tree may house several families or a dozen or so shops. The only buildings on the forest floor are businesses that require a large amount of heat in order to function – smithies, factories, etc.

Some grand homes take up not only the entire interior of the large trees but are also built on and around them. Graceful spires cling to the sides of ancient oaks and redwoods. The home of House Dannan is a cluster of these behemoth trees located in the center of the realm and surrounded by a nearly impenetrable living wall of thorns, brambles, and tower-like trees.

House De Veci

Prominent Members
    Matriarch: Quinan De Veci
    Consort: Nerissa De Veci
    Heir: Nolyn De Veci

Coat of Arms:

Notes: The Royal House for over 300 years. House De Veci ruled from the founding of the Empire until it was deposed by the now extinct House of Sheylar in 2081 YOLD, the House of De Veci is a proud family with a long history.

Archduke Quinan of Devecia makes a point to show his loyalty and support of the throne, much to the chagrin of his eldest son and heir; Nolyn who believes that the family should strive to regain what is rightfully theirs – namely the gilded throne.

Nolyn has gained a worrisome amount of support among the young people of Devecia. He is rumored to be creating a secret militia to form the core of his army when he makes his play for the throne. This group, known only as the Doves and spoken of only in whispers, has been accused of committing acts of deimism throughout the Empire and was one of the primary targets of Emperor Grigori II's "war on deimism."

- **Grand Duchy of Devecia**

Population: 153,000
    Human: 49%
    Elf: 7%
    Dwarf: 4%
    Halflings: 41%

Demographics
    Thralls: 4%
    Freemen: 37%
    Landed Freemen: 36%
    Artisans: 21%
    Other: 2%

Per Capita Income: 285 Brigs

Description: The Grand Duchy of Devecia is a peaceful realm, for the time being anyway. The people of Devecia are a hard working lot. They are loyal to the Empire, and are genuinely concerned about Nolyn's radical political beliefs.

Devecia is the heart and soul of the Empire. Both the Imperial Palace and Capital are located in this province. The countryside surrounding the city is strewn with noble villas. Serving and maintaining these estates forms the foundation of the Devecian economy.

Devecia is quickly becoming a military state. The Emperor, concerned about the idea of a rebellion fomenting in the Imperial capital, has more than tripled the number of Imperial troops stationed in this province. He has also taken it upon himself to bring in "advisors" from the Teksarian Rangers.

With the number of Imperial troops running around the Grand Duchy, crime in Devecia is at an all time low. While the younger generation welcomes this change, this troubles the older citizens who remember all too well the dangers of leaving too much power in the hands of one man.

The Rangers have done nothing to upset the lives of ordinary citizens yet, so this discontent is largely limited to barroom philosophers. However, if the seed of rebellion had been planted in Devecia, Emperor Grigori II is doing everything he can to water those seeds.

House Elgion

Prominent Members
 Patriarch: Dergin Elgion
 Consort: Hanalli Elgion
 Heir: Theron Elgion

Coat of Arms:

Notes: The Earl of Elbanin is short, even for a dwarf. He is a gruff individual who acts as if he is new to the nuances of court and etiquette despite sitting of the throne of Elbanin for over 120 years. The Earl is a cunning man and this gruff and uncouth demeanor is only part of his act to keep his opponents off guard. They expect him to be the battle crazed Dwarven drunkard and he puts them at ease by filling this role perfectly.

Compared to his father Theron, heir of Elbanin, appears to be the very picture diplomacy and refinement. Of course the truth is the Theron fails to understand the role society has delegated to him. This may turn out to be his greatest strength or his most exploitable flaw.

In the mean time, Lord Dergin takes advantage of this difference in the political arena. Often times he will enter negotiations with his abrasive personality and ruffle as many feathers as possible only to send his son in afterward to smooth things over. The contrast between them is so great that many people agree to Theron's demands if only to save themselves from having to suffer his father any longer. This suits the earl just fine as long as Elbanin comes out ahead in the end.

- **County of Elbanin**

Population: 159,000
 Human: 38%
 Elf: 4%
 Dwarf: 53%
 Halflings: 3%

Demographics
 Thralls: 7%
 Freemen: 65%
 Landed Freemen: 3%
 Artisans: 23%
 Other: 2%

Per Capita Income: 325 Brigs

Description: The mountainous province of Elbanin is rich in minerals. Though they are not taxed any less than the citizens of any other province, the great wealth found in the soil of this land translates into a wealthy population.

Almost all the dwellings in this province, and in fact entire cities, exist below the provinces surface. These cities appear to be veritable fortresses. Large stone or metal doors flanked by defensive towers both inside and out mark their entrances.

The few actual buildings that travelers do encounter on the surface tend to be either military outposts or the property of mercantile concerns. These outcroppings of civilization are usually capable of providing minor aid to travelers and restock their supplies…for a reasonable fee. There is no such thing as a free ride in the County of Elbanin.

Though the dwarves of this province prize craftsmanship and individual effort, theirs is a communal society. Every person is expected to do their job and pull their weight for the good of the county as a whole. Those few dwarves who are able to earn any appreciable amount of wealth usually due so by discovering some new and innovative way for others to more efficiently perform the more menial tasks of mining, refining, and transporting ore. This is why there are considerably less landed freemen in this society.

Males and females are considered absolutely equal in all things. This troubles some travelers from other provinces who are more accustomed to acknowledging the differences between men and women. Women are expected to work in the mines next to their husbands. Wages are paid by the family, not by the individual, and are paid based on the total hours worked and not for the amount of work done.

That is not to say that those in charge do not keep a watchful eye on the amount of work you are doing. Failure to perform your "fair share" of the work load is considered a very serious crime in Elbanin and often results in indentured servitude while your wages go to compensate the community for your lack of dedication, mutilation, or, in more serve cases, death.

The County of Elbanin does not have a military in the traditional sense. Instead every adult citizen of the county is trained in the use and maintenance of arms and armor. Each member of the community serves a period of time patrolling the county and keeping their fellow workers safe. When not in service to the military, these citizens work in the mines as other take their turn to provide protection. In the event of invasion, every person residing in Elbanin who is able to carry a weapon is called to help with the defending their homeland.

Goblin raids have become more prevalent in recent years. Political scientists throughout the Empire see this as a sign of some large event lurking on the horizon. Numerous other provinces have offered to aid Elbanin in turning back these raiders, but the proud dwarves will have none of it. Many believe they fear allowing other provinces to station troops in their lands. Others point to a more sinister reason for their refusal of aid. Whatever the reason, travelers to the County of Elbanin has best be on their guard.

House Honblas

Prominent Members
    Patriarch: Skerit Honblas
    Consort: None
    Heir: Garm Honblas
Coat of Arms:

Notes: The House of Honblas is the youngest of the Dwarven provinces in the Empire. It was founded in 2284 YOLD by a concession from Grand March of Khymbria in recognition of the service provided by Honblas himself, progenitor of this noble family, during the rebellion of 2281 YOLD. Lord Skerit Thane of Hanallas maintains strong ties with that family as did his ancestors before him. Lord Skerit has never married. The heir to the Barony's throne is his nephew Garm.

Garm is a level-headed and politically astute individual. His piercing blue eyes seem to be able to look into the very soul of those whom he speaks to. He is unusually tall for a dwarf. This is probably because he is the product of mixed elven and dwarven heritage. Garm was born of a union between an elven officer in the Khymbrian army and a Dwarven female from House Honblas during the failed coup of 3027 YOLD.

Despite his races natural aversion to the arcane arts, Garm was schooled at the Suidae Verruca. It was during this schooling that he met and befriended Baelyn Khembryl and Spyrodin Nefar. Their relationship ensures that the diplomatic ties between houses Honblas and Khembryl will continue for the foreseeable future.

- **Barony of Honallas**

Population: 216,000
    Human: 33%
    Elf: 12%
    Dwarf: 53%
    Halflings: 2%
Demographics
    Thralls: 4%
    Freemen: 16%
    Landed Freemen: 55%
    Artisans: 23%
    Other: 2%
Per Capita Income: 335 Brigs

Description: The Barony of Honallas is unique in Dwarven lands in that they earn almost no income from mining. Instead the people of Honallas are framers and brewers. Most of the grains produced are used in the production of alcoholic beverages and the ales and meads produced by the dwarves of Honallas are widely acknowledged as the finest in the Empire.

Honallas is a land of rolling hills lacking the mountains that usually mark Dwarven lands. This suits the Honallasians just fine. Most of the province has been cultivated and belongs to the families that grow the fruits and grains that are used in brewing. The vast majority of the artisans living in Honallas are master brewers and vintners.

Other Dwarven realms are suspicious of Honallasians because of the fact that they live above ground on flat land and have strong diplomatic ties to human lands. This does cause some problems between the realms and the people of Honallas have had to remind their kin on the field of battle that they are dwarves at heart.

Honallasian merchants travel throughout the Empire plying their wares. These dwarves are considered more worldly and civilized by both the humans and the elves of the Empire. This is due to the fact that they exist in a society that is less communal than those of their kin.

House Kadoch

Prominent Members
    Patriarch: Madar Kadoch
    Consort: Kennil Kadoch
    Heir: Nelar Kadoch

Coat of Arms:

Notes: Lord Kelvilar, the first Thane of Kargrave was ennobled by a decree of Emperor Vasyl I in 2081 for their support of house Sheylar's ascent to the Imperial throne. Since that time the House of Kadoch has loyally supported the throne…regardless of who has held it.

The Kadoch's support of Vandal Nefar in his rebellion strained the relations with the other noble families. When House Khembryl returned to the gilded throne, Emperor Alocer forced Kadoch to donate a portion of their realm to the House of Keroon. This caused enmity between the three houses that remains to this day.

The current thane, Lord Madar, is the great grandson of Kelvilar. Though well respected, age is finally taking its toll on the proud dwarf. Most people suspect it is just a matter of time before his son is sitting on the throne.

Nelar is a handsome, for a dwarf, young man in his mid one hundred and teens… While he has already distinguished himself on the field of valor at this young age, he is nowhere near the statesman that his father is.

- **Barony of Kargrave**

Population: 115,000
    Human: 12%
    Elf: 3%
    Dwarf: 62%
    Halflings: 23%

Demographics
    Thralls: 2%
    Freemen: 59%
    Landed Freemen: 14%
    Artisans: 23%
    Other: 2%

Per Capita Income: 295 Brigs

Description: The Barony of Kargrave is a small province created by forced allocation of lands once belonging to the County of Elbanin. This alone, though it happened years ago, is enough to sour relations between these two Dwarven lands.

The economy of Kargrave is sustained by lucrative Imperial arms contracts first instituted by Emperor Teos of the now defunct House Balasteer. These contracts have been honored by subsequent emperors giving Kargrave the nickname "Armory of the Crown." Most of its citizens are employed by the military-industrial complex. This economy was further bolstered when Grigori II declared war on all Deimist factions across the Empire.

As befits a people who earn their living making implements of wars, the people of Kargrave are a dour lot. They live as a testament to the old adage that wealth does not equate to happiness. Of course, being wealthy doesn't make them any less happy than anyone else either.

Kargrave is also notable for its incredibly lax weapons policy. All form of melee weapons and firearms are permissible unless they are used to threaten another being. This makes Kargrave a veritable military encampment. Heavy weapons are a noted exception to this policy. Anyone found to be carrying a heavy weapon without the proper authorization is handled quickly, efficiently, and without any unnecessary mercy.

House Keroon

Prominent Members
    Patriarch: Palan Keroon
    Consort: Naomalla Keroon
    Heir: Elena Keroon

Coat of Arms:

Notes: The members of the House of Keroon have pledged themselves to the service of our Lady of Discord. Their loyalty to the church is such that other nobles have remarked that the first non-human to ascend to the Imperial throne will probably come from this house.

- **Viscounty of Sylaire**

Population: 182,000
    Human: 41%
    Elf: 50%
    Dwarf: 6%
    Halflings: 3%

Demographics
    Thralls: 1%
    Freemen: 49%
    Landed Freemen: 19%
    Artisans: 29%
    Other: 2%

Per Capita Income: 245 Brigs

Description: The Viscounty of Sylaire is a largely self-sufficient province. Its primary industry is agriculture, though it actually exports very little of the goods produced.

The Viscounty boasts several Eristocratic schools and is considered the unofficial spiritual center of the Empire. Even the Polyfather maintains a vast estate in Sylaire, though what he uses this property for remains a mystery.

Sylaire has one of the most comprehensive schooling programs in the Empire thanks to the influence of the Eristocracy. This makes Sylaire one of the best educated provinces in the Empire. Many people continue on to earn advanced degrees even if they fully intend to live out their lives toiling in the provinces many fields.

House Khembryl

Prominent Members
- Patriarch: Jonfran Khembryl
- Consort: Marilla Khembryl
- Heir: Baelyn Khembryl

Coat of Arms:

Notes: The Khembryl family once sat upon the Imperial throne. Then the arch-necromancer Vandal Nefar rose to power in the province of Naergoth.

Soon the Imperial capital was over run by an army of soldiers that could not be killed…at least not a second time. The field of battle consumed many souls during that war. With each conflict the enemy grew strong as the bodies of the recently deceased rose to bolster their ranks.

The surviving members of House Khembryl went into hiding and secretly began to mount a rebellion against the upstart necromancer and his fiendish forces. After a bloody conflict lasting almost 7 years, Vandal Nefar was banished to the world beyond.

Despite their past differences, things appear to be mending between the Houses of Khembryl and Nefar. The Khymbrian heir and the heir of Naergoth attended the Suidae Verruca together with Garm Honblas and the three appear to have become friends. Exactly what this bodes for the empire as a whole remains to be seen.

The Khembryl family themselves earned their considerable fortune through investing in the provincial industries rather than through taxation. All contracts for such investments are freely entered into and negotiated by all concerned, otherwise House Khembryl withdraws from the deal.

More than any other noble house, the House of Khembryl works to maintain a separation between themselves, their holdings, and those that belong to the province. The house maintains a separate and distinct military force for their personal protection. They maintain separate financial records. Even their home is separate from the provincial palace, which houses the museum of Khymbrain history as well as the headquarters of the Khymbrian military.

These differences stem from the idea that has been at the core of House Khembryl's political philosophy. They see themselves more as administrators of the province on behalf of the people and not as rulers to lord over them.

- **Grand March of Khymbria**

Population: 279,000
- Human: 54%
- Elf: 25%
- Dwarf: 10%
- Halflings: 11%

Demographics
- Thralls: 0%
- Freemen: 32%
- Landed Freemen: 34%
- Artisans: 33%
- Other: 1%

Per Capita Income: 395 Brigs

Description: Khymbria is unique among Imperial provinces for several reasons. The most obvious of these reasons is the manner in which House Khembryl administers their domain. Their policy of allowing their people to reap the benefits of their own labor has made them well-loved by the people of the province. Of course, it has also earned them their fair share of enemies.

Khymbria is a truly free market. The government practices an extreme form of laissez faire capitalism that scares the rulers of other provinces. Contract law is both simple and explicit. Any two parties may freely enter into any agreement under any terms they so choose. The government steps in only to enforce such contracts and adjudicate contract disputes. In all other cases the market dictates its own regulations.

Municipal services are all provided by the private sector. There is no state run fire department or police agency. These functions are instead performed by private concerns that are contracted by the people of a given area. Those who do not wish to pay for the services are free to do so, however, they will not be able to utilize the services until such a time as their account has been balanced. This means that, unless you are a customer, the fire department will not stop your house from burning to the ground. They may act to limit the damage to property in order to protect that of their customers, but there is no charity work. It also means that no group or organization gains an advantage over any other. Everyone who wants protections pays for it.

While Khymbrians do pay taxes, they only pay those taxes mandated by the Empire. By tradition no additional taxes imposed by the House of Khembryl. This tradition has been upheld by every Grand Marquis since the founding of the March. The taxes that are collected by Imperial mandate go toward providing for defense and improving the infrastructure such as schools and roads. House Khembryl is also unique in that moneys collected by way of these taxes remains in the coffers of the March itself instead of lining the pockets of the nobles.

The Grand Army of Khymbria is a large and well-trained all volunteer force. Unlike other provinces, the Grand Army of Khymbria is not a tool of the nobles who rule the land. Instead it serves the people of the March by providing for their defense. While the Grand Marquis is the nominal head of this military force, the actual military leadership is made up of seasoned veterans who have risen through the ranks. The decisions made by these officers are subject to review by the Grand Marquis and kept in check by a well armed populous and the Marquis personal guard.

House Kreyes

Prominent Members
    Patriarch: Seston Kreyes
    Consort: Amira Kreyes
    Heir: Miceylla Kreyes

Coat of Arms:

Notes: The House of Kreyes is descended from the famous Dwarven general Therrod Kadoch.

When house Sheylar first wrested control from House De Veci in 1934 General Therrod was assign to govern the troublesome De Veci lands that had previously been controlled by an elven house whose name have been lost to antiquity.

Later, during the war of 2245, when house Rahun seized control of the Empire by obliterating House Sheylar, the Dwarven governor of this province took the opportunity to gain independence. Not wishing to upset the new Emperor, House Kadoch did not attempt to rein in their wayward children and the province of Cutharne was born.

When Vandal Nefar staged his coup, House Kadoch embraced the opportunity to lay claim to the land they had lost under House Rahun. The armies of Kargrave marched across the land of Cutharne. Soon the seasoned warriors of Kargrave had wrestled control of the province and established their own interim government.

When House Khembryl launched their counter-attack, the tattered remnants of House Kreyes were at their side. After the dust settled and the dead were finally laid to rest (again), Emperor Valdris gave Cutharne back to the House of Kreyes and bestowed the title of Viscount on the Lord of Cutharne.

Today house Kreyes is a strange blend of human Dwarven, and Elven blood. Members of this family are often short and muscularly built, but have a peculiar grace about them.

Miceylla, heir to the Viscounty, is an exotic beauty. She has the build of a gymnast, the grace of a dancer, and the tenacity of a cornered tigress protecting her young. She serves her father as a diplomatic envoy to other noble families handling all of Cutharne's most crucial negotiations. She has even been seen in the Imperial court when the occasion has warranted.

In spite of their mixed elven heritage, other elven nobility tend to look down upon House Kreyes more than they look down upon any other family. Likewise, dwarves remain skeptical of this house because of the animosity between them and House Kadoch. It is not an enviable position to be in, but it is one that the members of the House of Kreyes manage with a pose and grace that few would have expected.

- **Viscounty of Cutharne**

Population: 117,000
    Human: 49%
    Elf: 9%
    Dwarf: 41%
    Halflings: 1%

Demographics
    Thralls: 5%
    Freemen: 52%
    Landed Freemen: 33%
    Artisans: 8%
    Other: 2%

Per Capita Income: 205 Brigs

Description: Cutharne is a broken land. Most of its topography consists of vast deserts and harsh wastelands – the fall out of the mystical energies used to combat the "Lich King" who ultimately met his demise within the borders of this land.

Many of the structures within this province are built upon the shells and foundations of older buildings. New walls were added to those that remained intact after the war had ended. Roofs were replaced. Sometimes entirely new structures were built on, around, or in the skeleton of a structure long since destroyed. This gives the province's architecture a unique and somewhat foreboding appearance as if each building contains a specter from the past trying to intrude upon modern life.

The great battles that took place on this land not only decimated the landscape but damaged the very fabric of reality. Food planted in this soil tastes more bitter & ashy than that produced elsewhere in the empire. Each year, magic in the province ceases to function from the morning of the 26th of Bureaucracy until the morning of the 32nd.

During this time, flowers wilt and die, sickness runs rampant among the populace, and not a single creature is ever born. Collectively these effects are known as the "Curse of Cutharne" to those who have had to endure them. It is a burden that the citizens of this province bear with a stoic pride.

Still attempting to recover after all these years, Cutharne has little in the way of commercial exports. Relics of the Great War, though increasingly scarce, still fetch a good price at market. There are relatively few artisans in Cutharne. Those who do find their way to this province are usually of a scientific or mystical nature intent on studying the curse and its effects on the people. In spite of years of such study, no way to avert the curse has been found.

House Lecabel

Prominent Members
    Patriarch: Konel Lecabel
    Consort: Amiko Lecabel
    Heir: Andac Lecabel
Coat of Arms:

Notes: The House of Lecabel is a young house as noble houses go having only been ennobled 41 years ago in 3031.

The uprising of 3027 had failed. Those separatists who remained alive sought shelter and anonymity in the broken and unclaimed wastes of Cutharne. Desperate to maintain peace in a realm already wrought with trouble Viscount Seston petitioned Emperor Renaldo I to ennoble his niece, Lady Amiko, and her husband, the elven war hero Sir Konel of Duidan, who had been recently wed. Thus was born the house of Lecabela.

- **Barony of Lecabela**

Population: 123,000
    Human: 61%
    Elf: 5%
    Dwarf: 4%
    Halflings: 30%
Demographics
    Thralls: 5%
    Freemen: 48%
    Landed Freemen: 23%
    Artisans: 21%
    Other: 3%
Per Capita Income: 215 Brigs

Description: The Barony of Lecabela shares much with their neighbor Cutharne. Lecabel suffers from the same curse. Its people eat the same bitter food. In truth, if you were not told by someone you would never know that you had passed from one realm to the other.

Connected by bonds of blood as well as land, Lecabela has extremely close diplomatic relations Cutharne. So close, in fact, that the two might as well be one nation.

House Malgrin

Prominent Members
- Patriarch: Sevarius Malgrin
- Consort: Ceyl Janek
- Heir: None

Coat of Arms:

Notes: The House of Malgrin was founded in 2480 YOLD when Emperor Valdris I ennobled Sevarius Malgrin, a vampiric general in the army of Vandal Nefar who had turned against his master.

Lord Sevarius, now more than 700 years old, has ruled this province ever since. Due to his deathless vampiric nature he appears to be a human man in his mid thirties and in excellent physical condition. In spite of his advanced age, Sevarius has yet to name an heir and has no children.

His current consort is Ceyl Janek. A peasant woman born in the province, Lady Ceyl is merely the latest in a long line of lovers that Sevarius has taken over the year.

- **County of Maldinach**

Population: 203,000
- Human: 48%
- Elf: 19%
- Dwarf: 19%
- Halflings: 14%

Demographics
- Thralls: 35%
- Freemen: 31%
- Landed Freemen: 3%
- Artisans: 29%
- Other: 2%

Per Capita Income: 310 Brigs

Description: The County of Maldinach is strange indeed. Though it is ruled by a vampiric lord, the very practice of necromancy has been outlawed. In fact, even owning a necromantic tome is grounds for immediate execution.

Slavery is more common here than most other places in the Empire. Count Sevarius himself maintains a veritable harem of nubile young women from which he feeds regularly. Although they could be considered little more than cattle, Count Sevarius treats these thralls with genuine concern. He spares no expense in their medical care.

Maldinach boasts some of the finest medical care available throughout the empire. The teaching hospital in the province's capital is widely regarded as the finest of its kind. And people needing delicate surgical procedures flock to Maldinach for the superior care available. The vast majority of Maldinachian artisans are medical professionals specializing in everything from internal medicine to medicinal magic.

Few people in Maldinach outside of those practicing the medical arts own any real property. Instead they are freemen who work in the service and support industries.

House Markune

Prominent Members
- Patriarch: Pretas Markune
- Consort: Kandria Markune
- Heir: Maxarin Markune

Coat of Arms:

Notes: Most of the other noble families of the empire view the House of Markune as a dangerous throw back to a darker, less enlightened age.

Their deep and unwavering hatred of all things non-human has led to the oppression of their people…ostensibly for their own good.

- **Viscounty of Markesh**

Population: 124,000
- Human: 77%
- Elf: 6%
- Dwarf: 17%
- Halflings: 0%

Demographics
- Thralls: 34%
- Freemen: 25%
- Landed Freemen: 21%
- Artisans: 18%
- Other: 2%

Per Capita Income: 175 Brigs

Description: Oppression hangs over the Viscounty of Markesh like a thick blanket of fog. The Viscount's "peacekeepers" are ever present. And their cold touch can be felt throughout life in this province.

Only humans of pure blood are even considered citizens. All non-humans are either servants or criminals. They have no rights and are afforded no quarter. Halflings are hated more than any other species and are killed on sight.

Knowingly giving aid or comfort to a non-human is a high crime. Inter-racial marriages or even affairs are punishable by death. Elves and dwarves who find themselves in this province and on the wrong side of the law, which is to say outside of a dungeon, are beaten or worse.

Needless to say, life in Markesh is difficult, unless you are a human.

House Merelan

Prominent Members
- Patriarch: Taslin Merelan
- Consort: Nimea Merelan
- Heir: None

Coat of Arms:

Notes: The House of Merelan was founded by Lord Admiral Jevan Merelan in 2167 as a mercantile concern providing transportation across the aether. It was ennobled by Emperor Zoren I in 2352 for their assistance is protecting Imperial ships from pirates.

The members of House Merelan draw upon their rich nautical history and run their province much like a captain would run his ship. It's a tight ship, but a fair ship.

- **County of Kolopan**

Population: 167,000
- Human: 40%
- Elf: 38%
- Dwarf: 22%
- Halflings: 1%

Demographics
- Thralls: 6%
- Freemen: 35%
- Landed Freemen: 39%
- Artisans: 18%
- Other: 2%

Per Capita Income: 280 Brigs

Description: Floating in the northwestern part of the Erisian Sea the County of Kolopan is noted for its formidable navy the size of which rivals that of the Empire's own armada. In fact, Kolopan has no army to speak of. Instead they rely on their marines to carry them through any conflict. It comes as no surprise that Kolopan is home to the Imperial Naval Academy, or that many naval officers are born in this land.

Life in this province centers on the great sea of aether. The shipyards of Kolopan turn out the best aethereal ships in the Empire. And those Kolopanites who are not employed building ships use them to fish the heavy air just beyond their shores.

The County of Kolopan retains good diplomatic relations with the majority of the neighboring provinces. In the past, they did have several land disputes with both Canya and Khymbria. These disputes seem to have been resolved and the provinces seem to have amicable relations at this time even forming a joint task force to rid the region of pirates and brigands.

Kolopan is also home to the Imperial Center for Aethereal Studies. The ICES has at their disposal numerous aethereal vessels including one that was designed to venture into the deep aether. This vessel, the Vanguard, was built to replace a similar vessel, the Wanderer that was lost with all hands aboard during its initial dive.

House Millikan

Prominent Members
    Patriarch: Cavar Millikan
    Consort: Saduze Millikan
    Heir: Resk Millikan

Coat of Arms:

Notes: House Millikan stands alone as the only noble house in the Empire composed of Halflings. Lord Cavar, the Count of Oberlan, understands all too well the precarious position that he finds himself in. To the west, just across the Sound of Raxorn, lies the Viscounty of Markesh where being born a Halfling is a capital crime. To protect himself and his people, Lord Cavar maintains strong relationships with House Calydon of Aerondale.

- **Barony of Oberlan**

Population: 162,000
    Human: 13%
    Elf: 28%
    Dwarf: 10%
    Halflings: 49%

Demographics
    Thralls: 0%
    Freemen: 33%
    Landed Freemen: 41%
    Artisans: 24%
    Other: 2%

Per Capita Income: 195 Brigs

Description: Oberlan is an idyllic land of rolling hills and verdant plains. The people seem to live a care free life despite existing with the specter of a Markeshite invasion continually hanging over their heads.

House Molikroth

Prominent Members
    Patriarch: Lucien Molikroth
    Consort: Chasyn Molikroth
    Heir: Thorne Molikroth

Coat of Arms:

Notes: Lord Lucien Molikroth, Baron of Canya, is a strange an enigmatic man. He is rarely seen outside his palace of dark volcanic stone. His consort, Lady Chasyn, an elf born in Khymbria, came to the province just 13 years ago as a diplomatic envoy from that land. Their Daughter, Lady Thorne, was born just one year later.

- **Barony of Canya**

Population: 139,000
    Human: 41%
    Elf: 1%
    Dwarf: 31%
    Halflings: 27%

Demographics
    Thralls: 8%
    Freemen: 25%
    Landed Freemen: 37%
    Artisans: 28%
    Other: 2%

Per Capita Income: 225 Brigs

Description: The Barony of Canya is a small island nation covered in ice and snow. Its borders have recently expanded. These expansionist forces, under the command of Admiral Jaxom Rondach, seem to have stopped after wresting a few islands from the Realms of Kolopan and Saerlan.

Canya is a largely undeveloped land and the inhabitants of this barony work for every inch of existence they claim as their own.

House Mytherie

Prominent Members
    Patriarch: Veldor Mytherie
    Consort: Imoen Mytherie
    Heir: None

Coat of Arms:

Notes: Veldor Mytherie is the youngest noble in the Empire having ascended to the throne of his province just two years ago after the death of his father Lord Gaedon. Last year the Baron of Mytheria celebrated his wedding to Lady Imoen Camaysar, the youngest daughter of Lord Briziac Camaysar the Baron of Syandar, cementing the peace between these neighboring provinces. The pair has no children yet and no heir has been named.

- **Barony of Mytheria**

Population: 180,000
    Human: 37%
    Elf: 6%
    Dwarf: 53%
    Halflings: 4%

Demographics
    Thralls: 3%
    Freemen: 48%
    Landed Freemen: 34%
    Artisans: 13%
    Other: 2%

Per Capita Income: 200 Brigs

Description: The seaside province of Mytheria is enjoying the hope that comes from a young and vibrant leader. The economy, predominantly manufacturing, is booming and Mytheria currently produces more lev-vehicles than any other province.

House Nasredin

Prominent Members
    Patriarch: Kitsen Nasredin
    Consort: Hatha Nasredin
    Heir: Gandin Nasredin

Coat of Arms:

Notes: Restoria is run like a corporate entity with the Nasredin family making up the board of GMs and the Archduke chairing that august body. Every decision that the Restorian government faces is treated as a cost / benefit analysis and they rarely vote against the bottom line.

The two of the archduke's children, Gandin & Kalina, serve as ministers in the Imperial cabinet controlling both the departments of commerce and education.

- **Grand Duchy of Restoria**

Population: 154,000
    Human: 40%
    Elf: 19%
    Dwarf: 37%
    Halflings: 4%

Demographics
    Thralls: 5%
    Freemen: 48%
    Landed Freemen: 5%
    Artisans: 40%
    Other: 2%

Per Capita Income: 355 Brigs

Description: The Grand Duchy of Restoria is the center of the Empire's entertainment industry. Vast tracts of land are occupied by studios producing both vidcast programs and holopics. Many of the citizens of Restoria have advanced degrees in field related to production and Restorian schools have programs in everything from acting to WI-AT graphics.

House Nefar

Prominent Members
    Patriarch: Lucibryn Nefar
    Consort: Rayvenne Nefar
    Heir: Spyrodin Nefar

Coat of Arms:

Notes: The progenitor of House Nefar is Vandal Nefar, the famed rebel behind the coup of 2473 when an army of undead marched across the land. It was this uprising & the treacherous "slash & burn" tactics that his forces employed that gave us the words "nefarious" and "vandalism." It was a dark time, but that period also saw the largest growth in the history of the Empire. Fueled by the greed of their master, the undead legions expanded Imperial power more than doubling the lands under Imperial control.

After Vandal's death at the hands of the forces of House Khembryl, many thought that House Nefar would be obliterated. To their surprise, Emperor Valdris I, leader of the Khymbrian forces, did not order the death of the Nefar family or even remove their title. Instead he granted the house the full rights and honors accorded to a former royal house including a state funeral for Vandal Nefar and internment in the House of Lords, the Imperial mausoleum.

This act, of course, set events in motion that would ultimately lead to his assassination, the poisoning of his heir, and the ascension of House Petiron to the Imperial throne.

- **Grand Duchy of Naergoth**

Population: 184,000
- Human: 49%
- Elf: 46%
- Dwarf: 2%
- Halflings: 3%

Demographics
- Thralls: 5%
- Freemen: 50%
- Landed Freemen: 29%
- Artisans: 14%
- Other: 2%

Per Capita Income: 230 Brigs

Description: Most travelers to Naergoth are surprised at how alive the province is considering that it was once home to the most infamous necromancer in Imperial history and his legions of undead servants. Today all that remains of the Vandal's reign is a solitary tower in the center of the Naergothite capital.

The foreboding edifice rises up from the landscape like a skeletal claw grasping at the pale moon. No one knows what treasures lie hidden within its menacing walls. Legend has it that this tower was once home to Vandal himself and that the wards that protect the tower were placed by Vandal and not his descendants. Whatever the truth may be, no one is known to have entered the tower since Vandal's death in 2480 YOLD.

House Nerilka

Prominent Members
- Patriarch: Leonis Nerilka
- Consort: Selyna Nerilka
- Heir: Corthan Nerilka

Coat of Arms:

Notes: The Patriarch of House Nerilka was originally a pirate king of some repute. When the naval forces of Kolopan made it their mission to stamp out piracy on the open aether, the members of the House of Nerilka had a tough decision to make. They could either give up the life that had made them wealthy beyond their dreams, or face the mighty Kolopanite armada. They chose to retire to the life of luxury and were ennobled by Emperor Harbin II in 2753 YOLD.

- **Barony of Saerlan**

Population: 284,000
- Human: 46%
- Elf: 22%
- Dwarf: 22%
- Halflings: 10%

Demographics
- Thralls: 5%
- Freemen: 48%
- Landed Freemen: 33%
- Artisans: 12%
- Other: 2%

Per Capita Income: 195 Brigs

Description: Despite claims of having reformed, the many islands that make up this barony serve as a hideaway for all manner of miscreants. The Baron and his family tolerate their presence provided they show the proper tribute.

Many of these pirates operate with a Baronial Letter of Marque authorizing them to attack the vessels of warring nations and pirates. Since there are no warring states within the empire (at present) they restrict their activity to hunting pirates…or ships that appear laden with treasure that they can claim were pirates after the crew has been slaughtered.

House Nezathar

Prominent Members
    Patriarch: Elan Nezathar
    Consort: Kylana Nezathar
    Heir: Vetter Nezathar

Coat of Arms:

Notes: House Nezathar was ennobled by Emperor Marcin I of house Petiron in recognition for their service in deposing House DeVeci in 1934 YOLD. Their lands were conceded by House Petiron at the Emperor's request. Since that time, House Nezathar has pursued a policy of isolationism. They rarely involve themselves in the affairs of other provinces. This was their saving grace during Vandal's war which started in neighboring Naergoth.

- **Barony of Zarthen**

Population: 152,000
    Human: 41%
    Elf: 7%
    Dwarf: 30%
    Halflings: 22%

Demographics
    Thralls: 6%
    Freemen: 48%
    Landed Freemen: 29%
    Artisans: 15%
    Other: 2%

Per Capita Income: 190 Brigs

Description: The Barony of Zarthen is a small province populated by simple people. It is rare to see a Zarthenian trading ship or merchant outside of the Barony. There is little of interest to attract outsiders so the Barony remains a relative mystery to the rest of the Empire. As long as their taxes make it to the Imperial coffers, that is unlikely to change in the near future.

House Petiron

Prominent Members
    Patriarch: Colfek Petiron
    Consort: Serene Petiron
    Heir: Harlyn Petiron

Coat of Arms:

Notes: Founded by druids who were tired of the destruction of the Empire's natural resources under the reign of House DeVeci, the House of Petiron became the second House to rule the Empire.

Today they maintain their love of nature and this attitude has led to a high population of elves, one of the highest in a human controlled province. Of course, this familiarity with elves has, over the years, led to cross breeding between the nobles and their elven subjects. Now a race of mixed blood, House Petiron can no longer lay any reasonable claim to the imperial throne.

- **Grand Duchy of Bamkara**

Population: 192,000
- Human: 40%
- Elf: 47%
- Dwarf: 6%
- Halflings: 7%

Demographics
- Thralls: 1%
- Freemen: 43%
- Landed Freemen: 36%
- Artisans: 18%
- Other: 2%

Per Capita Income: 195 Brigs

Description: The Grand Duchy of Bamkara is beautiful blend of elven artistry and human ingenuity. It is a very environmentally friendly province and industry is heavily regulated. The province has banned many products that are viewed to have a negative environmental impact and those that are not banned are heavily taxed.

Lev-vehicles are common in the more affluent areas of the province, but regular rolling wagons remain the most common. Technomagically augmented mounts are unknown as it is viewed as defiling nature. Aetherships are extremely rare and the few that do exist were built outside of the province.

Bladed weapons larger than daggers and firearms of all types are outlawed completely. Being caught carrying one of these items results in confiscation of the item, arrest, and trial. These trials are often fair though they tend to be brief. Bamkarian law does not require anyone other than the magistrate hearing the case to believe you are guilty.

House Teldevar

Prominent Members
- Patriarch: Solonar Teldevar
- Consort: Vivaria Teldevar
- Heir: Herryk Teldevar

Coat of Arms:

Notes: The House of Teldevar was founded by a group of elves and their human sympathizers escaping the harsh treatment they received in the Viscounty of Markesh. They were ennobled in 2965 by Emperor Jemes III of House Tessadyl due to reasons that are as of yet unknown.

- **Viscounty of Exardonia**

Population: 197,000
- Human: 44%
- Elf: 27%
- Dwarf: 24%
- Halflings: 5%

Demographics
- Thralls: 2%
- Freemen: 52%
- Landed Freemen: 27%
- Artisans: 17%
- Other: 2%

Per Capita Income: 220 Brigs

Description: Exardonia is a small and relatively peaceful island nation. Its citizens earn their living by either farming or fishing and the province produces just enough to support itself.

House Tessadyl

Prominent Members
- Patriarch: Jemerick Tessadyl
- Consort: Naroni Tessadyl
- Heir: Willax Tessadyl

Coat of Arms:

Notes: House Tessadyl was once a royal house holding the gilded throne for a brief 66 years before the Emperor Jemes III died without naming an heir during the elven uprising of 3031. This instilled a deep hatred of all things elven in the members of House Tessadyl.

- **Grand March of Teslantis**

Population: 181,000
- Human: 66%
- Elf: 2%
- Dwarf: 19%
- Halflings: 13%

Demographics
- Thralls: 4%
- Freemen: 46%
- Landed Freemen: 34%
- Artisans: 14%
- Other: 2%

Per Capita Income: 240 Brigs

Description: The province of Teslantis is notable for its complete lack of all things elven. Even owning a piece of elven art is a crime. Harboring an elven fugitive, which is defined as any elf not in servitude to another being, is a capital crime.

House Valermos

Prominent Members
- Patriarch: Phyre Valermos
- Consort: Ember Valermos
- Heir: Phlame Valermos

Coat of Arms:

Notes: The House of Valermos was ennobled by Emperor Renaldo, the Impressive Commentator, as a punitive measure against House Dannan. Of course, this was largely for show because House Dannan didn't know what to do with the undeveloped volcanic hot bed that made up the south of their lands and was tired of paying the requisite taxes on it.

- **Barony of Valkonova**

Population: 119,000
- Human: 43%
- Elf: 9%
- Dwarf: 41%
- Halflings: 7%

Demographics
- Thralls: 5%
- Freemen: 51%
- Landed Freemen: 25%
- Artisans: 17%
- Other: 2%

Per Capita Income: 225 Brigs

Description: Valkonova is a mountainous province noted for its numerous active volcanoes. The main export of this province is sculptures crafted from the volcanic rocks that compose the land. The artisans of Valkonova also craft weapons out of these rocks, though they tend to be more brittle than the more common steel weapons and break or dull too often to be effective.

House Valturis

Prominent Members
    Matriarch: Tase Valturis
    Consort: None
    Heir: None

Coat of Arms:

Notes: Ennobled by Vandal Nefar when he served as Emperor, House Valturis is most well known for the assassination of Emperor Zoen II of the House of Khembryl. House Valturis is also the only noble family that marks succession through the females of the family.

- **Viscounty of Tserakhar**

Population: 187,000
    Human: 44%
    Elf: 27%
    Dwarf: 24%
    Halflings: 5%

Demographics
    Thralls: 13%
    Freemen: 32%
    Landed Freemen: 19%
    Artisans: 34%
    Other: 2%

Per Capita Income: 230 Brigs

Description: The Viscounty of Tserakhar is a matriarchy of the strictest order. While the citizens of Tseralhar do not discriminate based upon race, males of any species are considered slightly better than slaves.

Only females are allowed to own property or practice magic on the contineres. Males are not allowed to carry, own, or keep weapons of any kind unless he is serving as a bodyguard to a woman of some importance. They claim Eris as their patron deity, but denounce the male Eristocracy as a heresy.

House Vassago

Prominent Members
    Matriarch: Shayle Vassago
    Consort: Hemah Vassago
    Heir: Andreyan Vassago

Coat of Arms:

Notes: Gaining independence from Elbanin during the elven uprising of 3031, House Vassago was ennobled in 3075 by Emperor Grigori I. Though originally a Dwarven house, Lord Shayle took an elven maiden for his wife and their son, Andreyan, is of mixed heritage.

- **County of Valindar**

Population: 99,000
    Human: 13%
    Elf: 20%
    Dwarf: 59%
    Halflings: 8%

Demographics
    Thralls: 43%
    Freemen: 35%
    Landed Freemen: 8%
    Artisans: 13%
    Other: 1%

Per Capita Income: 235 Brigs

Description: The County of Valindar would be a stereotypical Dwarven enclave if not for the liberal dose of elven culture that was introduced. Today you can find an elven tree city towering over the entrance to a fortified Dwarven hall.

The province is in a state of continuing conflict with neighboring Elbanin. This conflict has yet to escalate beyond skirmishes, but the conflict has been going on since the founding of this province. The majority of Valindar's work force is thralls captured during these small battles.

House Vathek

Prominent Members
  Matriarch: Raym Vathek
  Consort: Fala Vathek
  Heir: Chandar Vathek

Coat of Arms:

Notes: The last of the Elven House in the Imperial peerage, House Vathek has the unenviable position of being a neighbor to the Grand Duchy of Teslantis. Raiding parties from both provinces continually cross the border to cause mayhem and sew chaos.

- **Duchy of Dizalakia**

Population: 185,000
  Human: 28%
  Elf: 46%
  Dwarf: 3%
  Halflings: 23%

Demographics
  Thralls: 3%
  Freemen: 35%
  Landed Freemen: 30%
  Artisans: 30%
  Other: 2%

Per Capita Income: 240 Brigs

Description: Dizalakia is a province divided. On one hand the people are generally peaceful. On the other hand a horrible travesty is being committed upon their people in the neighboring lands. Some call for war, others sue for peace. Exactly what will happen remains anyone's guess, but the Lord of Dizalakia prepares for a war he hopes will never come and prays to the Lady for a peace he knows cannot last.

Lord Raym has sent envoys in the hope of finding allies in what he believes to be the inevitable conflict between these two provinces.

House von Rohm

Prominent Members
  Matriarch: Illinor von Rohm
  Consort: Allia von Rohm
  Heir: Bardomus von Rohm

Coat of Arms:

Notes: The von Rohm family claims to have descended from a man named Regan who was born on another world in another time. The rest of the peerage dismisses these claims as crazy, but that doesn't change the fact that the House of von Rohm is shrewd and ambitious. They took advantage of the tragedy in Malinova to claim the land they now control as their own. They convince Emperor Vasyl the Unchaste to ennoble them in exchange for a small harem of elven slave girls. And before Lord Telos knew what was happening his province had shrunk by more than 30%.

- **Viscounty of Pleroma**

Population: 128,000
  Human: 49%
  Elf: 2%
  Dwarf: 13%
  Halflings: 36%

Demographics
  Thralls: 4%
  Freemen: 52%
  Landed Freemen: 27%
  Artisans: 15%
  Other: 2%

Per Capita Income: 145 Brigs

Description: Despite having a title of nobility, the von Rohms claim that theirs is a totalitarian democracy. As far as the rest of the Empire is concerned, there's no difference. Sure the people get to vote, but their choice is always the same.

Having "stolen" their nobility from House Chasmali, there is more than a little bad blood between the two provinces. This situation is exacerbated by the fact that families were separated when Pleroma was formed. This creates a very lucrative trade in people across the border, not as slaves but as a means to reunite with loved ones. The Military of Pleroma has sought to crack down on this trafficking of persons, but as much as they fight it, House Chasmali, backed by the Malinovian military supports these efforts.

Recently the Emperor ordered these two houses to attend arbitration at the Imperial Palace. The von Rohms fear that the Emperor will attempt to force them to open the border and allow person to freely cross and reunite with lost family members. The fear the many of their more productive citizens will use this excuse to emigrate to their wealthier neighbor.

No one knows what Lord Illinor, Viscount of Pleroma, has up his sleeve to foil any attempt to force an accord, but most people believe he has something. Whatever it is, it should be noted that Lady Regan von Rohm, eldest daughter of the Viscount, has recently been seen visiting the ancestral home of House De Veci. This leads many to believe that Lord Nolyn De Veci is somehow involved.

The Imperial Government

The Imperial Court

Emperor: His Imperial Majesty Grigori II

Prime Minister: Condallyn Rekis

Minister of War: Grumbar Donnar

Minister of Finance: Elyn Emeraldis

Minister of Art: Arawn Crisse

Minister of Science: Jodiah Mandon

Minister of Commerce: Gandin Nasredin

Minister of Health: Doctor Weyan Cloonek

Minister of Urban Development: Aryll Vohr

Minister of Education: Kalina Nasredin

Minister of Agriculture: Jaysan Glandyr

Minister of Transportation: Seydar Jollan

Minister of Labor: Jemes Hafora

Minister of Justice: Artol Gymhor

Sovereign Father: His Holiness Lord Tebryn

Imperial Demographics

Population: 5,820,000
- Human: 44%
- Elf: 26%
- Dwarf: 19%
- Halflings: 11%

Demographics
- Thralls: 5%
- Freemen: 49%
- Landed Freemen: 24%
- Artisans: 15%
- Other: 7%

Per Capita Income: 240 Brigs
Gross Imperial Product: 1,396,800,000 Brigs

Emperor Grigori II has sat upon the gilded throne since Emperor Vasyl the Unchaste abdicated after it was discovered that he kept a harem of elven slaves for his personal pleasure. This scandal may have blown over had it not been for the images of elven women clad in blue dresses sneaking into the throne room vidcast throughout the Empire for days on end.

Grigori II was appointed the 43rd Emperor by the Eristocracy on the 20th of Chaos, 3167 YOLD. Since that time he has instituted legislation that favors the Eristocracy including his "Chaos Based Initiative" granting the Eristocracy access to the Imperial coffers for the purposes of improving the quality of education in the empire.

The Loyalist Act, Grigori's second official proclamation as Emperor, established the Teksarian Rangers as an Imperial peacekeeping force and gave them tremendous power to deal with both real and imagined threats to the Empire. The Loyalist act grants the Rangers access to the telcom hubs allowing them to monitor any and all telcom traffic. It also grants then the ability to search and seize property that they suspect of being involved in the commission of an Imperial crime. They no longer require a magistrate's order to perform either the telcom tap or the search provided the Rangers are able to prove criminality within one year of the act in question.

Law & Order

The first Emperor to codify Imperial Legal System and transform it from a gross miscarriage of justice into a fair and (sometimes) honest institution was Vandal Nefar during his seven year reign. Subsequent Emperors have added to new laws to the books and have changed the means by which laws have been enforced. Yet none have significantly changed the system that Vandal created.

The first major change to the legal system was the idea that there were really five legal systems operating within the Empire. These levels, called the Orders of Grievance, separated the legal system into five distinct parts.

The **First Order of Grievances** is Ecclesiastic Law. This section of the legal system concerns itself with crimes against the goddess and her church. It includes such crimes as defiling a holy place and grave robbing to assault upon the Eristocracy and lesser clergy.

The **Second Order of Grievances** is Imperial Law. This section is devoted to crimes against the Emperor and the Empire as a whole. The crimes of High Treason, Espionage, and Impersonating an Imperial officer are found in this Order.

The **Third Order of Grievances** is Provincial Law. These laws change from province to province. Most provinces include such activities as attempted assassination of a Lord to poisoning a water supply in their laws.

The **Fourth Order of Grievances** is Tributarial Law. These are the laws that govern the territories of the lesser nobility, those not ennobled by Imperial decree.

Technically, a **Fifth Order of Grievances** does exist. It entails local laws and punishments. This order of grievances is seldom referred to as such. Instead people simply violate local statutes & laws. Local courts may or may not follow the conventions listed below.

Under this system of justice crimes are tried by courts that govern each particular Order of Grievance. In the event that multiple orders have been violated, the case it tried by the highest court responsible for the violation.

Within each Order of Grievance, laws are further separated by their severity. The Empire officially recognizes four levels of crime in each order. Should multiple charges be filed against the same person or persons, the trial will be held in a manner according to the highest severity of the charges. In the event that two or more crimes are of equal severity, they will be tried collectively as a crime one step more severe than the crime that they committed.

An advocate who represents the victim always presents the case to the court and the defendant is entitled to an advocate to present contradictory evidence as a defense. The magistrates involved in trying the case take an active role in determining the truth of the matter are able to ask questions of both the prosecution and defense. It is not uncommon, especially in important cases, to have magical means available to ensure that all testimony given is honest and true.

Each Order of Grievance is superseded by laws of higher orders. For example, The First Order of Grievance makes it a crime to blasphemy Eris. This law applies in all Imperial lands. It is not possible for a lesser lord to decree that it is forbidden to worship Eris or that she is not a deity. Should a lesser noble attempt such an act, they would be in violation of the First Order.

They would also be guilty of willful disobedience under the Second Order. This crime would also be tried in an Ecclesiastic court. Since blasphemy is a summary offense of the First Order and willful disobedience is a summary offense of the Second Order, this crime would be tried by the Ecclesiastic Courts as an Indictable offense following the conventions of that type of trial and incurring penalties accordingly at the discretion of the magistrate or magistrates.

Capital Offenses are crimes that always warrant the loss of the life of the offender. This may mean the death of the accused or it may mean life imprisonment or even life as a thrall. Other punitive penalties may be incurred as well as restitution. The discretion is left to the court hearing the case.

Capital crimes are always heard by a tribunal of magistrates. A jury of 10 people selected by the advocates and the magistrates hears the evidence and advises the tribunal.

Indictable Offenses are slightly less egregious than capital crimes. They may include the death penalty in some cases, and always require some form of incarceration. They may also require some form of restitution or punitive fine.

Indictable offenses are tried by a single magistrate who is advised by a jury of 12 selected by that magistrate and the advocates involved in the case.

Summary Offenses are crimes that are heard simply by a magistrate. These crimes may carry a short term of incarceration as part of the penalty, and almost always carry some form of fine and possibly restitution for damages.

Contraventions are the lowest classification of crime officially recognized by the empire. These crimes are considered too insignificant to bother a magistrate with. So the sentencing is carried out by the officer present provided he or she has enough evidence to believe that a crime has been committed. Contraventions include things like reckless operation of a lev-vehicle, public drunkenness, and unlawful dueling.

Persons who feel that the officer in the case was in error can appeal their conviction. However, doing so automatically upgrades the crime, if found guilty, to a summary offense. The accused has a right to demand that a jury be present, but doing so upgrades the crime further to an indictable offense.

Grievances of the First Order

Capital Offenses
- Assault on a member of the Eristocracy: The property, lands, and title of the guilty party is seized by the OCE and they are sentenced to death, life in prison, or life as a thrall.
- Defiling of a Holy Place: The guilty party, and their family, become thralls of the OCE and their property is seized by the church.
- Impersonating a member of the Eristocracy: death or life in prison.

Indictable Offenses
- Theft of Church Property: Return of the property and/or restitution plus a prison term or thralldom equal to 25 % of the guilty party's expected lifespan.
- Grave Robbing: Return of the property and/or restitution, prison term or thralldom equal to 10 % of the guilty party's expected lifespan.

Summary Offenses
- Assault on a lesser member of the clergy: Incarceration or thralldom of 10% of the guilty party's expected lifespan.
- Impersonating a member of the lesser clergy: Incarceration or thralldom of 5% of the guilty party's expected lifespan.
- Blasphemy against the Goddess: Fine of 100 Brigs and 1 week in prison

Grievances of the Second Order

Capital Offenses
- High Treason (including assault on the Emperor): Death, life in prison, or thralldom; seizure of the guilty party's property, lands, and titles.
- Espionage against the Imperial Court: Death or life in solitary confinement with the door permanently sealed.

Indictable Offenses
- Theft of Imperial Property: Return of the property and/or restitution plus a prison term or thralldom equal to 25 % of the guilty party's expected lifespan.
- Impersonation an Imperial Officer: Prison term or thralldom equal to 10% of the victims expected lifespan.
- Forgery of an Imperial document, order, or decree: Incarceration or thralldom equal to 5% of the guilty party's life span plus restitution of damages and loss of the offending extremity.
- Practicing necromancy: Death
- Possessing a necromantic tome: Death, life in prison, or thralldom; seizure of the guilty party's property, lands, and title.

Summary Offenses
- Willful disobedience of an Imperial order or decree: Incarceration or thralldom up to and including life plus restitution and punitive fines.
- Blasphemy against the Emperor: Incarceration or thralldom of up to 10 years plus punitive fines and restitution of damages
- Assault on an Imperial Officer: Incarceration or thralldom up to one year plus punitive fines and restitution of damages.
- Blasphemy against an Imperial Officer: Incarceration of up to one season plus fines and damages.
- Unlawful Entry of Imperial Property: Incarceration or thralldom of up to 5 years plus punitive fine and restitution of damages.

Contraventions
- Obstruction of Justice: Incarceration until information is provided plus charges as accessory to the crime.
- Bribery of an Imperial Official: Incarceration of up to five years plus punitive fines. (Accepting a bribe is considered enough evidence to convict the officer of "willful disobedience.")

Grievances of the Third Order

It is impossible to list the laws of each of the various provinces that compose the Empire. The various noble lords have very different opinions on what constitutes a crime and what level of penalty should be imposed for said crimes.

One realm, plagued by pirates, may view piracy as a capital crime. While another realm, whose economy is based largely on acts of piracy, may not consider it a crime at all. Suffice to say, most realms acknowledge treason, assault on the noble lord or his family, and espionage as capital crimes. This need not be the case, however, and it is important to learn the laws of the province that you are in.

The only thing that is certain about provincial law is that it cannot ignore crimes of Ecclesiastic or Imperial law nor can it enforce laws that are contrary to those Orders of Grievance.

Grievances of the Fourth & Fifth Orders

It would be impossible to detail the myriad of tributarial and local laws. Many governors do not even bother passing edicts beyond those of the provincial lord. Others view their charge as a personal kingdom and rule it with an iron fist. Suffice to say, you should learn the laws that govern the land you're in.

Organizations

Imperial Military

Description: The Empire of Eristonia maintains a large and well regulated standing militia. In the days of the early empire, these forces were used mainly for defensive purposes. Now that the Empire encompasses the entire known world, the Imperial military finds itself destroying rampaging hordes of goblins, hunting down traitors, and quelling the occasional rebellion.

Though the military has been used as a peace keeping for, the Imperial legions are a broad sword, not a surgeon's scalpel. They have two primary functions – kill people and break things. While they are very good at what they do, most people do not appreciate having their things broken and / or being killed. As such, many Emperors are wary of using the military in heavily populated areas.

Organization: The imperial military is divided into five primary divisions for strategic and administrative purposes. All parts of the Imperial military answer to the Emperor through the Ministry of War. Officials called legates oversee the troops and ensure that they remain loyal to the Empire.

The first division of the military is the Imperial legions. The Empire currently has 60 legions. Thirty-two of these legions are permanently assigned to the capitals of the various imperial provinces. Their official purpose is to maintain peace and support the provincial lord. However, it is suspected that they are there to ensure the loyalty of the lord himself as much as anything else.

The remaining 28 legions serve in various functions throughout the empire. Currently there are 3 legions stationed in fortresses just outside the Imperial capital. Another legion is stationed in the capital itself serving as the city watch. A third legion serves are guards for the Imperial palace and the Emperor. Other legions are stationed at Imperial bases all over the empire.

Most legions are named after the region in which they first served. Thus the provincial legion assigned to the capital of Devecia is named the First Devecian Legion. Other legions bear more colorful names based on their intended purpose. The Legion patrolling the Imperial Capital is known as the Emperor's Will. While the 3 legions stationed around the Capital are known as the Emperor's Wrath, Sword, and Blade respectively. The legion guarding the Imperial palace and the Emperor himself is known as the Emperor's Gonfalon because they bear the Imperial standard whenever the Emperor travels.

Each legion consists of 5,000 men and is led by a general. Legions are divided into cohorts of 500 men each under the command of a colonel. These cohorts are further divided into centuries of 100 men led by a captain. The smallest division of military personnel in the legions is the squad which consists of 10 men under the leadership of a sergeant.

The second portion of the military is the Imperial Cavalry. The cavalry maintains rank and structure similar to that of the legions, but each structural division bears a different name making it easier to differentiate between units serving in the same area. The Imperial cavalry is divided into wings of 5000 men. The Empire currently has 15 such units at its disposal. Wings are further divided into regiments of 500 men each. These regiments are broken down into sentinels of 100 men while cells of 10 men form the smallest subdivision of cavalry.

The third division of the military is the Imperial Navy. The navy is divided into four fleets of aether ships. One fleet is stationed near the capital. The other three are based out of Imperial facilities in Kolopan, Naergoth, and Lecabela. An officer with the rank of Fleet Admiral is in charge of each of these fleets. Individual ships are controlled by their respective captains.

Within the Imperial Navy there exist two more administrative divisions. The first governs the activities & operations of shore facilities including bases, shipyards, and supply stations. The second is composed of support personnel.

The fourth division of the military is the Imperial Air Corp. The air corps is the smallest division of the imperial military machine having only three bases in the empire. These air bases are located in Devecia, Canya, and Malinova.

The smallest unit in the air corps is the flight. It consists of two airships each controlled by its own captain and the flight itself controlled by a commodore. Two or more flights form a squadron under the command of a vice marshal. A marshal presides over a group composed of two or more squadrons. Groups are joined together to form wings under the command of an air marshal.

An air base may have several groups that operate out of it. An officer with the rank of sky marshal is responsible for all airborne operations out of each airbase. An officer with the rank of field marshal governs all ground based operations of the air corps at each facility.

The final division of the Imperial military is the Imperial Auxiliary. Each Imperial province is required by Imperial decree to provide the Empire with troops, ships, and supplies. In addition, the eldest male child of any peerage family must attend the Imperial College of War and becomes an officer in the Imperial military for a tour of duty no less than 5 year long.

The Knights of the Temple of Eris

Description: The official name of this organization is the "Our Lady of Discord's Benevolent & Impoverished Temple Coterie of Holy Eristocratic Soldiers" though it is more commonly known simply as the "Templars."

In spite of its religious and militaristic trappings, the Knights of the Temple of Eris serve the Eristocracy in several functions. Besides providing security for the high ranking members of the Orthodox Church they also serve as the covert operations arm of the church.

Organization: The leader of this organization is the Grand Master of the Order. He answers to the Polyfather of the OCE. The Grandmaster is served by four senior masters who are each responsible for a different branch of Templar operations.

The Voice of the Lady serves as the order's Public Relations arm and propaganda machine. Most of the information that people know about the Eristocracy comes from the spin-doctors working for the Voice. This branch is also responsible for managing all of the order's communications.

The Heart of the Lady is the branch that most people associate with the order. In fact, many Imperial citizens believe this branch to be the whole of the order. The Heart maintains several hospitals, clinics, and shelters throughout the Empire. In addition to providing the services one would normally expect to find in these facilities, the order uses them as safe houses and supply depots.

The Eyes of the Lady are tasked with monitoring the affairs of the various Imperial provinces and the Imperial court itself. Agents of this branch infiltrate the various noble houses serving in a variety of functions. They report their findings to the Eristocracy through secure couriers working for the Voice.

The Hand of the Lady serves as the covert action arm of the order. The hand performs any missions that the Polyfather deems in the best interests of the OCE. Members of this branch are trained in a wide array of specialties ranging from seduction to demolitions. They are organized into teams and are ready to do anything, anytime, anywhere, to enforce the Lady's will… as determined by the Polyfather, of course.

In addition to these branches, the order also ranks agent according to their abilities and level of training. Those entering the order are ranked as neophytes. Once they have completed their basic instruction agents are assigned as apprentices to a more senior member of the branch they will be serving in. After this period of apprenticeship the agent is then promoted to the status of knight.

Finally, knights who have demonstrated their abilities and are ready for positions of leadership are granted the title of master. Masters are able to train apprentices and may be asked to sit on an advisory council to the high master of their respective branch.

A single senior master administers each branch. These masters report directly to the Polyfather and are responsible for the operation of their particular branch.

Goals: The goal of this organization is simple. They protect the interests of the OCE at all costs. In order to accomplish this goal the Templars utilize a number of different approaches. Every action, no matter how innocuous, is designed to help them accomplish this goal.

The Templars run a system of hospitals across the Empire. These hospitals, funded by the OCE, provide medical treatment to all citizens regardless of their station or status. Many of these hospitals support research in an effort to develop new cures for disease. They also maintain shelters and soup kitchens & food pantries for those who are down on their luck, programs for helping trouble youth, and help rebuild areas ravaged by storms and other natural disasters.

These subsidiary charities provide excellent cover for the order's other operations. A hospital makes an excellent place to interrogate enemies of the church as well as recover from the injuries sustained during your latest mission. Soup kitchens and shelters provide safe and accessible safe house. All of these operations can easily hide a decent supply of weapons and other equipment that an agent might need.

This, of course, completely ignores the myriad of churches and schools that the OCE also controls which would happily provide an agent of the order with a place to sleep and recover without question.

Much of the information gathered by the Knights of the Temple is shared with the political allies of the church though they are never told where this information comes from. Most assume that Eris herself imparts this knowledge on the Polyfather. The order does everything that it can to foster this idea and help create an air of mystical importance around the Polyfather.

The Polyfather uses the order to ensure that, whatever the political climate of the empire may be at the moment, the Orthodox Church of Eris comes out on top. There have, however, been times when the order has acted on its own to promote the best interests of the church including the assassination of at least one Polyfather.

Watchmen

Description: The Watchmen is really more of an urban myth than an organization. A few years ago, a Teksaria Ranger chief lieutenant in charge of the narcotics division was found dead in his office. The rangers, as you might have guessed, suspected foul play.

The only evidence at the scene was a small slip of paper pinned to the corpse. On that scrap of paper was written a single phrase in a language that no one understood - *"quis custodiet ipsos custodies."*

The ranger detective in charge of the investigation consulted several scholars before they came up with the translation – "who watches the watchmen." The detective immediately declared that this attack was the work of a new deimist group he called the watchmen. Apparently, the actual meaning of the phrase was completely lost on him.

The organization that actually committed this crime was the "Watchful Holy Order of Reverent Erisian Soldiers." It is a secretive organization that, despite its name, operates completely independently from the Orthodox Church of Eris.

Organization: The watchmen appear to be organized into cells. Each member knows the members of his cell and possibly one or two other members of the organization. These cells may work together, but, more often than not, they operate completely isolated from the rest of the group. This structure works to ensure the security of the organization as a whole. Even when the authorities do manage to arrest or eliminate one cell, others move in to fill the void.

No one knows who if any one is at the head of this organization. No official orders are ever received. Instead, new members are recruited and trained by individuals or cells and then left to their own devices. It is assumed that anyone who is invited into the organization is capable of ascertaining viable targets, plan, and execute operations.

Periodically cells do help each other. This is not because they are in communication with each other but because the authorities make a point of vidcasting any arrests with all the pageantry and showmanship they can muster. They parade the unfortunate detainee around like a trophy trying to earn as much political credit as they can. This gives other cells plenty of opportunity to stage a rescue, complete an operation, or do something completely unexpected and get away with it.

Goals: The goals of this group vary from cell to cell. Some cells strive to overthrow oppressive rulers. Other cells may work to oppose the influence that the Orthodox Church has on Imperial society. A third group may oppose the wide reaching powers granted to law enforcement agencies. A fourth may oppose governmental restrictions on trade and industry. And another group may be anarchists working to depose the Emperor himself and abolish the Empire itself.

Don't mistakenly believe that these cells are full of compassionate people who work for the good of the common man. One of the common threads gleaned from interrogating the operatives that have been captured is the idea that people are responsible for their own actions and need to be held accountable. You can be sure that if a watchman is operating in a given area then he has a vested interest in that operations success.

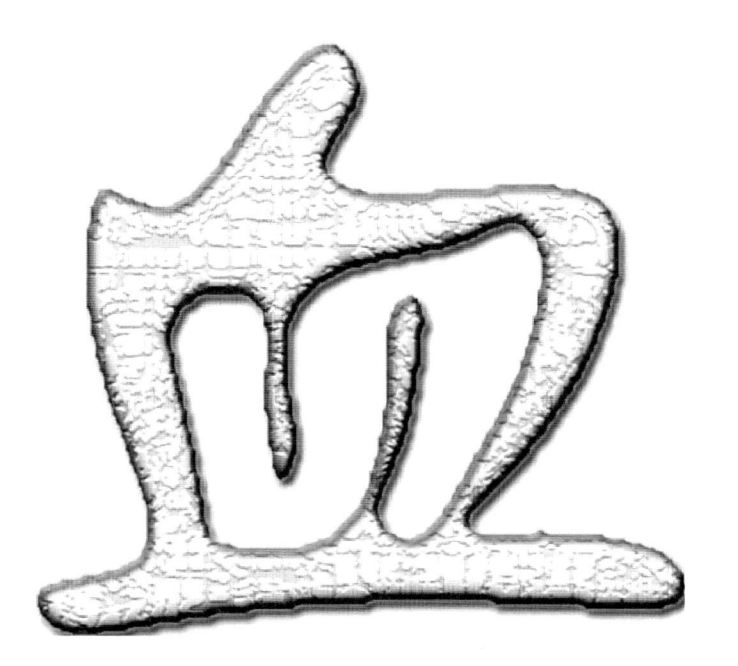

The Doves

Description: The Doves are another Deimist organization in the eyes of the Imperial government. And again, they are pretty close to the mark on this one.

History: The Doves have undergone many transformations over the years. Scholars generally believe that the organization that would become the Doves was founded in 1934 YOLD with the fall of the House of DeVeci. That makes it the oldest known Deimist organization on the Lady's Rock.

Organization: The Doves are a militaristic organization that follows a strict chain of command. The leader of this organization is known simply as the Praetor. The Praetor is the supreme commander of the Doves and his word is law.

Beyond this level of authority things get a little confusing. Directly below the Praetor are the pro-praetors – the lieutenants who lead the various operations.

However, roughly on par with the Pro-praetors are consuls. These individuals oversee the operations in a given province. They are assisted in their duties by a pro-consul who is assigned to each major city.

The Praetor issues his orders by way of an extensive courier network. The members of this network are known as legates. They are assumed to speak with the full authority of the Praetor.

A special group exists within this organization known as the cohors. This group serves as the Praetor's bodyguard and is used to carry out missions deemed to sensitive to trust to regular operatives.

Goals: The goal of the Doves is the one thing that is known about them with any level of certainty. The Doves seek to reestablish the Empire with a member of House De Veci on the Imperial throne.

In order to accomplish their goal, the Doves target Imperial Ministries, monuments, and anything else that has a reasonable chance of undermining the public's trust in the empire. They use whatever means are available to them showing more concern for the results than secrecy or discretion.

Archduke Quinan of Devecia has been very critical of the Doves and their tactics over the years even though he would ascend to the Imperial throne if they were to be successful. His ardent opposition to this Deimist threat has earned him the favor and support of the Emperor. Unfortunately, sources now indicate that Lord Quinana's son Nolyn may actually be a member of the Doves if not their leader.

While Lord Quinan denies these allegations, Nolyn is strangely silent on the matter. Nolyn's vocal criticism of the current royal house and his assertions that he is indeed the rightful heir to the Imperial throne have done little to ease the mind of the Empire. And it is believed that the Ministry of War has several plans drawn up in order to seize control of Devecia should the need arise.

The Gadbians

Description: The very existence of the Gadbians is a point of contention throughout the Empire. Some people maintain that the Gadbians are a conspiracy that has secretly been manipulating the course of Imperial history since the beginning. Others argue that this group is a myth. They cite the fact that no one has ever been able to provide even the tiniest bit of credible evidence to support their existence. Of course, those who believe in the Gadbian conspiracy claim that the lack of proof is evidence to the power this conspiracy possesses.

Organization: If the rumors are to be believed, the Gadbians are organized into a number of houses each with 13 members.

The leader of the first house is known as the Magister Montis or master of the Rock. The other 12 members of the first house each lead a house of the second tier. These leaders are known as Magister Imperium – the masters of the empire.

The Third tier houses are led by a Magister Provincia - the provincial master - who is also a member of a second tier house. A member of the third tier is known as Magister Regius and is in charge of the fourth house responsible for operations in the provincial capitals.

The members of the fourth house, having the title "Magister Urbanum," each lead a house of the fifth tier in a major city. The Magister Populi are members of the fifth houses who also lead the sixth and final houses. These sixth houses are composed of the soldiers who probably have little idea exactly what they are involved in. They are mindless cogs in a well oiled machine.

If this model of the organization was accurate and true that would mean that the Gadbians have somewhere around 3 million members. In other words, for this to be true almost 60% of the Imperial population would have to work for the Gadbians in some way shape or form. And while that's not impossible, it does seem highly unlikely.

It is believed that the upper echelon of the Gadbians consists of prominent bankers and businessmen who use their personal fortunes to finance the organization.

Goals: The Gadbians goal, if they do exist, is simply to control the entire known world. If the rumors about this organization are to be believed, they've done an excellent job thus far.

The Gadbians operate behind the scenes manipulating events on the Lady's Rock to accomplish their goals. They will use anyone that they believe is in a position to help them carry out their insidious plots.

Those who subscribe to the theory that the Gadbians are a real organization give them credit for many of the events recorded in the history of the empire. They are believed to have orchestrated the demise of the noble houses of Sheylar, Balasteer, and Salvenus. They are credited with the rise of Vandal Nefar and planting the seeds of the Elven Uprising that led to the death of Emperor Jemes III of House Tessadyl in 3031 YOLD.

The Gadbians are also given responsibility for many of the technological and magical advancements Imperial citizens enjoy today. Gadbian backed scientists are said to have developed the telcom network, vidcasters, and holopics. The Gadbians are believed to have created the ERP as an extra dimensional haven in which to hide from the authorities. Alternate theories claim that they merely discovered the gateway to this utopian realm.

Teksarian Rangers

Description: The Teksarian Rangers are the Emperor's personal force of "peacekeepers." They can be found operating in any province of the Empire thanks to the Loyalist Act.

Organization: The Teksarian Rangers are led by the Commission of Public Safety from their headquarters in Austyr in the Grand Duchy of Teksaria. The Commissioner is assisted by several deputies that help him keep track of the organization as a whole. Each province is assigned a Chief of Ranger Operations who is responsible for the Ranger's activities in that province. Many chiefs also appoint deputies to help them fulfill their duties, an extremely common practice in large or unruly provinces.

The average citizen rarely has to deal with Rangers at this level. Most people are more familiar with the operational end of the Rangers – the precinct. Each Precinct is headed by a Captain who oversees all precinct activities and reports to the provincial chief. To help control the workflow, precincts are divided into several divisions many of which are further divided into departments based on their area of expertise.

Patrol Division is responsible for, as its name suggests, patrolling the Empire in search of criminals. This division is broken down into departments based upon the type of patrol that the officers are engaged in. Most Precincts have street, highway, waterborne, and aethereal patrol divisions.

Tactical Division is called in whenever things become too much for patrol to handle. Departments within the tactical division are Special Weapons and Tactics, Bomb Disposal, and Riot Control. Many Tactical divisions also maintain a Fast Response Team and a Hostage Rescue Team as part of their S.W.A.T. department.

Investigative Division is responsible for handling those cases that cannot be immediately solved by the patrol office at the scene. Homicide, Forensics, Vice, Narcotics, Robbery, Surveillance, and Organized Crime are the most common departmental sections of the Investigative Division. Many of these divisions also support a Special Investigations Unit that handles crimes which do not conveniently fall into one of the previously mentioned categories.

Internal Affairs is the division responsible for keeping the rest of the Rangers on the straight and narrow. It is their job to investigate misconduct and ensure loyalty to the Chaparran family.

Administration handles all the mundane aspects of running an Imperial police force. They maintain personnel files, schedule training programs, and handle the Public Relations needs of the Rangers.

Penology is responsible for maintaining the various prisons that are under the jurisdiction of the Rangers. They oversee all prison operations from food services & laundry to probation & parole.

Psychology is tasked with evaluating the state of mind of officers, suspects, witnesses, and convicted criminals. They also provide counseling for victims.

Legal is responsible for presenting the evidence gathered by the other divisions to the Magistrate who will be trying the case. Theoretically they would also defend members of the Rangers if someone brought a suit against them, but people who disagree with the Rangers have a tendency to not be seen there after.

Research & Development is the last division in the Rangers. Unlike other divisions, R&D is not found in every province. Instead it is centrally headquarters out of Austyr with facilities existing in locations as necessary. R&D develops much of the proprietary equipment used by the Rangers in pursuit of their goals. They are constantly working on new weapons, vehicles, and enhancements to give the Rangers that extra edge in the field that has made them the most feared organization in the Empire.

Goals: The goals of the Teksarian Rangers have never been a secret. Their purpose is simply to protect the Chaparran family and enforce their will. They were first used as an Imperial force by Emperor Vasyl the Unchaste. But it was not until Grigori II sat upon the throne that the Rangers truly became a force to be reckoned with.

Grigori II passed into law the Loyalist Act that greatly expanded the Ranger's power and authority. Now, instead of just being the lap dogs of the Emperor, they had the law on their side. Of course, as is often the case in situations such as this, the people didn't really see any change at all.

The Loyalist Act was officially intended to provide the Rangers with the tools they would need in order to stamp out Deimism and Deimist organizations operating in the Empire. In reality, it gave them the power to search any building, seize any property, listen to telcom calls, and, worst of all, monitor any & all ERP activity.

It was the ERP tracking that gave Imperial citizens their first clue as to what had transpired. Soon WI-ATs across the Empire began to experience LAG. Of course, even if they had the power to put a stop to this travesty, by then it was too late to do anything about it. The damage had been done. Citizens were forced to live in fear not only of criminals but of their own government.

Unfortunately, the blanket powers possessed by feudal lords made fear of the government a common occurrence. People who were suspected of deimist activities simply disappeared in the middle of the night. Many of them, it is believed, were taken to Mons Praeclarum (the Beautiful Mountain). The Mons is prison secret complex rumored to be home to unspeakable tortures and other inhumane practices all carried out in the name of Imperial security.

Dolus Meretricis

Description: The Dolus Meretricis was founded in 2296 by decree of Emperor Andreyen I of Khymbria, as a trade association of professional persons of negotiable virtue. It served to protect the interests, and in some case the very lives, of its members. This was no easy task as the Dolus represents all types of professionals ranging from high paid courtesans and escorts to thralls purchased to satisfy the appetites of their masters.

The Imperial sanction established the Dolus Meretricis, commonly referred to simply as the "DM," as a force to be reckoned with. They routinely paid visits to brothels and slave markets alike. They worked to improve living conditions and ensure safe treatment of their charges. The Emperor granted them the power to arrest and try those who would abuse members of the Dolus.

The Dolus fell from grace when Vandal Nefar took control of the Empire. Though it was reinstated during the reign of Valdris Khembryl, it never again gained the prominence that had made it a driving force in the empire. Over the following years its influence continued to wane until it was officially disbanded by Emperor Callum II in 2663. Still the Dolus continued in secret. Even without Imperial sanction the Dolus continued to fight for the rights of courtesans, prostitutes, and sex slaves.

Under Emperor Reynaldo I attempts were made to round up the remaining members of this group. In 3076, under the decree of Emperor Grigori I it became a crime even to mention the Dolus Meretricis.

After the death of Grigori I at the hands of an assassin, Vasyl the Unchaste granted amnesty to all suspected Dolus members past, present, and future. Their brief reprieve from persecution ended when he abdicated the throne amidst the scandal for which he is now known.

Emperor Grigori II blamed them for the death of his predecessor and classified them as a deimist organization of the worst kind and authorized the Teksarian Rangers to use any means necessary to bring them to justice.

Today most Imperial citizens believe that the Dolus Meretricis no longer exists. They think it is merely a tale told by sex slaves in order to keep hope alive during unfavorable times.

Organization: The Dolus Meretricis is governed by the Council of Nine. No member of the council is known by name. Instead each council is identified only by their number on the council – one of nine, two of nine, three of nine, etc. The council members elect one of their own to direct meetings and speak for the council should the need arise.

Should a council position become vacant, a new member of the Dolus is elevated to the council and takes the same numeric designation as his or her predecessor. The current head of the council is believed to be a young elven woman known as Six of Nine. She is number one on the Ranger's "most wanted" list.

Other than the Council, the organization of the Dolus remains a mystery. They do not appear to have any other internal structure. No one has been able to ascertain how the members communicate with each other or the council, if they do at all.

Several suspected agents have been captured by the Teksarian Rangers. Even under torture none of these people would admit to the continuing existence of the Dolus Meretricis instead simply referring to it as Nostrum Res – Our Thing. In this way the Dolus has been operating as an open secret for the past 6 years. Some people in the industry watched over by the Dolus have even gone so far as to have what is believed to be the group's sigil tattooed somewhere on their bodies. Whether or not this is truly the group's insignia or even if the person bearing it is a member, its presence has been enough to stay the hand on more than one slave owner.

Goals: The goals of the Dolus Meretricis have not changed over the years. They still strive to better the conditions of courtesans, prostitutes, and sex slaves living in the Empire. However, with the loss of Imperial sanction, their methods have changed considerably. In many ways, they are more powerful now than they have ever been in the past.

In order to achieve their goals, the Dolus seeks to influence those in power. They accomplish this through a mixture of blackmail, intimidation, and outright murder. Those under the protection of the Dolus are often in position to acquire information that certain people would rather not have become public knowledge. Others are able to get close to powerful men and women and ply more subtle manipulations.

Those people who have done wrong by the Dolus soon learn the error of their ways. This is no more clearly illustrated than in the tale of Minase Camaysar, first born son of Lord Briziac Camaysar, Baron of Syandar. Minase was fond of young men. One day while attempting to impress his desires upon a young elven slave, the slave's father, also a servant in the house, took exception to the then heir's action. He took the serving tray he had been carrying and struck the young noble across his head cutting open his cheek and scarring him for life.

Minase was outraged. The slave was bound and banished to the dungeon. After a few weeks of surviving on his own waste, the slave was brought to Minase's chambers. There he was bound, gagged, and forced to watch as his son was brutalized by Minase. The boy's throat was finally slit and he lay on the floor bleeding to death while Minase turned his attentions to the slave's wife and other children. The slave watched helplessly as each member of his family was forced to endure unspeakable torment. Then Minase began to torture the man until he finally succumbed to pain and gained the sweet release of death.

No one knows what happened to Minase Camaysar the night he died, nor do they known the identity of his assailant. When the guards entered Minase's chambers the next morning they found the young noble suspended from the ceiling by his own intestines his body bruised and bleeding from hundreds of tiny cuts and punctures. On his chest burned into his very flesh was the Mark of the Dolus Meretricis

Amazingly he was still alive, kept from the peace of death by some strange magic. It was not until the Baron himself ordered that the slave and his family be given a proper burial that he found the peace of death. No sooner had the bodies been interred and Minase let out his last breath. He was buried in a small private ceremony.

The Watchful Order of Mages

Description: The average person sees the watchful order as a mutual admiration society for those who claim to be able to wield magic. They think of it more as an elitist gentleman's club than an actual guild. In fact, neither the Imperial Ministries of the Art or Commerce recognize The Watchful Order of Mages as an actual guild. Instead they claim that it is little more than a social club for affluent and influential gentlemen.

Conspiracy theorists, however, make a different claim entirely. They claim that the benevolent gentlemen's social club is merely a ruse to hide a much more insidious plot.

They claim that the Watchful Order is the source behind a carefully constructed plot to conquer the whole of the Lady's Rock. They claim that this group is competing with the Gadbians, controlling them, or controlled by them.

They make a point of trying to expose this dangerous threat for what it really is. Of course, few if any citizens actually listen to these rantings.

Organization: The Watchful Order is a very secretive organization. That being said, most of their secrets are cleverly hidden in plain view.

The order officially recognizes six ranks within their hierarchy.

The first is apprentice. An apprentice is a member new to the order regardless of ability. They are allowed supervised access to the order's library and apprentices are always assigned to a more senior member of the order for training.

The next rank is magus. These members make up the back bone of the order. They are full members of the order with unfettered access to the facilities of the order.

Arch-mages fill the next circle of the hierarchy. These powerful men and women are granted their position by a consensus of their peers. Not only do they have unfettered access to the order's facilities, but they have access to other resources as well.

The next ranking members of the order are the Lord Magi. There are two Lord Magi named for each element one representing each aspect of magical ability. These eight members represent the concerns of those mages who are of like aspect at the grand council of magi.

Four High Magi oversee the day to day affairs of the order. One of these is appointed to represent each of the basic elements.

A single member sits at the head of this organization and holds the rank of Lord High Magus. If this organization is truly at the center of a web of intrigue, the Lord High Magus is the spider at the center of that web.

Some believe that another rank exists within the order – that of master. This does not appear to be true. Instead master is an honorific used to indicate both a magus who has advanced sufficiently in the order's teachings that they can be trusted to train others and a magus in charge of one of the order's five towers.

Goals: As previously stated, the order appears, for all intents and purposes, to be exactly what it claims to be. They are a secret society that operates openly. Their declared goal is the pursuit of magic and knowledge.

The problem is not what they're doing, but what they plan to do next. What happens when the order has all the knowledge and magic that it craves? After all, knowledge is power and magic is… well… magic. And exactly what are they watching anyway?

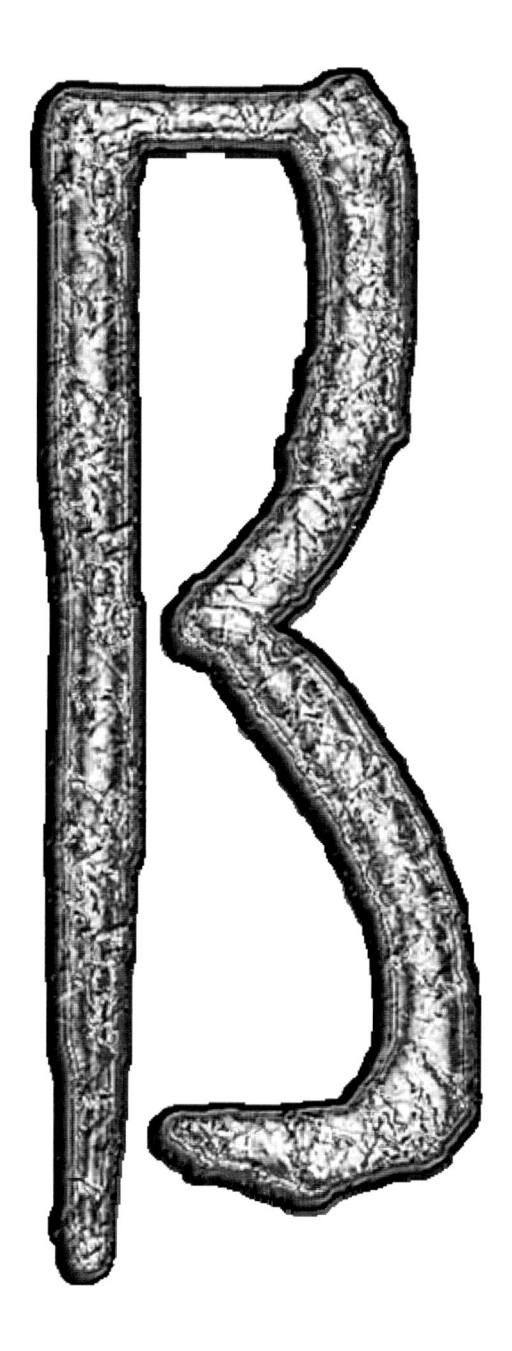

67

Glossary of Erisian Slang

Aether: a substance colorless, odorless, slightly warm to the touch, and contains a slight, almost electrical, charge (also known as "heavy air")

Alley Cat: A derogatory term for an urban ailure or fellen who earns a living entertaining others (often as a prostitute).

Athame: A ritual knife or dagger used in the detestable practice of sacrificial magic.

Black Ice: dirty money. Derived from the slang term ice (q.v.).

Chao: an ancient symbol of the goddess long abandoned by the Eristocracy. It is believed that chao is the singular form of Chaos.

Continere: a mass of land (or an island) floating through the aether.

Cooler: a fence. One who takes property of questionable ownership and disposes of it for you, usually for a cut of the profit.

Crimbils: the offspring of the mating between a Teg and member of another race, usually an elf.

D-Cells: see "dark cells" in techno-magical equipment

Dark: intentionally powered down so as not to be detected by spells or devices that detect magical energy, used in reference to an aethereal vessel.

Data-miner: a term used to describe a dwarven scholar or sage (often used derogatorily by other dwarves).

Deimism: the political ideology where acts of aggression against civilian targets are used to push forth a political agenda. The idea is that the government will succumb to your desires out of the fear that you will continue to attack them.

Deimist: one who practices Deimism. People and groups who oppose the empire or the Eristocracy are quickly labeled as deimists.

Dueker: slang for defecating, resulting from a mispronunciation of another slang phrase "to drop a duce".

Elven: of or pertaining to elves. Not to be confused with Elvish (see below).

Elvish: the elven language. Not to be confused with elven (see ablove).

Eristocracy: the hierarchy of the Orthodox Church of Eris

ERP: the "Electronic Repository of Pornography" is an alternate reality composed of electronic impulses that is very much different from our own. In this reality females of the species are willing to perform a variety of acts that few of their counterparts on the Lady's Rock would even dream of. Access to this alternative dimension is limited by the technology of today. Currently citizens are simply able to view the events taking place in this realm by means of a "Utopian Reality Link," a unique address that identifies which part of the ERP you wish to view.

Fellen: the half-breed offspring of an Ailure with a member of another species, most likely human.

Ferrocrete: A type of stone that is reinforced with steel through an alchemical process to create a substance that can easily be shaped in its liquid state, but cools to form a rock-like substance of superior strength and durability.

Fizz: power, usually used in reference to magical energy such as the charges in a magical or techno-magical item.

Flat: without power. This term is derived from the flat power output line on the magical reactor of an aethereal vessel when it is without power.

Flat-Line: to suddenly loose power.

Frost: A payment, usually a bribe, made in order to aquire some good or service.

Frosty: having sufficient funds available.

Grounding: forcing another creature into exile, usually in some dark, dank hole in the ground.

Groundling: a derogatory term for the half-breed offspring of a dwarf and other creature, usually a human with bad eye sight, a poor sense of smell and extremely low standards.

Ice: any hard currency.

Imager: a device used to capture images for later retrieval or transmission.

Half-Elf: a term used to denote the half-breed child of an elf and another creature, usually a human.

Half-Orc: a term for the offspring of an Orc and another creature, usually a human.

Holopics: three dimensional images meshed with sound usually displayed in a theater but also shown over the vidcaster once ticket sales die down significantly. Holopics are often used to educate, entertain, or brainwash an unsuspecting population. All Holopics are rated by the Holopic Association of Eristonia based on acceptability of content.

Knuckle Draggers: a derogatory term for goblins used because their stooped posture exaggerates the length of their arms giving them an almost simian appearance.

Lady's Rock: the planet itself

LAG: localized access glitch. The condition by which a users gateway to the ERP slows down considerably making the images appear jerky and unnatural adversely affecting the enjoyment of the medium.

Lahum: a contraction of "latent human," lahums are those humans with a latent talent for either magic or psionics.

Lev-vehicles: The primary for of conveyance on the Lady's Rock is a hovering wagon, carriage, cart, or chariot that stays afloat by means of levitation magic. Most of these vehicles require some additional form of power to move laterally, so horses, oxen, and other beasts of burden see tremendous use.

Some of the more affluent people are able to purchase chairs that move completely by magical means. These personal conveyances are extremely rare because of the expense involved in creating and maintaining them.

Malaclypse, the elder: the star that used to drain the darkness, but, due to its age, is not nearly as powerful as it once was. Today Malaclypse, the elder, serves as the moon of the Lady's Rock.

Malaclypse, the younger: the star that drains darkness from around the Lady's Rock allowing everyone to be able to see.

Mark: a target, usually of a bounty hunter, thieves or con-men

Mehum: a contraction of "mere human," mehums are normal humans like those you would expect to find anywhere on the material plane.

Mimic: a device used to record sound for later transmission or retrieval.

Nothum: a derogatory term for any unwanted or illegitimate children, especially half-breeds.

Peace-Bond: a techno-magical device attached to a weapon that notifies the authorities if the weapon is drawn.

Peerage: families ennobled by the Imperial edict

Polyfather: the supreme head of the Orthodox Church of Eris

Prancer: a derogatory term for an elf.

Quarterling: a derogatory term for a half-breed with one Halfling parent.

Rabbit: the mark, or target, of an assassin.

Reds: Slang for smoking stick because of the reddish color of the dried, ground Fumi Ficus leaves used in their production.

'Sucker: See "dark sucker" in techno-magical equipment.

Telcom: a device used for vocal communications over great distances.

Technomancy: the blending of magic with technology to produce items for use throughout the empire.

Templars: a slang term for the Holy Knights of the Temple of Eris.

Toast: anything that causes someone not to have money (used to mean that you were ripped off or that you ripped someone else off).

Toasty: not having any available funds.

Tributarial: having to do with the territories that compose an Imperial province. The nobles who govern tributarial realms are known as "lesser nobles" because they were ennobled by a member of the peerage and not by the Emperor.

Vidcaster: a device used to transmit mind-numbing pictures and sound over distances and distribute them to numerous houses.

WI-AT: a wireless image and audio terminal is by far the most common means of accessing the ERP (q.v.).

PLAYER'S SECTION

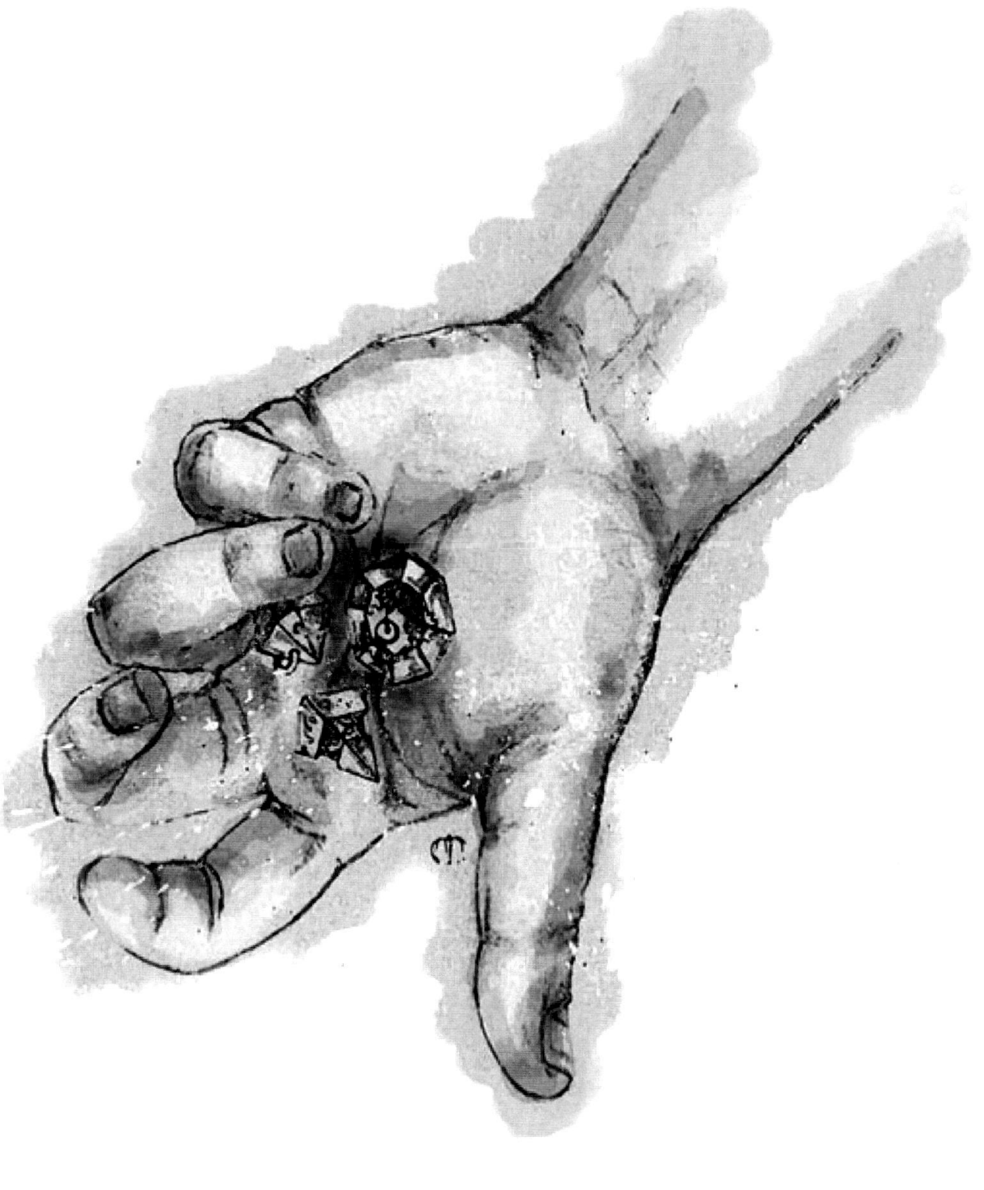

Creating a Character

Getting Started

In order to create your first character you'll need a few things.

- Scratch paper
- Pen or pencil
- Set of Dice
- This book
- Character Sheet or blank paper
- Your imagination

Now that you have all the tools you will need, we can get started making your first character. Other games may have different ideas on how a character should be created. Many of these ideas are the by-product of years of research and experience. Of course, that doesn't make them any less wrong.

The process of creating a good character really boils down to seven simple steps. If you follow these steps, and have two brain cells rubbing together in your head, you will have a fun and believable character to play

1. Come up with a character concept
2. Select a race
3. Determine attributes
4. Select skills
5. Choose Merits and Flaws
6. Purchase equipment
7. Add the finishing touches

Character Concepts

Before you put pen to paper, before you roll a single die, you should first decide on the concept for your character. It is the single most important part of character creation. It is also the part that is most often overlooked.

Having a firm grasp of your character concept will make it much easier to create your character. It will help you when it comes time to assign your attributes and select your skills. It will serve as a guide when purchasing equipment. It will even give you a good idea of how your character is going to act during the game.

This does not need to be a finalized version. We'll discuss fleshing out your character later on. Right now we just need a working idea of who your character is, what he or she does, and where they came from.

A smuggler who grew up on the mean streets of a coastal town is going to have different strengths, weaknesses, and skills from a smuggler who grew up the heir to a merchant's fortune but became disillusioned with the idea that his family earned their money off the hard work of others. Both are perfectly viable characters, yet their will be notable differences in their attitudes, attributes, and skills.

The smuggler who grew up on the streets may feel that others deserve to be taken advantage of. After all, no one helped her get to where she was. Why should she help others? She may have a more manipulative nature than her counter-part having relied on her wits to survive. She may also possess a more larcenous skill set with a few ranks in sleight of hand or hide to represent her start as a petty criminal. She may tend to horde the treasure paying only enough to keep her crew in line.

Meanwhile, the disillusioned heir might see it as his responsibility to help those he feels are unable to help themselves. He may rely on his charisma & his training with a rapier to get him out of tight spots. He might approach his smuggling operation more as a business than as a personal empire…a throw back to his earlier education. He may pay a wage that is more than fair to the members of his crew so that they may one day become free men.

As you can see, even two seemingly identical characters can turn out vastly different based on their initial concepts. Even before we've assigned statistics it's easy to see whose strengths will lie where. We also have a good idea what type of skills each character will have.

Lastly, we know what the characters will be like. We have a basic idea of how they will react in a given situation. We have a clue as to what their motivation is for adventuring. And we can start to draw a mental picture of each of these characters.

The smuggler that grew up on the mean streets will likely dress very practically; he will most likely wear armor that provides protection without limiting his mobility. His choice of weaponry will also reflect his harsh view of the world. He will probably choose a weapon that does a lot of damage, but can be easily concealed or wielded in close quarters.

The disillusioned heir is likely to dress more flamboyantly, reflecting his noble upbringing. He will likely don a chain shirt or possibly even half-plate armor. The weapons that he wields will also reflect his heritage. He may wield a rapier and a dagger or a traditional knight's sword. He is not likely to make use of weapons such as great axes that lack refinement.

We've done a good deal of character creation by simply writing a paragraph about each character. That is why this step is so important. It is this step that separates good characters from mediocre characters.

Character History

If you come up with a concept that you really like, consider writing a character history. Explore where your character came from and what specific events defined them. Determine the catalyst that drove them to the life of an adventurer. Figure out who the important people were in their lives and let the GM know what happened to them.

A character history, though not necessary, serves three purposes. Each is equally important, but for very different reasons.

First, it helps solidify your character concept. The more you know about what happened in your character's past, the fluid his or her behavior in the present will seem.

Second, it creates a finite number of things from your past that the GM can use. This helps make you a more integral part of the story arch. The party may travel through the town in which your character was born. You may encounter a long lost relative who needs your help. It also limits the number of relatives, rivals, and other miscellaneous plot hooks the GM can dredge up focused on you.

Third, a well-written character history also lets the GM know what sort of adventures you would enjoy. If your history contains dark conspiracies and sinister plots, the GM will know that you enjoy intrigue. Likewise, if you write about deciphering ancient maps and searching long forgotten tombs, the GM can make sure you have plenty of those as well.

It's really a win-win for everyone, and it won't take any more of your time than you let it.

You might also want to keep in mind this one simple (and time honored) axiom... "The more the GM's campaign depends on your character, the harder that character will be to kill."

Note on religion: Religion tends to be a much over looked aspect of character creation. Players think that religion only matters if you're playing a member of the clergy. That isn't true.

Take a look at the world around you. Most people have some sort of religious belief. Now imagine a world were the gods grant spells and perform miracles each and every day. Can you honestly say that religion would be less important in the face of this verifiable evidence of the existence of deities?

If you answered "yes" to the question above, you're only kidding yourself. The truth of the matter is that your character probably has a religion of some sort. Just as our religion shape our behavior today, it would also have an effect on your character. Take a moment to look at the pantheon of deities and select the one you think your character might worship. Keep that selection in mind when making your character.

Character History Questionnaires

For your convenience, I've included a list of questions that I ask about characters while I'm reading their character histories. The answers to some of these questions can have a direct affect on the course of the campaign. Other answers simply help round out the character and provide some motivation. You may not be able to answer all of these questions before you begin actually making your character. That's fine. Simply keep these questions in mind during the process. Answer the ones you can as you can.

- **Family**

1. Where is your character from?
2. How old is your character?
3. Does your character know their parents?
4. If so, are they still alive?
5. If they are alive, where are they?
6. Does your character keep in contact with them?
7. Does your character have any siblings?
8. Are they male of female?
9. Where does your character fall in the birth order?
10. Are any of the siblings still alive?
11. Does your character have any contact with them?

- **Appearance**

1. What does your character look like?
2. Does he or she pay attention to their appearance or do they care little for how they look?
3. What about hygene? Does your character try to bathe regularly or does he or she smell (and / or look) like they just crawled out of the grease dumpster behind a restaurant that should have been condemned at the turn of the last century?
4. What type of clothing does the character usually wear?
5. What state is that clothing in?
6. Does the character have any distinguishing features or characteristics? Physical quirks? Tattoos? Piercings?

- **Abode**

1. Where does your character live?
2. Does he or she own their home, rent it, or so they sleep wherever they can get out of the rain?
3. How is this residence furnished?
4. Where did the character get these furnishings?
5. How often are they home?
6. Do they maintain the residence?

- **Vocation & Education**

1. What did the character do before adventuring?
2. How did they learn this trade?
3. Why did the character choose that occupation?
4. Did they enjoy it?
5. Why did they choose to stop doing it?

6. Where did they learn the skills they'll use while adventuring?
7. Did the character attend any school?
8. How long did he or she attend?
9. How did they do while attending?

- **Personality**

1. Does the character have anything particular (or peculiar) likes or dislikes?
2. Does your character have a moral code he or she adheres to?
3. Does your character have any goals?
4. How does your character feel about other races?
5. Why does you character have those feelings?

- **Nature & Demeanor**

1. How does your character see themselves?
2. How does your character think other people see him or her?
3. How does your character want other people to see him or her?
4. How do others really see your character?
5. Does your character hide is true feelings from others?
6. If so, why?

- **Religion and Belief**

1. Does your character worship a deity?
2. If not, why is he or she different than everyone else on the planet?
3. If so, which deity and why?
4. How strongly does the character believe?
5. What effect does that belief have on the character's attitudes?
6. How does the character show this belief?
7. How does the character feel about other religions and deities?

8. How do these feeling affect his or her relationships with others?

- **Sordid Past**

1. Does you character have any deep regrets about his or her past?
2. Has your character done things in their past that they wish to keep secret?
3. What are those things?
4. Why did the character do those things?
5. What does the character do to try and keep his or her secret?
6. To what lengths would the character go to ensure that his or her secret stays a secret?
7. Is there anything the character would not do to keep the secret?
8. Does anyone already know the secret?
9. If so, what is the character's relationship with that being?

- **Adventuring**

1. Why did your character begin adventuring?
2. What does your character hope to gain by adventuring?
3. How will it change the character's life if and when they achieve their goals?
4. What will they do once these goals have been achieved?

- **The Party**

5. Why is he or she adventuring with this particular group?
6. Will he or she continue to do so once they have reached their goals?
7. If not, what will you as a player do when your character leaves the party?

Races

There are 11 base races, 10 subspecies, and 11 half-breed races available for play. For those of you who graduated from South-West, that makes for 32 available racial options for any starting character. (This only seems appropriate since 3+2=5 and 5 is a number sacred to the Lady.)

Each race has its own flavor as well as traits that distinguish it from the other available races. These traits make some races better at certain things and less adept at others.

Choosing a race is a very important step in character creation. Each race has qualities that will subtly influence the character's concept. Where the character was born, how the character was raised, and why the character became an adventurer rather than a blacksmith or a barmaid are all affected by the character's race.

Some player will opt for stereotypical roles for their character. Elven woodsmen and dwarven warriors are both fine character. There is a certain comfort to be found in playing things that are familiar to us.

Do not, however, discredit the unique role-playing opportunities available by choosing something people do not expect. The half-orc mage or the halfling barbarian can be interesting characters in their own right.

In my experience, when players are selecting a race, they usually choose the type of character that they wish to play and then pick a race whose attribute scores best fit that class. For example, if you're going to play an archer, you choose an elf because they have a high natural dexterity. The problem with this method is that you end up creating your concept to fit the character you have created.

While this time-honored method of character creation does what it needs to do, it only accomplishes the bare necessities. It creates a one-dimensional... or maybe two dimensional at best... character that will allow you to play the game. The character will undoubtedly lack the third dimension – Depth...

The racial descriptions that follow tell you a little about each race. These descriptions deal only with dominant racial traits for each species and give broad descriptions of average members of that race.

Characters, however, are not average members of their species. If they were "average" members of their race, they would be blacksmiths and barmaids, not warriors and mages... and the game would be really, really boring. ("I go to the table and see if anyone needs a drink. I rolled 3 successes on my 'flirt with customer check;' did they leave a good tip?")

If that's the type of game you where hoping to play when you opened this book, I have good news and bad news. The bad news is that you wasted your money. The good news is that the game you were looking for *does* exist. Most of us affectionately refer to it as "real life." It's a game most of us spend the majority of our adult lives playing, and, quite frankly, we role-play in order to get a break from it.

Read the description for each race and select the race that you feel best fits your character concept. Think of how your character is different from the average member of his species. Is he a liberal, flexible dwarf? Is she a stubborn and unyielding elf? Does he or she worship a different deity than is normal for his or her race?

As in the "real world," it is our shared interests that bind us to others, but it is our differences... and our flaws... that make us the unique individuals that we are.

Ailure

The ailure are a species of cat-like humanoids. They live in isolated tribes throughout the empire, staying in the fringes of imperial society. Some attempts have been made to integrate the ailure. Of course, integration does not mean that the ailure have been granted citizenship, so those found within imperial civilization are usually slaves of, or bodyguards for, the wealthy. A few rogue ailure have found a lucrative living as members of more liberal thieves' and assassins' guilds.

Personality: The ailure exhibit many of the same behaviors that domesticated cats do. They can often be found lounging in the sun or chasing birds that wander into their camps. This behavior has led many to conclude that the ailure are lazy. That is not the case.

Ailure are hunters by nature and see no reason to waste time on anything other than the hunt. Ailure children enjoy playing games that hone their formidable hunting skills. These games are encouraged by the elders of the tribe. Ailure continue to participate in these games well into their adult lives.

Ailure have an innate curiosity that leads them to search out new and interesting things. This leads many young ailure to leave the tribe of their birth and explore the world around them. Many of these travelers eventually return having grown bored with the world at large.

Physical Description: Ailure are a race of bipedal felines. Their bodies are covered with fur that bears a distinctive pattern. Members of the same tribe have similar patterns, so it is possible, though difficult, to determine an ailure's tribe of origin by carefully examining this pattern. Male ailure tend to have thicker hair on their heads. This mane is darker in color than the fur on their bodies, but retains the same pattern.

The eyes of an ailure reflect light and appear to glow in situations where light is limited. Their sense of hearing is also very well developed as is their sense of smell. An ailure can even identify people that they know by their sent and heartbeat.

Ailure have an average lifespan of 75 years. When ailure reproduce they usually bear litters of children. These children are born both blind and deaf. When they are about 17 days old their ear canals open and they are first able to hear the world around them. Their eye lids open and they are first able to see around day 25.

Despite being blind, young ailure begin to crawl when they are only 18 days old and take their first steps within their first season of life. They are considered fully grow by their third season and reach sexual maturity at about that same time.

All ailure are born with retractable claws. Most learn to use these claws as a deadly weapon. Young ailure are born unable to retract their claws and do not instinctively learn this ability until they are about 27 days old.

Both male and female ailure go through a period of heat one out of every three weeks. During this time frame they are extremely fertile and can even become pregnant or impregnate other humanoids that they have intercourse with.

Relations: Ailure view other races with a mixture of curiosity and disdain. They see themselves as the ultimate predators. They consider all other creatures on the Lady's Rock to be prey that they will one day kill. Even those ailure who serve masters of another species believe this to be true. If another ailure were to ask them why they serve such a creature, the ailure would explain that they are merely studying their prey.

This attitude of superiority is thinly veiled and often causes problems with members of other races. If the ailure realize this, they do not seem to care. If it is pointed out to them, most ailure will simply drop the veil all together.

Lands: The ailure are a tribal society. They are not considered civilized by the empire, so they are not accorded the same rights and privileges that others receive. Most ailure that are encountered living in the Empire are either nomadic tribes or thralls. They are commonly found as body guards or concubines for wealthy merchants and nobles. Because of their unique skills, those who own ailure often treat them well. Very few ailure thralls ever rebel against their masters.

Ailure tribes are governed by a chieftain. This ranking member of the tribe is almost always male. However, this hereditary position is passed down through the mother's bloodline instead of the father's. All male children of the ruling female are eligible to become the next chieftain regardless of their father or his status within the clan. This means that the next chieftain is always chosen from the nephews of the current ruler and not his own children.

This tradition leads to some very interesting social and political maneuvering. Males who desire to have their offspring rule will often combat each other for the opportunity to mate with the ruling female. Those who are unable to win a contest of arms may even resort to subterfuge to see their dreams realized. Since even offspring that would be considered illegitimate by other species are able to inherit leadership of a tribe, other less savory methods are sometimes employed.

Religion: As a race of warriors and hunters, ailure tend to venerate more martial deities such as Aren, or deities whose portfolios include stealth and subterfuge such as Ahbendon and Dumathan. Recently, as the ailure begin to take their place in the empire, Chalysse, the goddess of the cycle of life and death, is becoming more and more popular.

Few ailure still worship Zaphalus, the god of the forest. This deity was widely worshipped by the species as a whole before the empire began to encroach on their territory. Zaphlaus' worship tends to be limited to well established tribes with little contact with the rest of the empire.

Language: Ailure do have a native tongue. It is a complex collection of whines, mews, and body language. It is very difficult for a non-native speaker to learn the language and impossible for them to speak it.

In spite of their strange language, ailure are quite capable of learning to speak other languages. Many tribes make a point of teaching young ailure the tongues of neighboring races as well as the common tongue of the empire.

Though few know it, the ailure language does have a written form. It consists of a series of scratches representing a particular concept or idea. This language does not contain enough words to convey more than basic concepts and is unsuitable for discussing anything more than mere survival.

The few ailure texts are written on a medium such as bone or wood that can be easily marked by the ailure's sharp claws. Such messages are often simple indicating fresh water, safe haven, or imminent danger.

Names: An ailure will have four names by the time he or she reaches adulthood.

The first of these is given to him at birth. The name holds no significance to the ailure and is merely a way of distinguishing one cub in a litter from another. This name often reflects the ailure's position in the litter and the cub's mother is male or father is female. This causes some confusion among other species who do not understand the ailure culture.

The second name an ailure receives is bestowed upon him or her by their mother upon reaching adulthood and completing a rite of passage. Both male and female ailure must complete these rites before being considered an adult member of the tribe.

The exact rite varies from tribe to tribe, but the high birth rate among ailure all but guarantees that failure will be fatal. Because of the danger involved, completing the rites is a reason for celebration.

The last name by which an ailure is known is given to him before the moment of his birth – the name of his tribe. This name has no real equivalent in the Imperial Trade Tongue. Rough equivalents are used when dealing with non-ailure.

Adventurers: There are many reasons why an ailure might be adventuring. Foremost among them is the innate curiosity young adult ailure have about their surroundings. Many ailure leave the tribe to explore the world around them. Most return to the safety of the tribe before too much time has past. A few brave ailure do not return, however. They can be found wherever their curiosity takes them.

Ailure are also prized as skilled assassins and thieves. These ailure, in the employ of a wealthy imperial citizen, could be encountered during a mission for their masters. Such ailure rarely adventure for very long, however. Once their task is complete, they usually return because of the excellent treatment they receive from their masters.

Some ailure grow bored of the life as a slave to an inferior being. As soon as the ailure's bored outweighs its enjoyment, the master's time has drawn to a close. With their master dead, these former slaves often take what they have learned and make their own place in the world.

Ailure Racial Maximums

Strength:	5	Reason:	5
Coordination:	10	Insight:	8
Quickness:	9	Psyche:	5
Constitution:	6	Charisma:	6

Racial Traits

- **Size:** Medium
- **Low-Light Vision:** In conditions of limited illumination, Ailure can see as well as a human can under normal daylight conditions
- **Retractable Claws:** Ailure are born with retractable claws. These claws can be used as weapons with a difficulty of 5 and a damage rating of 2 + 1. They also provide 2 bonus dice to use for climbing tests.
- **Racial Advantages:** Ailure begin play with the Equilibrium and Quick Reflexes advantages at no cost to the player.

Fellen (Subspecies)

Fellen are the name given to the offspring of ailure and humans.

Personality: Most fellen are born to enslaved ailure concubines and the powerful human who own them. These fellen often become slaves themselves giving them a rather somber outlook on life.

Fellen exhibit many of the same personality traits as their ailure parent. They are innately curious about the world around them. They can also be found lounging in sunbeams and playing games that give voice to instinctive hunter buried deep within them.

Fellen, however, quickly realize that they are born to serve. This realization leads them to question the purpose of life itself. Most become despondent hoping to end it all but being kept from doing so by some primal urge to survive.

Physical Description: Fellen appear mostly human, though they do gain some feline characteristics from their non-human parent. All fellen have cat-like tails, vertical "slit" pupils, and cat-like ears. They have the same amount of body hair for a human of their gender, but that hair shares the distinctive tribal markings of their ailure parent.

When fellen breed with an other creature, the result is always another fellen. If the fellen bred with another fellen or an ailure, the distinctive tribal marks often appear on the offsprings skin as well as their hair. This is the only indication of the fellen's parentage.

Relations: Fellen, especially the females, are prized slaves. As a result, they are often treated very well by their owners. They are, however, slaves and have little choice in what they do, how they do it, when they do it, or whom they do it with... whatever "it" may be.

Some fellen resent this treatment and rebel against their owners. These fellen undoubtedly resign themselves to a life on the run. Escaped fellen slaves are worth a fair amount of coin. Many a bounty hunter earns his or her livelihood tracking them down and returning them to their owners... or anyone else willing to pay their price.

Other fellen embrace their existence. These fellen thrive and flourish. Because of their exotic appearance, a fellen courtesan often attracts wealthy and powerful clients. If the fellen is smart (and lucky) this can translate into some real influence in the world around them.

Lands: Fellen have no land of their own. They are less adept at hunting then the ailure, so they are seen as a liability in ailure lands. This makes them unwelcome even among members of their parent's tribe.

Humans, on the other hand, view the fellen as expensive playthings. While a particularly successful fellen may be given lavish gifts by potential clients, they rarely, if ever, hold any overt power in human lands.

Religion: As with many people who face a life of servitude, fellen regularly turn to religion. The deity of choice for most fellen is Jhaemaryl. The goddess of blood and lust calls to the fellen's more base urges, as well as having dominion over many of the deeds fellen are forced to perform as part of their servitude.

Language: Fellen have no language of their own. They are often taught the human tongue in order to better serve their masters.

Names: Because they are born as slaves, fellen are often named by their owners. This does not usually occur until the fellen is old enough to have some value to the owner... often on the open market.

Adventurers: Fellen go adventuring for many reasons. As you may have guessed by now, a fellen wishing to free themselves from the shackles of human servitude has little choice but to live by his or her wits traveling from city to city.

What most people fail to guess, however, is the number of fellen slaves who adventure as well. Some adventurers opt to bring fellen slaves with them for companionship. It doesn't hurt that a fellen's natural abilities make them well-suited for the adventuring life. Of course, more than one such "adventuring slave" has found a way to escape and join the former group rather than the latter.

79

Fellen Racial Maximums

Strength:	4	Reason:	5
Coordination:	9	Insight:	8
Quickness:	8	Psyche:	5
Constitution:	6	Charisma:	7

Racial Traits

- **Size:** Medium
- **Low-Light Vision:** Like the ailure, fellen can see as well during conditions of limited illumination as a human can see during normal daylight.
- **Retractable Claws:** Fellen also have retractable claws. They provide the same advantage to the fellen that they do to the ailure.
- **Racial Advantages:** Fellen begin play with the Equilibrium and the 1 point Sex Appeal advantages at no cost to the player.

Dwarf

Dwarves are the same "lovable" creatures that you would expect to find on any fantasy world. Legend has it that they were the second species of creature created by the goddess, after elves and other fey.

Personality: Dwarves are gruff and abrasive by most standards. They rarely show affection, gratitude, or acceptance to others… especially to non-dwarves. They expect perfection from themselves and demand it from those around them.

Of course, few things ever meet the dwarf's lofty expectations. Even the stoutest human ale is little better than dishwater when compared to dwarven ale. The orc you're facing may have just cleaved your arm clean off with his axe, but he still fights like an adolescent dwarven female… though he's probably less hairy. That dragon just melted off your face with his fiery breath, but it wasn't nearly as hot as the forge the dwarf worked every day, while attending school, when he lived in that active volcano.

No matter what you've done or what you will do, there is a good chance, the dwarf has lived through worse… and an even better chance that he's going to tell you about it. An elven bard once commented that dwarves appear to be born with a granite chip embedded in their shoulder. That same bard was found with his lute firmly implanted in small intestine and a barely legible note pinned to his silken blouse declaring that his singing sounded like dying goblin crooning to the tune of a poorly cast bell.

Physical Description: Dwarves are, as you may expect, shorter and stockier than humans. They also have an (over) abundance of body hair sporting long beards.

Female dwarves are rarely encountered outside of dwarven lands. Some people, mostly elves, claim that the reason this is true is because dwarven women are equally as hairy as dwarven men making it impossible to distinguish between them. These claims are only a slight exaggeration.

Dwarven females are almost as hairy as dwarven men. They even have beards. Despite elven criticism, however, dwarven females in human lands do adopt human standards and shave their beards, mustaches, armpits, backs, etc… usually.

Relations: Dwarves tend to get along well enough with most civilized races… as long as they aren't elves. This animosity between dwarves and elves dates back before even these ancient races began to record their history, so no one really knows why it exists.

Lands: Dwarves make their homes in some of the most inhospitable places on the Lady's Rock. The first dwarven enclaves were carved out of the heart of mountains. This tradition has been followed by most dwarven clans. These pockets of dwarven culture (and I use that term somewhat loosely) are veritable fortresses. Even the smallest dwarven town is well fortified appearing more like a military camp than a booming metropolis to the uneducated.

Because dwarves and humans do get along, for the most part, it is only natural that dwarven nobility control some portions of the empire. These realms tend to be mountainous, and their economies are often centered on the mining, refining, and forging of metals.

Dwarves follow the human ranks of peerage with one notable exception. Dwarves who hold the title of Baron, either as an imperial or provincial peer, use its dwarven equivalent – Thane.

Religion: Dwarves value a strong work ethic and skill at the forge making Semis a natural choice for the theologically minded dwarf. Their guarded natures ensure that there will be at least a few adherents of Dumathan in any dwarven city of significant size. Likewise, the more martial dwarves often worship deities like Valderon and Narsin who exemplify courage and honor, both of which are important to the dwarven military machine.

Language: The dwarves' native tongue is a harsh and guttural language. Like the creatures who speak it, Dwarven is a pragmatic and logical language. It is less flowery than even the Imperial Trade Tongue and has only a tenth of the adjectives and adverbs that elven possesses. Phonetically it is filled with hard consonants and abrupt sounds making it seem as if the speaker is angry no matter what he or she is talking about.

There is no language on the Lady's Rock better suited to discussing the processes of constructing something out of stone or metal. While it is not as descriptive as elven, it is considerably more precise.

Names: Dwarves tend toward ancestral names. Children are often named for famous members of their families. Durin, Thorfin, and Gundar are examples of male dwarven names. Female dwarven names include Brunhild, Gerda, and Valaer.

Adventurers: The most common dwarves leave their enclaves in search of adventure is the desire to make a name for themselves and have generations of dwarven children bear their names. These dwarves seek to accomplish great things is search of fame; fortune is a mere afterthought at best for most of them.

Common Dwarf Racial Maximums

Strength:	6	Reason:	6
Coordination:	8	Insight:	7
Quickness:	6	Psyche:	7
Constitution:	7	Charisma:	5

Racial Traits

- **Size:** Medium
- **Darkvision:** Dwarves can see in the complete absence of light. Darkvision is black and white, but subtle shades of gray allow the dwarf to distinguish between various metals.
- **Racial Advantages:** Common dwarves begin play with both the Poison Resistance and Resistant to Toxins advantages at no cost to the player.

Grey Dwarves (Subspecies)

The grey dwarves separated from shortly after the first elf-dwarf war. These dwarves refused to adhere to the Goddess's decree that elves and dwarves should try to live in peace and refuse to accept the humans as Eris's appointed agents of that peace. They see these events from ancient history as the Goddess's test for the dwarves. As such, any dwarf who has conceded to the preposterous idea that humans should rule has failed this test… and is a traitor to his or her race. This, of course, applies to any dwarf who isn't a grey dwarf.

Personality: Grey dwarves are callous, cold, and calculating. They are as stubborn and stoic as their distant kin, but there is a certain edge to a grey dwarf that can only come from knowing that you are the only species being true to your nature and all other variants of your race are traitors deserving only of death.

Physical Description: Grey dwarves are slightly shorter than other dwarves. Their skin has a gray pallor to it as a result of their many centuries living beneath the earth. There hair is almost universally white for the same reason.

Grey dwarven eyes are the one thing that truly separates then from their more common kin. While dwarves normally favor earthen tones of brown, black, and gray, grey dwarves have eyes that literally glow with the fires of the forge… or of the underworld if you ask a dwarven historian.

Relations: Grey dwarves view all other creature as either a foe to be killed or an asset to be used until it makes more sense to kill them. Fortunately, this also seems to apply to other grey dwarves making the chances of this species ever mounting a successful attack on the empire slim at best.

Lands: Unlike other dwarves, who make their homes in the mountains, grey dwarves carve their cities out of the bed rock of the floating land masses than make up the Lady's Rock. They rarely venture to the surface unless it is to kill something, steal something, or kill something while stealing something.

Religion: Grey dwarves cherish many of the same things that other dwarves do… though their idea of honor is twisted to say the least. They venerate Semis and Dumathan just like their cousins do. Unlike their cousins, however, many of the also worship dark deities like Aren (the god of war) Ahbendon (the god of deceipt), and Kyerhan (the god of murder).

Language: On the surface, grey dwarves appear to speak the same language that other dwarves speak. There are several important differences, however, that will cause the average speaker of Dwarven to end up dead. For example, every word in dwarven that conveys some level of trust or camaraderie… words like friend and ally… have a much different meaning to the grey dwarves. In the examples mentioned above this difference translates to something like "these people mistakenly choose to trust me, so I intend to use them until I can kill them and steal their things."

Names: Grey dwarves follow the same tradition in naming their children as do other dwarves. Of course, their idea of a hero is as different as their idea of honor. Typical male grey dwarven names include Sarak, Dorim, and Trebaine. A female grey dwarf might be names Kheimhild, Serya, or Helath.

Adventurers: Grey dwarves adventure for one reason and one reason only. They either need to kill someone or need to still something and they either do not have henchmen or cannot trust the henchmen they do have to do it right.

There is a very remote possibility that a grey dwarf could leave the enclave because he or she was pure of heart and couldn't take the cutthroat life of a grey dwarf any longer. Of course, there is a significantly larger possibility that this is a ploy by the grey dwarf to lull you into a false sense of security, kill you, and steal your stuff.

Grey Dwarf Racial Maximums

Strength:	5	Reason:	7
Coordination:	8	Insight:	8
Quickness:	5	Psyche:	7
Constitution:	7	Charisma:	5

Racial Traits

- **Size:** Medium
- **Darkvision:** Grey dwarves can see in the complete absence of light. Darkvision is black and white, but subtle shades of gray allow the dwarf to distinguish between various metals.
- **Racial Advantages:** Grey dwarves begin play with the Poison Resistance, Resistant to Toxins, and Magical Aptitude advantages at no cost to the player.
- Racial Disadvantages: Grey dwarves begin play with a moderate allergy to sunlight which they receive no points for.

Mountain Dwarves (Subspecies)

Mountain Dwarves are direct descendants of the dwarves who marched against the elves and were "grounded" by Eris. Other races would consider the descendants of the people whose actions resulted in condemnation by a deity to be cursed… or at least unlucky. Dwarves, however, are a strange breed. They view the mountain dwarves as the noblest and truest of the dwarves. Common dwarves want to be like them… and mountain dwarves want to kill them all.

Personality: Mountain dwarves tend to be arrogant and condescending to other creatures. It isn't that they lack social graces or compassion. They just know, without any doubt what-so-ever, that they are the noblest and purest of dwarves. After all, the mountain dwarves can trace their ancestry back to the very beginning. It was their ancestors who prayed to Eris and gained beards and brew… and what would dwarves be without beards and brew? It was their ancestors who waged war on the elves. And what self-respecting dwarf doesn't want to wage war on the elves?

Physical Description: Mountain dwarves look almost identical to common dwarves. They do tend to be stockier, however. Mountain dwarves generally pay close attention to their appearance, they are the noblest of dwarves after all. It would not do to be traipsing all over the Lady's Rock looking like a lesser dwarf.

Relations: Most races do not distinguish between mountain dwarves and common dwarves. This annoys mountain dwarves, but it is the common dwarves who feel obligated to correct them more often than not.

The mountain dwarves' condescending demeanor does grate on other creatures, but they generally believe they are simply dealing with a particularly annoying dwarf rather than a separate species.

Lands: Mountain dwarven lands are no different than the lands ruled by common dwarves. In fact, most dwarven lands are ruled by members of this species of dwarf.

Religion: Mountain dwarves worship Semis, as other dwarves do, as the divine representation of industry and commerce. They also venerate Steve, the god of status, because of their claim as noble dwarves.

Language: Mountain dwarves speak Dwarven. They do not alter the language at all, though they do tend to speak on a grander scale thaqn common dwarves.

Names: Mountain dwarves always name their children after great dwarven heroes. These heroes are not necessarily mountain dwarves, but the mountain dwarves will always claim them as such. Arbak, Kurdan, and Taras are examples of male mountain dwarven names. Females of this species may have names like Valaira, Korina, or Sundris.

Mountian Dwarf Racial Maximums

Strength:	6	Reason:	6
Coordination:	8	Insight:	7
Quickness:	6	Psyche:	6
Constitution:	7	Charisma:	6

Racial Traits

- **Size:** Medium
- **Darkvision:** Mountain dwarves can see in the complete absence of light. Darkvision is black and white, but subtle shades of gray allow the dwarf to distinguish between various metals.
- **Racial Advantages:** Mountain dwarves begin play with the Hyper Immune System, Poison Resistance, and Resistant to Toxins advantages at no cost to the player.

Dorcs (Half-Breeds)

Dorcs are the misbegotten offspring of a dwarven mother and an orcish father. (No self-respecting… or even self-loathing… dwarf would sink so low as to ever impregnate an orcish female.) These children are usually born several seasons after a skirmish between the dwarves and the orcs and their mothers rarely, if ever, consented to intercourse.

Female dwarves carrying a dorc child take their own lives. In the eyes of the clan, they will have forever tainted their bloodline by giving birth to the half-breed bastard growing in their womb. They have been ingrained with the importance of the clan and its lineage since birth and this black mark on their family's honor is simply too much for these women to bear.

Those who are strong enough to continue living despite their shame (or too weak to regain their clan's honor, if you ask a dwarf) usually leave their homeland. These unfortunate mothers live alone in the wilderness eching a living off of the land. They give birth to their children in solitude.

Many of them die during the rigors of childbirth. Those who survive are horribly scarred by the event and are forever after unable to bear children. Dwarves claim this is a sign of the god's curse upon the unfortunate mother.

Personality: Dorcs embody the worst characteristics of dwarves and orcs. They are aggressive and stubborn. Their mothers instill them with a love of family and a dedication to the clan that will never accept them. Unwanted and unloved, Dorcs have something to prove… especially to themselves.

Physical Appearance: Dorcs are a strange cross-breed of two unattractive species. They stand about as tall as the average human, but their bodies are very muscular. They are so muscular, in fact, that it appears as if their muscles are straining against their skin. Dorcs have a pair of tusks protruding from their lower lip, a throwback to their orcish heritage. Their dwarven ancestry gives them an abundance of body hair, which is mottled green and brown… like a decaying plant.

(The picture of the dorc that originally filled this spot was removed as a show of compassion to those among our readers who may have eaten in the last week. – the editor)

Relations: Dorcs are hated by dwarves, who view them as an abomination. The dorcs themselves idolize the dwarves and will often fight to defend the clan that their mother belonged to gladly giving their lives to save creatures who despise them.

Ironically, the orcs of his father's tribe would probably welcome the powerful warriors, if they knew of their existence. Unfortunately, their dwarven mother's indoctrination of the dorcs into the culture of their dwarven parents makes this a highly unlikely event. There are few things as hard to get over as racial hatred taught from birth.

The solitude in which the dorcs are raised keeps them isolated from other species. Since dwarves do not admit their existence… and the orcs don't know about it… other races are oblivious to their existence.

Dorcish Lands: Since dorcs are the unwanted offspring of a (now) clanless dwarf, they have no place in dwarven lands. They also have no place in the lands of other races since none of those races know that dorcs exist.

Furthermore, since dorcs are raised in isolation, the chances of dorcs banding together and forming a land of their own is extremely slim… so slim, in fact, that you might as well consider it non-existent.

Religion: Dorcs worship the same deities as dwarves… and for much the same reasons. Whether they do so because of genuine belief or because of their early indoctrination would be a matter of conjecture… if anyone knew they needed to ponder it.

Language: As part of their early education, the dorc's mother teaches the young dorc to speak the dwarves' native tongue.

Names: In a strange twist of fate, dorcs often bear the names of great dwarven heroes… following in the naming traditions of their dwarven ancestors.

Adventuring: Dorish adventurers are rare only because dorcs themselves are rare. Their everyday lives are no more difficult than a life of adventure making them well suited for this vocation. Those that do adventure are some of the most fearsome warrior on the Lady's Rock.

Dorc Racial Maximums

Strength:	7	Reason:	6
Coordination:	8	**Insight:**	7
Quickness:	6	Psyche:	6
Constitution:	7	**Charisma:**	4

Racial Traits
- **Size:** Medium
- **Darkvision:** Dorcs can see in complete darkness. This vision is black and white, but subtle shades of gray allow for some distinguishing between colors.
- **Thermal Vision:** Dorcs can also see in the infrared spectrum allowing them to see heat as it emanates from creatures and objects. This vision can be disrupted by sudden heat sources, like a fireball, just as normal vision is disrupted by sudden changes in lighting.
- **Racial Advantages:** Dorcs begin play with both the Poison Resistance and Resitance to Toxins advantages at no cost to the player.

Elves

Elves are fey creatures, the true children of Eris. Elves were instilled with the chaos of the Goddess herself. Much of her world was created for the benefit of the elves. The dwarves were made so that the elves did not need to trouble themselves with the maintenance of the Lady's Rock. The humans were created to keep peace between the elves and dwarves. Because of this, elves hold a special place on the Lady's Rock. As the human philosophers say, "Elves – anything you can do; they dan do better."

Personality: Most people on the Lady's Rock, including the elves themselves, see elves as whimsical creature – the embodiment of chaos itself. As is often the case with common perceptions, this is not exactly true.

Yes, elves seem more whimsical than other races, but this has more to do with elven life-spans compared to other races. What seems like a crisis to humans is merely another phase in the cycle of life for the much longer lived elves. This doesn't mean that elves don't understand the gravity of things. In fact, it is precisely *because* elves know the true importance of things that this is the case.

Physical Description: Elves are slightly shorter than humans on average. They are slight of build and move with a grace that few creatures can rival. Elves are agile creatures and elven males weight as much as a well-proportioned human female of comparable height. Elven ears are also slightly longer than humans and terminate in a graceful point. Their eyes are almond shaped.

Elven skin tones range from deep bronze to pink. They demonstrate the same variations in hair and eye colors as humans do.

Relations: As mentioned earlier, there is an animosity between elves and dwarves that predates recorded history. While the elves seem to have no problem with individual dwarves, the idea of having to deal with large quantities of dwarves amassed in one location sends shivers down the spine of even the most accepting elf.

Humans are another story. On one hand, elves love humans the way humans love their dogs. Just as a dog protects the human members of its pack, so to do the humans exist to protect the elves. This attitude is only amplified by the fact that humans tend to revere elves in much the same way dogs revere their human masters.

On the other hand, elves know that humans were put on the Lady's Rock by Eris herself in order to govern it. In this regard they are like children who, having once been trusted by the parent and left home alone, but having lost that trust is now being babysat. To make matters worse, the eldest human is barely an adult by elven standards.

It's like a 16 year old being told that his 9 year old sister is in charge while mom and dad are out. The nine year old experiences a strange mix of feelings. She feels adoration for her older sibling, but quickly becomes drunk with power. Meanwhile, the older sibling has no respect for the wishes of the younger and merely tries to humor her so that he doesn't have to listen to the inevitable whining.

Generally speaking, elves see other races as beneath their notice. No other race was created with a divine mandate from Eris, so no other race is of any importance. Hence, they are of no concern to the elves.

Elven Lands: The domains ruled by elves are a unique blend of nature and civilization. Elven cities are built to be one with the forest rather than being built over the forest. Elven homes are nestled securely in the branches of mighty oaks and redwoods. Some elves even use magic to craft their homes inside the trunks themselves.

Graceful spire and delicate metalwork are a hallmark of elven lands. While not as skilled as dwarven craftsmen, elves have had several millennia to learn how to do it. After that long, you're bound to figure it out by accident.

Elves tend to govern their lands loosely. If people do not cause trouble and everything runs smoothly, the elves allow great latitude to their people. That being said, the elves do not tolerate people who wantonly abuse the planet or the creatures who make it their home. If this ever does happen, the elves strike hard and fast to remove the blight form their realm.

Religion: As creature instilled with the essence of Eris herself, you would think that the majority of elves would worship the Goddess of Chaos and discord. As you may have guessed by reading the previous sentence, they do not.

Chalysse, the goddess of the cycle of life, has a strong following among the elves. Other popular deities include Laeroth (the god of wisdom), Solvarus (the god of the hunt), and Tchoren (the god of magic).

Language: The elven tongue, known as Elvish, is filled with subtle nuances that make it difficult for none native speakers to make full use of the language. Almost imperceptible changes in inflection or intonation can convey a spectrum of emotions and feelings that other languages lack the words to describe.

To give you an example, humans often say they are feeling blue when they are sad. Elves, on the other hand, know the different levels of sadness associated with sky blue, baby blue, royal blue, navy blue, and midnight blue.

Despite these difficulties, elven is still a truly beautiful language. It has a melodic quality that makes it mesmerizing to those who are unfamiliar with it. People can get an elven phrase stuck in their heads in much the same way a catchy tune can bounce around in their head.

Names: Elven names are often difficult to pronounce for non-native speaker of the language and practically impossible for those who do not speak it at all. Like the language itself, elven names tend to have a melodic quality. Two names that sound identical to the untrained human ear may have vastly different meanings.

Because of these difficulties, elves tend to shorten their names for use in human society. If they do not do it themselves, the humans will undoubtedly do it for them.

This can be very embarrassing when whether you're talking about art, an artist, an expert, or treasure is simply a matter of intonation.

Male names include Aelemar, Gareth, and Kethean. Female names include Nimue, Hatae, and Syllia.

Adventurers: Adventuring elves may have an interest in history that leads them to study ancient tombs. They might be studying magic and traveling to learn things that they could not learn from the extensive elven libraries. It might be a desire to study other races or cultures that drives them. Regardless of their reasons, most elves see adventuring as an means to an end rather than the end itself.

Common Elf Racial Maximums

Strength:	4	Reason:	6
Coordination:	9	Insight:	8
Quickness:	8	Psyche:	6
Constitution:	5	Charisma:	7

Racial Traits

- **Size:** Medium
- **Low-Light Vision:** In conditions of limited illumination, elves can see as well as a human can under normal daylight conditions.
- **Charm Resistance:** Elves receive two extra die for the purposes of resisting charm and enchantment spells.
- **Sleepless:** Elves do not require sleep. Instead they enter a meditative trance to rest and rejuvenate. This means that the elves do not suffer penalties to perceive things while "sleeping."

Aquatic Elves (Subspecies)

Aquatic elves are the least common of all elves. This is probably due to the fact that the Lady's Rock does not possess large oceans of water for them to inhabit and only has a limited number of lakes and inland seas large enough to support these elves in any significant numbers.

Personality: Aquatic elves tend toward the extremes of elven personalities. They are more passionate… and at the same time more slothful… like the lazy rivers and tumultuous seas they occupy.

Physical Description: Aquatic elves look like common elves except that their skin tones range from light blue to emerald green. Their eyes tend toward silvers and grays. Their hands and feet are webbed to allow them to swim better… which makes sense considering they live underwater.

Like dolphins, aquatic elves are mammals and do not breathe water. Most of them are able to hold their breath for extended periods of time, however.

Relations: Aquatic elves have little use for other races. Other species pollute the rivers lakes and streams in which the aquatic elves make their homes. These races exploit the waters for their resources with little concern for the impact that they have.

Lands: Aquatic elven towns are built beneath the surface of large lakes and inland seas. Their homes are crafted from coral and aquatic plants. Debris from surface vessels is also used. Better to make use of it than allow it to clutter up the sea floors.

Theses cities make extensive use of aquatic plants to produce the oxygen that the aquatic elves need in order to survive. This oxygen is then trapped in the vaulted ceilings of their dwellings providing them with a steady supply of breathable air without venturing to the surface. This leads some scholars to mistakenly assume that aquatic elves can actually breathe water. They are not fish.

Religion: Two deities are highly revered among the aquatic elves. They are Barak, the god fo storms, and Manak, the god of the waters. Other deities may have a small following in some cities, but there are not many aquatic elves on the Lady's Rock, so their worship is rather miniscule.

Language: Aquatic elves speak a dialect of Elvish that accentuates the melodic nature of the tongue making it more of a song written as needed than a language. Speakers of Elvish can understand this dialect if they pay close attention to what the singer is singing.

Names: Aquatic elves follow the same naming conventions as their land-dwelling kin, but they make heavy use of prefixes and suffixes having to do with water. Male aquatic elves might be names Sumavin, Nafel, or Dushor. Females have names like Sumae, Quilynda, or Kellara.

Adventurers: There are few aquatic elves and therefore few aquatic elven adventurers. Their periodic need for water limits their ability to travel very far from shore… and therefore limits their ability to explore dusty old ruins and crypts.

Aquatic Elf Racial Maximums

Strength:	5	Reason:	6
Coordination:	9	Insight:	8
Quickness:	8	Psyche:	6
Constitution:	6	Charisma:	6

Raqcial Traits

- **Size:** Medium
- **Sonar:** Aquatic elves use a form of echolocation to navigate their underwater realms. This sonar functions out of the water as well. It can be disrupted by loud abrupt noises just as vision is disrupted by abrupt changes in lighting.
- **Low-Light Vision:** In conditions of limited illumination, aquatic elves can see as well as a human can under normal daylight conditions.
- **Charm Resistance:** Aquatic elves receive two extra die for the purposes of resisting charm and enchantment spells.
- **Sleepless:** Elves do not require sleep. Instead they enter a meditative trance to rest and rejuvenate. This means that the elves do not suffer penalties to perceive things while "sleeping."
- **Deep Breath:** An aquatic elf is effectively breathe underwater.

Drow (Subspecies)

Drow were the first elves created by Eris. Legend has it that these elves decided to exile themselves to the depths of the earth when Eris grounded the dwarves. Other elves claim the drow were banished because of the great evils they wrought upon the world and call them dark elves for these sins. The drow, if they had been asked, would say that they went because they knew they were equally deserving of punishment.

Personality: Drow, more than any other elves, are the embodiment of chaos. Their erratic behavior confuses other races. They don't understand the drow, and people tend to condemn what they do not understand.

Physical Description: Drow have the same height and build as other elves. Drow ears are longer than normal elven ears. While the ears are longer, they do not protrude above the drow's head as some artistic reditions might lead you to believe.

Because they live underground where there is no light, they have no "natural" skin tones, hair color or eye color. However, when on the surface, the following traits have been witnessed: Drow have skin as black as coal. Their hair colors tend toward white. Blonds and grays are less common, but not enough to be considered rare. Rare drow have been born with metallic silver, gold, or bronze hair.

Drow eyes are not limited to colors normally displayed by humans. Because eye color is really a function of reflected light, drow eyes can appear to be any color of the rainbow - violet, red, and gray eyes seems to be the most common.

Relations: Drow are feared by most surface races. This doesn't really bother the drow, but it does limit their desire to deal with surface species. Of course, this limited contact simply increases their mystery… which increases others' fear of the drow… which increases others' misunderstanding of the drow… which increases others' condemnation of the drow. It's a vicious cycle.

Lands: Drow live in caverns beneath the Lady's Rock. They carve their cities in much the same way that grey dwarves do, but drow cities have a form over function quality that leaves little doubt of their elven creators.

As befits creatures instilled with chaos, drow lands are filled with contradictions. On one hand a drow city is a seas of chaos. Skirmishes between rival drow houses keep the population in check. On the other hand, a rigid system of laws keeps the even this chaos in check.

How can something be chaotic and governed by laws? That's a good question. If you ask a drow, they'll probably say something to the effect of, "Is that what you would expect? No? Then it is unexpected… illogical… and, therefore, the very embodiment of chaos." Then they'll probably kill you.

Religion: Drow, more than any other race, tend to venerate Eris above all other deities. Other deities may be worshipped in drow cities, but these deities are always viewed as servants of the Goddess. Drow see spiders as a living symbol of their Goddess - the eight legs of the spider representing the eight rays on the Star of Chaos. The fact that the legs move about constantly changing position only increases this association in the eyes of the drow.

Language: The drow dialect of Elvish is similar to other dialects. The elves claim it is a corrupt form of their tongue while the drow claim they speak the original tongue of the elves. In either case, a speaker of one language need only pay close attention to understand a speaker of the other.

Names: Drow names follow typical elven conventions for naming, though they do use more hard consonants then other elves. Malagaun, Brizerd, and Nalryn are examples of male names. Belarayne, Jhaelafae, and Charanna might be female names.

89

Adventurers: Drow adventurers are usually surface raiders looking to secure those goods that cannot be gained through trade… mostly because few races trade with the drow.

Every once in a while a scimitar wielding drow gets fed up with life in the drow lands and ventures to the surface. These drow usually find a blind ranger to train them before they actually convince someone that they aren't dangerous. Then they become soft and wishy-washy before regaining that little lavender twinkle in their eyes that made them an interesting character in the first place… but I digress…

Drow Racial Maximums

Strength:	4	Reason:	7
Coordination:	10	Insight:	8
Quickness:	9	Psyche:	7
Constitution:	4	Charisma:	8

Racial Traits

- **Size:** Medium
- **Darkvision:** Unlike other elves, drow possess darkvision. This black and white vision functions even in the absence of light. While it cannot see colors, subtle shades of gray allow the drow to distinguish between them.
- **Charm Resistance:** Elves receive two extra dice for the purposes of resisting charm and enchantment spells.
- **Sleepless:** Elves do not require sleep. Instead they enter a meditative trance to rest and rejuvenate. This means that the elves do not suffer penalties to perceive things while "sleeping."
- **Racial Advantages:** A drow begins play with the 3 point Magical Resistance advantages (granting 1 bonus success) at no cost to the player.
- **Racial Disadvantages:** Drow also begin play with a severe allergy to sunlight for which they receive no additional build points.

Eburnae (Subspecies)

The eburnae are a strange race that many believe to be the result of elven necromancers cavorting with members of the undead during the time of Vandal Nefar. Though they do exhibit some qualities of the undead, eburnae are very much alive.

Personality: The eburnae tend to have a very serious outlook on life, spending your life being hunted as an abomination against nature can have that effect on a species. They tend to be quiet and reserved. An old eburnae proverb reads, "It only takes one farmer to rouse a mob." Most eburnae know this to be true from first hand experience.

When an eburnae does feel safe, he or she makes a point of enjoying themselves as much as possible. They believe that each day may be their last, so they cherish the times when they do not need to fear for their lives.

Physical Description: Eburnae resemble elves in that they are slender with well-defined musculature. They have chalk white skin with crimson hair. Their eyes are often bright colors, so vivid that they appear unnatural. Blues, greens, and reds are dominant, though some rich chocolate browns have been encountered.

The ears of an eburnae are slender and pointed like those of elves, but they are much longer. Eburnae tend to decorate their ears with numerous piercings and cuffs.

The eburnae encountered thus far have displayed an interesting characteristic, their bodies are in a constant state of flux making them semi-intangible. When one of these eburnae is attacked their bodies flow around the foreign object limiting the amount of damage caused by the attack.

This ability does have a drawback, however. Sometimes an eburnae looses control of their connection to the physical world. This results in any of their tangible equipment to fall through their bodies causing immense pain. Magical attacks disrupt this ability causing the same damage to an eburnae that they would a human.

For some unknown reason, ghost wood also seems to disrupt this ability. An eburnae's body is unable to pass through ghost wood like other living creature. They also are unable to "flow around" weapons made of ghost wood even if they are non-magical. This is often used as evidence that the eburnae are undead. Eburnae, however, are not undead. They are affected by positive and negative energy just like any other living creature.

Relations: Eburnae are very distrusting of other races. As mentioned earlier, a lifetime of being hunted as the spawn of the undead can have that effect on a species.

Despite this inherent distrust, it is possible for eburnae to breed with other races. The child resulting from such a union is always an eburnae regardless of the race of the other parent.

Lands: As a race of outcasts, eburnae have no lands that they call their own. Instead they try to exist on the fringes of imperial society.

Several times during the history of the empire, eburnae have tried to found remote villages where they could live unmolested by the rest of the world. Each of these attempts has failed. Once the imperial citizens found these enclaves, they razed them to the ground.

Religion: Ahbendon and Dumathan, both deities of stealth and subterfuge, are often worshipped by the eburnae. Another deity that is highly revered is Chalysse, the goddess of the cycle of life and death.

Language: The eburnae do not have a language all their own. Instead they speak Elvish and the Imperial Trade Tongue. Scholars use this fact to support their classification of the eburnae as an offshoot of elves.

Names: Eburnae give their children either human or elven names depending on which species dominates the area where the child is born.

Adventurers: Eburnae adventure for many reasons, but none call to them more than their desire to stay alive. Two things tend to be true about adventurers. Adventurers travel from place to place seeking treasure. This nomadic life style suits the eburnae quite nicely. The more they move around, the less likely they are to be discovered. The treasures that adventurers acquire are also appealing to the eburnae. Many of them are powerful aids to the eburnae and finding them negates the need to deal with a merchant who may be less than helpful when dealing with the "walking damned."

Eburnae Racial Maximums

Strength:	5	Reason:	6
Coordination:	9	Insight:	7
Quickness:	8	Psyche:	6
Constitution:	5	Charisma:	8

Racial Traits

- **Size:** Medium
- **Life-Sight:** Eburnae eyes are not as sensitive to light as the eyes of other elves. Instead, the eburnae's senses are attuned to the energies of life itself. Living creatures give off a bright green light when using this vision. This light illuminates the world around them. Dead creatures or objects that were once alive (wooden tables, for example) have a pale green glow representing their former lives. Undead creatures appear as utter blackness against the gray background.
- **Charm Resistance:** Eburnae receive two extra die for the purposes of resisting charm and enchantment spells.
- **Sleepless:** Eburnae do not require sleep. Instead they enter a meditative trance to rest and rejuvenate. This means that the eburnae do not suffer penalties to perceive things while "sleeping."
- **Semi-Intangible:** When an eburnae is attacked by a piercing, slashing, or crushing weapons they add their insight to their quickness and roll the total number of dice to dodge. Moreover, the damage from piercing and slashing weapon is recorded as mind damage if it is not dodged or gaffed. Only weapons that do crushing damage immediately do physical damage to an eburnae.

However, should an eburnae ever critically fail on any roll or lose control of their body (either by losing consciousness or falling victim to a poison, toxin or spell), the eburnae is unable to maintain "tangibility" and their possessions "fall" through his or her body causing intense pain. The character takes 1 point of mind damage per point of armor value for any armor they are wearing. Normal clothing is treated as padded armor for this purpose. Jewelry and other items cause pain, but no damage unless they are magical in which case they do 1 point each.

Grey Elves (Subspecies)

Grey elves are considered the most scholarly of elves. When people speak of elven high magic, it is the power of the grey elves that they speak of.

The first grey elves were a band of wizards renown for their mastery of the mystic arts. As they gained in magical power and prowess, these wizards began experimenting on ways to enhance the elven race. An extensive breeding program was begun in the lands controlled by these elves. They did not succeed in breeding the uber-elf they had hoped for, but their selective breeding did create a new species of elf.

Personality: Grey elves are the most serious of the elves. They place a high degree of importance on reason and logic. They see the world as a complex mathematical equation and believe that mastery of this equation is the source of unbridled power… if they could just unlock its secrets.

Physical Description: Grey elves have a slighter build than common elves. Their skin, hair, and eye are paler shades of those common to other elves. The early breeding programs promoted mental aptitude over physical prowess, and the living grey elves still share these traits.

Relations: Grey elves look down upon other races, even other elves. Because of the emphasis they place on intelligence and learning… and the fact that they have centuries to study… few other species can live up to the grey elves expectations.

Though they would never admit it, humans frighten most grey elves. The short lived humans often fail to see all the consequences of their actions… some of which won't come about until long after the human has died. This makes them dangerous.

Grey Elven Lands: Areas ruled by grey elves are a strange contradiction of things. They have the same forms as other elven areas, but rather than allow nature to dictate art, the grey elves strive to force nature to conform to the rules of architecture and design. This gives even their forest cities an unnatural feel to them.

Religion: Grey elves favor Semis (the god of craftsmen) and Steve (the god of status, fashion, and hair styles). While they worship other deities, they shy away from those deities whose actions cannot be consistently predicted… like Eris,. Tchoren, and Barak.

Language: Grey elves speak the same tongue as other elves, but their rigid adherence to rules of grammar and form has taken much of the beauty out of the language. Like a picture you're forced to draw, a story you're forced to write, or, in this case, a song you are forced to sing… there is no life to the grey dialect of Elvish.

Names: Grey elven names are often long, drawn-out titles more than actual names. Unlike other elves, they rarely shorten them for the convenience of others. Typical male grey elves have names like Lafrethyr, Dredrimnal, and Kerlynael. Females names are equally lengthy and difficult to pronounce such as Sehamaera, Thaliavanna, or Rhysarrae.

Adventurers: Grey elves rarely adventure. They spend their time locked away in libraries, towers, and other places where they can perfect their art. Those few that do adventure usually do so in an attempt to regain some lost sliver of knowledge or ancient artifact.

Grey Elf Racial Maximums

Strength:	4	Reason:	8
Coordination:	9	Insight:	8
Quickness:	8	Psyche:	6
Constitution:	4	Charisma:	7

Racial Traits

- **Size:** Medium
- **Low-Light Vision:** In conditions of limited illumination, elves can see as well as a human can under normal daylight conditions.
- **Charm Resistance:** Elves receive two extra die for the purposes of resisting charm and enchantment spells.
- **Sleepless:** Elves do not require sleep. Instead they enter a meditative trance to rest and rejuvenate. This means that the elves do not suffer penalties to perceive things while "sleeping."
- **Racial Advantages:** Grey elves begin play with the Magical Aptitude advantage at no cost to the player.

Wood Elves (Subspecies)

Wood elves are viewed as primitives by other races. They are only slightly more civilized than orcs as far as most people are concerned. They would probably be treated little better than orcs if it wasn't for the fact that they are elves.

Personality: Wood elves are a very practical race. Some people would say "simple." They are acutely aware of their place in the great cycle of life. They do not fear death, but they do not long for it either. They are fearful of arcane magic, though they embrace magic of a divine nature. They use tools, but only those which they make themselves preferring bows and spears to swords. They wear armor made from the skins of animals and spend most of their time barefoot.

Wood elves see themselves as the protectors of the forests. More than any other elf, a wood elf will mercilessly hunt those who exploit the woodlands. The woodsman who chops down trees without planting new ones, the person who burns a forest to make room for a pasture, and a large hunting party may all find themselves the targets of these stealthy stalkers.

Physical Description: Wood elves look like very muscular elves. Their skin is often bronze in color, though it is usually covered with dirt or paint to help camouflage them in the wild.

Wood elves care little for their personal appearance. While they bathe regularly, they do not go to the great pains with their appearance that other elves do.

Relations: Wood elves are very reclusive. They rarely venture out of their woodland homes. They are uncomfortable in cities and other highly civilized areas. After all, if they were intended to live in cities, then cities would grow naturally.

Some people have tried to explain that there is really little difference between building a house and making leather clothing. Wood elves usually attribute such talk to the corrupting influence of civilization… as they chase the speaker through the woods.

Lands: It is difficult to describe wood elven territory to people because most people wouldn't know a wood elf controlled forest if they were sleeping in the middle of it. While the other elves were learning how to build cities, forge weapons, and cast spells, the wood elves were perfecting the skill that the other elves had long since abandoned. If a wood elf is in a forest and does not want to be found, you will not find him or her.

Wood elves are hunters and gatherers that live in tribes organized along matriarchal lines. These tribes are semi-nomadic in behavior. They rarely, if ever, form a permanent community, but they restrict their movement to a particular forested area.

Religion: Wood elves favor nature deities, but shun those deities they see as corrupted by society such as Durian, a nature goddess who now governs agriculture.

Language: Believe it or not, wood elves still speak a recognizable dialect of Elvish. Much of the elven language has been lost to the wood elves, however. While they can describe a sunset over s pristine lake in a virgin forest in such detail that it would make an ogre weep, they have no words to describe any of the complex social structures that other people living in the empire take for granted. For example, wood elves speak of the tribe, but have no words to differentiate between this extended family and smaller familial units.

Names: Wood elves tend to have names easily translatable into other languages. These names often depict some notable event in the elf's past or some aspect of nature that the elf wishes to exemplify. A wood elf who saved a bear from a hunter might be known as Rethar, a name that easily translates to Bear-friend. If the wood elf ventures into human lands, he or she would likely go by the translation of his name rather than the actual elven equivalent.

Adventurers: Wood elves usually adventure to avenge some terrible wrong… whether it is real or perceived… that has been committed against nature. These adventurers make some of the most implacable foes you will ever have the misfortune of encountering.

Wood Elf Racial Maximums

Strength:	6	Reason:	5
Coordination:	9	Insight:	7
Quickness:	8	Psyche:	6
Constitution:	6	Charisma:	6

Racial Traits

- **Size:** Medium
- **Low-Light Vision:** In conditions of limited illumination, elves can see as well as a human can under normal daylight conditions.
- **Charm Resistance:** Elves receive two extra die for the purposes of resisting charm and enchantment spells.
- **Sleepless:** Elves do not require sleep. Instead they enter a meditative trance to rest and rejuvenate. This means that the elves do not suffer penalties to perceive things while "sleeping."

Elfling (Half-Breed)

Elflings are to elves what halflings are to humans. They are the offspring of elves and halflings. They tend to be found where halfling shires abut elven woodlands.

Personality: Elflings are fun-loving pranksters. They see life as a game… a myriad of different jokes that all have the same punchline. All you can hope to do is live your life more interesting… tell your joke better… than the next guy.

Physical Description: Elflings look like miniature elves. Adult elflings stand about half as tall as full grown elves. They often have the same skin tone, hair and eye color as their elven parent. Elflings rarely grow facial hair. Elflings, both male and female, tend to wear their hair long. Ornate braids a ponytails are seen as status symbols. This obsession with hair borders closely on the dwarven obsessions with beards.

Relations: Elflings are both loved and hated by other races. Their child-like appearance and natural charisma causes them to be well-liked among most species. However, these races often grow tired of the elflings continuous pranks… especially if they happen to be the butt of those jokes.

Lands: Elflings control no lands of their own, but are welcome in the lands of the elves, halflings, and humans. They enjoy all the benefits of imperial citizenship… though the empire makes no distinction between elflings and halflings.

Religion: Elflings religious practices trouble other races. The dark god Ahbendon, the god of deception, is a elfling favorite because they see practical jokes as part of his portfolio. Semis is often worshipped by elflings who favor elaborate, humorous, and mostly harmless traps as pranks. Tchoren is another favorite, especially among elflings who use magic.

Language: Elflings have no language of their own and are generally raised to speak both Elvish and the Imperial Trade Tongue.

Names: As a half-breed, elflings share the same naming patterns as their elven and halfling parents.

Adventurers: Elfling adventurers are actually quite common. Until recently, elflings were simply considered to be halflings, so more than one tale of a halfling hero could, in fact, be an elfling.

Elflings are innately curious. Shortly after reaching adulthood, this curiosity changes to a full-blown wanderlust. The elfling leaves his homeland and journeys out into the world to see what he or she can see. The elflling may return once thie wanderlust is satiated, but many are never heaqrd from again.

Elfling Racial Maximums

Strength:	3	Reason:	6
Coordination:	9	Insight:	7
Quickness:	8	Psyche:	7
Constitution:	4	Charisma:	8

Racial Traits

Size: Small

- **Low-Light Vision:** In conditions of limited illumination, elflings can see as well as a human can under normal daylight conditions.
- **Charm Resistance:** Elflings receive two extra die for the purposes of resisting charm and enchantment spells.
- **Stealthy:** An elfling receives a bonus die to any roll to hide, move silently, or otherwise be stealthy.
- **Racial Advantages:** Elflings begin play with the Light Sleeper advantage a no cost to the player.

Gelf (Half-Breed)

Whenever two species of humanoids live in close proximity to each other, there is bound to be some mixed relationships. Gelf are the result of such a relationship between an elf and a gnome.

Personality: Gelf are simple folk. They appreciate the simple things in life and see no need for extravagance. As long as they have a roof over their heads and food to eat, Gelf are happy.

Physical Description: Gelf stand sligthly shorter than their Elfling cousins. Their noses are longer than any other elven species or half-breed. Gelven ears seem too large for their heads, but not grotesquely so. The skin of a gelf is often tanned bronze because of the time they spend working outdoors. Their eyes are narrow and their eye brows protrude slightly in order to protect them from the bright sun. Eye color is predominantly greens and browns. Hair color favors shades of brown as well.

Relations: Gelf get along with most other species. They enjoy working the land and willingly trade the products of their labor for the goods they cannot produce on their own.

Gelf often act as liaisons between communities of elves and dwarves. Dwarves trade forged items for the produce from the gelven fields. Gelf, in turn, trade these dwarven goods to elves for woodwork.

Of all races on the Lady's Rock, Gelf get along best with the halflings. The two races share a love of the rural lifestyle that has created a deep bond between them.

Lands: The gelf live in small farming communities, usually on the edges of an elven forest. Gelf have no desire to rule over the lives of others. Instead, gelf are content to work the land and live off its bounty.

Religion: Most gelf pay homage to Durian, the goddess of agriculture. This deity plays an important part in the everyday lives of the gelves, and every elven household has a small shrine to their patron.

The few gelf with martial inclanations worship Barak, the god of storms. The violent nature of this deity satiates their desire for a strong deity and his capacity as the bringer of rain satisfies their more naturalistic instincts.

Language: Most gelves speak Elvish, Gnomish or both as well as the Imperial Trade Tongue. Depending on where the gelves live determines which language they speak most prevalently.

Names: Gelf raised by an elven parent often have an elven name while those raised by gnomes have a gnomish name. Gelves born to gelven parents usually take names from whatever culture rules the lands in which they live.

Adventurers: Sometimes a rare gelven child is not content with life as a simple farmer. These children leave their homes and seek to make a name for themselves among the people of the Lady's Rock. To date, none of them have returned to tell the tales of their adventures… and the histories do not hold the tales of great gelves of the past.

Gelf Racial Maximums

Strength:	3	Reason:	7
Coordination:	9	Insight:	7
Quickness:	7	Psyche:	7
Constitution:	4	Charisma:	7

Racial Traits

- **Size:** Small
- **Low-Light Vision:** In conditions of limited illumination, elves can see as well as a human can under normal daylight conditions.
- **Thermal Vision:** Gelf are able to see in the infrared spectrum of light. This allows them to see the heat emanating for creatures, objects they have had contact with, or other warm things. This vision can be disrupted by sudden changes in temperature in the same way normal vision is disrupted by sudden changes in light.
- **Racial Advantages:** Gelf begin play with the Scientific Aptitude advantage at no cost to the player.

Half-Elves (Half-breed)

Half-elves have existed since humans and elves have existed. A half-elf is a child born to an elf and a human. These children are almost always born to a loving couple and are given all the comforts and opportunities that their parents can afford.

Personality: Many half-elves have an "outcast" mentality. This idea that they do not belong to the cultures of either parent is often manufactured by the half-elves themselves. This self-imposed exile often turns into either loners or reckless warriors with something to prove.

These attitudes are a source of confusion for the parents of the half-elf who strived to give their child every opportunity. The half-elves often mistake this confusion for some negative emotion and use it as justification to further their self-image as a being trapped on the fringes of two societies that don't want them.

Physical Description: Half-elves look like short humans with one notable difference, their ears terminate in points. Otherwise half-elves have the same physical characteristics as a human of the same height and weight.

Lands: Half-elves are readily accepted in both human and elven societies. As such, half-elves have come into positions of power in some human or elven lands from time to time. These lands usually stay true to their roots even with a half-elven ruler.

Religion: Half-elves worship a variety of deities based upon their individual interests and the land in which they were born.

Language: Half-elves, like most half-breeds, do not have a language of their own. Almost every half-elf learns the Imperial Trade Tongue and many of them learn Elvish in order to connect with their elven heritage.

Adventurers: Half-elven adventurers are actually quite common. Only humans have more members in the adventuring community. Each half-elf has his or her own reasons for adventuring and many of these reasons exist only in the half-elf's own mind.

Half-Elf Racial Maximums

Strength:	5	Reason:	6
Coordination:	9	Insight:	7
Quickness:	8	Psyche:	6
Constitution:	5	Charisma:	7

Racial Traits

- **Size:** Medium
- **Low-Light Vision:** In conditions of limited illumination, elves can see as well as a human can under normal daylight conditions.
- **Charm Resistance:** Elves receive two extra die for the purposes of resisting charm and enchantment spells.
- **Racial Advantages:** Half-elves begin play with the Presence Advantage at no cost to the player.

Gnomes

The role of gnomes on the Lady's Rock has long been a point of discussion among philosophers. They appear to be somewhat akin to both elves and dwarves. There are differences between them, but those differences aren't really that numerous to justify Eris creating this creature. So why are they here?

Though the dwarves would deny it if they ever learned the truth, gnomes actually descended from early dwarves. Before Eris made the dwarves smelly or hairy, a small number of them realized that the elves found their appearance troubling. Rather than pray to Eris for help, these dwarves took matters into their own hands. They strove to be more like the elves, and they succeeded.

Eventually these dwarves evolved enough that they appeared to be a completely separate species. They developed a language all their own to further distinguish themselves from their dwarven ancestors. Now the schism is so complete than only evidence of their true descent lies in dusty tomes locked in secret gnomish libraries.

Personality: Gnomes share many personality traits with elves. Both races love the natural world. Both races appreciate beauty. Both races love to dance and play. Gnomes, however, maintain a love of strong brew, one of the few holdovers from the time before the grounding when they were still dwarves.

Physical Description: Gnomes are shorter than halflings, but they lack the pleasant proportions that halflings have. Gnomish arms appear to be longer than they should be and their legs appear shorter. Last, but not least, gnome noses are longer than would be aesthetically pleasing by most.

Relations: Gnomes seems to get along best with elves. Humans tolerate gnomes, but, like most races, wonder what the gnome's role in in the cycle of life. Dwarves have a strong reaction toward gnomes. Either they treat them as brethren or as enemies. Rarely is a dwrf ambivalent toward them. Other races are content to let the gnomes live with the elves and have no strong feelings about them one way or another.

Lands: Gnomes often make their homes in elven controlled areas. They seem content to allow the elves to rule and concern themselves more with support roles in the communities.

Religion: Gnomes favor industrious deities such as Durian and Semis. Other deities may be worshipped by individuals or small groups, but these deities hold the reverence of the majority of gnomes.

Language: The gnomish language is a strange blend of elven and dwarven that can best be described as "pig-elven." It based on Dwarven with a smattering of Elvish thrown in where Dwarven falls short. The gnomish language uses the grammatical constructs and word forms of Elvish. This makes it one of the most difficult languages to master.

Names: As befits the gnomes, they use a mixture of elven and dwarven names when naming their children. Gnomes tend to give male children dwarven names and female children elven ones.

Adventurers: Gnomes can go adventuring for a variety of reasons. At the root of these reasons, if anyone bothered to dig that deep, you would probably find greed. If anyone knew the real history of the gnomes, they would probably contend that there was some genetic desire for metal coins and gemstones that was a hold over from when they were dwarves.

Gnome Racial Maximums

Strength:	3	Reason:	8
Coordination:	8	Insight:	7
Quickness:	6	Psyche:	6
Constitution:	4	Charisma:	6

Racial Traits

- **Size:** Small
- **Low-Light Vision:** Gnomes are able to see as well during conditions of limited illumination as humans are during daylight conditions.
- **Thermal Vision:** Gnomes can see in the infrared spectrum of light allowing them to see heat emanating from creatures and objects. This vision can be disrupted by abrupt changes in temperature much in the same way normal vision is disrupted by sudden changes in lighting.
- **Racial Advantages:** Gnomes begin play with the Mechanical Aptitude advantage at no cost to the player.

Goblins

Goblins were first encountered by the humans as they expanded their empire. Tribes of the primitive creatures raided military supply chains and sabotaged equipment. After a failed attempt to exterminate the pests, the empire decided to allow them limited admittance into the empire. Now they are treated like any other primitive race trying to make their way in imperial society.

Personality: Goblins are cowardly by nature. A goblin's first, and often only, concern is for him or her self. Everything and everyone else is either a threat or a potential target.

Physical Description: Goblins are short, misshapen humanoids with green tinted skin and large black eyes. Their hairy is stringy, greasy, and almost always black in color. Goblins have long ears and small porcine noses.

Because they are always expecting attack, goblins walk in a crouched position, like a coiled spring. Their long arms would drag on the floor if they did not hold them up.

Relations: Goblins living in imperial society are usually slaves or thieves. This does not give them a good reputation with other races. Dwarves especially hate goblins, but dwarves hate most non-dwarven races.

Lands: Goblins only have control over small pieces of wilderness. In the wild, goblins are a primitive people and have a tribal society.

In civilized lands, goblins are viewed as either slaves or pests.

Religion: Many of the goblins alive in the empire today worship Manak, the god of disease, for the role they believe the deity played in eliminating rival tribes. They also venerate Ahbendon and Dumathan for the treachery inherent in each of their portfolios.

Langauge: Goblins speak a language, called Goblinoid by scholars, which they share with their larger hobogoblin kin. It is a harsh language with a very limited vocabulary.

Names: Goblin names are short consisting of a single syllable. Goblins usually follow this given name with an honorific os some sort… usually something outlandish and obviously untrue. Male goblin names might include Ter, the dragon killer; Drob, the castle render; or Zard, the well-hung.

Females do not use honorifics unless they are ranking members of the tribe. Exam ples of female goblin names include Mar, Fray, and Her.

Adventurers: Goblins do whatever they need to in order to survive. Sometimes skulking through an abandoned castle seems more appealing than avoiding the city watch. Therefore, goblins sometimes venture into abandoned castles.

Goblin Racial Maximums

Strength:	3	Reason:	6
Coordination:	8	Insight:	7
Quickness:	7	Psyche:	5
Constitution:	5	Charisma:	5

Racial Traits

- **Size:** Small
- **Low-Light Vision:** Goblins can see in conditions of limited illumination as well as a human can see during daylight hours.
- **Racial Advantages:** Goblins begin play with the In Tune advantage at no cost to the player.

Hobgoblins (Subspecies)

It might seem strange to classify the larger hobgoblin as a subspecies of goblin, but the evidence presented by the Imperial Ministry of Science was overwhelming… and completely incomprehensible to this author…

Personality: Hobgoblins are bullies. They rely on brute strength to accomplish their goals. If they can not accomplish their goals with sheer strength, the hobgoblins try to use numbers. If numbers are not enough, the hobgoblins will flea. They have no desire to face off against a superior foe.

Physical Description: Hobgoblins appear to be larger, more muscular goblins. They stand about as tall as a short human. Their arms and legs are proportional to their bodies. They have the same green-tinted skin, greasy black hair, and dark pit-like eyes as their goblin cousins.

Relations: Hobgoblins hate almost everyone. They see goblins as their personal servants and often lead goblins tribes. Orcs, in turn, see the hobgoblins as fodder and use them to thin out the defenders during raids. Everyone else either wants them dead… or in a slave market.

Lands: There are no hobgoblin lands. A mating pair may take over a goblin tribe. Orcs may capture some of them for use for tasks the orcs do not wish to do themselves. Wealthy humans may purchase them as guards or menial laborers. Other than that, the best the hobgoblin can hope for is a small section of road to rob regularly without too much interference from the authorities.

Religion: The hobgoblins respect strength so they worship strong deities. Aren, god of war, is a favorite as is Jhaemaryl, goddess of blood and lust.

Language: Hobgoblins speak Goblinoid. While they can learn other languages, few do… with the exception of the phrase "give us your gold" in the Imperial Trade Tongue.

Names: Hobgoblins name their children in much the same way goblins to. Tark, the mighty; Kadu, the ravager; and Ghul, the insane are the names of some hobgoblin heroes. Bera, Tril, and Rowe are the names of some female hobgoblin brigands.

Adventurers: Hobgoblins are small fish in a big pond. They want to be big fish and do what they can to foster that image for themselves. Some rare hobgoblins choose to do this by looting dead people rather than the living. So they find their way into crypts and catacombs rather than waiting by the roadside.

Hobgoblin Racial Maximums

Strength:	5	Reason:	5
Coordination:	7	Insight:	6
Quickness:	6	Psyche:	5
Constitution:	7	Charisma:	5

Racial Traits

- **Size:** Medium
- **Low-Light Vision:** Hobgoblins share the same keen vision as their smaller cousins.
- **Racial Advantages:** Hobgoblins begin play with the High Pain Tolerance advantage at no cost to the player.

Halflings

Created from the left over primordial clay Eris used to make the first humans, halflings have been struggling to establish their place int eh world ever since.

Personality: Halflings are a race of creatures who would rather not get involved in the affair of the "big folk." They are content to live in their hillside homes nestled in the plans of the empire. They are content to tend their crops, puff on smoke-weed, and drink ale. They enjoy singing, dancing and eating... but care for little else.

Physical Description: Halflings stand half as tall as a human giving them a child-like appearance. There ears have a slight point to them, but it is not as pronounced as that of elves. Male halflings often sport neatly trimmed beards.

Relations: The live and let live halflings tend to get along with humans, gnomes, and elves. Dwarves do not think halflings take life seriously enough. Other races see them as easy targets.

Religion: Halflings venerate Durian, the goddess of agriculture, because her portfolio includes the plants that bring smoke-weed and alcohol.

Language: Halflings do not have a language of their own. They speak the Imperial Trade Tongue.

Names: Halfling names are usually two syllables and make extensive use of long vowel sounds. Halflings often use parts of names from other languages and make them their own. Dildo Faggins is a famous halfling bard.

Adventurers: Halflings so adventure frequently, but their motivation is often down right strange. A halfling doesn't adventure to become a hero. The halfling adventures in order to become the cook of heroes.

Halfling Racial Maximums

Strength:	3	Reason:	6
Coordination:	8	Insight:	8
Quickness:	7	Psyche:	6
Constitution:	4	Charisma:	7

Racial Traits

- **Size:** Small
- **Low-Light Vision:** Halflings can see in conditions of limited illumination as well as humans can see in daylight
- **Stealthy:** Halflings receive 2 extra dice to roll for any test involving hiding, moving silently, or otherwise being sneaky.

Quarterlings (Half-Breed)

Quarterlings are the children of humans and halflings. The name of this species began as a joke among scholars at the Ministry of Science who wondered what you would call half a halfling. A half of a half is a quarter, so "quarterling" was the answer they came up with… It stuck.

Personality: Quarterling adults are almost always very aggressive. They scowl continually and always seem angry about something.

Physical Description: Despite the implications of their name, quarterlings are not miniature halflings, in fact, quarterlings stand almost as tall as elves. They have the same skin tones and range of hair and eye color as humans do. Their ears are less pointed than those of halflings, but not as rounded as human ears. Because of their similarity in appearance, quarterlings are often mistaken for short humans.

Relations: Quarterlings truly are outcasts. Quarterlings have a difficult existence. They are too tall to live comfortably with their halfling parent and too short to live among the humans an escape ridicule… but at least they can walk through the doorways without hitting their heads.

They are seen as curiosities in both human and halfling societies. No matter how loving their families might be, the outside world rarely is. The quarterling is often the subject of scorn and ridicule. The rage resulting from this mistreatment simmers inside the quarterling until it finally boils over.

Lands: Quarterlings have no lands of their own to call home… and they can find no solace in the lands of their parents. Quarterlings wander the countryside until their aggressive nature and self-destructive behavior finally ends their miserable lives.

Religion: For the most part, quarterlings are not religious. They often reject the religions of their parents after wondering why a deity would allow them to be born into such misery. Those quarterlings that do turn to religion often pray to deities of death asking to be removed from this world.

Language: Quarterlings spoeak the Imperial Trade Tongue.

Names: Quarterlings usually hqave human sounding names. Their parents know that they will never fit in among halflings and hope that at least having a normal human name will save them some small portion of ridicule.

Adventurers: Quarterlings usually see adventuring as a means of finding death. They do not feel that death is coming fast enough for them, so they seek it out. Most of them succeed.

Quarterling Racial Maximums

Strength:	4	Reason:	6
Coordination:	8	Insight:	7
Quickness:	7	Psyche:	5
Constitution:	5	Charisma:	6

Racial Traits

- **Size:** Medium
- **Low-Light Vision:** Quarterlings enjoy the same acute vision as their halfling relatives.
- **Stealthy:** Quarterlings receive an addition die to any roll to hide, move silently, or otherwise be stealthy.

103

Humans

Humans are the dominant species on the Lady's Rock… by divine decree. They have formed an empire that spans the known world. Their greed has caused the collapse of their empire… and their hope brought it back from ruin… time and time again. The greatest heroes and most horrendous villains in the history of the empire have all been humans.

Normal, or common, humans are known as mehums, short for mere humans.

Personality: Humans are the most diverse of all races on the Lady's Rock, so much so that we describe other races in terms of humanity. Any personality trait you have witnessed, that you can imagine, or that you have has been a human trait at some point.

Physical Description: Humans average about 6 feet in height, with females being slightly shorter than the males. Their skin tones range from pale pink to dark brown. Hair can be black to blond and turns gray or white with age. Eye color ranges from blue to brown.

Human males average 6 feet in height and 180 pounds. Females tend to be slightly shorter and lighter than males.

Relations: As the rulers of the empire, humans enjoy a place of virtually uncontested power in the empire. The major races of the Lady's Rock know that humans are in control… and they've seen what humans are capable of to regain that control should it be take from them. As such, most races give humans quite a bit of latitude.

Lands: Technically speaking, all lands within the empire are human lands. That being said, of the provinces ruled by humans, they run the gambit from corrupt to almost altruistic. Some human rulers see their domain as a means to enrich themselves. Other see their position as a means to enrich the people living within their domain.

Religion: Humans are an adaptable species. This is also true when it comes to religion. Many of the deities worshipped in the empire today began as racial or even tribal deities. Humans leaqrned of them and incorporated them into their own pantheon of gods spreading their myths and legends to the corners of the empire.

The predominant human religion, and the most powerful religion in the empire, is that of Eris, the Goddess of Chaos and Discord. The worship of Eris is the state religion of the empire and crimes against this church are viewed more harshly than crimes against the Emperor himself.

Language: The human language is known as the Imperial Trade Tongue. As its name suggests, it is the language of commerce throughout the empire. Most creatures who travel will speak Imperial Trade Tongue giving the humans yet another advantage.

Names: Human names are drawn from a number of places. Some are taken from myth and legend. Others harken back to professions once practiced by ancestors… or practiced still today. Others still are made up by parents who want their child to stand out. Kaiden, Gunnar, and Kivan are examples of names given to male humans. Corinne, Sarah, and Jadacey are examples of female names.

Adventurers: As with most things in the empire, humans make up the majority of adventurers. They strike out seeking fame, fortune, or simply acceptance.

Mehum Racial Maximums

Strength:	5	Reason:	6
Coordination:	8	Insight:	7
Quickness:	7	Psyche:	4
Constitution:	6	Charisma:	6

Racial Traits

- **Size:** Medium
- **Racial Advantages:** Humans receive an additional 1d10 build points to spend on advantages at character creation.

Laham (Subspecies)

Legend has it that Eris once visited the Lady's Rock (Her rock). During this visit, she encountered a subset of the human race that had a unique and insightful understanding of Her divine plan. She immediately recognized these humans for their latent potential even though they could not recognize it themselves.

As the legend spread, all manner of humans began to claim that they were among these chosen elite, known as the "laham." In a twist of fate befitting the Goddess of Chaos & Discord, few humans who identify themselves as laham actually are. Instead they are mehums with delusions of grandeur.

Personality: Lahams exhibit many of the same personality traits as mehums. They can be cruel, vindictive, loving, and compassionate. What sets them apart from others of their species isn't their personality, but their insight. This insight allows lahams to accomplish many things.

The laham can almost feel the strands of fate, the ties that bind other creatures together. With the skill of a master weaver, the lahm can manipulate these stringsand alter the fabric of reality. Luckily, this insight also means that few laham have the desire to upset the universal balance. Innately knowing where creatures belong in the grand scheme of the multiverse means that you know what role you're supposed to play as well.

Physical Description: Lahams are indistinguishable from other humans. They have the same hair, eye, and skin color range. They also have the same average height and weight.

Relations: One might imagine that laham feel themselves superior to others because of their unmique abilities and place in history. This is not the case. As one human philosopher, thought to be a laham, "In the race we call life, the superior man does not win. In fact, most times the superior man isn't even races. He's too busy living his life to worry about where he falls in the army of mediocrity."

Lands: If it is impossible to tell a laham from a mere human, it is equally impossible to tell laham lands from mehum lands. Those rulers who are particularly enlightened are often declared to have been lahams post humously.

Religion: Considering that the origin of this subspecies is tied in the legends of a divine entity, it is surprising to note that most lahams view religion as a tool rather than as an independent force.

These laham believe that the gods gain their power from people's belief in them rather than people deriving power from the gods. This does not make their faith in a religion less real, however. In fact, it often bolsters that faith even in times of great duress. While others might lose faith in times of need, lahams understand that even more faith is needed to empower the deity… so that it can help them.

Language: Laham speak the Imperial Trade Tongue.

Names: Laham are humans for all intents and purposes, so laham names are the same as human names.

Adventurers: Reading through the history books, one might assume that every human who has ever adventured was a laham. This is because of the human propensity to declare those who achieve to be more than mere humans. After all, there has to be some reason why the people of myth and legend were capable of accomplishing great tasks while the readers of myth and legend are barkeeps, blacksmiths, and farmers.

Laham Racial Maximums

Strength:	4	Reason:	7
Coordination:	7	Insight:	8
Quickness:	6	Psyche:	8
Constitution:	5	Charisma:	6

Racial Traits

- **Size:** Medium
- **Racial Advantages:** Humans receive an additional 1d10 build points to spend on advantages during character creation.

105

Tiefling (Subspecies / Half-Breed)

Tieflings are a largely misunderstood race. Many believe that they are the offspring of humans and diabolic or demonic entities… the children resulting in mating with a succubus, for example. Others believe that having a teifling child is the price a parent pays for making a deal with such entities. The truth is that both of these ideas hold some grain of truth.

Personality: Tieflings represent the darker side of the human psyche. They have many of the same personality traits as humans, but the darker side of those traits seems to be amplified.

A tiefling can be just as passionate as a human, but that passion often slides into obsession. They can be as cruel as humans, but that cruelty usually becomes sadistic. They can fall in love, but that love is always tinged with jealousy and lust rather than simple adoration.

Physical Description: Tieflings share the same average height and weight as humans. Tieflings, however, all bear some taint of the demonic or diabolic forces that influenced their birth.

This taint can take any number of forms and no two tieflings display exactly the same characteristics.

Commonly seen traits include:
- Horns on the temple or forehead. Some have a single horn while others have a veritable "crown of horns". These may resemble traditional horns or be more like antlers.
- "Unnatural" hair or eye color.
- Goat-like legs.
- Scaly skin. Scales may be so fine as to appear like normal skin except under close inspection.
- An unusual number of fingers or toes.
- Hands or feet ending in claws.
- Fins or feathers rather than hair.
- Bony protrusions resembling spikes on the body.
- Mysterious marking on the body.
- Strange odors that cannot be covered or removed.
- A touch that kills plants.
- A devilish splayed tail.

This list is far from being "all inclusive." Most times, tieflings display a number of characteristics related to a central theme. This theme may be unknown to the tiefling themselves.

One of the most famous tieflings alive today is Baelyn Khembryl, first born son of the Grand Marquis of Khymbria and heir to that Imperial province. Baelyn has deep blue skin and coppery-red hair. His eyes are a sickly yellow. The young heir's body temperature is so unnaturally cold that touching his bare skin causes burns. Baelyn's temperature remains constant no matter what the temperature of his environment is protecting him from extremes of temperature that would cause serious harm to others.

Exactly why young Khembryl has these particular traits in unknown to all save his parents… and they do not seem willing to discuss the subject. The theme of his demonic attributes, however, is pretty clear.

Relations: In primitive times, tieflings were feared and hated by other races. Today, the empire is more enlightened. While tieflings are still give a wide berth in more rural communities, the more civilized portions of the empire treat them as just another citizen.

Lands: Tieflings have made their mark on imperial history, but few have ever risen to a position of authority. Those that have are wise enough to surround themselves with advisors capable of curbing their darker natures.

Religion: While individual tieflings may worship any deity they choose, they do have a noted tendency to favor darker such as Kyerhan (the lord of murder) and Dumathan (the god of secrets).

Languages: Tieflings normally speak the Imperial Trade Tongue. Most tieflings also learn to speak Infernal and / or Abyssal in order to connect with their demonic heritage.

Names: Tieflings are named by their parents and have names that reflect the culture and area in which they were born.

Adventurers: Tiefling adventurers usually venture out on that road for one of two reasons. They are either trying to fulfill the instinctual desires of their heritage or run from them. A good number of tiefling heroes became heroes in order to fight their dark heritage. An equal number of tieflings struck out in order to satiate their dark desires.

A tiefling who is drawn to violence can battle brigands and monsters without fear of reprisal. Those same tendencies would cause trouble for the tiefling if they remained in a city and engaged in violence against imperial citizens.

Tiefling Racial Maximums

Strength:	5	Reason:	7
Coordination:	9	Insight:	8
Quickness:	7	Psyche:	7
Constitution:	6	Charisma:	7

Racial Traits

- **Size:** Medium
- **Darkvision:** Tieflings are able to see even in the absence of light. This vision is black and white, but subtle shades of gray allow for distinguishing between two objects of different colors.
- **Racial Advantages:** Tieflings begin play with the Magical Aptitude advantage at no cost to the player

Decani (Subspecies)

The decani were created long ago by human mages to serve as their assistants in magical research. Because ordinary golems were too uncoordinated to be of much use and other humans may have questioned the moral implications of the mage's studies, it became necessary to develop a creature that would serve the mage faithfully and capably without arousing too much suspicion if suffered a horrible death. The answer to this dilemma was the decani.

Personality: Decani tend to be inquisitive and willing to learn new things. They see each new experience as an opportunity to learn and each repeated experience as an opportunity to reexamine what they believe they already know. They are, however, naïve to the way the world functions outside a laboratory environment.

Physical Description: Decani were created in the image of their creators. They appear human in almost every way. The notable exception to this is hair… decani have none. They are bald and possess no body hair. The mages who created them were concerned that the hair might interfere with their experimentation so they did not add this feature to their creation.

Despite not having hair, decani due have eyebrows, or at least the semblance of eyebrows. The sight of the hairless decani was a bit unnerving to humans, so a darker patch of skin was added above the eye to simulate an eyebrow.

Though decani began life as little more than a sentient construct, their creators did an excellent job. Physiologically, decani are almost identical to humans. Because of this, and because they are cheaper to breed than build, no new decani have been created in several centuries.

Relations: Decani were created to serve humans. While other servitor races rebel against their masters, the decani seem content to serve so long as there remains new things for them to learn. A bored decani can be very dangerous as they tend to have a little knowledge of several subjects, but rarely master any of them.

Lands: As you may have guessed, decani have no lands of their own. That being said, some decani have earned the trust of their human masters and do serve in a civil capacity, some even going to far as to be appointed as their lord's right hand man.

Religion: Decani generally practice whatever religion their master practices. The rare free decani may practice any religion, though they give preference to deities who favor knowledge and industry, two traits bred into their species.

Language: Decani have no language of their own; instead they speak the Imperial Trade Tongue. Decani are intelligent and may learn any language their master allows them to learn.

Names: Decani children are often named by their master. This is done more to tell several decani apart and keep track of lineage for breeding purposes than anything else. As such, decani names tend to reflect the role they serve in their master's household.

Podius, for example, might be the decani responsible for holding the master's spell book during rituals.

Adventurers: Decani adventurers are rare. Those encountered are usually doing so at the behest of their master. Decani explore ruins on behalf of aging mages who are unable to do so themselves. They travel to places their masters fear to go to gain knowledge or items their masters desire.

This desire to serve sometimes drives the decani even after the death of their master. These decani continue their master's life's work even after that life has ceased to exist.

Decani Racial Maximums

Strength:	6	Reason:	7
Coordination:	7	Insight:	5
Quickness:	6	Psyche:	4
Constitution:	5	Charisma:	4

Racial Traits

- **Size:** Medium
- **Low-Light Vision:** Decani are able to see in limited light as well as human can during the day.
- **Racial Advantages:** Decani receive any one aptitude advantage (mechanical, scientific, magical, etc) at character creation to represent the type of research they were bred to perform.

Mephisti

The word "mephisti," both singular and plural, comes from a long forgotten dialect of elven and means "those who shun the light." The few sages that know the origin of this word assume that the mephisti are evil because of it. This comes from the natural propensity of living creatures to equate light with goodness. The light that the mephisti shun is not the light of goodness. Instead, they shun the light at the end of the tunnel most people claim to see then moment that they die.

All mephisti alive today were once something else. Then they died. The intense and conflicting emotions surrounding the events of their death stop the mephisti from being drawn into the astral plane and on to the outer planes to enjoy their eternal rest. They are instead drawn to the plane of shadow where they are reborn and return to the Lady's Rock.

Personality: Mephisti are created from intense conflicting emotions. These emotions tend to have a profound affect on the newly formed mephisti even if they do not remember the circumstances of their death. Rather than being amplified by the experience, these emotions tend to become more subdued.

A devotedly religious individual who was, from birth, designated to be sacrificed to a deity in order to earn said deity's favor might simultaneously long for and fear the moment of her death. Such a person might return as a mephisti if these emotions were strong enough. She may be utterly fearless, but may be filled with despair at the pointlessness of existence.

Likewise, a warrior who has been bitten by a werewolf that is killed by his friends in order to save him from the horrible curse might return as a mephisti. Such a person might be incapable of love or hate seeing people as one would view any other animal.

Physical Description: Mephisti are a created race. They are born of a melding between the shadow that makes up the plane of shadows and the chaos from which Eris formed the Lady's Rock. As such, mephisti come into existence as adults. They have no navel. They do not age and have no known lifespan.

Mephisti males average approximately six feet in height and weigh around 180 pounds. Females are generally shorter and lighter. A mephisti's skin is always dark in color ranging from black to a dark charcoal grey. Their hair color is similar, though it is usually a slightly lighter tone than their skin.

Mephisti have no visible iris or pupil. Instead their eyes are a solid color. The color of a mephisti's eyes changes to reflect their dominant emotional state. This would provide a helpful clue when dealing with these mysterious creatures, if there was a standard by which the colors could be judged. Unfortunately, there is not.

Like all sentient beings, the emotions of a mephisti are a complicated and personal thing. While this chromatic representation remains consistent for each individual mephisti, the same emotion may be displayed differently for different individuals. One mephisti, being fearful of what lies behind the next door, may have yellow eyes while another may have orange.

Relations: Mephisti are misunderstood by most people on the Lady's Rock. This fear and misunderstanding drives

109

many mephisti away from "civilized" lands, though they rarely stray too far from civilizations itself.

Many Mephisti, shunned by society, enter into self-imposed exile living among the subterranean races. Because of their appearance, they are easily able to blend into drow society and their unique abilities often translate into positions of authority among the dark elves. This only adds to their fearsome reputation among the more "civilized" races.

Lands: Mephisti have no lands of their own. They usually make their home among the drow living in their vast underground cities. Many consider these caverns to be their homes.

Religion: Mephisti may worship any deity and many of them chose to worship deities that reflect their newfound purpose in life.

Language: Despite being a race of created beings, mephisti speak a language all their own. They are intuitively able to speak, read, and write this language upon their rebirth,

Names: Many mephisti choose to keep their original names upon their rebirth. Other members of this race select new names in order to hide from those they knew in their former lives.

Adventurers: Mephisti may adventure for many reasons. Often these reasons are tied to the circumstances of their death and rebirth. They make seek to avenge a real or perceived wrong, or to protect those whom they knew in their previous life.

Mephisti Racial Maximums			
Strength:	5	Reason:	6
Coordination:	9	Insight:	8
Quickness:	8	Psyche:	7
Constitution:	6	Charisma:	7

Racial Traits

- **Size:** Medium
- **Darkvision:** Mephisti possess the ability to see in the absence of light. This vision is black and white, though shades of gray allow distinguishing between colors.
- **Ether Vision:** Mephisti also have the same Life Sight vision as Eburnae.
- **Racial Disadvantages:** All Mephisti suffer from the past life regression disadvantage. The character receives no points for this disadvantage.

110

Minotaurs

Minotaurs are a recent arrival to imperial lands. They came to the empire across the great Erisian Sea in ships made to look like sea serpents rising out of the aether. This provided the first evidence that the empire was not alone on the Lady's Rock. Since them, minotaur raids have increased in frequency and small minotaur villiages have sprung up on the fringes of imperial society.

Personality: Minotaurs are a brutal species. They understand only one thing – strength. While they form familial bonds, these bonds are created more from pride than love. They see emotions as a weakness… one a warrior cannot afford.

Physical Description: Minotaurs appear to be bovine humanoids. The average minotaur stands about 1 ½ times taller than his human counterpart. Both male and female minotaurs sport large horns on either temple. Their bodies are covered with a short, coarse hair. This coat is usually solid brown in color with some rare minotaurs having reddish coats. Even more rare are white minotaurs with black spots. Such minotaur are seen as weak by other members of their race and almost always killed at birth. Minotaurs have deep brown eyes that change to green when angered. Minotaurs have hooves instead of feet. They tend to favor nose rings and harnesses over more traditional clothing.

Relations: The minotaurs encountered by the empire thus far have been raiding parties. This is not conducive to forming healthy relationships between the various races… minotaurs are more hated than any other "civilized" race.

Religion: Minotaurs predominantly worship Barak (god of stroms), Vastra (goddess of the aether), and Jhaemaryl (goddess of blood and lust).

Lands: Aside from a few small outposts along the coastal wilderness, no one has encountered minotaur lands as such.

What little has been determined from discussion with captured minotaurs is that theirs is a rigid society where might truly does make right. Everything from election of leaders to determining guilt or innocence during a trial is determined by who is the victor in some test of combat.

Language: Minotaurs speak a language of their own known as Tauran, in human lands. It is a harsh language that is vaguely reminiscent of dwarven. While scholars unanimously agreed that the two languages are not related, the average citizen of the empire does not have time to read scholarly works. So rumors persist that dwarves are somehow related to these behemoths.

Names: Mintoaur names reflect character traits that the minotaurs appreciate. Names already encountered are Grodar, Vykel, and Traldor, When translated into the Imperial Trade Tongue these names mean things like "strong," "vicious," and "implacable."

Adventurers: As raiders, minotaur are not native to imperial lands. Those minotaurs who go adventuring are probably the sole survivors of a failed raid… or raiders who were marooned by their former comrades for some reason.

Minotaur Racial Maximums

Strength:	7	Reason:	4
Coordination:	8	Insight:	7
Quickness:	7	Psyche:	5
Constitution:	9	Charisma:	5

Racial Traits

- **Size:** Large
- **Thermal Vision:** Minotaurs are able to see heat emanations in the infrared spectrum of light. This vision can be disrupted by sudden changes in temperature.
- **Reach:** Minotaurs are big. The reach for any melee weapon they use is 5 feet longer than it normally would be… *NOTE: reach, NOT range…*

Baphan (Half-Breed)

The purpose of a raid is to gather wealth and supplies for the homeland. As is often the case with raids, minotaurs often favor their victims with physical affection during the course of the pillaging. When the victims are humans, the result is a baphan.

Personality: Baphans usually raised by their minotaur fathers, their mothers dying during the course of their birth. They are treated as slaves by the minotaurs... fodder for human cannons, firearms, and arrows. Baphan grow to resent their minotaur heritage and, those with the courage, flee their parental captors.

Physical Description: Baphan stand head and shoulders over a human of the same age and weight nearly twice as much. They have horns like a minotaur, but these horns are on their foreheads rather than their temples.

Baphan do not have the same coarse body hair that minotaurs do. Instead their hair grows in patterns similar to humans. This hair is almost always brown, though rare blond baphan have been born. Their eyes are the same brown as their minotaur parents. They do not have hooves, but their feet end in two claw-like toes.

Relations: Because baphan are only ever encountered in the presence of minotaur, most people assume that they are some sort of slave species that the minotaurs brought with them from their mysterious homeland. As such, the baphan are more pitied than feared. If people ever learned the truth, their horror might outweigh their pity.

Lands: Baphans are a slave races to a species that is far from home. Needless to say, they have no lands.

Religion: Those few baphan who have any religious leanings favor Chalysse, the goddess of life and death. They usually pray for a swift death in order to be free from their brutal captors.

Language: Most Baphan are illiterate and know only those words in Tauran that they need in order to comply with their master's orders and avoid being beaten or killed.

Names: Baphan do not have names. They are seen as work animals, not pets. They are referred to by a variety of colorful and derogatory words by their minotaur captors. Being illiterate, the baphan often confuse these epitaphs for names.

Adventurers: Any baphan adventurers are escaped slaves. They fight to survive, not for fame or fortune.

Baphan Racial Maximums

Strength:	6	Reason:	6
Coordination:	7	Insight:	7
Quickness:	6	Psyche:	6
Constitution:	8	Charisma:	5

Racial Traits

- **Size:** Medium
- **Thermal Vision:** Baphans are able to see heat emanations in the infrared spectrum of light. This vision can be disrupted by sudden changes in temperature.

Morc (Half-Breed)

Humans aren't the only victims of minotaur raids. In fact, the most common victims are other primitive species who are less able to defend themselves. Orcs, the premier native raiders, are often the targets. Morcs are the result of some of these raids.

Personality: Despite the circumstances of their birth, morcs take well to life with the minotaurs. Orcish women are better able to survive the rigors of bearing a half-minotaur child, and often remain to raise the child among the minotaurs. These children, born of two species who value strength, become skilled fighters and fight along side their minotaur fathers. They are blood-thirsty and relentless warriors. They respect strength in combat above all else. As such, any creature incapable of defending itself deserves death.

Physical Description: Morcs are only slightly shorter than full-blooded minotaurs. They have a fine coat of coarse green-tinged hair over their bodies and thick, greasy black manes on their heads. Like minotaurs and baphan, morcs have horns, but these horns grow from the back of the morc's head and sweep forward.

Rather than having a bovine snout, morc's noses are more porcine in keeping with their orcish heritage. They lack the tusks of other orcs, however.

Relations: Unlike baphan, morcs have earned the respect of the minotaurs. They are effective warriors and are a welcome addition to any raiding party. This makes them just as hated as their parents, a sentiment shared by the orcs.

Lands: Morcs live with minotaurs and are second-class citizens in whatever lands the minotaurs control.

Religion: Morcs favor the same deities as minotaurs.

Language: Morcs are often taught Tauran by the minotaurs in order to make them more effective raiders. If their orcish mother survived childbirth, the morc usually learns orcish from her as well.

Names: Morcs usually bear the name of their minotaur father preceded by the word "bal" or "bel" (depending on if the child is male of female respectively). This word means "bastard of" in Tauran. If a minotaur has more than one such child, the names are again preceded by its borth order.

Adventurers: Adventuring morcs are rare, as you probably have guessed. Morcs are content with their lot in life as the grunts of the minotaur forces. A morc who is the sole survivor of a failed raid might seek vengeance against those who killed the raiders and end up on the road of adventurer by proxy.

Morc Racial Maximums

Strength:	6	Reason:	5
Coordination:	8	Insight:	7
Quickness:	7	Psyche:	6
Constitution:	8	Charisma:	4

Racial Traits

- **Size:** Medium
- **Thermal Vision:** Morcs are able to see heat emanations in the infrared spectrum of light. This vision can be disrupted by sudden changes in temperature.
- **Darkvision:** Morcs are able to see in the absence of light. This black and white vision does allow for shades of gray, so it is possible to distinguish between colors even though you cannot see them.

Orc

Orcs have just recently begun integration into imperial society... mostly as slaves. Orcs are a savage and proud people. At one time, nomadic tribes of orcs roamed the empire hunting and gathering in order to survive. They were a practical people in tune with nature. The advancement of the human empire into orcish territory has changed all that.

Today the remaining tribes survive largely by raiding settlements on the edges of the empire as the civilized races encroached further and further into their tribal lands. Only a few pockets of free orcs live in the wilds of the most remote imperial provinces.

Personality: Orcs take great pride in their warrior tradition. Constant skirmishes with the empire have turned the orcs from mostly peaceful primitives into blood-thirsty barbarians bent on human destruction.

Physical Description: Orcs stand slightly taller than humans. They have broad shoulders and bulging muscles. The ridge above their eyes is more pronounced and covered with a thick greasy, black eye brow. They have short porcine noses and large tusks protrude from their lower jaw like those of a wild boar. Orc skin tones are sickly shades of green and their hair is almost universally stringy and black.

Relations: The orcs who live within the empire as slaves have the look of a caged lion. You can see it in their eyes. These orcs have been broken by captivity. Some of them view their new masters as the chieftain of a new tribe. Others plot his or her demise in the hopes of regaining past glory.

Lands: Traditionally, orcs live in a tribal society. A chieftain is selected from among the warriors and a high priestess is selected from among the clergy. These two people hold joint authority over all aspects of tribal life. The dual leaders help to ensure that no orc tribe succumbs to whims of one person bent on personal glory.

As the human empire grows, these tribes are becoming fewer in numbers. Today, free orc tribes can only be found in outlying imperial provinces.

Religion: Orcs favored nature deities in ages past. Ruins of a now lost orcish empire have temples to Chalysse (goddess of the cycle of life), Durian (goddess of agriculture), and Barak (god of storms). Tribal orcs paid homage to these deities even after the mysterious fall of their empire and their reversion to a more primitive lifestyle.

As their wars with humans have increased, orcs have turned to more war-like deities. Aren (god of war) has joined the war-like Barak as the chief deities of the orcs.

Language: The orcs speak a language of their own, known in the empire as Orcish. Orcish is an interesting language in that it lacks words to describe many modern conveniences and weapons. Instead these ideas are expressed conceptually. An aether ship, for example, is "a great wooden bird that carries men on its back" in Orcish. A lev-wagon is "a large canoe that floats like a leaf in the wind."

Names: Orcs traditionally name their children after the first thing the chieftain or priestess (depending on if the child is male or female) sees after the child is born. Burzaan (meaning dark sun) might be the name of a child born during an eclipse. Gurghaamp (meaning trembling earth) might be the name of a child born during an earthquake.

Adventurers: The orcs have a rich heritage as adventurers. Before they encountered the humans, orcish legends were filled with heroes who accomplished great deeds. Members of the tribe sought to accomplish deeds of equal or greater magnitude to ensure that they would be remembered. This tradition holds true today as well. Even among enslaved orcs, these legends are kept alive.

Orc Racial Maximums

Strength:	6	Reason:	5
Coordination:	7	Insight:	6
Quickness:	7	Psyche:	6
Constitution:	8	Charisma:	5

Racial Traits

- **Size:** Medium
- **Thermal Vision:** Orcs are able to see heat emanations in the infrared spectrum of light. This vision can be disrupted by sudden changes in temperature.
- **Darkvision:** Orcs are able to see in the absence of light. This black and white vision does allow for shades of gray, so it is possible to distinguish between colors even though you cannot see them.

Half-Orcs (Half-Breed)

Half-orcs are the offspring of humans and orcs. These children are considered imperial citizens if they are born to a human mother. If they are born to an orcish mother, the empire sees them as no different than orcs... which is to say that they are slaves.

Some unscrupulous merchants have gone so far as to purchase female orcish slaves and breed with them to create a slave population to use or sell.

Personality: Half-orcs personalities depend largely on the circumstances of their birth. A half-orc born to a human mother is an imperial citizen, but he or she is still half orc. They lack the beauty of half-elves, and are often ridiculed by other children. This causes them to feel alone even when surrounded by others. These half-orcs often grow to resent the communities in which they live.

Half-orcs born to orcish mothers in imperial lands are born into slavery. While that may seem like the worse of the two alternatives, these half-orcs find acceptance and have a genuine sense of belonging. While they often resent their masters, they are usually better adjusted than their human-born kin.

Sometimes half-orcs result from raids on imperial lands. The mothers are brought back to the tribe as prizes and latter become pregnant. These children are accepted as members of the tribe without reservation.

Physical Description: Half-orcs are about the same size as a human of similar age. The green tinged to their skin tone marks them as half orc. Their hair and eyes can be color normally found in humans.

Half-orcs have enlarged incisors on their lower jaw. These fangs are not nearly as large as orcish tusks, but are noticeable nonetheless. Half-orcs often have slightly upturned noses as well.

Relations: Half-orcs born to a human mother officially enjoy all the benefits of imperial citizenship. Of course, a half-orc born to a human and one born to an orc look identical, so it becomes the responsibility of the half-orc to prove that he or she deserves these benefits.

Language: Half-orcs born in human lands, regardless of parentage, are taught the Imperial Trade Tongue. Half-orcs born to orcish tribes are taught Orcish.

Names: Half-orcs are named by their mothers, so what name is given to a particular half-orc depends on where it was born and who is was born to.

Adventurers: Like half-elves, half-orcs make up a sizable percentage of adventurers on the Lady's Rock. Many of these half-breeds feel as though they have something to prove, both to the world around them and to themselves. This desire for approval and acceptance (especially self-acceptance) causes them to journey beyond the comfortable confines of their birth and seek the fame and fortune of the open road.

Half-Orc Racial Maximums

Strength:	5	Reason:	6
Coordination:	7	Insight:	6
Quickness:	7	Psyche:	6
Constitution:	8	Charisma:	5

Racial Traits

- **Size:** Medium
- **Thermal Vision:** Half-orcs are able to see heat emanations in the infrared spectrum of light. This vision can be disrupted by sudden changes in temperature.
- **Darkvision:** Half-orcs are able to see in the absence of light. This black and white vision does allow for shades of gray, so it is possible to distinguish between colors even though you cannot see them.

Teg

The teg are a race of fey creatures. Teg are not born, rather they spring into existence spontaneously, the children of magic and chaos. They can be found anywhere throughout the realm, though they are very rare. Seeing a teg is said to be a sign that the goddess is watching you personally. Knowing Eris, that is not always a good thing.

Personality: Teg are whimsical and playful. They see life as a game. Teg do not care whether they win or loose; they merely wish to play. If the game of life becomes boring for one reason or another, a teg simply changes the game in whatever way is likely to provide the least amount of boredom.

Physical Description: Teg look like tiny elves with insect-like wings. They stand about a foot in height (if they ever stood still long enough to measure). Their skin, hair, and eyes can be almost any color. Teg wings can be patterned and brightly colored like those of a butterfly or transparent like those of a dragonfly.

Teg are not born. Instead they spontaneously appear as the children of the magic and chaos left behind when Eris created the world. They have no natural life spans. Teg live as long as life remains interesting to them, unless they meet their fate through combat. When a teg dies or chooses to cease living, the experiences and power they have gained during their lives goes back into the world creating more teg. In this way, the teg race perpetuates itself and grows.

Every 500 years, the teg gather for a special rite. These teg spend a week drinking, dancing and cavorting. At midnight on the fifth day, the teg simply disappear leaving just five of their fellow teg behind to continue their eternal cycle.

Relations: Few races who have encountered teg enjoy spending time with them. Of all the races on the Lady's rock, only the elves tolerate teg to any degree… and even they tire of them after a short time.

Lands: Teg are highly revered throughout the empire, but no one has been foolish enough to grant them leadership over a realm. Periodically, groups of teg gather to celebrate various holidays, events, or simply because it's a day ending in Y. At these times, small hills ringed with mushrooms spontaneously appear to give the teg a safe haven. These hills have given rise to the legends of faerie kingdoms beneath the Lady's Rock, but they are most likely the things of legend.

Religion: Few teg become members of any clergy. The few teg that do often become bored with their deity after a few days, weeks, or years. Because the teg are Her children, Eris continues to grant them spells regardless who they pray to.

Language: Teg have no intelligible language of their own. They pretend to, however. When two teg meet, they will converse in a hodge-podge collection of mismatched languages and nonsensical words. The meaning of these conversations is conveyed by means of a special telepathic bond that all teg share.

Names: Since teg are not born in a traditional sense, there is no parent to name them. So, they name themselves. As with everything else that the teg do, there is no rhyme or reason to the names that they choose. Sometimes these names are eloquent and sylvan sounding as would befit a fey. Other times they can only be described as odd. One teg might name herself Willow Moonglamour while another might simply call himself Bill. History records some famous teg tricksters who named themselves after common items that they saw. The legendary thieves Dead-Cat and the Bearded Clam were two such teg.

Adventurers: Teg adventure for the same reasons that they do anything else – they're bored. The problem is that few people want to go adventuring with a teg. Stealing from an ancient dragon is dangerous enough. Trying to steal from an ancient dragon while adventuring with someone who might cast a spell to awaken the sleeping beast because he thinks fighting a dragon might be fun is doubly… or even triply… so.

Teg Racial Maximums			
Strength:	2	Reason:	6
Coordination:	10	Insight:	9
Quickness:	9	Psyche:	7
Constitution:	3	Charisma:	8

Racial Traits

Size: Tiny

- **Life-Sight:** Teg eyes are not as sensitive to light as the eyes of other elves. Instead, the eburnae's senses are attuned to the energies of life itself. Living creatures give off a bright green light when using this vision. This light illuminates the world around them. Dead creatures or objects that were once alive (wooden tables, for example) have a pale green glow representing their former lives. Undead creatures appear as utter blackness against the gray background.
- **Charm Resistance:** Teg receive three extra die for the purposes of resisting charm and enchantment spells.
- **Limited Flight:** Teg seem to possess the ability to fly. In reality, teg have the innate ability to levitate allowing them to hover up to 5 feet above any flat surface.
  Levitation only allows for vertical movement, so the teg rely on their wings in order to move through the air. They are able to do this at their normal movement rate and are even able to run and sprint while "flying." Normal rules for fatigue apply.
  Teg may force themselves to levitate above the 5 foot ceiling they innately have, but doing so is strenuous and is considered combat, even if it isn't, for the purposes of fatigue (see page XXXX).
- **Racial Disadvantages:** All Teg begin play with the impulsive disadvantage. The character receives no addition points for this disadvantage.

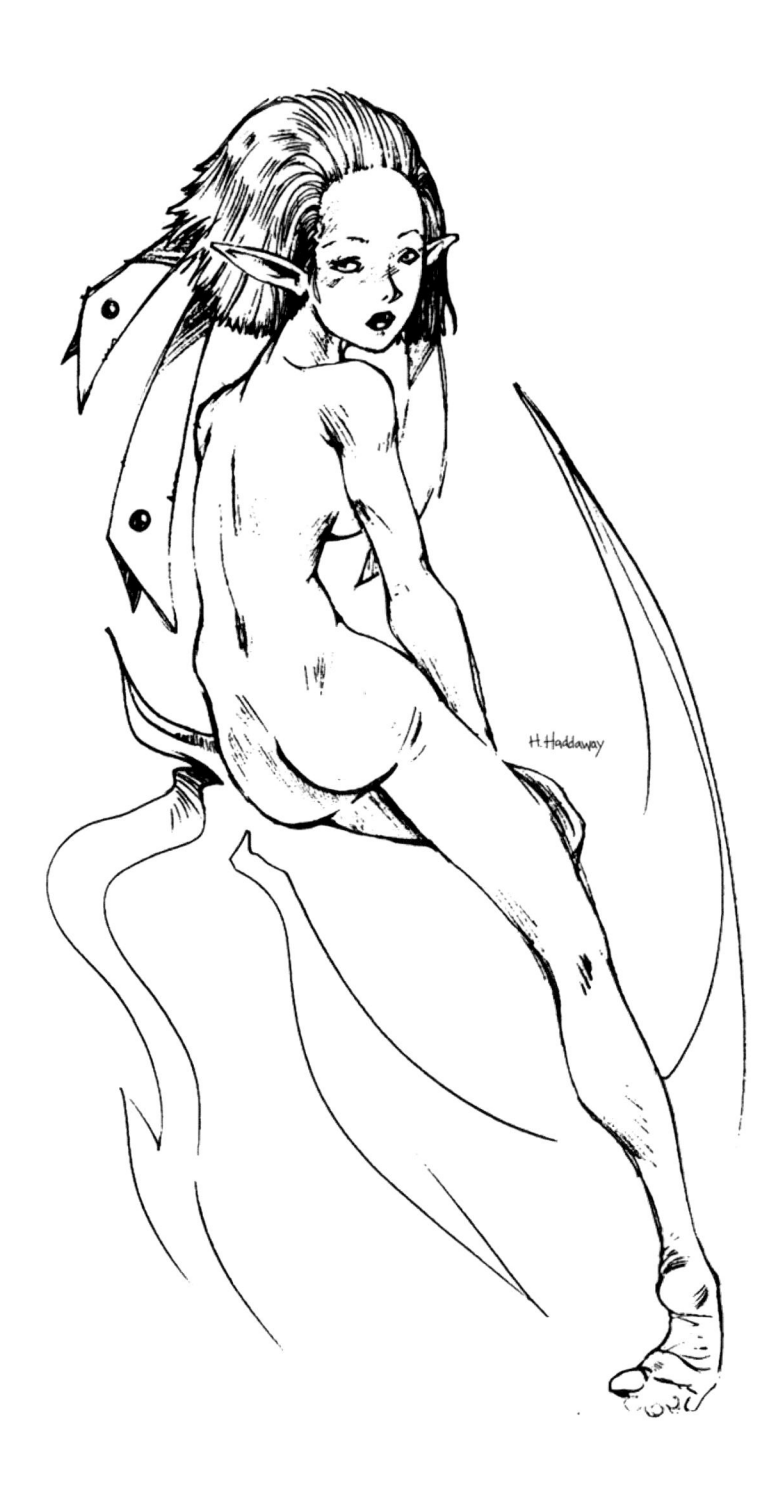

Crimbils (Half-Breed)

When a teg has the desire to mate with something, the result is a crimbil regardless of the species of the other parents. These children are always raised by their non-teg parent. Child rearing grows tiresome too quickly for the teg to be involved for long.

Tegs who mate with each other simply do so for pleasure. No offspring is ever created in that way.

Personality: Crimbils are not as whimsical as the teg that spawn them. Crimbils instead take human behavior and personality to the extreme. They play hard and fast with the rules of man and the laws of nature. Like a candle bruning at both ends, the crimbils burn bright, but for a very short time.

Physical Description: Regardless of what races breeds with the teg, the resulting crimbil appears the same. A crimbil resembles an elf with longer ears. They are graceful creatures with an other-worldly beauty. Crimbils do not have wings like the teg. They do have other features that mark them as children of chaos.

A Crimbil's skin, hair, or eyes, often demonstrate markings resembling creatures of nature. They might have a frog-like pattern on their skin or a peacock-like pattern in their hair. In addition to this pattern, the crimbil, like the teg, may have skin, hair, and eyes of any color.

Relations: Crimbil are viewed as a gift from the Goddess herself. Whether that gift is a cherished treasure or a hand-made sweater given to you for Christmas by an aunt you rarely see depends on the person. Eris is the Goddess of Discord, after all.

Lands: Crimbil are the offspring of the teg, no sane person would willingly give them control of any realm… and crimbils, like teg, grow bored with the process of gaining land long before it is complete.

Religion: As creatures blessed by the Goddess, you might imagine that crimbils worship the Concubine of Confusion. While some of them do, this is not a universal trait. Crimbils worship any being that strikes their fancy. They do, however, tend to favor deities with a chaotic bend.

Language: Crimbils do not possess language of their own. Instead they are taught the native tongue of their non-teg parent.

Names: Crimbils who are named by their non-teg parent usually have names similar to others of the non-teg parent's species. Crimbils whose teg parent helps select a name could have any name… literally.

Adventureres: Crimbil adventure for only one reason, because they can. There is a certain freedom to the adventuring life that appeals to the crimbil. That freedom draws them like moths to a flame.

Crimbil Racial Maximums

Strength:	4	Reason:	6
Coordination:	9	Insight:	8
Quickness:	8	Psyche:	7
Constitution:	5	Charisma:	7

Racial Traits

Size: Medium

- **Life-Sight:** Crimbils posses the same life sensing vision as their teg parents. Their eyes are not as sensitive to light as the eyes of other elves. Instead, the eburnae's senses are attuned to the energies of life itself. Living creatures give off a bright green light when using this vision. This light illuminates the world around them. Dead creatures or objects that were once alive (wooden tables, for example) have a pale green glow representing their former lives. Undead creatures appear as utter blackness against the gray background.
- **Charm Resistance:** Crimbils receive two extra die for the purposes of resisting charm and enchantment spells.

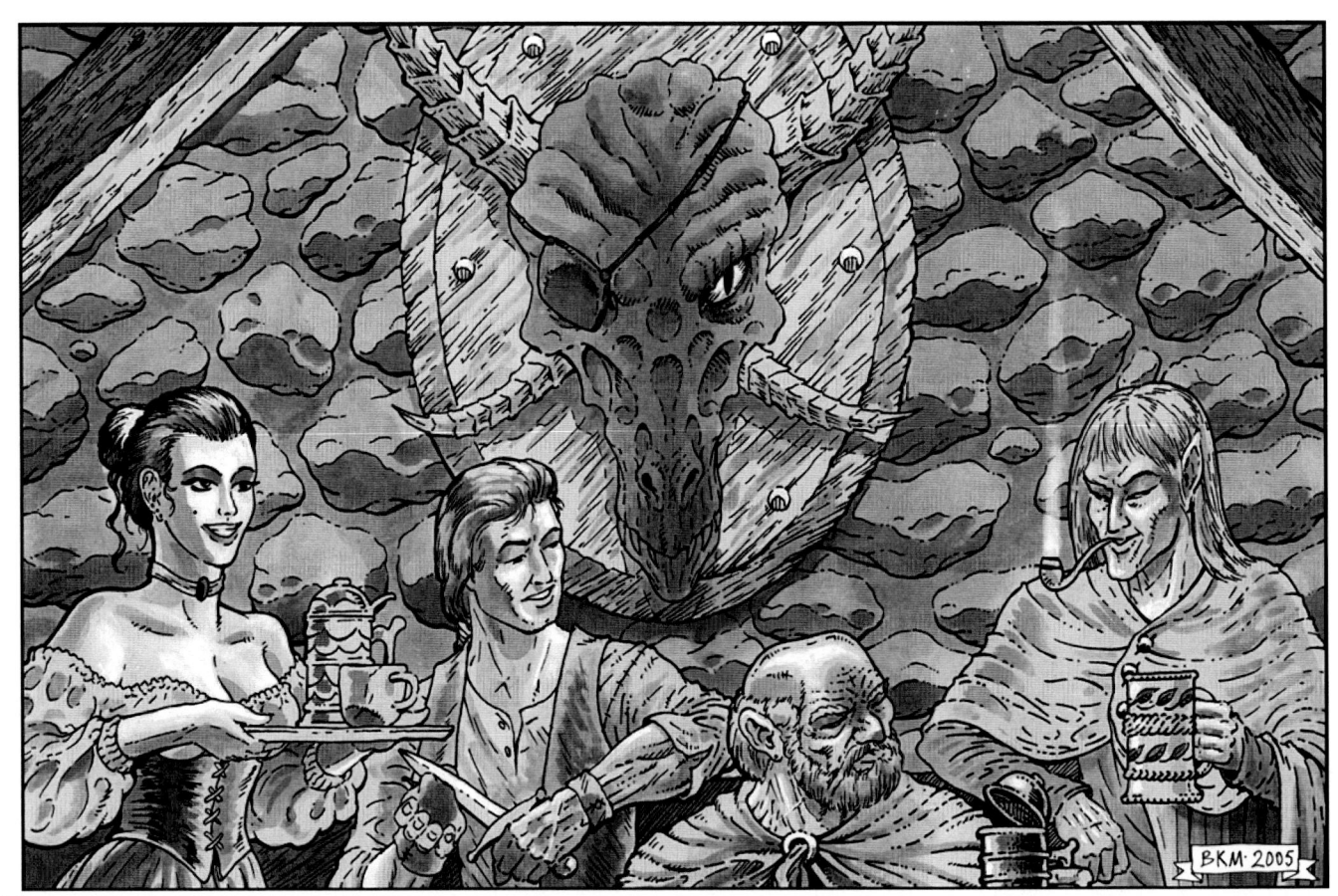

Build Points

While reading the racial descriptions, you may have noticed that each entry ends with a "Bonus Build Points." This is the number of extra build points your character receives for being a member of that species.

Each character starts with a base of 100 character points, 1-18 bonus build points, and the bonus points for race. To determine the number of points your character begins with, roll 2 10-sided dice and add the results. Remember that the 0 or 10 on your die counts as 0 in the d10 system. This means that every character will begin with between 100 and 118 build points plus the points for his or her race.

These points are spent to purchase not only your race but your attribute scores and active skills as well. In addition, you can purchase advantages with character points. And, if you happen to run out of points before you make the perfect character, you can gain addition points by taking disadvantages.

Race

Each race has a build point cost listed at the end of its entry. This is the number of points that is costs in order for your character to be a member of that race. Once the character has paid this cost, he or she gains all the traits inherent in their species.

Attributes

Attributes are purchased at a cost of 2 build points per attribute point. Characters must begin play with at least 1 in each of their attributes after racial modifiers are applied. Depending on the race you select, it may cost several build points to gain an attribute of 1.

For example, Teg begin play with a -4 modifier to their strength score. This means that a teg character must spend 10 build points to have a strength of 1.

No more than 12 build points can be spend on any one attribute (6 attribute points) and no more than ½ of your initial build point total can be spent on attributes.

Dice Pools

Once you have your attributes assigned, you can determine your character's dice pools. Exactly how these come into play will be covered latter. For now, just remember that it needs to be done.

Hit Points

Next, you'll determine how much damage your character can take before they die.

Active Skills

Once you've purchased your race and assigned your attributes, the next task is to choose your active skills. The cost of an active skill varies depending on the attribute score that governs it.

It costs 1 build point per skill point until the skill equals the attribute. Once the skill is equal to the attribute, it costs 2 build points per skill point. No character can begin play with a skill greater than twice its governing attribute.

For example, Dauphin has a quickness of 5. He wants to purchase the acrobatics skill. It costs him 5 build points to have an acrobatics skill of 5 (1 build point for each skill level). If he wants to have a higher acrobatics skill, it cost two build points for each skill point. Dauphin cannot begin play with an acrobatics skill of higher than 10.

Knowledge Skills

Knowledge skills represent things that your character knows. Knowledge skills do not cost build points. Instead, the character receives a number of points to spend on knowledge skills equal to 7 times their reason score. These points can only be spent on knowledge skills.

Advantages

Any remaining build points can be spent to purchase advantages. These advantages provide your character with an edge during play separating him or her from other members of their species.

The character can have as many advantages as he or she can afford to purchase. However, it is the player's responsibility to know what advantages their character has and what each does. If you select too many advantages you run the risk of hearing yourself say, "Damn, I forgot I could do that!"

121

Disadvantages

If you find yourself running short on build points… or you just want an interesting character… you can choose from a long list of disadvantages. Each disadvantage provides you a number of additional build points. These points can be used to purchase or improve active skills, knowledge skills, or advantages.

Of course, they're called "disadvantages" for a reason. Each disadvantage represents a physical, mental, or social flaw that your character possesses. Disadvantages can have a profound impact on the game, so choose them…wisely.

Wealth

Each character begins play with a certain amount of money that he or she can use to purchase clothing, equipment, and weapons. Roll 5d10 and add the result to 250. This number (between 250 and 295) represents the number of brigs that the character has. Roll another 5d10 to determine how many lances the character has.

Purchase Equipment, Weapons, and Apparel

Now that you know how much money your character has, you can begin to purchase the things your character will use when you begin to play. Yes, this is your chance to purchase the weapons you will use to become the embodiment of death on the mortal plane.

Remember to keep your character concept in mind while selecting weapons, equipment, and items of apparel. A great sword might do a lot of damage, but it doesn't fit with the idea of a dashing swashbuckler. Likewise, full plate armor provides a lot of protection, but it is impractical for a thief or assassin to wear regularly.

Attribute Score

Since characters exist only in our minds, we need a means of figuring out how they affect their equally fictional environment. To do this, our game uses dice in order add a measure of chance. The challenge then becomes figuring out how many dice the players roll when their character attempts a particular action. That's where attributes come into play.

Attributes represent your character's natural talents and aptitudes. They are useded anytime the character's natural abilities come into play rather than their learned skills.

Attributes are an abstract concept rather than concrete ideas. They are meant to symbolize how well your character can use his or her natural talents to affect the world around them. For this reason you will not see any charts telling you how much weight you can lift because of your high strength score. That's what dice rolls are for, and anyone can get lucky… well, almost anyone.

There are 8 different attributes – 4 physical & 4 mental – that will form the foundation for your player character.

In addition, your character will have 3 dice pools you can use to augment your character's actions. These dice pools are derived directly from your character's attributes.

Remember, attributes cost 2 build points for each attribute point you assign, no more than ½ of your total build points can be spent on attributes, and no more than 6 points can be assigned to any attribute before racial modifiers are applied.

The average ability score for an adult human is between 2 & 3 (2 is low average, and 3 is high average). The averages for other races are, not surprisingly, 2 and 3 plus or minus their racial modifiers to a minimum of zero.

Physical Attributes

Four physical attributes will define your character's ability to interact with the real world.

Strength (*STR*): This attribute embodies the character's ability to apply physical force on the world around him or her. Strength affects the amount of damage done in a melee attack. It also affects how much the character can lift and carry.

Coordination (*CRD*): Coordination is a measure of your character's hand-eye coordination, balance, and fine manipulation. This attribute governs your ability to hit things with both ranged and melee weapons. It's also the skill you use when you're playing video games. Coordination also governs your ability to your ability to nail that dismount during the Olympics… of course, if your ankle is broken, wound penalties will come into play.

Quickness (*QCK*): This attribute is how quickly your character can move. Quickness also governs a number of dexterous skills that are not merely hand-eye coordination such as athletics & acrobatics.

Constitution (*CON*): Your character's constitution is representative of his physical health, endurance, and ability to resist damage. A high constitution also helps you resist the effects of drugs and alcohol.

Mental Attributes

Reason (*RSN*): In short, your character's reason is his or her intelligence. It is your character's understanding of logic and basic problem solving skills. Reason is used to solve puzzles , riddles, and any other similar things a strange frog-like creature might throw your way if it stumbles upon you while searching for its "precious."

For spell-casting characters, reason is the attribute that governs the skills used to design, develop, and learn new spells.

Insight (*INS*): Insight is a more passive version of reason. It's your character's intuition. It also represents your character's ability to see the subtle undertones in a social situation. Hunches, gut feelings, and empathy are all examples of insight at work.

For spell-casting characters, insight is the attribute that governs the character's casting skill.

Psyche (*PSY*): Your character's force of will is symbolized by psyche. Psyche is used to resist mental damage and trauma.

For spell-casting characters, it is also important. Psyche determines whether the caster risks taking mind or body damage for casting spells.

Dice Pools

Each character has 3 different dice pools that can be used to augment certain activities.

Most often, these pools will come into play during combat. Once the dice in these pools are used, they are unavailable until the character rolls for initiative again.

When used outside of combat, the pools refresh at the end of a given scene. For this purpose, a scene is defined as a specific encounter or section of the story that has the same basic theme. If there is any question as to what a scene is, the director will make the official determination.

Dice from one of these pools used to augment a roll to resist fatigue or the effects of sleep deprivation do not refresh until the character either rests or sleeps. In effect, being tired or fatigued reduces the characters dice pools.

Action Pool: The character's action pool is derived from adding together their coordination, quickness, reason, & insight and dividing the result in half.

For the mathematically inclined, the equation would look like this:

$$(CRD+QCK+RSN+INS)/2$$

Dice from the action pool can be used to augment almost any active skill. Action pool dice are also used to dodge attacks (see dodging on page XXXX).

Vigor Pool: The number of dice in your vigor pool is determined by adding together your strength, quickness, constitution, & psyche and dividing the result by 2.

For the mathematically inclined, the equation looks something like this:

$$(STR+QCK+CON+PSY)/2$$

The dice from your vigor pool are use to resist physical damage. They may also be used to augment rolls where the character's health comes into play, such as resisting a disease or the effects of alcohol.

Willpower Pool: Your willpower pool is determined by adding all of the character's mental attributes and dividing that result by 2.

For the mathematically inclined, the equation would look like this:

$$(RSN+INS+PSY+CHA)/2$$

Willpower dice are used to resist mental damage. These dice can also used to resist enervation from casting spells. They may also be used to bolster the character's resistance to seduction, bribery, or other feats of will.

NOTE: Even if a particular roll might qualify for augmentation by more than one dice pool, only the dice from one pool can be used.

Skills

Skills represent the things that your character has learned either through training, schooling, or self-study. Skills are divided into two distinct categories. Your character should have some skills from each of the three groups.

When selecting these skills, be sure to keep your character concept in mind. Think not only about what skills you want your character to have, but what skills they should possess based on your concept. Think about what your character did before becoming an adventurer. A character that was raised by a weapon-smith should have some weapons crafting skill.

Not every skill you select has to have an apparent affect on game play. Don't forget to include a skill or two simply to round out your character. A grizzled warrior with an appreciation, and knowledge, of operas is a more believable character than the warrior who is little more than a walking armory.

This game takes place in a semi-feudalistic society. In such a society most people simply grow old, take over the family business, and die doing what their parents did. Player characters are not most people, but that doesn't mean that mom and dad didn't start teaching them all there was to know about farming before they struck out on their own.

Keep in mind that to a large degree skills are abstract concepts. Their purpose is to provide a mechanic with which to play the game. They are not intended to represent realistic representation of human ability.

In the real world wielding a battle axe is different from wielding a fencing foil. In the game world, making a separate skill for each weapon would slow down play, drastically limit the character's abilities, and put a serious damper on the player's level of enjoyment.

Skill Tests

Any time a player rolls dice in order on behalf of their character it is a "test." Skill tests are, by far, the most common type of tests in the game, though others do exist.

There are four different types of skill tests. They can each be applied to a different situation in the game. The different types of tests are detailed below. It is up to the discretion of the director which type of test is most applicable to the skill use based on the situation that the character is in when the test takes place.

- A **Standard Test** (ST) is a test where the player is given a target number by the director. It is, by far, the most common type of test in the game. The player rolls a number of dice equal to his attribute versus the modified target number.

- An **Open Test** (OT) is a test without a set target number. Open tests are usually used when the character's skill will be directly challenged by an NPC or monster. The highest result of an open test becomes the target number for your opponent. Tests used to sneak into a building or hide from a guard are the most common type of these tests.

- **Parallel Tests** (PT) usually result when two characters are set against one another, but some other important factors come into play that have an effect on the outcome. They are resolved by both players rolling against a set target number and comparing the number of successes.

    If two hackers are simultaneously trying to boot each other off of a system, they are competing against each other and the computer system. In this case, both players roll their reason attribute versus the target number assigned by the director to represent the difficulty of the system and modified by their computer skill. The character with the most successes wins the test.

- The last type of test is a **Direct Test** (DT). Direct tests occur when one character is directly competing against another. In a direct test both characters roll a number of dice equal to one of their attribute scores versus a target equal to their opponents score.

    An example of this type of test would be if one character is trying to open a door while another character attempts to hold it shut. Each character would roll a number of dice equal to their strength score versus a Target number equal to their opponent's strength score.

Unskilled Tests

If your character does not have the particular skill required to complete a task, they can default on the roll. This means that the character rolls the attribute associated with the test versus the target number. When defaulting to an attribute, however, the character needs twice as many successes to achieve the same goal. This means that two successes are required for even a minimal success. It also means that, when using a weapon that the character is not skilled in, the damage rating is multiplied by ½ the total successes. The target number is also increased by two.

Critical Successes

Anytime all of the dice used to make a roll achieve a result that is higher than the assigned target number the result is a critical success. The outcome of this role is the best possible outcome imaginable.

Critical Failure

Conversely, anytime all of the dice used for a skill test come up zero, the result is a critical failure. The outcome of the test yields the worst possible results. This may mean that the string on your bow breaks or that the gun you're firing jams. It might mean that the character drops his weapon and must use an action to retrieve it. Or, if you have a particularly devious director, it may mean that you just shot another member of your party.

Rule of Zero

Unlike many games that utilize the 10-sided die, in the d10 system, a zero on a role counts for zero, not 10. Because zeros are failures no target number can ever be less than 1… regardless of how skilled the character may be.

Rule of Fives

Five is the sacred number of the goddess Eris. As such, anytime all of the dice used in a skill test come up 5, it is assumed the Eris herself was watching the character and personally influenced the results of the check. This may mean success on a roll that might otherwise have failed. It may mean failure on a roll that might otherwise have succeeded.

Eris' motivation for manipulation fate is likely to remain a mystery to the players. The director himself might not know what Eris hoped to achieve. She is the goddess of chaos and discord after all.

Rule of Nines

Any time a nine is rolled naturally on a die, that die is rolled again and the results of the two rolls are added together.

Concentration

Sometimes a character needs to succeed on a roll. Maybe he or she is trying to defuse a bomb; maybe they're trying to shoot to disarm an opponent that needs to be taken in alive. Whatever the reason, a character can improve his or her chances of success by spending a few rounds concentrating on the task at hand. For each round spent in concentration, including aiming a projectile weapon or firearm, the character receives an extra die on the applicable skill test up to a maximum of three dice.

This concentration, or aiming, does not affect the target number in anyway. The bomb does not miraculously become less difficult to defuse because you've thought about it for a few seconds. Likewise, your opponent does not become less difficult to hit because you looked at them down the barrel of your gun and took a few deep breaths. Instead, the character becomes more centered and focused giving them a higher chance of success at the crucial task. This focus is represented by the bonus dice.

Pulling Your Punches

Sometimes you want to succeed, but not by as much as you could if you were really trying. This most often happens during combat, but it might have other applications during play.

When a character "pulls a punch" in the d10 System, he or she simply uses less dice than they are able, rolling only 5 though they have a skill of 10 for example. This is a risky proposition because it reduces you odds of rolling a success, but limiting your results is what pulling a punch is all about.

Active Skills

Active skills are those most likely to have an affect on game play. The active skill list includes all of the combat skills, some mental disciplines, and many social skills. Your level of aptitude in these skills is reflected by your ranks in them. Ranks in these skills are purchased using build points at a straight one for one conversion.

A character can have as many, or as few, active skills as the player desires. The only stipulation to the number of points you can spend on skills is that no skill can be ranked higher than the attribute most commonly associated with it.

For example, skill with a rapier (edged weapons) is governed by the character's finesse score. If the character has a starting finesse of 3, they cannot begin play with 4 ranks in bladed weapons.

It is important to note that skill checks will not always involve the attribute most commonly associated with them. Sometimes it makes sense to use a skill in conjunction with another attribute. Throwing a football is a function of the athletics skill, but it seems to have more to do with finesse (hand-eye coordination) than quickness (agility).

Though many of the things you will encounter in this game have correlating skills listed in this section, this list could not possibly include every strange and deviant idea that players come up with. If you want your character to be able to do something that isn't covered by one of the skills below, discuss it with your director and create a new skill.

Acrobatics (QCK) - This is the skills used to determine your character's ability to jump and grab a swinging chandelier, vault over a wall, or flip over a balcony railing only to land safely and ready to fight on the floor below.

Acting (CHA) – Acting is more than pretending to be something you aren't. That's dating and is covered under the seduction skill. Acting is, for all intents and purposes, becoming another person. Being able to mimic mannerism, accents, and do it believably.

Appraise (RSN) – Appraising is used to determine the market value of a person, place, or thing.

Athletics (QCK) – Athletics is used to represent you aptitude for sports related activities.

Awareness (INS) – Most people are able to notice the world around them with little trouble. They might not notice a picture slightly askew, but they certainly would notice a 500 foot lizard rampaging through town eating people. This skill represents the refined ability to notice the skewed picture. It is useful for detectives, archeologists, and interior decorators.

Beguile (CHA) – Beguile is used in situations where the character is attempting to lie, con, or mislead the person he or she is talking to. This skill is the one that you use to explain to your wife why your girlfriend is in the house.

Build/Craft X (RSN) – Creating an item is what this skill is used for. It is handled slightly differently than other skills in that you must select what it is you know how to build/craft when you select the skill.

Cartography (RSN) - This is the ability of the character to produce clear and understandable maps based upon their observations.

Climb (STR) – This skill is used whenever your gym teacher makes you climb the rope in gym class. It also is the skill used to determine if you are able to get up and over the wall before the authorities.

Command (CHA) – Command is used to measures a character's ability to lead other people.

Cryptography (RSN) – The art of making and breaking codes, cryptography can also be used to decipher ancient languages or encrypt messages to your co-conspirators.

Dance (QCK) – This is your character's ability to move in time with music that is pleasing to those who witness it. It is used for all styles of dance from ballroom and waltzes to the electric slide and break dancing.

Demolitions (RSN) – Explosives are tricky to work with even if you know what you're doing. If you don't know what you're doing, get used to living without opposable thumbs. Demolitions is the skill that will help you keep your digits.

Discern Lie (INS) – Sometimes when your talking to someone you just get that feeling that they're lying to you. The value of this skill to anyone in law enforcement cannot be measured. This ability to notice when someone is being less than honest with you can be learned and improved. This skill represents that learning and improvement.

Disguise (CHA) – Disguise is the ability to appear to be something other than what you are. The disguise skill is more than applying make-up. It's changing stance and stature, changing facial structure, and being able to do it all for extended periods of time. It is important to note that even with an obscene level of disguise there are still things that cannot be accomplished. A halfling cannot disguise himself as an ogre no matter how hard he tries without stilts, padding, and a lot of prosthetic make-up. You cannot appear to be more than one size category smaller than you are, and appearing more than one size category larger requires things like stilts.

Drive (CHA) – Drive is *not* the ability to operate an automobile. They don't exist on the Lady's Rock… yet. Instead, the drive skill is a measure of a character's ability to steer a vehicle pulled by beasts of burden – horses, oxen, donkeys, other characters, and ex-girlfriends – in a safe manner. It also governs less conventional types of vehicle operation such as evasive maneuvers.

Edged Weapons (CRD) – This skill covers the use of swords, daggers, axes, and other weapons with sharp edges.

Escape Artist (QCK) – This skill is the characters ability to slip out of bonds and other restraints. It does not allow a character to pick a lock. That's covered under its own skill.

Fast-Talk (CHA) – Fast-talking is *not* lying. Fast-talking is the fine art of representing the truth is a particular light so that the person you're talking to believes what you want them to believe and you have not lied to them. Though you have deceived, misled, and otherwise bamboozled them, you were being completely honest at the time.

127

Firearms (CRD) – This skill governs your use of handheld ballistics weapons such as shortarms (pistols) longarms (Rifles) and blunderbusses

Forgery (CRD) – Forgery truly is an art form. It is the ability to reproduce signatures and documents that appear to be authentic. Forgery is used to make counterfeit currency, create licenses you could not otherwise legally obtain, and provide note from your mother explaining why you weren't in school yesterday.

Gambling (CHA) – Gambling is the fine art of wagering money on a game of chance. The gambling skill is the fine art of manipulating that chance so that you win the money.

Gunnery (RSN) – Gunnery covers all direct fire weapons that are *not* man-portable. This includes cannons, ballistae, and the 120mm main gun of an M1A1 Abrams tank.

Hide (QCK) – Hiding represents your ability to know when, how, and where to hide.

Impact Weapons (CRD) – This skill covers all melee weapons that do not have an edge (blunt weapons, chains, whips, etc).

Interrogation (CHA) – Interrogation is the ability to forcibly gain information from an unwilling character through intimidation, torture, and other less savory means.

Interview (CHA) – This skill is the benign form of interrogation. It's knowing what questions to ask and how to ask them to get a character to give you the information you're after.

Intimidation (CHA) – This skill represents a character's ability to instill fear in another character.

Jump (STR) – Even character can jump, but a character with this skill is particularly adept at it.

Launch Weapons (RSN) – Launch weapons is used to resolve indirect fire. Weapons like catapults, trebuchets, mortars, and badminton birdies are all examples of indirect fire and would be governed by the Launch Weapons skill.

Navigation (RSN) – This skill is used to determine where you are, where you're headed, and how to get from point A to point B. It is possible to navigate without the aid of maps, star, and other devices. However, it is extremely difficult.

Negotiation (CHA) – Negotiations is used any time a character is trying to honestly deal with another character. It covers haggling about price and hammering out the details of a contract.

Orate (CHA) – Oration, or "Speechifying" as Emperor Grigori II likes to say, is the character's ability to speak to and motivate a large crowd.

Play Musical Instrument X (CRD) – Whether your character is a violinist, guitarist, or a drummer who just likes to hang out with real musicians, this skill governs your ability.

Pick Locks (CRD) – This skill is used when a character wants to gain access to something that has been secured by a lock. This skill does not cover combination locks. That is the province of the safecracking skill.

Pilot (CRD) – Piloting represents the character's skill at operating all manner of flying or hovering craft not propelled by beasts of burden. Since these are the major forms of transportation on the Lady's Rock, this skill tends to be of value.

Projectile Weapons (CRD) – Any weapon that fires a projectile without the aid of an explosive chemical reaction (i.e. bows & crossbows) is classified as a projectile weapon.

Ranged Weapons (CRD) – This skill covers the use of grenades, baseballs, and shuriken (that's ninja stars for those of you who are unfamiliar with the term). In short, any time you throw something, whether you hit your target or not is determined using this skill. Unless you happen to be throwing dice at a craps table, that's covered under gambling.

Reach Weapons (CRD) – This skill governs the use of polearms, spears, staves, and other melee weapons that provide extended range.

Repair X (RSN) – Repair skill is handled slightly differently than other skills. Each time you select a repair skill you must specify what you are able to repair. You are still able to repair other things by defaulting to this skill and still have a higher chance of success than someone who does not know how to repair anything.

Ride (QCK) – The ride skill indicates the character's proficiency with controlling, directing, and staying on a mount.

Safecracking (RSN) - This skill allows the character to open combination locks. It does not cover the use of explosives, which is part of the demolitions skill, in order to open a safe.

Search (RSN) – Search is your character's adeptness at finding items. Everything from secret doors and hidden compartments to lost vidcaster remotes and lev-carriage keys can be found using the search skill.

Seduction (CHA) – Seduction is the art of getting other people to fall in love with you, usually for a period of 24 hours. It is used in any social situation where the terms alcohol and rooffie might also be applied.

Sense Motive (INS) – Sense Motive is used whenever the player wished to determine if another character is hiding something. If the character has knowledge of the person in question, at the director's discretion, the character may be able to determine what they are hiding.

Sing (CHA) – This is the character's ability to carry a tune and impress Randy, Paula, and Simon.

Sleight of Hand (CRD) – Sleight of Hand covers a variety of things that characters might find useful. From picking pockets to slipping room keys in other character's pockets, any quick, deceptive manipulation of small objects uses this skill. It's also great for birthday parties, corporate retreats, and bar mitzvahs.

Sneak (QCK) – This is the character's ability to move without making any undo noise. It is used anytime you want to move about without drawing attention to yourself whether that's moving through a lord's castle or getting home a few hours past curfew.

Spell Casting (INS) – This spell represents the character's ability to manipulate the mystic energies that surround the world of the Lady's Rock and bend then to his or her psyche. See magic page XXXX for more information.

Summoning (CHA) – This skill is the character's ability to summon and control various elemental and spirits. Details of summoning can be found on page XXXX.

Summoning should not be mistaken with "conjuring" which is a type of magical spell.

Tracking (RSN) – Tracking is the ability to follow a trail. In order to track a creature, the tracker must have a sense capable of following the trail. For example, an intangible ghost that smells of flowers could be tracked by scent, but not by sight.

Treat Injury (RSN) – This skill is used to resolve the effectiveness of efforts to aid in another's recovery. Its use is actually covered under the section on healing (see page XXXX).

Unarmed Combat (QCK) Unarmed Combat is used to measure the character's aptitude for hand-to-hand combat. Street brawling, Boxing, or mastery of the ancient spoonerian martial art of Yuck Fou are all specializations of this skill.

WI-AT Operations (RSN) – An indispensable skill, WI-AT Ops is a measure of a character's aptitude for using a Wireless Image & Audio Terminal. It is used to search databases for valuable data or the ERP for suitable "reading material."

<u>**Knowledge Skills**</u>

A character receives 7 times their character's reason attribute in points to be spent on knowledge skills. These skills represent things that the character has learned. They may be useful during the course of play, but usually have a more passive role.

Quite literally, knowledge skills can be anything you want your character to know. An elven scholar who is fascinated by orcish tribal culture could be fun and interesting to play as could a teg with a fondness, and extensive knowledge of, dwarven ales. These little quirks go a long way to making a character come to life.

Below is a list of sample knowledge skills. It is not all inclusive by any means. If you are unable to fine a skill that perfectly suits your character, feel free, with the director's approval, to create skills that are more appropriate to your particular character.

Alchemy: Alchemy is equal parts chemistry, philosophy, mysticism. This skill deals with more magical applications of other sciences. Things like brewing magical potions, creating golems, and transmuting lead into gold are the province of alchemy.

Anthropology: This skill deals with the study of the physical, social, and cultural development of player races.

Arcane Theory: Arcane Theory is used in two ways. First, it can be the purely academic study of magic by someone who is not able to utilize magical energies. Second, it can represent the magical education & study necessary for a magically adept person to develop new spells. (See Magic on page XXXX)

Archeology: The systematic study of past life and cultures by recovery and examination of material evidence like burial sites, buildings, tools, earthenware, and personal items.

Architecture: Architecture is the art and science of the design and construction of buildings, ships, and other things inhabited by people.

Area Knowledge X: This skill represents the character's knowledge and understanding of a particular region or the facilities used by a particular agency. The player must select the area that the character has knowledge of at the time this skill is chosen. The director has the final say on whether a skill selection is too vague. Area Knowledge: Khymbria might be too vague; while Area Knowledge: Imperial Military Bases might be perfectly acceptable depending on the scope of the campaign. Area Knowledge for a particular city is always acceptable.

Art: Art is the study of paintings, sculptures, etc.

Ballistics: Ballistics is the knowledge and study of the dynamics of projectiles and the weapons that fire them. A character skilled in ballistics is able to determine the type of weapon used based on a recovered projectile and can even match that projectile to the weapon that fired it. The character is also familiar with the effects of ballistic weapons on various substances, like the human body, and could determine such things as the location of the shooter based on the angle of an entry wound.

Biology: The study of life and living organisms including their structure, function, growth, origin, and evolution.

Chemistry: Chemistry is the scientific study of the composition, structure, properties, and reactions of matter.

Conspiracy Theory: Conspiracy theories abound in any world, especially one heavily laden with politics and intrigue like the Lady's Rock. This skill represents the study of those theories.

Contraband: This skill represents the character's knowledge of contraband items – drugs, weapons, etc. A character with this skill knows what items are wanted where and what laws govern those items.

Cosmology: The metaphysical study of the nature, origin, and structure of the universe is cosmology. This field of study includes not only the creation of the Lady's Rock, but of other worlds, planes of existence, and dimensions. It also covers theories about traveling between these places.

Criminology: Criminology is the study of crime, criminals, criminal behavior, and the process of correcting that behavior. A criminologist may be able to create a profile of a criminal based upon the particulars of a crime provided that the criminal in question left enough evidence at the scene. They may also be able to determine the likely course of action that a criminal may take based on past behavior of that criminal or other criminals like him.

Dwarven Ales: This skill represents an extensive knowledge of the production and consumption of dwarven alcoholic beverages. The character possessing this skill is somewhat of a connoisseur.

Ecclesiastic Law: This skill represents a working knowledge of the First Order of Grievances. A person with this skill is qualified to prosecute or defend someone accused of violating laws of this order.

Economics: This social science deals with the production, distribution, and consumption of goods & services. It also deals with business management, commercial finances, and economic theories like supply & demand.

Elven Wines: This skill represents an extensive knowledge of the production and consumption of elven alcoholic beverages. The character possessing this skill is somewhat of a connoisseur.

Engineering X: Engineering is the application of scientific and mathematical principles to more practical ends, such as design, construction, and operation of an object, structure, or system. Engineering is *not* a theoretical field of study. IT cannot be used to develop new ideas, only to apply existing ideas in a practical manner.

This knowledge skill is one of those skills requiring the choice of a specialization. A character can be an electrical engineer, mechanical engineer, WI-AT engineer, transportation engineer, economic engineer, political engineer, or any other type of engineer you can imagine. It is impossible, however, to simply be an engineer and not have a field of specialization. The very concept of what engineering is makes the very idea both impractical and unrealistic. This skill can be taken multiple times.

Eristocracy: This skill represents more extensive knowledge of the hierarchy of the Orthodox Church of Eris. Characters with this skill are familiar with the membership, structure, and capabilities of this group of power brokers.

Etiquette X: Etiquette is the art of knowing what practices and forms are prescribed by social convention or by authority. It is concerned with behavior, modes of address, and other social customs. Each time etiquette is chosen, the player must decide what portion of society the skill applies to. Some possibilities include: Court, Guild, Street, Magical Groups, & the ERP. The etiquette skill can be taken multiple times.

Fringe Cults: This skill represents a working knowledge of religious cults, their icons & symbols, prominent members, and ideologies.

Fey Lore: The study of all things relating to the mysterious Fey is covered under this skill. A person with this skill can identify faerie mounds, art, and weapons. They know the myths, and many of the truths, about this enigmatic race.

Geology: The scientific study of the origin, history, and structure of the solid matter that makes up the Lady's Rock.

History: History is the branch of knowledge that analyzes and records past events.

Imperial Law: This skill represents a working knowledge of the Second Order of Grievances. A person with this skill is qualified to prosecute or defend someone accused of violating laws of this order.

Language X: This skill represents the ability to speak and, at higher levels, read a particular language. Like some other skills, a specific language must be chosen. One cannot simply put a few ranks in "languages" and be able to read every language any more than you could write "various medicinal herbs" on your character sheet and expect to be carrying something with which to produce the antidote to the venom of a creature thought to long be extinct.

Literacy is far from common on the Lady's Rock, however, for the purposes of the game, anyone who has more than one rank in a given language skill is assumed to be able to read & write it as well as speak it unless the character specifies otherwise.

Languages test, when appropriate, are best handled with a Parallel Test with a difficulty assigned by the director based on the concept that the speaker is attempting to convey. Things like foot and shelter should be fairly simple to convey. While concepts like the afterlife or the nature of women should be very difficult.

All player characters receive one language skill at rank 9 at no cost at character creation. This is the language that the character grew up speaking. It is usually a racial language, though it is not uncommon for different members of different races to raise their children knowing to speak the Erisian tongue especially in urban areas.

The languages commonly spoke on the Lady's Rock include the following:

- **Ailuran:** Spoken by the Ailure, this language contains purrs, hisses, and other sounds that most races are incapable of making. While they can still speak the language and get their point across, native speakers may find their performances quite comical.
- **Dwarven:** The native tongue of the dwarves is a very harsh and guttural language. While it is not difficult for other races to learn the tongue, many do not like to speak it because its rigid structure…and the fact that everything you say in dwarven sounds like you're cursing.
- **Elven:** A flowery and melodic tongue, the native language of the elves is filled with subtle changes in tone and inflection. It is not impossible for other races to learn, but they always tend to sound "forced" in some way. Because of this it is always possible to distinguish a native speaker from someone who has learned the tongue.
- **Goblinoid:** The native tongue of the goblin races, this language is also spoken by other "uncivilized" creatures.
- **Gnomish:** This language is, as you may have guessed, the native tongue of the gnomes.
- **Erisian (Imperial Trade Tongue):** The "common" trade tongue of the Empire of Eristonia. It is the native tongue of humans and is spoken by almost every race.
- **Orcish:** Probably the only common language more harsh than dwarven is Orcish. For example, there are roughly 187 different ways to translate the work "kill" into orcish depending on the means and motive behind the death. On the other hand, there is no Orcish word for love and the word for sex is the same regardless of consent.

Linguistics: Linguistics is the study of language, its structure and evolution. In this game linguistics is the skill used to specifically mean the study of ancient languages and their evolution into modern tongues. A linguist is not necessarily able to speak these languages but a character with this skill may be able to translate them if he hears them or decipher ancient texts if he finds them.

Music: This skill is the study of musical composition including tone, pitch, measure, melody, harmony, and any other word you can think of that is involved in music. While a person with this skill may be able to compose music, they cannot necessarily play a musical instrument or sing these are covered under their respective active skills. However, a person with the musical skill would be able to critique someone who was performing either instrumentally or vocally.

Occult Lore: This skill represents knowledge of various myths and legends found throughout the Empire. It can be used to recall the tales of great heroes, how orcs believe the world was created, or the healing properties believed to exist in certain herbs. Like most legends, whether or not this knowledge is accurate is a matter for scholars & scientists.

Pathology: Pathology is the study of diseases and their causes, processes, development, and consequences. Someone with the pathology skill would be able to diagnose a disease based on its symptoms. Though it may take some research if the disease was not previously known, the character would also be able to make predictions about the diseases behavior in the body and level of contagiousness.

Pharmaceutical: This skill represents knowledge of medicinal drugs, their production, uses, and side effects. Pharmaceutical knowledge is part chemistry and part pathology, though not enough of either to do anything outside of the pharmaceutical world.

Philosophy: This skill gives the character a general knowledge of the writings, theories, and ideas of various philosophers. A person with this skill can engage in philosophical debate with another and understand the theories behind philosophical arguments.

Politics: This skill represents an understanding of political structure. A character with this skill understands the hierarchy of political bodies as well as their procedures.

Prostitution: A character with this skill has a working knowledge, and maybe a practical one, of the sex industry. They can identify prostitutes, courtesans, and other industry workers. And they understand the various laws regulating and restricting that industry.

Provincial Law X: This skill represents a working knowledge of the Third Order of Grievances. A person with this skill is qualified to prosecute or defend someone accused of violating laws of this order. Unlike the two previous law skills, the character must select the particular province that this skill applies to.

Psychology: The scientific study of mental and emotional processes and behaviors. Psychology can be useful to determine someone's motivation, likely course of action, or emotional state.

Religion X: This is the knowledge of the beliefs, scriptures, and practices of a particular religious group. A character with this skill as knowledge of the group's doctrines & dogma as well as their rituals, customs and any sacraments they may have.

Seamanship: This skill governs the character's knowledge of ship operations on both the inland waterways and on the aether.

Since travel by aether is by far the safest route between provinces, this skill is vital to the economy of the Lady's Rock as well as to the lives of those who make their living plying these trade lanes.

Smuggling Routes: Knowing what items will sell on a particular black market is completely different from knowing how to get them there. This skill deals with the various routes commonly used by smugglers throughout the empire and the difficulties that can be expected on each route.

Sociology: Sociology is the study of social behavior including the origin, organization, and development of societies. This skill can be used to the influence of an individual or group might have on a given area. It can also be used to make intelligent estimates about the role of various individuals in a particular society or the relative rank of people in a social structure.

Strategy: Strategy is the ability to formulate a plan to effectively and efficiently complete a large scale operation. Characters with this skill have the ability to put together an effective plan of action in order to achieve a long term goal.

Tactics: A tactic is a procedure, plan, or set of maneuvers engaged in to achieve a particular end, aim, or goal. It is the means by which the objectives identified by the strategy are achieved.

Theology: Theology is the rational study of deities, religious truths, and their relationship with society and the people who compose that society.

Skill Specialization

A character can choose to specialize in an aspect of any skill once they have achieved rank 3 in the base skill. A specialization is a focus on a particular category within a skill. Most skills can be specialized in, as most skills encompass more than one thing.

For example, the use of swords is governed by the edged weapons skill. A character who primarily uses swords might decide to specialize in their use and eschew the use of other edged weapons. Once he or she achieves rank 3 in edged weapons, he can freely do so.

Specialization does not affect the way the skill is used during play. However, it is easier to improve a specialization than a standard skill and easier still to improve a concentration. (See Character Improvement on page XXXX)

If a Character chooses to specialize in a skill during character creation, reduce the value of the parent skill by 1 and record a specialization at one point higher than the score of the original skill. After character creation, it costs 3 mana points to specialize (see Character Improvement on page XXXX).

For example, Charlie has the firearms skill at rank 5. He wants to specialize in longarms, so he reduces his firearms skill to 4 and records longarms 5 on his character sheet. From this point forward they are treated as two separate skills with the noted exception that the parent skill can never exceed the specialization. (i.e. you cannot have a specialization at rank 7 and raise ita parent skill to 8)

Advantages & Disadvantages

The next step in creating a character is completely optional. Selecting advantages and disadvantages may add depth to the character, but they should not be selected lightly. As always, the director has final say on which advantages and disadvantages will be allowed in a particular campaign.

Every advantage and disadvantage has a point value assigned to it based on the impact that it has on game play. Advantages can be purchased using build points. If you run out of build points, you can acquire more by taking disadvantages. However, no character can have more than 15 points worth of disadvantages.

Before selecting advantages and disadvantages check with your director to be sure they will be used in your campaign. The advantages described below provide some serious benefits to characters that may unbalance the game if they are not countered with disadvantages. If a director feels that keeping track of a character's advantages and disadvantages will be too difficult, they are strongly encouraged not to use them in their game.

Unless it is specifically listed in the description, any given advantage or disadvantage can only be taken once by a given character.

Advantages

Academic Aptitude (-2 pts): The character is naturally gifted when it comes to his studies. Any time the character rolls a purely academic skill, excluding scientific or linguistic knowledge skills and all active skills, they receive an additional die.

Adeptness (-4 pts): The character is adept at a particular skill. All target numbers directly involving this skill are reduced by one. This advantage can be taken multiple times, but each time it is taken it must be applied to a different skill.

Ambidexterity (-6 pts): When a character with ambidexterity fights with a weapon in each hand, they can use their full skill rating for each hand..

Bi-Lingual (-2 pts): The character was raised in a household that spoke more that one language regularly. As such, the character speaks both languages as fluently as any native speaker. In game terms the character receives a second language at rank 10.

Bland Appearance (-2 pts): A character with this advantage has a uniquely average appearance. People who are asked to describe the character will say that he or she was of average height and build… and that's about it. If the character attempts to hide in a crowd of people, anyone attempting to spot him or her suffers a +2 penalty to their target number.

Cleric (-10 pts): A character with this advantage is a member of the clergy of some deity. They have access to spells that a mage does, but they have the additional strictures imposed upon them by their deity. Clerics begin with 30 points worth of spells just as mages do (see magic page XXXX). Teg clergy need the "Mage" advantage because they do not adhere to religious strictures.

Common Sense (-2 pts): A character with this advantage has more sensibility than the average person. Anytime the character is about to attempt something that the director deems foolish or impractical, he or she must warn the player and give them an opportunity to reconsider their chosen course of action.

Contact (-1 to -5 pts): The character has an acquaintance that may be of use. This person could be a local beggar who feeds the character information. Otherwise they could be the personal valet of a local lord. They may be any person that the director approves, but they *must* reside in the character's home area (large city, rural tributarial province, etc.) and they can only provide the character with information.

The director and the player should work together to develop the exact nature of the contact. The point cost of this advantage is determined by the director based on its impact on the game. The beggar may be worth only one point, while the merchant may be worth any number of points based on the goods in question. The valet, however, may have access to sensitive information and might be worth significantly more because if it.

Keep in mind that the relationship between the character and the contact needs to be maintained. A contact may, from time to time, ask the player to perform a task for him or ask for some other type of favor. Likewise, contacts that are ignored are not apt to help you out when you need them.

Criminal Family (-3 pts): The character's family business is not something that the authorities approve of. They may be smugglers or pirates. They may run a local gang of street toughs or control the local thieves' guild.

While this may have some detrimental effects on the character's life, it does entail some unique benefits. A criminal family can help a character gain access to contraband items or dispose of stolen property. But be warned, families often have a knack for showing up and needing your help at the most inopportune times.

Cunning Linguist (-1 pt): A character with this advantage has a knack for learning languages. Anytime the character makes a language or linguistics skill test they receive an additional die.

Eidetic Memory (-5 pts): Some people have good memories. A person with an eidetic memory doesn't have a good memory. They have a superb memory. A character with this advantage remembers everything that they see or hear. The character always recalls significant details. Any target number to recall obscure data is half of what it would be for a character without this handy trait.

Energy Resistance (-2, -4, or -6 pts): The player selects a particular type of energy that his character is better able to resist. Each level of this advantage gives the character an extra die to soak damage from that energy type.

Note: This advantage may be taken multiple times, but each time it must apply to a different type of energy.

Equilibrium (-2 pts): A character with this trait has an excellent sense of balance. All target numbers involving balance are reduced by 2.

Exceptional Peripheral Vision (-2 pts): The character with this trait has superb peripheral vision and gains an extra die on any perception test involving vision.

Exceptional Attribute (-4 pts): The character receives an additional attribute point. In addition to this boon, the character's racial maximum for that attribute is raised by one.

Famous (-3 pts): For some reason the character earned a modicum of fame before they began adventuring. This may be well deserved fame, or it may be a legend that has been blown way out of proportion. The player and the director are encouraged to come up with the reason that the character is famous. The character receives an extra die on any social tests involving a person that would have knowledge of this event.

Favor (-1 to -5 pts): Someone owes the character a favor. It may be a farmer whose barn the character saved from burning to the ground or it might be a tributarial lord whose daughter was saved from vicious bandits by the character. In either case, the character has a boon that they can fall back on. Once this boon is spent, however, it is gone. The director has final say regarding who can owe a favor to the character and what the cost of this advantage will be based on the favor and who owes it.

Flexible (-2 pt): The character is double-jointed. This makes it easier for the character to slip out of bonds, ropes, and other areas of confinement. The character receives an extra die on any test where this flexibility would come into play.

Focused (-1 pt or -3 pts for mages/clerics): The character with this advantage is more centered than most people. Any time they are attempting a feat requiring concentration, the character is able to shut out the distractions of the outside world and focus on the task at hand, and they receive an extra die on any such test.

This advantage costs more for magically active characters because it has an additional benefit for those who practice the arcane arts. If a mage chooses to maintain a spell such as invisibility, he suffers a penalty to all target numbers while the spell is active of +2. A mage with this advantage cuts that penalty in half suffering only a +1 to his target numbers. (See magic page XXXX)

Friends Abroad (-1 to -5 pts): This advantage is the same as the *contact* advantage except that this person *cannot* reside in the character's home area. Instead this contact is located in a different imperial or tributarial province.

Friends in High Places (-3 pts): Somewhere along the line the character made a friend who is in a position of power. This may be a childhood friend who inherited the family business or a child of a local lord that the character met while attending school. This friend may use his or her influence to help the character from time to time. But they will not do anything that would cost them their position and power.

Like other contacts, these friends need to be maintained. More importantly, high placed contacts have a tendency to be more of a hindrance than a help.

Friends in Low Places (-3 pts): This is effectively the same advantage as above except that this friend is not on the "right" side of the law. This could be the head of a local thieves' guild or the well connected fence. Whoever this friend is, the same warning above apply… maybe even more so than before.

Good Reputation (-1 pt): The character with this advantage has a good reputation. They are seen as an honest and trustworthy person by the people in their local area. One the bright side of things, honest merchants and citizens treat the character with respect. On the down side, dishonest merchants may try to take advantage of the "goody two shoes" character. The net result is a -2 bonus on all diplomacy checks.

Like fame, a good reputation isn't necessarily something that the character earned. It could be the result of a fortunate misunderstanding.

High Pain Tolerance (-4 pts): Some people are better able to deal with pain than others. The high pain tolerance advantage reduces the penalties to initiative and skill test as a result of damage by 1.

Higher Education (-2 pts): This advantage represents the fact that the character has completed more schooling than the average Imperial citizen. Instead of receiving just the standard 7 points per point of knowledge attribute, a character with this advantage receives an additional 3 points per point of reason or 10 total points worth of knowledge skills per point of reason.

Hyper Immune System (-1 pt): A character with this advantage has a heightened immune system making them more capable of resisting diseases than most people. The character receives an extra die on any test involving catching or overcoming a disease.

In Tune (-3 pts): A character with this advantage is more in tune with their surroundings than most people. They receive an additional die on all awareness tests.

Internal Compass (-1 pt): This advantage provides the character with an innate sense of direction. This gives them an extra die on navigation checks and similar tests.

Life of Purpose (-3 pts): Some people have something that they feel the need to accomplish before they die. A character with this advantage is one of them. The player needs to establish this purpose at the time of character creation. From that moment forward, the player can opt to re-roll any one failed skill test during a gaming session provided that test will help them advance toward their goal.

Light Sleeper (-2 pts): A character with this advantage is still somewhat aware of the world around them even when they're asleep. They suffer ½ of the normal penalties a character suffers when roused from sleep. They take only a -4 to awareness checks rather than -8 and only have their dice pools reduced to ¾ normal rather than ½ (see sleep on page XXXX).

Mage (-15 pts): The character with this advantage gains the ability to bend the universe to his will by manipulating magical energy. The character must select the element that he is aspected to and begins the game with a number fo spells equal to the number of dice in his or her Willpower pool (see magic page XXXX).

Magic Resistance (-3, -6, or -9): For each level of this advantage the character has grants him a bonus die on a test to resist the effects of magic. These dice cannot be used to resist enervation.

Magical Aptitude (-5 pts): Some people are just naturally good at certain things. For the character with this advantage that thing is magic. Characters with magical aptitude receive an additional die to roll for each magic test. This does not include tests for summoning, controlling, or banishing spirits… or resisting enervation from the same.

Mechanical Aptitude (-3 pts): This is the same as magical aptitude except that this advantage applies to mechanical skill test such as building, repairing, and modifying mechanical devices.

Mystic Chameleon (-3 pts): Normally when a mage casts a spell he imprints the space around him with his magical signature. A mage with this advantage still leaves a signature, but it is dynamic rather than static. That is to say that the signature is rarely the same twice. Any time a spell is cast, roll a single d10. Record the number that comes up. If someone looks at the signature, this is the variation they see. The next time the character casts a spell, repeat this roll. If the numbers match, the signatures are similar enough that someone might be able to make the connection.

This advantage does stack with Magical Aptitude. That means a mage with both advantages would roll 2d10, adding the results, each time a spell is cast and have 19 different possible signatures instead of only 10.

Perfect Time (-1 pt): The character has an innate sense of timing. They are able to accurately estimate the current time within a few seconds and rarely miss their cues when performing plays. Their comedic timing is unparalleled.

Planar Adept (-3 pts): This advantage grants the character an additional die to all summoning test (see summoning on page XXXX).

Poise (-4 pts): A character that has poise is cool under fire. They are rarely shaken and are able to react, even if surprised. A character with this feat receives a -1 bonus to all target numbers to resist fear.

Poison Resistance (-2 pts): The character with this advantage is better able to resist the affects of poisons than other members of the same race. They receive an additional die on any test involving the effects, including damage, of any poison that they come into contact with.

Note: for the purposes of this game, poisons are substances of an inorganic nature that cause injury, illness, or death.

Presence (-2, -4, or -6 pts): The character has an air about them that draws other people like a moth to a flame. This skill is similar to a "Sex Appeal" advantage, but it applies to anyone who does not have a relationship with the character. Characters can benefit from both advantages at the same time.

Quick Healer (-5 pts): The time required for a character to heal from a given wound or condition is cut in half provided they are no longer taking damage.

Quick Reflexes (-4 pts): The character is quick to react to dynamic situations. As such, he or she receives an additional die to roll for initiative tests.

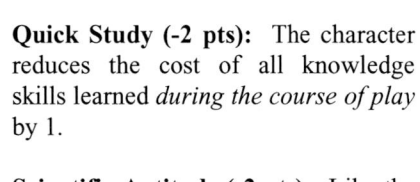

Quick Study (-2 pts): The character reduces the cost of all knowledge skills learned *during the course of play* by 1.

Scientific Aptitude (-2 pts): Like the other aptitude advantages, the character is able to add an extra die to any test involving a particular set of skills, in this case sciences.

Sex Appeal (-1, -2, or -3 pts): The character has features that people who are attracted to their gender find appealing. The character is able to add a number of dice to their charisma tests involving persons attracted to them equal to the level of this advantage purchased.

Resistant to Toxins (-2 pts): Like the resistance to poisons, the character is able to better resist the effects of toxins. He receives an additional die on any such tests.

Note: for the purposes of this game, toxins are substances of an organic nature that cause injury, illness, or death.

Tough as Nails (-4 pts): The character is more resistant to damage than others of his race. Anytime the character takes damage he suffers 1 less point than the results indicate.

Valiant (-1 pt): The character receives a -1 bonus to all target numbers to resist fear.

Wealth (varies): A character with this advantage begins play with more money than the average character. Players are encouraged to come up with a source for these funds.

Cost	Brigs
5	250
10	500
15	1,000
20	2,500
25	5,000
30	10,000
35	25,000
40	50,000

Well Connected (-5 pts): At character creation the character selects one type of merchandise that he or she is always able to purchase & sell at favorable rates. Like other contacts, this relationship must be maintained by the character.

Will to Live (-4 pts): Most people have a strong desire to continue living. The character has a stronger desire than most. Once per gaming session, the character can use willpower pool to modify any one dice roll not normally augmented by willpower.

Disadvantages

Addiction (Varies): The character is addicted to some substance. The cost of this disadvantage is based upon the substance that the character is addicted to and the frequency with which they must indulge their addiction.

A common substance is one that is readily available and can be easily found in civilized areas. Sugar is an example of a common substance. It can be found in even the most rural areas with little difficulty.

An uncommon substance is one that is more difficult to find, but that is more difficult to come across outside of larger cities. Smoke Sticks and alcohol are examples of uncommon substances. Remote rural communities rarely have the facilities available to process these goods.

A restricted substance is something that is legal, but there are laws regulating it. The berries of the blood vine are an example of a restricted substance. Their transportation and sale is regulated in an attempt to stop this plant from spreading further. Certain medicinal herbs fall into this category as well.

Points	Substance	Points	Frequency
1	Common	1	1 / CON Weeks
2	Uncommon	2	1 / CON Days
3	Restricted	3	1 / CON Hours
4	Illegal	4	Continuous

Illegal substances are things that cannot legally be purchased. Narcotics are just one example of an illegal substance.

The character with the addiction must use the substance to which they are addicted at least once in the time allotted. If you use the substance multiple times within the allotted time frame, you still must take it at the next interval. If you could store up uses of an addictive substance, I wouldn't need another cigarette until I'm 153 years old.

If the character fails to use the substance at the prescribed interval, they must make psyche check verses a target number equal to the rating of the addiction and score a number of successes equal to the dosage(s) missed. If they succeed, their Constitution drops by one point. If they fail, they go into immediate withdrawal and suffer a penalty to all rolls equal to the ranking of the addiction. In addition the character still loses a point of Constitution. This roll repeats itself each time the character fails to use the substance. The penalty does not increase, but the character continues to lose Constitution. Once their Constitution reaches zero, the character falls into a coma.

NOTE: Constitution points lost in this manner cannot be healed through natural rest until the character has indulged their addiction.

Once the character begins to indulge their addiction again, their constution points return at a rate of one for each interval in which the character uses the substance he is addicted too. Additional uses do not increase the rate at which these points return.

If, and only if, the character chooses to end his addiction they must stop using the substance and make the requisite will test as described above. If the character achieves more successes than necessary on subsequent tests, the rating for their addiction decreases by one. However, if they use the substance again before they have completely weaned themselves off of it, their addiction instantly returns to full strength.

Even after they have conquered their addiction, they're still not clear of danger. If they ever use that substance again, they must make a Psyche test versus a target number equal to their original addiction rating. If they fail, their addiction returns in full force.

Addiction is a dangerous thing. It isn't funny or fun. It destroys families and lives. And, more often than not, the addicted person is consumed by the addiction. It is included as a disadvantage for the sake of realism. Both players and directors are strongly cautioned about using this disadvantage in the game.

Allergy (varies): The strength of an allergy depends on the severity of the allergy and how common the substance is. Allergies develop for a variety of reasons. Most people remain allergic to a given substance for the rest of their lives though medication may help alleviate the affects of the allergy.

Points	Substance	Points	Severity
1	Rare	1	Mild
2	Uncommon	2	Moderate
3	Common	3	Severe

A rare substance is one that the average person is not likely to encounter. Of course, player characters are not average people, so be prepared to encounter it regardless. Dragons are an example of something that is rare.

Uncommon substances are things that are more easily found but, for some reason are not as common as others. An example of an uncommon allergy might be a precious metal such as gold.

An allergy to a common substance is something that the character will probably encounter regularly. Cats, dogs, milk, and cotton are all examples of common substances.

The severity of an allergy is another story each level of severity results in a +1 penalty to all of the character's target numbers while the substance is present (i.e. +1 for mild, +2 for moderate, and +3 for severe).

Bad Reputation (+2 pts): For some reason the character has a reputation as a liar, cheat, and scoundrel. This may be an undeserved reputation or the character might actually be a rotten person. Whatever the truth may be, people always expect the worst. They always assume that the character is either lying or has some sort of ulterior motive. The net result is a +3 penalty on all social interactions.

Berserk Rage (+5 pts): While most characters enjoy combat, a character with this flaw is obsessed with it. If the character enters combat, he or she cannot willingly disengage from the conflict unless they succeed on a Psyche test with a difficulty equal to 5 plus the number of enemy combatants. Each success achieved on this test allows the character to spend an action disengaging from combat. It does not, however, stop his or her opponent from chasing them and reengaging.

Blind (+6 pts): The character is blind. This is not the result of some physical or psychological ailment but rather the result of some magic that affected the character while he was still in the womb. Spells that provide magical means of sight function normally until the end of the duration, but such magic cannot be made permanent no matter how hard the mage may try.

Blinders (+2 pt): A character with this disadvantage has notable blind spots in his peripheral vision. This results in having 1 less die to use when making a vision based perception test.

Blowhard (+1 pt): The character is a braggart and everyone knows it. While they may not automatically ignore what the character tells them, they do assume the character is exaggerating the details. This results in a +2 penalty to all diplomacy tests.

Color Blindness (+1 pt): The character sees in black, white, and shades of gray. It is impossible for them to distinguish colors in anyway. Any tests involving colors, such as clipping the red wire on the explosive device in the corner of the room, are subject to a +5 penalty.

Combat Paralysis (+4 pts): The character freezes up in combat situations. On the first round of combat he only receives one action for every two successes on his initiative roll. (See combat on page XXXX)

Criminal Record (varies): The character has a criminal record. If he has violated Ecclesiastic or Imperial Law, this disadvantage is worth 3 points. Provincial Law is worth 2 points while Tributarial and local laws are worth only 1 point.

Cycloptic Vision (3 pts): The character has only one functioning eye. As with blindness, this disadvantage cannot be removed via magic, though the cause of this ailment may be more mundane. Because of this disadvantage, the character has little or no depth perception. He suffers a penalty of +4 on all rolls involving accurately estimating distance. This includes, but is certainly not limited to, ranged combat.

Deaf (+5 pts): The character cannot hear. Again, as with blindness, this cannot be cured by magical means, though magical spells and devices may alleviate the handicap.

Deep Sleeper (+3 pts): The character is all but oblivious to his surroundings when he is asleep. The character is able to use only half (round like you were taught in school) his perception dice on any perception test made to notice something while the character is asleep. This includes taking damage, though the character does receive a bonus to his target number equal to the number of points of damage taken.

As someone who suffers from the disadvantage in real life, I can assure you that, despite what you may think, people who are deep sleeper do not always notice that they are being hurt. This is something that my children test and reaffirm every single morning.

Enemy (+1 to +5 pts): The character has an enemy. It could be a jilted ex-lover or it could be a noble lord. The player is encouraged to work with the director to determine who the enemy is, why they hate the character, what resources they have at their disposal, and how much this disadvantage is worth.

Fear the Reaper (+6 pts): After character creation the director rolls a number of dice equal to the character's Constution score and adds the results together and secretly records the number. This is the number of gaming sessions that the character has to live. Once that time has passed, the director should instruct the player to make a constution test with a target number of 10 plus the number of times that the character has made this test. If the character fails, he dies. If he succeeds, the director re-rolls a number of dice equal to the characters constitution as before to determine the new time limit. The process continues until the character fails and dies.

For example, Joey is playing a human mage with a constitution of two. The director rolls 2d10 and gets a 5 and a 2. Seven gaming sessions later he tells Joey to make a constitution test with a target number of 10. Joey rolls a 9 and a 4. Joey re-rolls the nine and adds the results of the second die to the 9 getting a total of 12 on that die. The director then re-rolls the dice and gets a 3 and a 2. Five sessions later, Joey rolls another constitution test, this time at target number 11 (10 plus 1 for because he has rolled this test once before.) The process continues until either Joey's mage or that campaign dies.

Frail (+4 pts): The character is weaker and more susceptible to damage than most people. Each time the character takes damage, she takes one more point than the results would indicate.

High & Dry (+3 pts): A character with this disadvantage cannot take any advantage that provides them with friends, contacts, or other allies. Nor can they take advantages like good reputation. Instead the character has been abandoned by everyone he or she knew. Furthermore, the character suffers a +2 penalty to all social interaction rolls.

Horrible Secret (+2 pts): The character has some secret that she fears will be revealed. It could be the love affair that he had with the son of the local baron. Or it could be the fact that his family's mercantile empire consists of a fleet of pirate ships. Regardless of what the secret is, the

139

character has a real and pervasive fear of it becoming common knowledge.

Hunted (+1 to +5 pts): Someone is after the character and not to invite them over for tea. Someone wants the character either dead or in some other extremely bad situation. This could be the farmer whose livelihood was ruined when his field was burnt as a fire break by the character, while she tried to stop a rampaging wild fire from destroying a small town. Or it could be the local crime lord who used to own that diamond necklace the character wears all the time.

As before the point cost for this disadvantage should be determined by the director based on who's hunting the character and why.

Impulsive (+3 pts): The character with this disadvantage lacks the filter between their brain and the rest of their body that allows then to think before they speak or act. In short, anything that the player says, even in jest, the character does. If the player looks across the gaming table and says, "I'm going to kill you" because another player drank the last Mountain Dew, his character attacks the character of the player who drank the Mountain Dew.

Ineptitude (+3 or +5): We all have things we're good at. This character has one particular skill that he or she is terrible at. If it is a knowledge skill, this disadvantage is worth 3 points. If it is an active skill, it is worth 5 points. Regardless, it must be a skill that the character has actually put points into. Whenever the character attempts a test for that skill, he receives one less die than his score would normally indicate.

Lethargic (+2 pts): Some people hate to do more than they have to. This character is down right lazy. Anytime the character is attempting to perform a task, and his life is not in danger, it takes him twice as long as it would anyone else.

Low Pain Tolerance (+4 pts): When a character suffers damage, they receive penalties to certain actions. A character with this disadvantage has those penalties increased by 1.

Lowered Immunity (+1 pt): The character with this flaw has a weaker immune system than others of his race and age. She receives one less die for the purposes of resisting diseases than her scores indicate.

Missing Limb (+5 pts): The character is either missing a limb completely or has a limb that does not function at all. As usual, neither magic nor science can cure this ailment.

If the character is missing a leg, their movement (q.v) is cut in half. If they are missing an arm, they can only apply half of their strength dice to most strength tests. The director should adjudicate when this disadvantage affects the game.

Mood Swings (+2 pts): The character is prone to rapid changes in both mood and demeanor. This should be role-played to function appropriately; however, if the player does not role-play this disadvantage, the director should feel free to penalize social interactions to reflect the changing moods… and issue reduced experience points at the end of the session.

Mute (+6 pts): The character cannot talk. It goes without saying that this is a permanent problem. To simulate this, the player should not talk to anyone at the gaming table other than the director. The character may communicate with other players through pantomime or drawing.

Mysterious Past (+6 pts): The character knows nothing of his past. Players who want to select this flaw are encouraged to tell the director and have the director to create the character.

Night Blindness (+2 pts): The character sees only half as far at night as a normal character of his or her race and age.

Notorious (+3 pts): Everyone gets 15 minutes of fame and this character used theirs for something very bad. The character receives 1 less die on social rolls with the authorities. However, their notoriety does earn them an extra die when dealing with the criminal element.

Obvious Magic (+3 pts): When a character casts a spell, they leave their arcane signature in the immediate area. This signature dissipates over time. However that dissipation happens much slower for a character with this flaw. The magical signature of a character with this disadvantage lasts twice as long as those of other spell casters.

Out of Touch (+6 pts): The character with this disadvantage is simply out of touch with the world around them. They suffer a +4 penalty to any reason or insight test related to noticing things. This includes, but is not limited to, searching for hidden or secret people, places, or things, discerning lies, and initiative. It does not, however, apply to attack rolls.

Overweight (+2 pt): The character is "big boned" though as many times as I've heard this expression, I have yet to see a "big boned" skeleton… including my own. The character's carrying capacity is only ¾ what it would normally be for a person with their strength because of the extra weight they are carrying naturally. In addition, they fatigue at a faster rate. Whenever there is a variable involved in how fast a character is fatigued, it is halved for the overweight character.

Again, while this may seem harsh to you, as a person who has this disadvantage in the real world, I assure you that these affects are realistic.

Pacifist (+8 pts): The character is a pacifist. They will not draw a weapon or take the life of another living creature under any circumstances. Should the character cause harm to another creature, they will be over wrought with guilt. In addition, they will earn no experience until they have atoned for their misdeed.

Paralyzed (+6 or +8): the character is paralyzed. This may be just their arms or legs (-6 pts) or their entire body from the neck down (-8 pts). In any case, this will obviously cause some major problems for the character.

Past Life Regressions (+4 pts): Quite a few people believe that our souls return to the earth and we are reborn. For the character with this disadvantage, this isn't just a belief, it's a reality. This character can actually remember glimpses of his or her past lives. Unfortunately, these glimpses come in the form of flash backs and seem to happen at the most inopportune times. The character receives no additional skills or abilities as a result of these memories.

Phobia (varies): The character with this disadvantage has an irrational fear of something. The number of additional points earned by this disadvantage varies depending on the object of this fear and the frequency in which this object would be encountered.

Rare objects are things the character is not likely to encounter during the course of play. This category includes things like plants that exist only in a remote corner of the Lady's Rock & animals only encountered in the depths of the aether.

Uncommon objects are things that the character will probably encounter, but not too often. Uncommon objects include things like magical potions. This category also included those things which are common, but can be easily avoided. Like a particular type of alcohol.

Common items are things that the character is likely to encounter in everyday life. These are things that can only be avoided with great care and caution. Common items include the metals used to mint coins, craft jewelry, and forge weapons. This category also includes animals used throughout the course of everyday life such as horses. While it is possible to avoid common items, it can only be done at a great inconvenience to the character.

Very common objects, on the other hand, are things that the character has no hope of avoiding no matter how careful they may be. This category includes things like player races.

For each level of severity, the character loses one die for the purposes of any test made while in the presence of the object of his or her fears.

Points	Substance	Points	Severity
1	Rare	1	Mild
2	Uncommon	2	Moderate
3	Common	3	Severe
4	Very Common	4	Crippling

As an example, Thorfin, the dwarven warrior, has a severe allergy to elves. This disadvantage earned him an extra 7 build points. However, anytime there is an elf present,

Thorfin suffers a penalty of 3 dice on all tests. This includes his initiative, attack rolls, and skill tests. Thorfin would be in sad shape if the elves ever attacked his home en masse.

Poor Vision (Varies): The character with this disadvantage is either near-sighted or far-sighted. This disadvantage is worth 1 point for every two points of penalty that the character incurs.

This cost may seem disproportionate, but this disadvantage can be overcome through the use of corrective eyewear.

Near-sighted characters suffer a penalty to any action where they must see something further away than their PER score in yards. Far-sighted character's, meanwhile, suffer a penalty to any action where they must observe something closer than their Reason score in yards.

Sanctity of Life (+5 pts): Most character's value life…especially their own. A character with this disadvantage values all life. In fact, he values it so much that he will not take a life unless there is absolutely no other choice.

The character can only take up arms in defense of himself or others. Furthermore, he must always attack to subdue or cause the least amount of injury possible to any person he attacks.

Secret Life (+3 pts): Some how the character has managed to lead two separate lives. The player must decide what two lives the character leads and which is common knowledge and which is secret. If the character has other advantages such as contacts or disadvantages like enemies, it must be decided which identity those advantages and disadvantages belong to.

Uncouth (+2 pts): For some reason a character with this disadvantage doesn't comprehend simple social etiquette as well as others. The character constantly says and does things that are inappropriate and crude. The character suffers a +2 penalty on all social interactions.

Uneducated (+3 pts): Though basic education is fairly common through out the empire, this character managed to slip through the cracks. He or she received significantly less of an education than most people. Because of this, a character who is uneducated receives only 5 points worth of knowledge skills per point of knowledge instead of the standard 7 points.

Vindictive (+4 pts): Most characters have a vindictive streak. This character has one a mile wide. The character must avenge any slight to his or her "honor" whether that slight is real or imagined. If the character fails to take revenge, he or she earns no experience until the scales are balanced.

Wanted (varies): The character not only has a criminal record, but he has yet to stand trial for his offense. In other words, this character is a fugitive. If he has violated Ecclesiastic or Imperial Law, this disadvantage is worth 6 points. Provincial Law is worth 4 points. Tributarial violations earn 2 points while local violations are worth only one point.

Ward (varies): The character has someone who depends on them for their very survival. This might be a spouse, child, or other family members. Or it might be the son of famous circus acrobats who were killed by a mob boss who was extorting money out of the circus and sabotaged their trapeze equipment as a warning to those who might try to defy him that you met while investigating the murder. Though that seems a bit far fetched, don't you think?

The director should determine the point value of this disadvantage based on the needs of the dependent. Someone who merely needs you to help with the rent once a month is worth much less than someone who needs medical attention.

Weak-Willed (+5 pts): The character is one of those people who have a hard time saying no. He almost always helps those who ask for it… even at significant personal cost. He is generally considered to be a push-over… a sucker… an easy mark.

Equipment

Despite the best efforts of the Imperial Navy, trade on the Lady's Rock is still a dangerous venture. Sometimes goods that are common in more developed areas are nearly impossible to come by in more rural regions and completely unknown on the fringes of civilization. What might be common in one city may be precious and rare in another.

The market places of large cities are full of merchants peddling their wares. Specialized weapon and armor smiths compete to provide the highest quality merchandise at competitive prices. Bower and fletchers import the most flexible and resilient branches for the construction of bows. It is a buyer's market.

The rural communities are a much different story. Often one lone blacksmith handles all the metal working needs of the area. The local cooper might also build wagons. It is a rough existence and people are forced to make due with what they have in order to survive.

Regardless, in most rural areas, trade is accomplished through bartering. The local farmer might trade eggs or other foodstuffs from the things he needs from the blacksmith. The blacksmith might, in turn, pay off his bar tab by producing metal tankards for the tavern.

Weapons

Combat is an important part of most role-playing games. That being the case, many players can not wait to purchase weapons for their characters. Many players read through the weapons list trying to squeeze every last ounce of damage out of their attacks.

In the d10 system, the damage dealt by a weapon has more to do with the character's skill with that weapon than with the weapon itself. This allows you to select a weapon based on your character rather than something simply intended to inflict the most damage on your opponent.

Weapon Qualities

Every weapon in the game can be broken down into statistics that are used to determine how the weapon behaves and the damage it does.

Hands: This column lists the number of hands that are normally required to use the weapon effectively.

Some weapons have two numbers listed meaning that the weapon can be used with either one or two hands. If this is the case, the other statistics for the weapon will also be separated to show the differences between one-hand and two-hand use.

Difficulty: Some weapons are more difficult to effectively wield than others. This number is the character's target number to hit a target with his or her chosen weapon.

Damage Rating (DR): The damage rating of a weapon indicates how many points of damage are done to the target *per net success* of the attacker (see combat page XXXX).

Damage Bonus (DB): Just as some weapons are more accurate than others, some weapons are deadlier… and some are less deadly. This trait is accounted for by the weapons damage bonus. This number is added to the total damage inflicted after all other calculations have taken place. (For those of you who don't know, adding a negative number is the same as subtracting a positive number.)

Note: A character using a melee weapon can add his or her strength score to the damage as well. A character who uses a one-handed weapon with two hands can add 1 ½ times his strength. Thrown weapons only receive ½ of the character's strength as a bonus to damage.

Range Increment (RI): All weapons have a range increment. This increment represents the size of each of 5 range categories - close, short, medium, long, and extreme range.

Range	Penalty
Close	+0
Short	+1
Medium	+3
Long	+6
Extreme	+10

The difficulty of using a ranged weapon is for use at close range. At each range category beyond close, it becomes more difficult to hit the target. The adjacent table shows the increase to difficulty based on the range category.

For example, a throwing axe has a range increment of 10. Targets between 0 and 10 feet are in close range. Targets from 11-20 feet are in short range and the difficulty to use the weapon increase from a 5 to a 6. Targets from 21-30 feet are at medium range and the target number to hit them is a 7. This pattern continues until the weapon reaches the end of its 5th range category – extreme. Beyond this point, the weapon is no longer effective.

Type: This is the type of damage inflicted by the weapon. There are 7 types of damage in the d10 system – Stun, Bludgeoning, Piercing, Slashing, Crushing, Energy, and Supernatural (see Damage Types on page XXXX).

Cost: The final category is the average price of the item. Keep in mind that this price may vary based on availability, quality, and how much the merchant likes you.

Note: A character can only effectively wield a weapon whose damage rating is less than or equal to his STR attribute plus 1. In other words, a character with a strength of 3 can only effectively wield weapons with a damage rating of 4 or lower.

- **Hand-to-Hand Weapons**

Gauntlets: Gauntlets provide one of the few means of doing actual physical damage with an unarmed strike. They are normally composed of interconnecting metal plates attached to a leather surface. They provide some protection to the wearer's hands.

Gauntlets, Locking: One example of specialty gauntlets, locking gauntlets are designed with a unique mechanism that allows them to lock in place when grasping a weapon or other item. Locking the gauntlets is a free action, but releasing the locking mechanism does require one full action.

Gauntlets, Spiked: Adding spikes to any weapon causes a portion of the damage dealt to become piercing damage. Spike gauntlets have a damage rating of 3. Two points of that damage is considered impact while one is considered piercing. The damage bonus is always considered to be piercing damage in these cases.

- **Impact Weapons**

Chain: A chain is simply that – a length of chain. When used as a weapon, the chain is usually weighted at one or both ends. Some wielders even attached spikes to the chain to increase the damage.

Club: Technically anything from a chair leg to a baseball bat qualifies as a club. Clubs are generally large blunt wooden objects. They can be found almost anywhere; however, some craftsmen do fashion these implements out of hardwood and sell them to the populace.

Flail: A flail is a blunt weapon composed of three pieces - a handle, a chain, and a head. The head of the weapon may be another shaft or it may be a ball like the head of a mace. Heavy flails are larger and inflict more damage than light flails.

Hammer: A hammer, both light and heavy, consists of a wooden shaft and a metal or stone head usually rectangular is shape.

Mace: A mace consists of a handle, usually constructed out of wood, topped with a dense ball of metal or wood.

Maul: A maul is a large weighted hammer used predominantly by military and law-enforcement personnel for the purpose of opening locked doors. Incidentally, it can also be very effective against non-door opponents though its use in this capacity is somewhat limited.

Morning Star: A morning star is effectively a mace that's head has been adorned with spikes.

Quarterstaff: A quarterstaff is a long wooden staff typically ranging from 6 to 9 ½ feet in length. It is most often wielded two handed and has a variety of alternative uses. Some people shod their quarter staves in iron so that they cause additional damage.

Sap: A small device consisting of some blunt material covered in leather with a short and flexible strap or shaft attached to one end. It is most often used in an attempt to knock a foe unconscious.

War Hammer: A war hammer is a large hammer usually with a shaped metal head that is specifically designed for use in combat.

Some war hammers are designed with a blunt hammer-like face opposite a sharp pick-like face. In this case use the war hammer statistics for the blunt face and the heavy pick statistics for the piercing face.

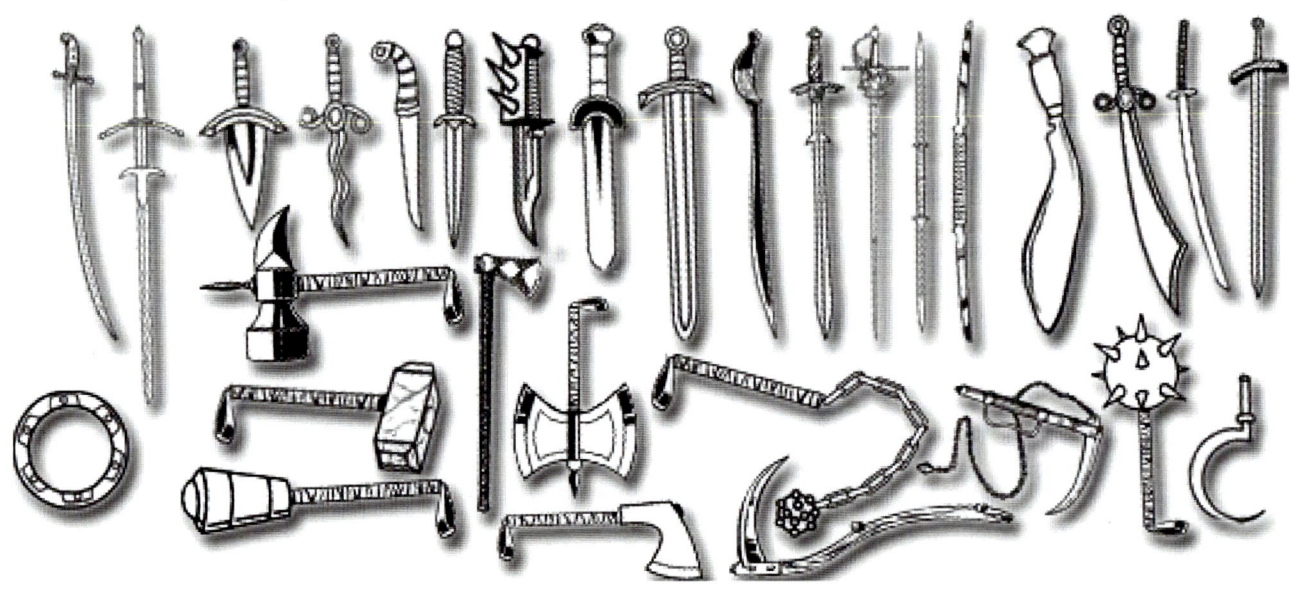

Whip: A whip is a piece of braided leather. In the hands of an expert, or an archeologist, it can be a tool and weapon of nearly unparalleled versatility. In the hands of an amateur, it can be more dangerous to the wielder than their foe.

- **Edged Weapons**

Axe: Axes are a staple of combat on the Lady's Rock. An axe consists of a wooden shaft topped with a broad blade-like head.

Four common variations of war axes are known to exist. The *hand axe* is the smallest and resembles a hatchet. The *battle axe* is slightly larger and most often used by military forces. The *bipennis* is a double headed battle axe. The extra blade adds weight and damage. By far the largest is the *great axe*. It is a hulking weapon designed to cleave foes in twain.

Cutlass: A cutlass is a short sword with a slightly curved blade. It was designed for use by naval officers fighting in the cramped quarters aboard ship and is incredibly accurate.

Dagger: A dagger is a small bladed weapon with two cutting edges that functions both as a tool and a weapon. Most people carry a dagger somewhere on their person whenever they venture outside of their home.

Dirk: A dirk is a specialized type of dagger. It is slightly longer than a standard dagger. A dirk comes to a very sharp point and is primarily used for thrusting rather than cutting though it does have dual cutting edges.

Dirks are usually sheathed on the sword arm of the wielder and are popular among warriors. The traditional warrior greeting of shaking hands high on the arm developed to check and see if your opponent was carrying a dirk so sheathed.

Falchion: A falchion is a short, broad sword with a convex cutting edge. The falchion combines the weight and power of an axe with the shape and versatility of a sword.

Pick: A pick is a weapon fashioned from a metal rod that is pointed at both ends and is attached perpendicular to a wooden handle. Of course, heavy picks are heavier than light picks and do more damage because of it.

Rapier: A rapier is a light, sharp pointed sword often with a cup or basket-like hilt used for thrusting. Rapiers do not, as a general rule, possess a cutting edge.

Saber: The land-borne cousin of the cutlass, the saber is also a short sword with a slightly curved blade. However, because it is most often used on land, and therefore against armored opponents, it is heavier than the cutlass. This causes it to do slightly more damage at the expense of accuracy.

Sickle: This weapon was originally created as a farming implement. It is a semi-circular blade attached to a handle made of wood, though some sickles have handles of horn.

Sword: The sword is, by far, the most common weapon used on the Lady's Rock. A sword is composed of a blade, a handle, and a cross-guard called a hilt. Some swords are very ornate and have jewels set into the hilt or the end of the handle, called the pommel.

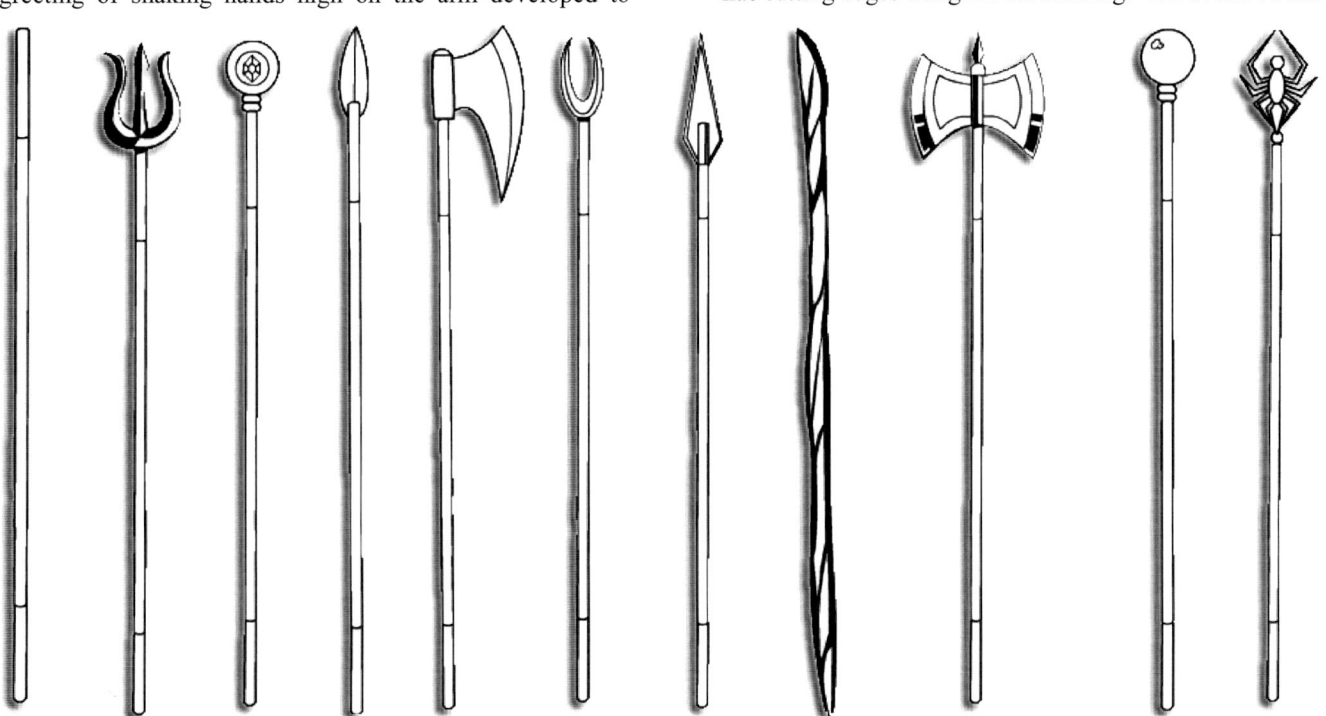

Five major varieties of sword can be found in use throughout the empire. The *short sword* is a piercing weapon with a short, narrow blade ending in a sharp point. The *long sword* is a longer version of the short sword and has cutting edges designed for slashing. The *broad sword* is effectively a heavier version of the long sword. The *great sword* is a longer than the average man is tall and must be wielded in two hands to be used effectively.

The last type of common sword, the *bastard sword* is unique in that it is designed to fall somewhere between a long, broad sword and a great sword. It can be wielded either one or two handed. When wielded in two hands, the bastard sword two-handed, the wielders effective strength score is considered 1 ½ times his normal rating. (See the section entitled "*Two Hands on a one-handed weapon*" on page 134.)

The *Double-Bladed Sword* can also be found though it is exceedingly rare. It consists of two sword blades attached at opposite sides of an elongated handle. A double-bladed sword can be equipped with piercing points, slashing edges, or a combination of both.

- **Polearms**

Glaive: A glaive is a knife-like blade crossed with that of a cleaver and attached to a long wooden shaft

Guisarme: A guisarme is similar to the glaive except that the point of the blade is reversed to form a hook.

Halberd: A halberd is a cross between a spear, an axe, and a pike all melded together and placed on top a pole to form a brutally effective weapon.

Ranseur: A ranseur is a long spear with a broad spear-like head and a crescent shaped hilt directly beneath the point. It is shaped much like a trident, but unlike that weapon, only the center spear point is capable of inflicting damage.

Scythe: A scythe is a farming implement adapted for use as a weapon. It's long curved single-edged blade is attached to a crooked handle. Its association with death gives this weapon a fearsome appearance that far outweighs its effectiveness.

- **Ranged Weapons**

Axe, Throwing: A throwing axe is an axe-like blade attached to a handle and weighted to be thrown effectively.

Bow: Several types of bows exist on the Lady's Rock. Each type has a different effective range and causes a different amount of damage depending on the ammunition used.

Crossbows: Crossbows look like little bows turned sideways and mounted to a rifle-like stock. They come in 4 basic types – Hand, Light, Heavy, and Arbalest. The arbalest is a heavy crossbow made of flexible metal instead of wood.

Dagger, Throwing: A throwing dagger is a dagger specifically designed for use as a throwing weapon. It is perfectly balanced and, in the right hands, can be deadly.

Dart: A dart is similar in appearance to an arrow or a bolt except that the shaft is thicker.

Firearms: Even though firearms have been around for a while, they still remain rare. This is largely due to the costs involved in owning one.

Firearms are another example of techno-magic. Smoke powder is added to bullets that are then placed in a special chamber in the handle capable of holding 25 bullets. The act of pulling the trigger causes an enchanted crystal to teleport a bullet from the handle to the firing chamber and detonates the smoke powder. The resulting explosion propels the bullet toward the target at an outrageous speed. The weighted "hammer" then serves to reset the mechanism for the next shot.

Three basic styles of firearm currently exist in Eristonia. The first is the Blunderbuss. This weapon was devised specifically to fire a large number of bullets covering a large area. Each shot fired by the blunder buss expels 5 bullets giving the blunderbuss a 5 shot capacity.

The second is the short arm, commonly referred to as a pistol. This single-handed weapon was created for use by officers as a last line of defense. Its effectiveness has caused it to find more widespread use today. It fires a single bullet with each shot.

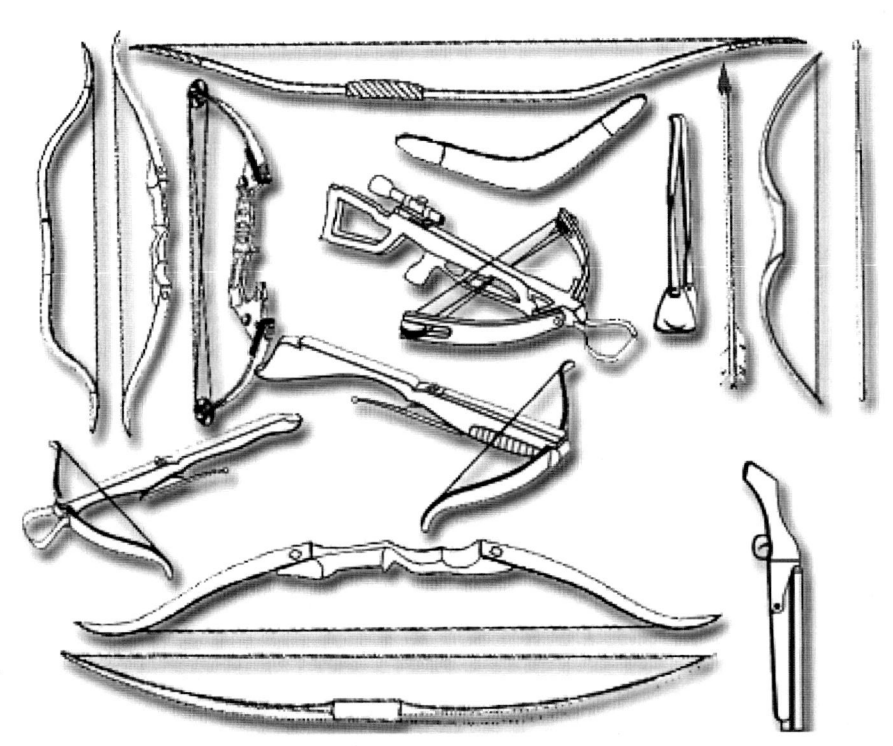

The last of the three is the long arm, or rifle as it is often called. The long arm is effectively a techno-magical heavy crossbow that fires bullets rather than bolts. If it wasn't for the increased penetrating power offered by the firearm, it probably wouldn't see much if any use.

Javelin: A javelin is a light spear crafted to be used strictly as a thrown weapon.

Spear: A spear is long flexible pole tipped with a metal point.

- **Ammunition**

Arrows: The projectiles fired by bows are called arrows. Arrows can be purchased with a variety of arrowheads each with a different purpose.

Flight arrows are small and unobtrusive providing excellent accuracy at the cost of some potential damage. The statistics for the bows on the weapons table show the statistics for the flight arrow because it is the most common.

Broad head arrows do more damage than flight arrows but are not as accurate. The Difficulty of using the bow increases by 1 and the weapon gains a damage bonus of 1 as well.

Swept Head arrows look like a "V." The long barded ends tear into flesh as the arrow pierces the body. This arrow is expensive. It is no less accurate than a flight arrow and as deadly as a broad head arrow.

Tri-foil arrows are the most highly sought after. They are constructed of three blades sharing a common point and provide a good mix of accuracy and damage. The difficulty of using a bow firing tri-foil arrows decreases by 1 while the damage bonus increases by two. Of course, only a master fletcher can craft these fabulous arrows.

Forked arrows see little use. They were designed for use cutting rigging aboard ship, but, as techno-magic became more popular, the use of riggings decreased drastically. The accuracy of using these arrows decreases by 1, but their damage rating (*NOT bonus damage*) is decreased by 1.

Bolts: Bolts are the ammunition used by crossbows. They look very similar to arrows but they are about half as long. They come with the same variety of tips that arrows do with the same affect on the crossbows statistics.

Bullets: Bullets are deceptively simple in form appearing to be small spheres of metal. Alone they are not dangerous at all, but, when mixed with smoke powder, they become one of the more dangerous weapons ever developed.

Ammunition*	Difficulty	Damage Rating	Damage Bonus	Type	Cost	Cost per 10
Arrows						
Broad Head Arrows	+1	+0	+1	P	7 Secs	7 Lances
Flight Arrows	+0	+0	+0	P	5 Secs	5 Lances
Forked Arrows	-1	-1	+0	S	6 Secs	6 Lances
Swept Head Arrows	+0	+0	+1	P	8 Secs	8 Lances
Tri-Foil Arrows	-1	+0	+2	P	1 Lance	1 Brig
Bolts						
Broad Head Arrows	+1	+0	+1	P	1 Lance 4 Secs	1 Brig 4 Lances
Flight Arrows	+0	+0	+0	P	1 Lance	1 Brig
Forked Arrows	-1	-1	+0	S	1 Lance 2 Secs	1 Brig 2 Lances
Swept Head Arrows	+0	+0	+1	P	1 Lance 6 Secs	1 Brig 6 Lances
Tri-Foil Arrows	-1	+0	+2	P	2 Lances	2 Brigs
Ballistics						
Bullets	+0	+0	+0	B&P	2 Lances	2 Brigs
Cannon Balls, Round Shot	+0	+0	+0	N	3 Brigs / Pound	3 Stars / Pound
Cannon Balls, Grape Shot	+1	0	-1	N	5 Brigs / Pound	5 Stars / Pound
Cannon Balls, Chain Shot	-1	0	+1	N	1 Star / Pound	10 Stars / Pound

* The numbers listed on this chart are added or subtracted to the statistics listed for each weapon type.

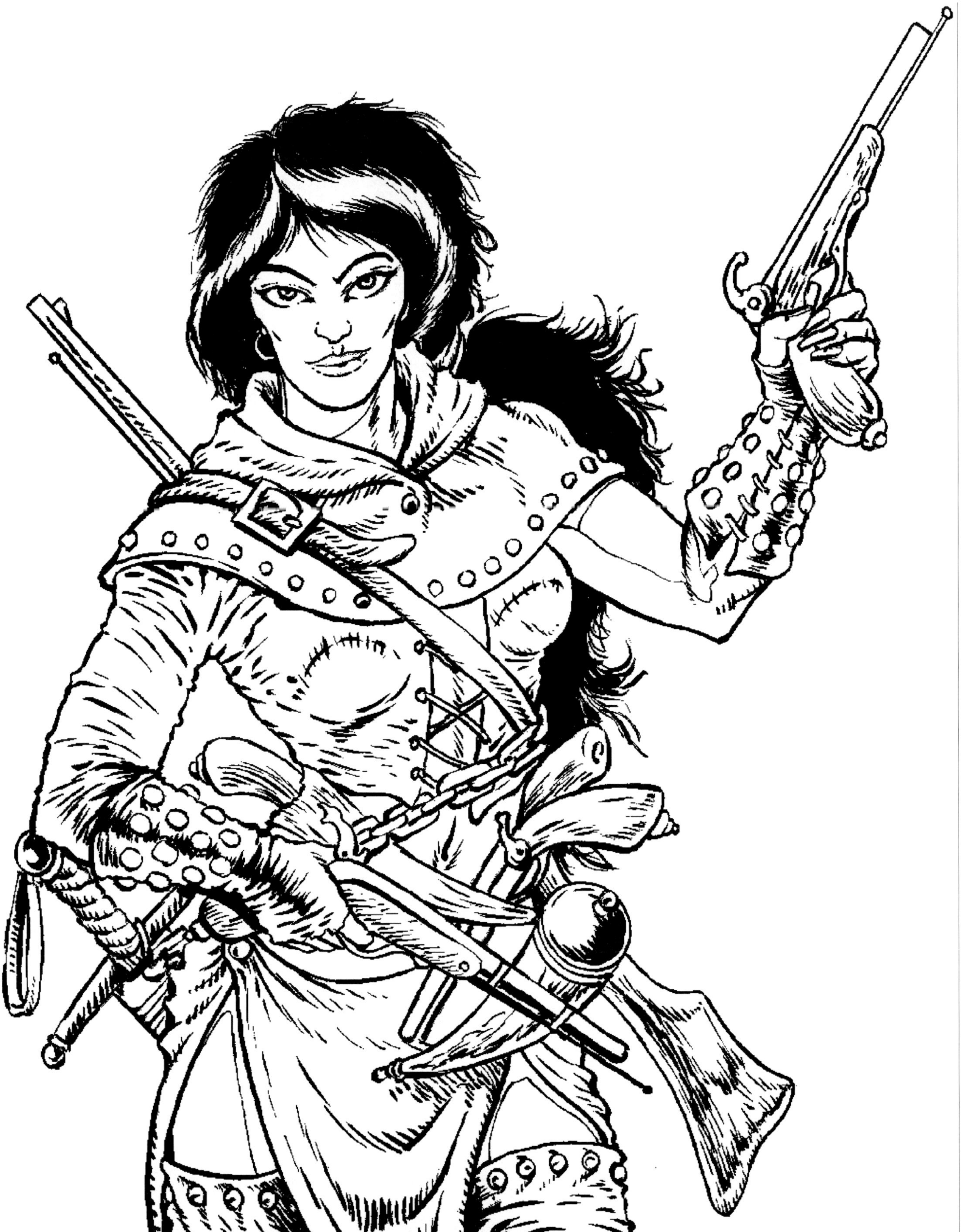

Weapons Skill	Weapon	Hands	Difficulty	Damage Rating	Damage Bonus	Range Increment	Damage Type	Cost
Basic	Claws	1	3	2	+1	-	P/S	N/A
	Club	1	5	2		-	B	8 Lances
	Dagger	1	3	1		5	S/P	2 Brigs 5 Lances
	Dagger, Punching	1	3	1		-	P	3 Brigs
	Gauntlet	1	3	1	-1	-	B	2 Brigs
	Horns (Gore)	1	3	3		-	P	N/A
	Quarterstaff	2	4	2		-	B	1 Brig
	Sickle	1	4	2		-	S	6 Brigs
Edged	Axe, Battle	1	6	3		-	C	15 Brigs 5 Lances
	Axe, Bearded	2	6	3	+1	-	C	37 Brigs 5 Lances
	Axe, Bipennis	2	6	4		-	C	27 Brigs 5 Lances
	Axe, Dwarven War	1	7	4		-	C	30 Brigs
	Axe, Great	2	7	5		-	C	20 Brigs
	Axe, Hand	1	6	2		5	S	6 Brigs
	Axe, Orc Double*	2	6	3/3		-	S	60 Brigs
	Urgosh, Dwarven*	2	6	3/2		-	S/P	50 Brigs
	Falchion	2	5	3	+1	-	S	75 Brigs
	Scimitar	1	4	2		-	S	15 Brigs
	Sword, Bastard	1/2	6/5	3/4		-	S/C	35 Brigs
	Sword, Broad	1	5	3	+1	-	C	25 Brigs
	Sword, Great	2	5	5	+1	-	C	50 Brigs
	Sword, Long	1	5	3		-	S	20 Brigs
	Warsabre	1	5	3	+1	-	S	20 Brigs
	Dagger	1	3	1		5	S/P	2 Brigs 5 Lances
	Dagger, Punching	1	3	1		-	P	3 Brigs
	Rapier	1	4	2		-	P	20 Brigs
	Sword, Short	1	4	2		-	S	10 Brigs
	Sword, Two-bladed*	2	7	2/2		-	S	100 Brigs
Impact	Chain	2	6	2		-	B&EN	15 Brigs
	Chain, Spiked	2	6	3	+1	-	B&P	25 Brigs
	Flail	1	6	3		-	C	8 Brigs
	Flail, Dire*	2	7	3/3	+1	-	C	90 Brigs
	Flail, Heavy	2	6	4		-	C	15 Brigs
	Whip	1	5	1	-3	-	B	4 Brigs 5 Lances
	Club	1	5	2		-	B	8 Lances
	Club, Great	2	5	4		-	C	5 Brigs
	Mace, Heavy	1	5	3		-	C	12 Brigs
	Mace, Light	1	5	2		-	B	5 Brigs
	Morningstar	1	6	3	+1	-	C	8 Brigs
	Quarterstaff	2	4	2		-	B	1 Brig
	Sap	1	4	2		-	B	1 Brig
	Hammer, Gnome Hooked*	2	7	3/2		-	B/P	20 Brigs
	Hammer, Light	1	5	1		10	B	1 Brigs
	Hammer, War	1	5	3		-	C	12 Brigs
	Maul	1	5	4		-	C	22 Brigs
	Maul, Great	2	5	5	+2	-	C	35 Brigs
	Pick, Heavy	1	5	2		-	P	8 Brigs
	Pick, Light	1	5	1		-	P	4 Brigs
	Scythe	2	6	3	+2	-	S	18 Brigs

Weapons Skill	Weapon	Hands	Difficulty	Damage Rating	Damage Bonus	Range Increment	Damage Type	Cost
Reach	Glaive	2	7	4		-	S	8 Brigs
	Guisarme	2	7	3	+1	-	S	9 Brigs
	Halberd	2	6	4		-	S	10 Brigs
	Quarterstaff©	2	4	2		-	B	1 Brig
	Ranseur	2	7	3	+1	-	P	10 Brigs
	Javelin	1	6	2		30	P	1 Brig
	Lance	1^M	7	5		-	P	10 Brigs
	Spear	1	6	3		20	P	2 Brigs
	Spear, Long®	2	6	3		-	P	5 Brigs
	Spear, Short©	1	5	2		20	P	1 Brig
	Trident	2	5	3	+2	10	P	15 Brigs

Weapons Skill	Weapon	Hands	Difficulty	Damage Rating	Damage Bonus	Range Increment	Rate of Fire	Damage Type	Cost
Firearms	Blunderbuss	2	3**	4		10	1/3 Acts	B&P	200 Brigs
	Longarms (Rifles)	2	4**	4	+1	40	1/2 Acts	B&P	575 Brigs
	Shortarms (Pistols)	1	4**	4		20	1/1 Acts	B&P	300 Brigs
Gunnery	Ballista	N/A	6**	2		120	1/6 Acts	N	500 Brigs
	Cannon, 1-pounder	N/A	6**	1		15	1/4 Acts	N	3500 Brigs
	Cannon, 6-pounder	N/A	6**	2		30	1/4 Acts	N	6500 Brigs
	Cannon, 9-pounder	N/A	7**	3		45	1/4 Acts	N	12000 Brigs
	Cannon, 12-pounder	N/A	7**	4	2	60	1/4 Acts	N	20000 Brigs
	Cannon, 18-pounder	N/A	8**	5		90	1/4 Acts	N	35000 Brigs
	Cannon, 32-pounder	N/A	9**	8		125	1/4 Acts	N	65000 Brigs
	Cannon, 60-pounder	N/A	10**	12		250	1/4 Acts	N	120000 Brigs
Launch	Catapult, Light	N/A	6**	2		150	1/5 Acts	N	550 Brigs
	Catapult, Heavy	N/A	6**	3		200	1/6 Acts	N	800 Brigs
	Trebuchett	N/A	6**	4		250	1/8 Acts	N	1000 Brigs
Projectile	Bow, Long	2	5**	3		100	1/1 Act	P	75 Brigs
	Bow, Long Composite	2	5**	3		110	1/1 Act	P	100 Brigs
	Bow, Short	2	5**	2		60	1/1 Act	P	30 Brigs
	Bow, Short Composite	2	5**	2		70	1/1 Act	P	75 Brigs
	Crossbow, Hand	1	4**	1	+1	30	1/1 Acts	P	100 Brigs
	Crossbow, Heavy	2	4**	4	+1	120	1/3 Acts	C&P	50 Brigs
	Crossbow, Light	2	4**	3	+1	80	1/2 Acts	P	35 Brigs
	Crossbow, Repeating Heavy	2	5**	4		120	1/1 Act	C&P	400 Brigs
	Crossbow, Repeating Light	2	5**	3		80	1/1 Act	P	250 Brigs
Ranged	Bolas	1	5**	1		10	-	B&EN	5 Brigs
	Grenades	1	4**	Varies		20	-	Varies	Varies
	Net	1	5**	-		10	-	EN	20 Brigs
	Sling	1	5**	2		50	-	B	1 Brig 5 Lances
	Axe, Throwing	1	5**	2		10	-	S	8 Brigs
	Dagger, Throwing	1	5**	1		10	-	P	2 Brigs 5 Lances
	Dart	1	5**	1	+1	20	-	P	5 Lances
	Javelin	1	5**	2		30	-	P	1 Brig

^M = This weapon is designed for Mounted use. Using it when not mounted requires 2 hands and the difficulty increases by 3

* = You must be specialized in this weapon in order to use it.

** = Difficulty adjustment for range increment applies to this weapon.

© = Despite this weapon being usable by those proficient in "Reach" weapons, it does not provide a "reach" benefit in combat.

® = Weapon provides an additional square of "reach" to the attacker.

Armor	Armor Value	Cost
Light		
Padded Armor	1	5 Brigs
Soft Leather Armor	2	9 Brigs
Studded Leather Armor	3	23 Brigs
Hard Leather Armor	4	15 Brigs
Medium		
Chain Shirt	4	97 Brigs
Hide Armor	3	15 Brigs
Ring Armor	5	50 Brigs
Chainmail	5	126 Brigs
Heavy		
Scale Armor	7	60 Brigs
Breastplate	5	168 Brigs
Splint Armor	8	184 Brigs
Banded Armor	8	130 Brigs
Half-Plate Armor	7	666 Brigs
Full Plate Armor	9	1,310 Brigs

* = A character who wears armor suffers a penalty to all physical skills (those based on STR, CRD, QCK, & CON, as well as initiative, equal to ½ the difference between the armor value and the character's strength.

Armor & Shield

Now that we've covered how to hurt other people, let's discuss the equipment that's going to keep you from getting killed… or at least slow the moment of your impending doom.

Defining Armor

First and foremost, armor only protects you from physical attacks that attempt to penetrate the armor. Armor does not protect you from the effects of poisons or toxins; it does not shield you from the effects of fatigue. It does not protect you if you are not wearing it. This may seem like too obvious a statement to make, but that doesn't mean that some people in the audience don't need to hear it.

Armor is divided into three categories – light, medium, and heavy. Each category of armor has a particular type of damage that it is more susceptible to than other damages. Slashing weapons have their target number to gaff increased to a 5 (rather than 3) versus opponents in light armor. Medium armors do the same for piercing weapons. Heavy armors are more vulnerable to crushing weapons.

- **Armor Value**

Armor Value is used to determine how well the armor protects the character. Reduce the power of the weapon by the armor value of the attack to a minimum of one (see Gaffing Damage on page XXXX).

Armor does not protect against magical spells that do not protect against magical damage.

One of the big problems with armor is that, in general, the more protective the armor is, the heavier it is. Heavier armor is less flexible restricts movement. To represent this fact, any character whose strength is less than the armor value (q.v.) of the armor they are wearing suffers a penalty to all defense tests & skill tests based on physical attributes, as well as, initiative checks equal to the ½ the difference between the character's strength and the armor value.

For example, a character with a strength of 4 who is wearing scale armor looses 2 dice from each of their skill tests, defense test, and his initiative rolls.

Armor Descriptions

Armor is more than just a means of defending oneself from attack; it is also a status symbol. The average farmer could not hope to afford full-plate armor and a member of the imperial peerage would never be seen on the battlefield wearing padded armor.

Not only does the armor you wear reflect your status in society, the way you refer to your armor betrays your place in the social hierarchy as well. Those who do not know better, who did not have the luxury of private tutor, often refer to all metal armors as "mails."

Strictly speaking, the term "mail" should be applied only to those armors constructed of interlocking links of metal that form a mesh. Other armors may include portions of mail, especially around joints, but they are simply armor, not "mail."

Padded Armor: Padded armor consists of several quilted layers of cloth and batting. Padded armor is hot, causing its wearer to sweat profusely. This makes the armor smell like a cross between wet dog and dirty gym socks after even a short time "out on the road." Padded armor is a breeding ground for lice and other parasites.

Soft Leather Armor: Soft leather armor is a supple type of leather that is tanned using tannin primarily derived from oak bark, animal brains, and other animal fats. The leather is then heavily smoked to prevent it from rotting.

Studded Leather Armor: Studded leather is similar to soft leather except that a myriad of metal studs have been attached to. These metal studs provide additional protection.

Hard Leather Armor: The soft leathers that make soft leather armor are boiled in oil or wax causing the armor to harden. The resulting leather is harder than soft armor, but it is less flexible.

Chain Shirt: A chain shirt is a simple shirt of chainmail the covers the wearer's torso, pelvis, upper arms and upper thighs. It is lighter than a full suit of chainmail offering greater mobility. However, it leaves are portions of the character's body unprotected.

Hide Armor: Hide armors are crafted from several layers of leathers and animal hides. It is common among tribal peoples who do not have access to advanced techniques to tan and treat leather & hides available in more civilized areas.

Ring Armor: Ring armor is made by attaching metal rings onto a backing of stiff leather.

Chainmail: The most advanced of the medium armors, chainmail is a mesh of interwoven metal links.

Scale Armor: Scale armors are made from overlapping metal scales. These scales are often shaped like the scales of a serpent, but can be stylized by more affluent wearers. Wealthy merchants often wear armor that has scales shaped like coins. Elven nobility wear scale armor that has scales shaped like oak leaves.

Breastplate: A breastplate covers your torso, front and back. When sold as armor, a breastplate comes with greaves to protect your shins, a helmet, and a skirt of studded leather to protect your thighs.

Splint Armor: Splint armor is crafted by attaching thin, vertical strips of metal to a leather backing.

Banded Armor: Banded armor is very similar to splint armor except that the strips of metal run horizontally rather than vertically.

Half-Plate Armor: Half-plate armor is a suit of chainmail with metal plates attached to protect the torso, legs, and arms.

Full-Plate Armor: Full-Plate is the type of armor you think of when you think of knights in shining armor. Each suit of full-plate is custom fitted for the person who will be wearing it.

Defining Shields

As with Armor, a shield can only protect you from something that you can use the shield to deflect.

Using a shield counts as fighting with two weapons (see two-weapons fighting on page XXXX).

- **Difficulty**

Shields are used to parry melee attacks (see parrying on page XXXX). This number represents the difficulty of parrying a melee attack with a particular shield.

- **Defense**

When you are parrying a blow, you are rolling an attack against your opponent's attack (see parrying on page XXXX). The defense rating of a shield is used to calculate the shield's damage for parrying… and only for parrying.

- **Damage**

Sometimes you need to hit someone and the only thing you have at hand is your shield. The number listed in the "damage" column is the damage rating of the shield when used as a weapon. Shield use is governed by either the impact weapons skill.

Shield Descriptions

Bucklers: Bucklers are small disks of wood or metal that are strapped to your forearm leaving your hand free.

Light Wood / Fabric Shield: These shields consist of cloth or thin pieces of wood attached to a wooden frame. They provide minimal protection from attacks, but are light and do not inhibit the wielder as much as some larger shields.

Light Steel Shields: These shields consist of a thin wooden framework covered with thin metal plates.

Heavy Wooden Shield: Heavy wooden shields are large planks of wood banded together by metal straps, much like a banded door. They are heavy, but provide good protection.

Heavy Steel Shield: These shields are crafted completely out of a thick piece of steel. They are large and, as you probably guessed, heavy.

Tower Shield: Tower shields are large and unwieldy. They are most often planted in the ground and used as cover, like a portable wall, rather than as a shield. In this game, tower shields can be used in either fashion.

When used to parry, tower shields function just like other shields. Using them as a means of cover, please see cover on page XXXX.

Shield	Difficulty	Defense	Damage	Cost
Buckler*	3	1/2	0	10 Brigs
Light Wood / Fabric	4	1	0	6 Brigs
Light Steel	5	2	1	29 Brigs
Heavy Wood	6	3	1	18 Brigs
Heavy Steel	7	4	2	47 Brigs
Tower**	9	5	3	65 Brigs

* = Bucklers cannot be used to parrying ranged attacks
** = Tower shields can be used as cover rather than to parry.

Adventuring Equipment

Most of us know what a tent is. I don't think I need to take the time to explain what a tankard is or what a shovel might be. That being the case, we're not going to waste your time or ours describing these things to you.

However, any item that has "superior" listed with its entry is of higher quality than a standard example of an item and adds or subtracts one from the target number as appropriate. Superior theives' tools reduce the target number of picking a lock by one while a superior lock increases the target number to pick it by one.

Technomagical Equipment

Technomagical equipment, as the name indicates, is a merger between magic and technology through a process called technomancy. These items are magical items that are so common that they are available in large cities and many smaller towns.

Aludel: The aludel is a special crucible that is used by alchemists to distill elemental essences for use as material components. Once a suitable vesswel is created, the aludel must be fired for 2 weeks in order for it to cure properly and be suitable for its intended use.

The aludel can hold 1 pound of material. Because coins require special treatment if distilled for elemental essence, only 12 of them can be processed at one time.

Athanor: The athanor is a special furnace used to distill the essences of elements from common objects. It takes quite a bit of time and skill to make an athanor. Once it has been constructed, it must be fired fired for a full lunar month in order to cure properly and be suitable for use in creating elemental essences.

The athanor is just large enough for an aludel to fit inside.

Dark Cells: Dark Cells are the small cylindrical objects that store the darkness drained from an area by dark-suckers (q.v.). Dark cells measure about two inches long and are about 1 inch in diameter. Dark Cells are more commonly referred to as "d-cells" by the general populace.

Dark-suckers: Dark-suckers are cylindrical objects usually about one foot in length and an inch and a half in diameter. Some varieties are as many as three feet long, reinforced, and often double as clubs. One end of the dark sucker is bell shaped and contains a mirrored concave surface that collects darkness and focuses it into the receptacle where it is transferred into the d-cells located inside the shaft.

Dwarf Goggles: Dwarf Goggles are constructed out of a pair of smoky lenses fitted into a large leather frame. The goggles are nearly impossible to see through even during the brightest days. However, in the complete absence of light, the Dwarf goggles allow the wearer to see clearly out to a range of 60 feet.

Elf Eyes: This eyewear is also composed of a set of lenses. These, however, are clear and easy to see through. These lenses are set into a delicate metal framework. The entire apparatus is worn like a normal pair of eyeglasses. Elf eyes do not obstruct vision in any way. As a matter of fact, they are enspelled to maintain a constant level of light to the wearer's eyes. This allows the wearer to see at his or her normal range even in conditions of limited light.

Floater: A floater is a device that looks much like a modern life jacket and serves a similar function. Characters wearing a floater are able to remain aloft in the aether. Characters without this device have the buoyancy of a rock of similar size and weight.

Imager: An imager is a roughly rectangular box measuring 4 ½ inches by 2 ½ inches by 1 inch. Directly in the front of the center of the device is a round opening covered with a convex mirror. This mirror serves to capture an exact image of whatever is directly in front of the imager.

Just to the right of the mirror as you are looking at the device is honey combed collection of mirrors. This device measures the ambient light of the area and adjusts the imager accordingly so that the images appear as if taken in broad daylight. A button located beneath this appliance turns it off allowing you to capture images at night without intensifying the light.

On the back of the device just above the center point is the "sighting box" which allows the user to see exactly what the imager sees. Some models have a selector lever near the sighting box that allows the user to change the device's field of vision.

Other models include a small screen on the back allowing for immediate review of the image. A rocker button allows scrolling through the images stored on the imager while another button allows you to keep or delete images depending on whether or not you like them. This is an expensive option and it increases the cost of the imager by a factor of three.

On the top of the imager is the capture button. Pressing this button causes the imager to capture the image. If the user holds this button down, it causes it to continuously capture the scene before it for viewing as a silent holopic. Some imagers include a dedicated mimic (q.v.) for use creating holopics with full sound.

On the bottom of the imager is the TP, or transfer port. This allows the user to transfer images from the imager to his or her WI-AT (q.v.) for viewing or printing.

A typical imager can hold up to 3000 still pictures or as many as 3 hours of holopic footage.

Mimic: A mimic is a small device much like an imager except that it captures sound rather than images. It is about 2 inches, by 1 ½ inches by ½ inch.

The top of the mimic contains a high powered microphone. The front contains a speaker while the back contains a view screen showing the amount of sound recorded and the time remaining on the device. The bottom of the device contains a TP for transferring the sound to a WI-AT.

On the side of the mimic are a series of seven buttons by which the user controls the device. Their functions are self-explanatory (Record, Play, Stop, Fast Forward, Rewind, and Delete) and a mimic requires no training before it can be effectively used.

NIC Card: The Nascent Interface Catalyst Card is the device that allows your WI-AT to make a connection to the ERP. It is a thin piece of metal on which numerous arcane symbols are engraved. The NIC card plugs into the network port of your WI-AT. It is an internal port, so most users never see this piece of hardware. Some don't even know it exists.

Peace Bond: A peace bond is a specially enchanted cord used to secure a weapon in its scabbard or sheath. If a peace-bonded weapon is draw, the cord breaks releasing a long "ping" (like a submarine using active sonar) to alert those nearby that a weapon has been drawn.

Peace bonds are often used by guards and city watchmen to ensure that visitors do not cause trouble… at least that's the theory.

Smoke Powder: A fine powder made from the leaves of the Fumi Ficus tree. It is black in color and volatile when exposed to heat. It is used to propel the bullet out of a firearm.

Smoke Sticks: A mild & legal narcotic made by grinding the leave of the Fumi Ficus tree. These ground leaves are then rolled in paper and smoked. Smoke sticks are sold either in packs of 20 sticks.

Making smoke sticks is a dangerous profession because grinding the leaves too much creates smoke powder and the friction of the grinding machines often ignites this powder causing explosions. This is why smoke mills are never located within population centers.

Telcom: Telcoms come in a variety of shapes, sizes, and colors. Regardless of form, the devices function identically. An alphanumeric pad located on the device allows you to make contact with other telcom units. A microphone in the device transmits the sound of your voice to the speaker of the other unit. This allows nearly instantaneous two-way conversations over great distances.

Thermal Box: This device is a special chest that is able to modify and maintain the temperature of items that are placed inside it. A series of buttons and dials on the front of the box allows the user to control exactly how hot or cold you would like the interior of the box to be.

Vid-Caster: A Vidcaster is a device measuring 3 feet high, 5 feet wide, and 3 inches thick. The front of the device contains a convex glass piece covering a metal board inscribed with mystic symbols. Speakers are located on either side of the glass.

Holopics are transmitted by various holo-stations throughout the empire. These holopics are then translated into sound and image by the metal board and displayed on the glass. Buttons on the top of the device allow the user to operate it by selecting a particular holo-station's transmission to display.

WI-AT: A wireless audio & image terminal is, by far, the most common means of accessing the ERP. It is 10 ½ inches long, 11 ½ inches wide, and 1 inch thick. Hinges at the back of the unit allow it to be opened revealing a keyboard, screen, and speakers. A small panel on the right side of the device pivots out to reveal the cursor pad allowing the user to move the cursor around the screen by tracing across the pad with his or her finger tip.

Several ports are located on the front of the machine. One, the transfer port, allows you to transfer images to the WI-AT from an imager, mimic, or other similar device. A second port allows you to insert small mirrored disks containing data. Another port allows you to connect multiple WI-ATs together for playing multi-player games. Yet another port allows you to plug in specialized control pads into the WI-AT for use with various applications.

Adventuring Gear

Item	Cost
Back Pack (cloth)	2 Brigs
Back Pack (leather)	5 Brigs
Barrel (empty)	2 Brigs
Basket (empty)	4 Lances
Bedroll	7 Lances 5 Secs
Bell	1 Brig
Blanket, light	5 Lances
Blanket, heavy	1 Brig
Block and tackle	5 Brigs
Bottle, wine, glass	2 Brigs
Bucket, wooden	5 Lances
Bucket, metal	5 Lances
Caltrops	1 Brig
Candle	1 Sec
Canvas (sq. yd.)	1 Lance
Case, map or scroll	1 Brig
Chain (10 ft.)	30 Brigs
Chalk, 1 piece	1 Sec
Chest (empty)	2 Brigs
Crowbar	2 Brigs
Firewood (per day)	1 Sec
Fishhook	1 Lance
Fishing net, 25 sq. ft.	4 Brigs
Flask (empty)	3 Secs
Flint and steel	1 Brig
Grappling hook	1 Brig
Hammer	5 Lances
Ink (1 oz. vial)	8 Brigs
Inkpen	1 Lance
Jug, clay	3 Secs
Ladder, 10-foot	5 Secs
Lamp, common	1 Lance
Lantern, bullseye	12 Brigs
Lantern, hooded	7 Brigs
Lock, keyed	
Very simple	20 Brigs
Average	40 Brigs
Good	80 Brigs
Amazing	150 Brigs
Lock, tumbler	
Very simple	25 Brigs
Average	50 Brigs
Good	100 Brigs
Amazing	200 Brigs
Manacles	30 Brigs
Manacles, superior	60 Brigs
Shackles	25 Brigs
Shackles, superior	55 Brigs
Mirror, small steel	10 Brigs

Adventuring Gear *(continued)*

Item	Cost
Mug/Tankard, clay	2 Secs
Mug/Tankard, metal	4 Lances
Oil (1-pint flask)	1 Lance
Paper (sheet)	4 Lances
Parchment (sheet)	2 Lances
Pick, miner's	3 Brigs
Pitcher, clay	2 Secs
Piton	1 Lance
Pole, 10-foot	2 Lances
Pot, iron	5 Lances
Pouch, belt (empty)	1 Brig
Ram, portable	10 Brigs
Rations, trail (per day)	5 Lances
Rope, hempen (50 ft.)	1 Brig
Rope, silk (50 ft.)	10 Brigs
Sack (small)	1 Lance
Sack (large)	3 Lances
Sealing wax	1 Brig
Sewing needle	5 Lances
Signal whistle	8 Brigs
Signet ring	5 Brigs
Sledge	1 Brig
Soap (per lb.)	5 Lances
Spade or shovel	2 Brigs
Spyglass	1000 Brigs
Tent, A-frame (1-man)	10 Brigs
Tent, A-frame (2-man)	13 Brigs 4 Lances
Tent, A-frame (4-man)	16 Brigs 7 Lances
Tent, Pavilion (1-man)	13 Brigs 5 Lances
Tent, Pavilion (2-man)	47 Brigs
Tent, Pavilion (4-man)	60 Brigs
Tent, Pavilion (8-man)	86 Brigs 6 Lances
Torch, untreated	1 Sec
Torch, treated	3 Secs
Vial, ink or potion	1 Brig
Waterskin	1 Brig
Whetstone	2 Secs

Clothing

Item	Cost
Apron	4 Lances
Belt	4 Lances
Blouse	1 Brig
Bodice	7 Lances
Cap	5 Lances
Doublet	1 Brig 5 Lances
Dress	1 Brig 2 Lances
Dress, fancy	2 Brigs
Jacket, fur	5 Brigs
Jacket, heavy	2 Brigs 5 Lances
Robe, heavy	1 Brig 8 Lances
Robe, hooded	2 Brigs
Hose	8 Lances
Knit Gloves	9 Lances
Hat, large-brimmed, cloth	8 Lances
Hat, large-brimmed, leather	1 Brig 5 Lances
Jacket, leather	4 Brigs
Jacket, light	1 Brigs 5 Lances
Robe, light	1 Brigs 2 Lances
Cape, long	2 Brigs
Cloak, hooded	3 Brigs
Glove, leather, long	1 Brig 8 Lances
Night Gown	1 Brig
Night Robe	1 Brig 2 Lances
Coif, padded	5 Lances
Gambeson, padded	1 Brig 8 Lances
Trousers, padded	1 Brig
Scarf	2 Lances
Hat, short-brimmed, cloth	6 Lances

Clothing *(continued)*

Item	Cost
Hat, short-brimmed, leather	1 Brig 1 Lance
Cape, short	1 Brig 1 Lance
Gloves, leather, short	1 Brig 4 Lances
Lingerie, silk	2 Brigs 5 Lances
Shirt, silk	2 Brigs
Skirt	7 Lances
Socks	2 Lances
Surcoat, emblazoned	2 Brigs 5 Lances
Surcoat, plain	1 Brig
Trousers, cotton	9 Lances
Vest	8 Lances
Muffler, wool	8 Lances
Shirt, wool	1 Brig
Trousers, wool	7 Lances
Boots, leather	2 Brigs 5 Lances
Boots, cloth	1 Brigs 2 Lances
Boots, leather, hip-high	6 Brigs
Boots, leather, knee-high	4 Brigs
Boots, leather, reinforced	4 Brigs
Sandals	8 Lances
Shoes, cloth	1 Brig
Slippers, cloth	8 Lances
Slippers, silk	1 Brigs 6 Lances
Boots, leather, soft	2 Brigs

Tools and Skill Kits

Item	Cost
Artisan's tools	5 Brigs
Artisan's tools, superior	55 Brigs
Climber's kit	80 Brigs
Disguise kit	50 Brigs
Healer's kit	50 Brigs
Holy symbol, wooden	1 Brig
Holy symbol, silver	25 Brigs
Hourglass	35 Brigs
Magnifying glass	100 Brigs
Musical instrument, common	5 Brigs
Musical instrument, superior	100 Brigs
Scale, merchant's	2 Brigs
Spell component pouch	5 Brigs
Spellbook, wizard's (blank)	15 Brigs
Thieves' tools*	30 Brigs
Thieves' tools, superior*	100 Brigs
Tool, superior	50 Brigs
Water clock	1000 Brigs

Food, Drink, and Lodging

Item	Cost
Ale	
Gallon	2 Lances
Quart	7 Secs
Pint	4 Secs
Banquet (per person)	10 Brigs
Bread, per loaf	2 Secs
Cheese (per pound)	2 Lances
Inn stay (per day)	
Common Room	5 Lances
Basic, single	1 Brig
Basic, double	1 Brig 5 Lances
Luxury, single	3 Brigs
Luxury, double	5 Brigs
Meals (per day)	
Good	5 Lances
Common	3 Lances
Poor	1 Lance
Meat (per pound)	3 Lances
Wine	
Common (pitcher)	1 Lance
Fine (glass)	1 Brig
Fine (bottle, 12 glasses)	10 Brigs

Mounts and Related Gear

Item	Cost
Barding	
Medium creature	x2 cost of armor
Large creature	x4 cost of armor
Bit and bridle	2 Brigs
Dog, guard	15 Brigs
Dog, riding	75 Brigs
Donkey or mule	29 Brigs
Draft Horse, heavy	200 Brigs
Draft Horse, light	100 Brigs
Feed (per day)	5 Secs
Horse, heavy	300 Brigs
Horse, light	138 Brigs
Pony	25 Brigs
Warhorse, heavy	500 Brigs
Warhorse, light	225 Brigs
Warpony	80 Brigs
Saddle	
Military	20 Brigs
Pack	5 Brigs
Riding	10 Brigs
Saddlebags	4 Brigs
Stabling (per day)	5 Lances

Transportation

Item	Cost
Ground Vehicles	
Carriage (single team)	120 Brigs
Carriage (double team)	195 Brigs
Wagon, enclosed	150 Brigs
Wagon, cloth covered	105 Brigs
Chariot	45 Brigs
Cart, small	23 Brigs
Cart, large	55 Brigs
Lev-Vehicles	
Carriage (single team)	400 Brigs
Carriage (double team)	650 Brigs
Wagon, enclosed	500 Brigs
Wagon, cloth covered	350 Brigs
Chariot	150 Brigs
Cart, small	75 Brigs
Cart, large	175 Brigs

Mounts and Related Gear

Item	Cost
Barding	
Medium creature	x2 cost of armor
Large creature	x4 cost of armor
Bit and bridle	2 Brigs
Dog, guard	15 Brigs
Dog, riding	75 Brigs
Donkey or mule	29 Brigs
Draft Horse, heavy	200 Brigs
Draft Horse, light	100 Brigs
Feed (per day)	5 Secs
Horse, heavy	300 Brigs
Horse, light	138 Brigs
Pony	25 Brigs
Warhorse, heavy	500 Brigs
Warhorse, light	225 Brigs
Warpony	80 Brigs
Saddle	
Military	20 Brigs
Pack	5 Brigs
Riding	10 Brigs
Saddlebags	4 Brigs
Stabling (per day)	5 Lances

Special Substances and Items

Item	Cost
Aludel	150 Brigs
Athanor	300 Brigs
Dark Cells (2/pack)	2 Brigs
Dark-Sucker	50 Brigs
Dwarf Goggles	150 Stars
Elf Eyes	50 Stars
Floater	25 Brigs
Imager	50 Stars
Mimic	10 Stars
NIC Card	50 Brigs
Peace Bond	5 Lances
Smoke Powder	30 Brigs
Smoke Sticks (20/pack)	5 Brigs
Telecom	100 Brigs
Thermal Box	89 Brigs
Vid-Caster	375 Brigs
WI-AT	680 Brigs

Transportation

Item	Cost
Ground Vehicles	
Carriage (single team)	120 Brigs
Carriage (double team)	195 Brigs
Wagon, enclosed	150 Brigs
Wagon, cloth covered	105 Brigs
Chariot	45 Brigs
Cart, small	23 Brigs
Cart, large	55 Brigs
Lev-Vehicles	
Carriage (single team)	400 Brigs
Carriage (double team)	650 Brigs
Wagon, enclosed	500 Brigs
Wagon, cloth covered	350 Brigs
Chariot	150 Brigs
Cart, small	75 Brigs
Cart, large	175 Brigs

159

Combat

A lot of people seem to think that combat is the purpose of a role-playing game. Some systems even go so far as to only issue experience points if you kill something. Others have modified this view slightly and are gracious enough to give you experience points if you merely "defeat" an encounter. Of course, killing things is still the primary way of ending an encounter.

Though the d10 system is designed to promote the actual role-playing aspects of the game from which this type of game draws its name, we strive to take a more realistic approach. Combat and killing things are still going to be an important part of most games regardless of what we write on these pages. That being the case here are the rules involved.

How Combat Works

Like most role-playing games, combat in the d10 system is cyclical. Each player rolls initiative for their character. This determines both the order in which actions take place and the number of actions each character can take.

The players then take turns describing the actions of their character starting with the character that scored the most successes on the initiative test. These actions are resolved in order and the process begins again.

The Sequence of Battle can be viewed as follows:

1. Determine Initiative
2. Resolve Actions
3. Apply Damage
4. Rinse
5. Repeat

Of course, this is a simplified view of the combat process. There are numerous variables that can have an affect on how combat actually plays out.
But once a character has been through a few combat situations, this process will be second nature for both GMs and players.

On the Lady's Rock, certain aspects of combat work a little differently than they do elsewhere on the material plane. These are optional rules designed to enhance play. They may seem a bit strange at first, but they add a dynamic element to combat. Once you've used them for a few sessions, they will seem second nature. You may even find yourself using them in other d20 based games.

Time Keeping

To control the flow of combat, it is broken down into semi-abstract units of time. These units help to govern the duration of spells and other effects in the game. The base unit of time is a round. One combat round is the amount time it takes for all characters acting in that round to perform all of the actions they are allotted due to their initiative check.

The round is broken down into phases. The round has a number of phases equal to the highest initiative result rolled. In other words, if the highest number of successes on an initiative test is 9, then the round has 9 phases. A phase is the amount of time it takes to complete a single action.

A round of combat should take roughly six seconds. Ten rounds equal a minute. Ten minutes make one combat turn. Six turns make an hour. Twenty-four hours make a day. Five days make one week. Seventy-three weeks make a year…etc…etc…etc…

Initiative: At the start of combat, each combatant rolls a number of dice equal to his or her "Action Pool" versus a target number of 5. Each success the character achieves is an action that the character may take in that combat round.

If the character fails to achieve any successes, he or she is overwhelmed by the situation that they find themselves in and is unable to act.

The round begins with the initiative phase corresponding to the highest number of successes achieved on the initiative test. A player character or non-player character can act (perform an action) on any phase equal or less than the number of successes they achieved… provided they have not spent those actions elsewhere.

For example, the characters Tom & Jim pick a fight with the NPCs Bill and Joe. Tom gets 5 successes on his initiative test. Jim gets 2. Bill and Joe score 3 and 4 respectively.

The directors begins with phase 5, corresponding to the highest number of successes rolled. In phase 5, Tom can choose to act or he may hold his action for a later phase (see "Special Action" on page XXXX). One phase 4, both Tom and Joe can act. On phase three Tom, Joe, and Bill can act. When they reach phase 2, all four characters may act. If any of the characters still have actions remaining, they may also act on phase 1.

Optionally, the player with the least number of successes declares his or her character's intended actions. The player with the next lowest number of successes states his or her character's actions next. This pattern continues until the person with the greatest number of successes states his character's planned course of action. Once the actions have been declared, initiative is resolved normally. This optional rule does slow combat, but it provides those with a higher initiative the benefit of knowing what their fellows are planning and stops "slower" characters from changing

161

their actions based on the actions of those with higher initiatives… which adds realism.

- **Special Actions**

Holding an Action: Sometimes a character may have initiative, but may not wish to act first in a given combat round. The character may wish to see what his or her opponent does before committing to a particular action. This is called "Holding Your Action," and a character who holds their action is said to have a "readied action."

When a character holds their action, they can immediately act on any subsequent initiative phase. This allows the character to act a split second before others acting in that phase.

For example, Tom (from our previous example) may elect to hold his action to see what Bill and Joe intend to do. When Joe moves to draw a gun during the fourth initiative phase, Tom can act immediately attacking Joe (if he has a weapon ready), knocking the weapon from Joe's hand as he draws it, or some other course of action Tom's player thinks will be beneficial.

Once the character acts, combat is resolved normally. If the character does not act (takes no action) during the initiative phase, the character is considered to have "Maximum Initiative" (Max Init) in the following round. This character does not roll for initiative and is instead considered to have rolled a success on every die for the next initiative test.

"Max Init" is only possible following a round in which you hold your action and do not act. Once you act, initiative is calculated normally on the subsequent rounds.

Rushing an Action: Sometimes, a character may want to act before an opponent even though they did not achieve more successes on the initiative test. When this occurs, the character's only choice is to rush his or her action.

When rushing an action, the character moves up in initiative round, but loses one die from each test that round for each phase so moved.

For example, Joe see Tom prepare to act (holding his action). He wants to draw his weapon (an action) and shoot Tom (another action) before Tom has a chance to act. Tom needs to move from phase 4 to phase 6 in order to accomplish his goal. He can do this, but he loses 2 dice from every roll he makes that round.

Action: As stated earlier, the number of successes acquired on the initiative test determines the number of actions a character has in a single round. Examples of actions are as follows:

- Attacking someone
- Dodging an attack by someone
- Parrying an attack (each subsequent parry after the first costs an action)
- Drawing or sheathing a weapon
- Reloading a missile weapon
- Adding smoke powder to a firearm
- Reloading a firearm
- Moving up to the character's movement rate in feet.
- Dropping to or rising from crouched position
- Rising from a prone position

Free Actions: Sometimes a player will want a character to do something that shouldn't require a full action to accomplish. The vast majority of these things are "free actions." That is, something that the character can do that does not cost them an action. Examples of free actions are the following:

- Speaking (though if this gets excessive, I recommend limiting players to a number of words equal to their character's reason score)
- Dropping an item
- Dropping to a prone position
- Canceling a spell
- Urinating (though opening and / or removing clothing *should* cost the character an action)

Attack Test: This is the character's attempt to hit his or her target. To make an attack test or roll, the player rolls a number of dice equal to the applicable skill for the weapon he or she is using against a target number equal to the difficulty for using a particular weapon.

Each success that the character achieves on this roll has the potential to cause damage to his or her opponent.

Damage: The number of successes achieved on the Attack Test is multiplied by the Damage Rating of the weapon used.

Certain weapons have a "Damage Bonus." This number is added to the total damage of the weapon once all other factors are taken into consideration.

Melee and thrown weapon also receives a number of additional points of damage based on the strength of the character wielding them. Add the character's strength to the damage from any melee weapon and ½ of the character's strength to the damage from any thrown weapon.

The target of the attack can still act to minimize this damage by making a "Defense Test."

- **Types of Damage:**

There are three basic types of damage that a character can suffer in the d10 system – Body, Mind, & Soul. These damage types are further divided into subcategories based on the cause of the damage - Crushing, Slashing, Piercing, Bludgeoning, Stun, Energy, Naval & Supernatural.

Crushing Damage is done primarily by heavy objects and weapons such as great swords, battle axes, and falling mountains. These weapons may have an edge (as is the case with the axe and sword) or may be blunt (like the mountain). The sheer size and weight of weapon causes damage, its edge, if any, is largely inconsequential. A battleaxe may slice into your flesh, but it will also crush your bones, which is why they cleave off arms.

Slashing Damage is done by smaller bladed weapons such as a scimitar or short sword. They lack the size and weight of crushing weapons, but are often easier to use… and, therefore, no less deadly.

Piercing Damage is done by sharp pointy things like spears and arrows. Piercing weapons do a fair amount of damage and are well-suited puncturing certain types of mail armor… and hot air balloons.

Bludgeoning Damage is done by blunt weapons that are not large enough to do crushing damage. Unlike other weapon damage, bludgeoning damage is treated as stun damage *unless* the weapon's damage rating exceeds the character's constitution score.

Stun Damage is any damage that is applied to the character's mental condition monitor rather than their physical condition monitor.

Energy Damage is most often done by magical spells such as fireball, lightning bolt, and blinding sphere of death.

Naval Damage is done by siege weapons. These weapons are not designed for use against small targets like player characters. Weapons that do naval damage are used to attack castles, fortified towns, and ships on the aether. Naval weapons cannot be parried, though they can be dodged.

The biggest difference between naval damage and other damage types is that naval attacks completely ignore armor. In addition, every two successes on a gaffing test only reduces the damage by a single point (instead of each gaffing success reducing the damage per the normal gaffing rules). This makes them extremely deadly.

Supernatural Damage is caused by certain monster, like the undead. Supernatural damage is applied directly to the character's "soul damage" and will quickly result in the character's death.

Entanglement: Some weapons cause entanglement, listed as "En" in the damage type of the weapon. These weapons reduce the quickness, and therefore movement rate, of their target by the damage rating of the weapon. In order to free themselves, the character must make a strength test against twice the damage rating of the weapon. Each success reduces the entanglement by one.

- **Hierarchy of Damage**

Damage is applied to the character in a strict hierarchy.

- Mind Damage
- Body Damage
- Soul Damage

When a character takes more mind damage than his or her condition monitor allows, the excess damage is applied as body damage. When the character has taken more damage than his body damage condition monitor allows, the excess damage is applied as soul damage. A character who has taken all the soul damage his or her character can is dead.

Damage is always applied in this manner. It never works the other way. Body damage is never applied to mind damage condition monitor and soul damage is always applied only to the soul condition monitor.

Defense Test: Characters can defend against attacks in one of two ways - dodge or parry. Some attacks can not be parried or dodged (see page XXXX).

Dodging: Dodges are resolved by rolling a number of dice equal to the character's quickness plus any dice from the character's action pool versus a target number of 5. Each success that the defender achieves cancels out one of the attacker's successes.

The exception to this is damage caused by firearms. If a character is attacked by a firearm, the dodge roll is done as normal, but the defender needs two successes in order to negate one of the attacker's successes. (See dodging a bullet on page XXXX)

Dodging costs the character one of their available actions.

Active Dodge: A character can spend all of their available actions to actively dodge all attacks aimed at him or her. In order to do this, the character rolls all of their action pool against a target number of 5. All of the successes achieved are used for each attack targeting the character during the round.

The character cannot attack or parry. He or she can only use their actions to move. The target number to hit the character increases by 2.

Parrying: In order to parry the player makes an attack test (see above) with his or her weapon.

The total damage for each attack is determined and compared. If the defender's total damage is higher than that of the attacker, no damage is done. If the attacker's total damage is greater, the difference between the two is applied to the defender.

A character can parry one melee or hand-to-hand attack each round without expending one of their available actions. However, there are drawbacks to parrying an attack.

If the base damage rating of the defender's weapon is less than that of the attacker, the damage rating of the defender's weapon is reduced by one. Likewise, if the base damage rating of the defender's weapon is more than double the damage rating of the attacker's weapon, the damage rating of the attacker's weapon is reduced by one.

The director needs to decide whether the weapon that the character is using is capable of parrying the attack leveled against him. A character cannot parry a melee weapon with their bare hands. If such an attempt is made, the defender simply takes damage.

If the player opts to use a ranged weapon to parry a melee blow, compare the base damage ratings and apply the results as follows:

If the base rating of the attacker's weapon is within one point (higher *or* lower) than the base damage rating of the defender's weapon, the defender's weapon can parry the blow, but it will not function until it is repaired.

If the damage rating of the attacker's weapon is more than the base of the defender's ranged weapon, the weapon is destroyed, cannot be repaired, and the wielder takes damage normally.

If the damage rating of the defender's weapon is more than double that of the attacker, it may be used to parry.

Note: These rules apply to using a bow or rifle to block a sword, axe, or other melee weapon. A character cannot fire an arrow to parry a melee weapon.

Gaffing Test: If the defense test does not negate the damage caused by the attack, the defender's only hope is to gaff, or soak, the damage. In order to accomplish this, the character rolls a number of dice equal to his or her applicable attribute - constitution for body damage & psyche for mind damage – against the power of the attack.

Though it is not all inclusive, the chart bellows lists many of the attacks a character is likely to encounter. Special attacks from monsters will have the gaffing target number listed in their description.

Attack	Power
Melee Weapon	Damage Rating + 3
Ranged Weapon	Damage Rating + 3
Damaging Spell	Spell Power + 3
Naval Weapon	Damage Rating + 9

Each success that the defender achieves reduces the damage by a number of points equal to your ½ Constitution for physical attacks or your ½ Psyche for mental ones. The only exception to this is naval damage which is reduced by a single point for every 2 successes achieved regardless of your Constitution. (Siege weapons – ballistae, catapults, trebuchets, and cannons – do physical damage… just so that we're clear.)

Dice from your vigor pool can be used to help you gaff body damage, but once those dice are used, they will not refresh until you roll for a new initiative. Likewise, willpower dice can be used to augment a roll to gaff mind damage, but suffer the same refresh rate as other dice pools.

Soul damage is gaffed in a similar manner using your character's charisma dice. No dice pool can augment a roll to gaff soul damage. In fact, each level of soul damage you suffer reduces your pools just as it would any other dice roll.

There is one exception to these rules – Enervation.

Enervation is the backlash a mage or cleric feels from channeling though themselves. Such is the dangers of a meager mortal trying to harness the power of the gods. It will be covered in the section on magic (see magic page XXXX).

Micellaneous Combat Modifiers

Of course, as anyone who's ever been in a combat situation will tell you, there is more to fighting than hitting the enemy and trying not to be hit by them. The cover, visibility, and a host of other things come into effect. We're not going to be able to cover every situation that might arise. We do hope, however, to cover some of the more common.

Visibility Modifiers

Visibility is a serious concern during combat. It's hard to hit something you cannot see. This is further complicated by the different type of vision available to different races. The table at the bottom of this page outlines the target number modifiers for different conditions of visibility. Remember to apply these modifiers, not only to the attack difficulty, but to the dodge difficulty as well. After all, it is just as hard to dodge something you can't see.

Complete Darkness: This is the complete absence of light. Rooms with no lights or windows, a subterranean cavern, or magically induced darkness are all examples of complete darkness.

Minimal Light: This, as you may have guessed, is a very miniscule amount of light, such as a match or candle, light leaking in around a door or shutter, or moonlight less than a full moon.

Partial Light: This category includes torch light, lamp light, the light of a full moon, and the light given off by a hearth.

Visibility Modifiers					
Condition	Normal	Low-Light	Darkvision	Thermal Vision	Ether-Sight*
Complete Darkness	+8	+8	0	+2	+8 / 0
Minimal Light	+6	+2	+1	+2	+6 / 0
Partial Light	+2	0	+2	+1	+2 / 0
Glare	+2	+2	+2	+2	+2 / 0
Mist	+2	0	0	0	+2
Light Fog or Rain	+4	+2	0	0	+4
Heavy Fog or Rain	+6	+4	0	0	+6
Light Smoke	+4	+2	+2	+2	+4
Heavy Smoke	+6	+4	+4	+4	+6

* The number before the slash is for targeting non-living or non-magical objects. The number after the slash is for targeting magical or living things.

Glare: This modifier includes abrupt flashes or light as well as looking into a source of bright light. Glare from an abrupt change in lighting usually lasts for a single round. Glare from looking at a light eource remains as long as you continue to look at it.

Mist: A mist is a light drizzle or flurry. There is not enough precipitation to quality as rain or snow, but there is enough to hamper vision to some degree.

Light Fog or Rain: Light fog or rain is just that. It is light, inland fog or or rain shower. It has a larger effect on Ether-Vision than other visions because of the organic, living attributes of water as the source of life.

Heavy Fog or Rain: This condition is similar to the conditions above except that the precipitation is significantly more substantial. A torrential downpour, blizzard, or thick coast fog are all in this category.

Light Smoke: This condition is the presence of a thin smoke, probably from a fire. The smoke must be a prevalent condition in order to hamper vision. The smoke given off by a candle isn't going to affect your ability to shoot someone. The smoke generated by burning refuse, however, might. The director will determine is this condition applies.

Heavy Smoke: This is a heavier version of the above condition. A room filled with smoke is a good example of this category.

Illumination

Different types of light sources affect vision very differently. For example, a blazing fire might make it easier for a human to see, but being right next to it makes an orc's thermal vision next to useless. Furthermore, no matter how large the fire is, it does not provide the same crisp, clear that the sun provides. Beyond the immediate area of the fire's immediate light is a region of flickering light and undulating shadows. On the previous page we explained how different conditions of visibility affect each particular type of vision.

The problem now is trying to decide which modifiers apply and when to apply them.

The light given off by a campfire, for example, offers partial illumination… but how far away from the fire can you be and still benefit from it? Surely people do not benefit perpetually from a fire no matter how far from it they travel… or how long it's been burning.

More importantly, a fire doesn't provide illumination equally for everyone. A person using Thermal Vision, for example, would be blinded by a raging campfire. If that fire was made from fresh, green wood, the person using Ether Vision would be in the same boat.

Likewise, a torch in an otherwise dark room would cause a glare to those using thermal vision. Darkvision wouldn't work at all in the cone of light provided by a Dark-Sucker. Being able to see in complete darkness is useless when the darkness is gone.

These may seem simple enough to adjudicate, but, as with most rules, if it isn't in black and white, some player some where will try to argue the point. This simply slows down the game and annoys the other people who are actually trying to play and have a good time.

To curb this unfortunately occurrence, the following page contains illumination charts for each type of special vision available in the game. These charts cannot hope to cover each and every possible situation. They should, however, serve as a guideline to help you realistically portray those events we have not covered… at least as realistically as you can get when you're playing an orcish cleric.

A Brief Note on Magic and Light

At some point in time a player is going to demand that the party's orcish opponents suffer from a "glare penalty" for a round due to the "fireball" he or she just created. The mage may, in fact, be correct. That, however, is not necessarily the case.

Though we'll deal with magic more in depth in a later chapter, some aspects of spell-craft are appropriate here. Because each spell is unique and only contains the attributes that the mage who designed the spell includes, spells may not function in a manner that their names might indicate. The fireball, in the example above, will only affect vision if the mage that designed the spell chose to include "elemental effects" in the spell's design. Without that element, the damage caused by this "fireball" is not fire at all. It has no heat. It gives off no light. It isn't really fire. And because it isn't fire, it doesn't behave like fire.

Likewise, an illusion spell may include visual, auditory, and tactile elements... it *may*... but that is not necessarily the case. Unless the mage includes visual effects in the spell's design, it gives off no light at all. Since heat is something you *feel* when in the presence of fire, without a tactile element, there is not heat. Furthermore, if the illusion is not realistic, it will not behave as its real world counterpart would.

Both players and directors are encouraged to examine the design of each spell carefully to determine its effects on the game, particularly those effects that people might not otherwise consider... like illumination...

Visibility Ranges (*Normal Vision*)

Light Source	Duration	Normal Vision	Partial Light	Minimal Light	Complete Darkness	Glare
Candle	1 hr	-	-	5 ft (radius)	Beyond 5 ft	-
Torch	1 hr	-	20 ft (radius)	40 ft (radius)	Beyond 40 ft	-
Camp Fire	1 hr / log	-	30 ft (radius)	60 ft (radius)	Beyond 60 ft	-
Lamp, Common	6 hr / pint	-	15 ft (radius)	30 ft (radius)	Beyond 30 ft	-
Lantern, Bullseye	6 hr / pint	-	60 ft (cone)	120 ft (cone)	Beyond 120 ft	-
Lantern, Hooded	6 hr / pint	-	30 ft (radius)	60 ft (radius)	Beyond 60 ft	-
Dark-Sucker	6 hr / D-Cell	60 ft (cone)	90 ft (cone)	180 ft (cone)	Beyond 180 ft	-

Visibility Ranges (*Low-Light Vision*)

Light Source	Duration	Normal Vision	Partial Light	Minimal Light	Complete Darkness	Glare
Candle	1 hr	-	-	10 ft (radius)	Beyond 20 ft	-
Torch	1 hr	-	40 ft (radius)	80 ft (radius)	Beyond 40 ft	-
Camp Fire	1 hr / log	-	60 ft (radius)	120 ft (radius)	Beyond 120 ft	-
Lamp, Common	6 hr / pint	-	30 ft (radius)	60 ft (radius)	Beyond 60 ft	-
Lantern, Bullseye	6 hr / pint	-	120 ft (cone)	240 ft (cone)	Beyond 240 ft	-
Lantern, Hooded	6 hr / pint	-	60 ft (radius)	120 ft (radius)	Beyond 120 ft	-
Dark-Sucker	6 hr / D-Cell	120 ft (cone)	180 ft (cone)	360 ft (cone)	Beyond 360 ft	-

Visibility Ranges (*Darkvision*)

Light Source	Duration	Normal Vision	Partial Light	Minimal Light	Complete Darkness	Glare
Candle	1 hr	-	-	-	-	-
Torch	1 hr	-	-	-	-	-
Camp Fire	1 hr / log	-	-	-	-	-
Lamp, Common	6 hr / pint	-	-	-	-	-
Lantern, Bullseye	6 hr / pint	-	-	-	-	-
Lantern, Hooded	6 hr / pint	-	-	-	-	-
Dark-Sucker*	6 hr / D-Cell	-	180 ft (cone)	90 ft (cone)	Within 90 ft	-

* Because Dark-Suckers absorb the darkness in the cone, the make Darkvision less effective in their area of effect. Their cone of illumination is inverted for those with Darkvision.

Visibility Ranges (*Thermal Vision*)*

Light Source	Duration	Normal Vision	Partial Light	Minimal Light	Complete Darkness	Glare
Candle	1 hr	-	-	-	-	Within 5 ft
Torch	1 hr	-	-	40 ft (radius)	-	Within 20 ft
Camp Fire	1 hr / log	-	-	60 ft (radius)	Within 30 ft	-
Lamp, Common	6 hr / pint	-	-	15 ft (radius)	-	Within 5 ft
Lantern, Bullseye	6 hr / pint	-	-	-	-	Within 5 ft
Lantern, Hooded	6 hr / pint	-	-	-	-	Within 5 ft
Dark-Sucker	6 hr / D-Cell	-	-	-	-	-

* Because Thermal Vision works by seeing heat energy, light sources using a flame of any sort have a negative effect on Thermal Vision

Visibility Ranges (*Ether Vision*)

Light Source	Duration	Normal Vision	Partial Light	Minimal Light	Complete Darkness	Glare
Candle	1 hr	-	-	-	-	-
Torch	1 hr	-	-	-	-	-
Camp Fire*	1 hr / log	Beyond 90 ft	90 ft (radius)	60 ft (radius)	Within 30 ft	-
Lamp, Common	6 hr / pint	-	-	-	-	-
Lantern, Bullseye	6 hr / pint	-	-	-	-	-
Lantern, Hooded	6 hr / pint	-	-	-	-	-
Dark-Sucker	6 hr / D-Cell	-	-	-	-	-

* If a Camp Fire is made with "green" branches, the burning essence from those branches inhibits Ether Vision because it sees life energy. Dead, dry branches and logs do not have this effect.

Cover

In order for someone to be considered "covered," they must be hiding behind some object, such as a half-wall, overturned table, or another person. The object must be large enough for the character to hide behind. A good guideline is that the object should be at least ½ as tall as the character.

Use reasonable judgment to determine if cover should apply. You're not playing Scooby-Doo® the RPG here. It is not possible for an normal adult human to hide behind lamp pole.

Targeting someone who is behind cover incurs a +4 penalty to the difficulty to hit your target.

Note: There is no such thing as a modifier to hit someone who has "Total Cover." As the term "total cover" implies, the person is totally covered. You can't shoot around "total cover." Your only hope is to shoot through it. Of course, you would be "firing blind" (see below).

Firing Blind

Firing blind occurs anytime the character is trying to hit a target that he or she cannot otherwise see or detect. This may happen because the attacker has been blinded, because the target is hiding behind an object that completely conceals him or her, or because the attacker is firing in a general direction hoping to hit a target he has not taken the time to identify.

This modifier works both ways. As mentioned earlier, it is just as difficult to avoid an attack you cannot see as it is to make the attack in the first place.

Firing blind always invokes a penalty of +8 to your target number.

Knockdown

If a target suffers a hit by a weapon that he cannot dodge and target number to gaff damage exceeds the target's strength score, the target suffers a knockdown.

A target that suffers a knockdown is knocked prone. They may avoid this by making a strength test with a target number equal to the target number to gaff damage (vigor pool can be used for this roll). If they score a number of successes that exceeds the attacker's strength score, they are not knocked prone and are knocked back 5 feet instead.

For example, Steven is a Teg. He has a strength of 2 and a vigor pool of 7 dice. Matt attacks him with a great sword. Matt is a human with a strength of 4. The magic number to see if steven is knocked down is 8 (3 plus 5 for the damage rating of the great sword). Since 8 is greater than 2, Steven is knocked down. He can roll a strength test versus the gaffing target number (8 in this case) and needs 4 successes to not be knocked prone. Steven will need dice from his vigor pool and he will need 4 or more dice to roll an 8 or higher. If he achieves this lofty goal, Steven will merely be pushed back 5 feet otherwise he is lying on the ground and needs to spend

Charging

A character can charge an opponent in order to deal a more devastating attack. In order to charge, the character must be able to move in a direct line to his opponent and must move at least 5 feet. Charging does not increase the amount of damage from the attack, but it does increase the power of the attack by the character's quickness attribute.

For more information on running and sprinting, see movement on page XXXX.

Basic Weapons

As you may have noticed, there is not skill for using basic weapons. This is because basic weapons are…well… basic. Using these weapons borders on instinctual. As such, no special skill is required to wield them. Any character can wield basic weapons at a skill level equal to their coordination without suffering the normal penalty for defaulting to an attribute. In other words each success counts.

Fighting with Two Weapons

Characters can only fight with two weapons at the same time if they have a ranking of two or higher in the applicable skills for each weapon held and are using two one-handed weapons.

The character receives full skill rating with his primary weapon, but cannot use more skill dice with his secondary weapon than he or she has points in coordination. If the weapon in their "off hand" is a light weapon, he or she can use up to twice their coordination attribute in skill dice.

The character only adds ½ of their strength score to the damage from his primary attack regardless of whether or not they have ambidexterity. No strength bonus is received by the secondary weapon unless the character is ambidextrous. Then they receive ½ of their strength as a damage bonus with that weapon as well.

A character fighting with two weapons can choose to engage two targets simultaneously. If this happens, the difficulty of using the weapon increases by 2 for the weapon in the primary hand and by 4 for the weapon in the off hand. (Since characters with ambidexterity are equally skilled with each hand, the difficulty of both of their weapons is increased by two.)

A Spell-caster who wishes to cast spells requiring somatic or material components while wielding a weapon is also considered to be fighting with two weapons. Material components are considered to be "light weapons" as are simple gestures.

Sizes and Combat

As you probably noticed when reading through the races section, different creatures have different sizes. Those sizes have two noted effects on combat.

First, it is easier to hit larger objects than it is to hit smaller ones. A teg trying to hit a human would be the same as a human trying to hit a giant... or a shed... Meanwhile, the giant trying to hit the teg would have as much luck as a human trying to swat a fly.
The second is the amount of damage done. A teg short spear is little more than a toothpick. And a giant's short spear is a tree. Even though these are the same weapon, they cannot do the same damage to a human. If you disagree, sign the damage waiver at the end of the book, come up to Green Bay, and we'll drop one of each on you. Then we'll know for certain which of us is correct.

The weapons listed in this book have difficulty and damage ratings listed for medium creatures. If you are playing a creature that is not medium sized, you'll have to make some changes to the weapon statistics for your character. The table below lists everything you need in order to make adjustments for size.

Compare the size of the attacker to the size of the defender. This will give you the modifier. Add or subtract it from both the weapon's difficulty and its damage rating.

For example, a teg with a strength score of 2 is using a bearded axe to attack a human. The teg is a tiny creature and the human is a medium creature. The difficulty of the bearded axe is reduced by 2, from a 6 to a 4, because it is easier for the small teg to hit the comparatively larger human. The damage rating is reduced by 2, from a 3 to a 1, because the teg-sized bearded axe lacks the weight and leverage of its human-sized counterpart. The teg still gets its full strength as a damage bonus as well as the +1 damage bonus from the weapon itself.

Special Rules

Regardless of the disparity, neither the difficulty nor the damage rating can be reduced below 1 due to size. If applying the modifier from the table would cause this to happen, apply the following rules.

- **Difficulties less than 1**

Should the size modifier reduce the difficulty to less than one, take the absolute value of the modifier (-1=1, -2=2, -3=3, etc.) and apply it as a damage bonus. Then set the difficulty of the weapon at 1.

- **Damage Ratings less than 1**

If the size modifiers reduce the damage rating to less than one, the damage rating becomes one, and the weapons damage is considered stun (mind) damage. If the initial damage rating was greater than one, subtract one from the initial damage rating and apply the remainder as a damage bonus. (A weapon with a damage rating of four that is reduced below 1 would now have a damage rating of one and 3 points added to its bonus damage.)

For example, Steve, our teg from before, is attack a dragon with a dagger. A dagger normally has a difficulty of 3 and a damage rating of 1. This particular dragon is an adult and is huge in size. The size chart gives us a modifier of -4 for a tiny creature attacking a huge creature. This reduces the difficulty to -1 and the damage rating to -3.

Since neither of these ratings can be reduced below 1, both are set at one. The dagger receives a +1 to its damage bonus because of the adjustment to its difficulty, and the damage dealt by the danger becomes stun (mind) damage.

Steve rolls his edged weapons skill versus a target number of one and gets a 5, 6, 3, 9, 12, 4, & 6. Steve does 7 points of mind damage from successes and an additional point in bonus damage because of the difficulty modifier. He also

Modifiers for Size

Attacker's Size	Height or Length*	Defender's Size: Fine	Diminutive	Tiny	Small	Medium	Large	Huge	Gargantuan	Colossal
Fine	6 ft or less	0	-1	-2	-3	-4	-5	-6	-7	-8
Dimunitive	6 in to 1 ft	+1	0	-1	-2	-3	-4	-5	-6	-7
Tiny	1 ft to 2 ft	+2	+1	0	-1	-2	-3	-4	-5	-6
Small	2 ft to 4 ft	+3	+2	+1	0	-1	-2	-3	-4	-5
Medium	4 ft to 8 ft	+4	+3	+2	+1	0	-1	-2	-3	-4
Large	8 ft to 16 ft	+5	+4	+3	+2	+1	0	-1	-2	-3
Huge	16 ft to 32 ft	+6	+5	+4	+3	+2	+1	0	-1	-2
Gargantuan	32 ft to 64 ft	+7	+6	+5	+4	+3	+2	+1	0	-1
Colossal	64 ft or more	+8	+7	+6	+5	+4	+3	+2	+1	0

* Humanoids always measure size based on their height. For non-humanoid creatures, use the larger of the creatures height or length to determine its size.

receives 2 bonus points from his strength for a grand total of 10 points of mind damage. The dragon is then able to dodge or soak the damage normally His target number to do so is only 3 (the power of the attack), so chances are he'll score a success or two... or three... or four..

Over-sized Weapons

After reading the rules for sizing and combat, some player is going to try and have their human character wield a giant-sized sword. If that happens, aimply consider the human to be an attacker the size of the weapon he or she is using.

For example, a human (medium size) who picks up an axe once wielded by a minotaur (large size) is treated as a large creature for the purposes of assigning a difficulty and damage rating to the weapon. In this case, the difficulty and damage rating would increase by one. The weapon is heavier so it does more damage, but it is also unwieldy for the human to use.

Unarmed Combat

In unarmed combat, characters do bludgeoning damage. A punch has a damage rating of 0.5 (or ½ a point per success) and a kick has a damage rating of 1. The attackers strength is added to the total damage for these attacks.

Object Rating

Every object has an object barrier rating. This rating represents the amount of damge that the object can take before the attack penetrates the object. It is not the number of points the object can take before it is destroyed, however.

If a character is hiding behind an object made of this substance and someone attempts to harm them, then the object rating is subtracted from the total damage before any defense from armor is applied... assuming, of course, that the attacker can manage to hit them firing blind.

Object	Rating
Cloth	1
Glass	2
Thin Wood	3
Thick Wood	4
Field Stone	6
Worked Stone	8
Thick Stone	12
Reinforced Stone	16
Ferrocrete	24
Reinforced Ferrocrete	32

Object Damage

An object can take a number of points of physical damage equal to its object rating times its area in square feet. Unlike living creature, and magical constructs or items, inanimate objects do not receive rolls to gaff damage. If an object takes of points of damage described above, it is reduced to rumble.

Dodging a Bullet

In the d10 system, a character that has available actions can always spend one of those actions to dodge an attack. This is part of game mechanics and is not always "realistic." Of course, you're playing a game where "mage" is a viable profession, so you shouldn't get too high up on the realism horse…

There may, however, be players who argue against our ruling that two successes are required to negate a single attack success when attempting to dodge a firearm.

Some of those people will argue that you shouldn't be able to dodge a bullet. Those people are right. Remind them that this is just a game.

Others might, erroneously, claim that their character should be capable of this superhuman feat. These people are idiots. Tell them… often.

If that doesn't work, here is the math behind dodging a bullet. Explain it to them… slowly… use small words…

If they still insist, follow the instructions found at the end of this section… and find a cheap florist so you can send flowers to their funeral.

First, according to the 1998 edition of *World Book Encyclopedia*, the average speed of a bullet varies between 600 and 5,000 feet per second. As a general rule, pistols have a lower muzzle velocity (bullet speed) than rifles. Most of us can't think in feet per second, so let's translate that into something that's easier to imagine shall we?

A bullet traveling at 600 feet per second travels 36,000 feet in a minute (600 feet x 60 seconds in a minute). That means in an hour it travels 2,160,000 feet (36,000 feet per minute times 60 minutes in an hour). Since here are 5280 feet in a mile, we can determine that the bullet is traveling at 409 miles per hour on the low end. On the high end, using the same basic equations, we see that a bullet can travel as fast as 3,409 miles per hour. That's pretty fast, I don't care who you are.

The M9 Beretta, a 9mm pistol that officially became standard issue for the US Marine Corps in 1982, has a maximum effective range of 152.5 feet and a muzzle velocity of 1200 feet per second (approximately 818 miles per hour).

Even at the furthest edge of its effective range watching the shooter pull the trigger, you don't stand a chance. It would take the bullet approximately 0.13 seconds to cover that distance. Since the hand to eye reaction time of the average human being is 0.16 second, the bullet would tear through your flesh 3 hundredths of a second before you even realized it was coming. It would take another 0.16 seconds for your muscles to react to the signals from your brain and try to get out of the way. Of course, you would have already been bleeding for 0.19 seconds.

Now, the longest confirmed kill by a sniper was set by a Canadian sniper team in Afghanistan at just under 7973 feet. The gun they were using was an M107 (pictured below) with a muzzle velocity of 2800 feet per second (approximately 1,909 miles per hour). That gives you 2.8475 seconds to get out of the way… oh wait… 2.6875 seconds… I almost forgot it takes a little bit of time for your mind to react. Sorry… 2.5275 seconds… I forgot that your mind needs time to tell your body what to do.

Of course, that's assuming that you notice the sniper lying prone just over a mile and a half away from you. The bullet is traveling somewhere around mach 2.5 so it would hit you before you even heard the shot… Of course, with the silencer that any competent sniper would use, you probably wouldn't even hear the shot at all. Flash suppressors would make the muzzle flash a moot point, though at that distance, it's questionable whether you'd recognize it anyway.

All of this is really moot since none of the firearms in this game have the range we're talking about here. So, as you can see it is simply impossible for anyone to believe that they can dodge a bullet. If someone is shooting at you with a ballistic weapon, the character's only hope is that either the shooter is incompetent or that his armor does its job.

If your players find the need to continue to argue this point, remind them that this is just a game and they should relax.

If that doesn't work, have them fill out the liability waiver included in the appendix of this book. Send it to Erisian Entertainment and we'll be happy to invite them up to balmy Green Bay, Wisconsin so they can demonstrate their uncanny quickness to our staff.

If they succeed, we'll publish an apology and revamp the rules in our next release. If they fail, well, that's what the damage waiver is for.

Movement

Normal Movement

The distance a character can normally move in a single action is 5 feet per point of quickness. The character can only spend one action to move per initiative phase. And, as you might expect, the character can choose to move less than this maximum distance.

Running

A character can choose to run, moving at double their normal movement rate. However, moving at this speed increases the target number to dodge by 2.

Note: Characters are not assumed to be standing still waiting to be shot, stabbed, or hit over the head with a big stick. They are assumed to be trying not to be hit.

A character who is running is trying to get from point A to point B quickly. Their attention is on their destination, not their opponents. This is the reason for the modifier to dodge target number.

Sprinting

Characters, like real people, are capable of attaining greater speeds for a brief period of time. Sprinting allows the character to move at three times their normal movement rate.

Sprinting takes its toll on the character physically. After sprinting, a character is physically exhausted. They're movement rate is halved until such a time as they are able to rest for a period of time equal to what they would need to rest if they had engaged in strenuous activity for one hour.

Overland Movement

A character can march one mile per hour per point of quickness. Walking isn't strenuous activity, but it does take its toll on a body after a while. Marching for a number of hours equal to your constitution score is considered the same as an hour of strenuous activity.

Characters can also run overland. However, the character can only run for a ½ hour (30 minutes) per point of constitution.

All of these rules serve merely as guidelines. The truth of overland movement is that "the party will arrive precisely when the person running the game intends them too."

Let's face it. You're going to go trekking into the woods. You'll camp for the night and some brigands, wolves, or other "random encounter" will interrupt your night's rest. After the combat, you'll quickly grow bored with uneventful nights sleeping under nature's blanket or wolves trying to eat you while you sleep, and you'll "fast forward" to the nearest city, ruin, or point of interest. You'll mysteriously arrive exactly at the point the director wants you to arrive and the adventure will continue.

I've been role-playing for more than half of my life (I am such a nerd), and I have yet to arrive at a location in time to avert a major plot development. It just doesn't happen. So getting caught up in overland movement rates in order to add some credibility where experience has clearly demonstrated that there is none is a waste of your time and mine. Trust me.

Speed & Size

Creatures that are larger than medium size add 1 to their quickness for each size category that they exceed medium (+1 for large, +2 for huge, etc.). Likewise, creatures that are smaller than small subtract one from their quickness for every size categories below small that they are. This is intended to represent the differences in stride of creatures of different sizes. As such, it applies only to movement on land. Other modes of movement, like the Teg's flight, are unaffected by this rule.

Quadrupeds & Other Multi-pedal Creatures

Creatures with more than two legs multiple all running modifiers by the number of pairs of legs they possess, to a maximum of 5. A centaur, for example, would run twice as fast as a human with the same quickness score and size.

Health and Healing

Healing

The amount of damage that a character heals is based on several factors. The first of these is the character's normal level of mental and physical fitness.

Normally, character heals a number of body damage points equal to his or her constitution score for every night (8 hours) of rest. Mind damage is healed at a rate equal to the character's psyche score each full hour of rest. Soul damage is healed based on the character's cha score each week (5 days on the Lady's Rock) regardless of whether or not you're resting.

Characters that suffer more egregious wounds heal slower than characters that are relatively unscathed. To represent this in game, the character heals one less point per 8 hours of rest for each wound category above light that he or she suffers (q.v. a character who is moderately wounded heals 1 less point per 8 hours, a character that is seriously wounded heals 2 less points, etc).

If this penalty drops the character to zero points, he or she cannot heal the wounds without aid, either magic or mundane.

For example, Stephan has a constitution of 3 and suffers from a critical wound. His wound level causes the amount of damage he heals to be lessened by 3 leaving him with 0 points healed per 8 hours of rest. Stephan will not recover without medical attention or healing magic.

If this modifier causes the character to heal a negative amount of damage, his or her condition worsens. Such a character suffers additional wounds equal to the net modifier each day until he or she heals enough to negate the penalty.

For example, Evilynn has a constitution score of 2… she's a squishy mage, what do they need constitution for? Evilynn becomes critically wounded. This produces a penalty of -3 (-1 for moderate, -2 for serious, -3 for critical). This penalty actually brings the number of points she can heal each day to -1 (2 Constitution plus -3 for wound level equal -1). Evilynn suffers one point of damage each day until she has healed to at least "seriously wounded" when she will net 0 points per day. She will not heal naturally until she reaches "moderately wounded."

Body, Mind, & Soul damage have their own condition monitors and only penalties from the corresponding monitor apply. Therefore, your mental condition monitor does not affect your physical healing and soul damage does not affect either of them.

This healing is a gradual process that takes place throughout the night. Therefore, a character that is only able to rest for 4 hours will heal ½ of the damage he or she would heal had they rested for the full 8 hours.

Treat Injury Skill

When a character attempts to treat someone's injuries, they roll a number of dice equal to their "treat injury" skill versus a target number equal to 5 plus 1 per wound level. Each success adds one to the number of points the character can heal each night to a maximum of double their applicable score. Separate rolls are required for physical and mental damage.

A wounded character can attempt to treat his or her own injury, but they require twice as many successes to achieve the same results.

For example, Matt is fighting a troll. He wins, but not before the troll wallops him a few times. Matt has a constitution score of 4 and has taken serious damage. Matt would normally heal 4 points for every 8 hours of rest (or 1 every 2 hours). However, his wound level reduces this amount from 4 to 2 (-2 penalty for serious wounds.

Drew, being a nice guy, tends to Matt's wounds. He rolls a number of dice equal to his Treat Injury skill (5 dice) verses a target number of 8 (5 plus 1 each for light, moderate, & serious wounds). Drew scores 3 successes, so Matt heals 5 points of damage for his 8 hours of rest (2 for his constitution minus wound level plus 3 for Drew's successes). Had Matt tried to tend to his own wounds, he would have needed 6 successes to achieve the same results.

Death and Dying

If your character takes all his or her available points of body damage, he or she is dead… well, dying. Any additional damage the character takes is applied to his or her Soul Damage. In addition, the character takes one point of Soul Damage each day until they have healed at least 1 point of Body *and* Mind Damage. If the character loses all of his or her Soul Damage points, he or she traverses the threshold between "mostly dead" and "all dead." The character can no longer be healed and has gone on to the realm of his or her deity.

Fatigue & Rest

Like real people, strenuous activity takes its toll on the characters. Also, like real people, the character's health plays a large role in the amount of sleep or rest necessary to recover.

Every time a character engages in strenuous activity, they will need to rest or suffer the effects of fatigue. The chart below outlines the amount of rest needed based on the character's physical or mental health. (Remember, mental activity can be strenuous too.)

Compare the character's Constitution or Psyche to the table below depending on the type of strenuous activity. The "Rest" column shows how long the character must rest after a given interval (usually 1 hour) of strenuous activity.

If the character fails to rest, he or she incurs the damage listed in the "Damage" column (bet you didn't see that coming, huh?). The character continues to take damage at a set interval (usually 2 hours) until he or she rests, sleeps, or passes out from exhaustion.

For example, Heinrich is building a makeshift wall to defend his farm from a coming goblin attack. He's a young farmer, so he's in decent physical condition having a constitution score of 3. Heinrich must rest 15 minutes for every hour that he works on the wall. If he does not, he takes 3 points of mind damage every 2 hours.

Likewise, Oretta is researching a new spell. She's a practiced mage and has a psyche score of 4. She must also rest for 15 minutes for each hour of research she does. If she fails to rest, she also takes 2 points of mind damage every 2 hours.

NOTE: Combat is a very strenuous activity. Despite what you see in the movies, running around in full plate wielding a great sword isn't easy on the body. Any combat that lasts more rounds than the character has points of either constitution or psyche (whichever is higher) is considered the same as 1 hour of strenuous activity.

This fatigue kicks in once combat is complete. Prior to that adrenaline and endorphins will keep the character operating at peak efficiency.

Characters that did not actually fight in melee, including dodging melee attacks, are not considered to have been in combat.

This is not to say that the character actually fought for an hour. We're simply saying that fighting for your life is just as hard as building a makeshift wall... Frankly, I think we're being generous.

Attribute	Rest	Damage
0	30 Minutes / 1 Hour of Activity	6 Points of Mind Damage / 2 Hours
1	20 Minutes / 1 Hour of Activity	4 Points of Mind Damage / 2 Hours
2	20 Minutes / 1 Hour of Activity	4 Points of Mind Damage / 2 Hours
3	15 Minutes / 1 Hour of Activity	3 Points of Mind Damage / 2 Hours
4	15 Minutes / 1 Hour of Activity	3 Points of Mind Damage / 2 Hours
5	10 Minutes / 1 Hour of Activity	2 Points of Mind Damage / 2 Hours
6	10 Minutes / 1 Hour of Activity	2 Points of Mind Damage / 2 Hours
7	5 Minutes / 1 Hour of Activity	1 Point of Mind Damage / 2 Hours
8	5 Minutes / 1 Hour of Activity	1 Point of Mind Damage / 2 Hours
9	5 Minutes / 2 Hours of Activity	1 Point of Mind Damage / 4 Hours
10	5 Minutes / 2 Hours of Activity	1 Point of Mind Damage / 4 Hours

Sleep

Characters also need to sleep periodically. Sleep allows both the mind and the body to rejuvenate and prepare for the day ahead. It is essential to maintain good health and function.

That being said, I cannot think of anyone I know who actually gets a full 8 hours of sleep every night… and we're not fighting (real) dragons. Obviously, seasoned adventurers cannot be expected to need more sleep than we do; so how much sleep do they need?

Compare your character's constitution score to the table on this page. The column labeled "Sleep" shows the minimum amount of sleep that the character needs during a given 24 hour period.

If the character does not get this amount of sleep, he or she must succeed on a constitution or psyche check (whichever is higher) to stave off the effects of sleep deprivation. The target number for this test is equal to 5 plus the number of tests already made to remain awake.

The character is able to remain awake for 1 hour for each success he or she achieves on this test. Once that time has expired, the character makes another check, but the difficulty increases by 1.

If the character fails to achieve any successes, his or her constitution & psyche are effectively reduced by 1 to represent the effects of sleep deprivation. This does not affect any dice rolls unless the character has already taken damage that has not been healed. However, it does reduce the amount of damage he or she can take for each wound level (see hit points on page XXXX).

Constitution	Sleep
0	10 Hours (minimum)
1	8 Hours (minimum)
2	8 Hours (minimum)
3	6 Hours (minimum)
4	6 Hours (minimum)
5	4 Hours (minimum)
6	4 Hours (minimum)
7	2 Hours (minimum)
8	2 Hours (minimum)
9	1 Hours (minimum)
10	1 Hours (minimum)

Regardless of how well the character rolls, he or she cannot go without sleep forever. Even if you can force the body to continue, the mind needs rest. Any character who succeeds at a number of tests equal to their psyche score is only stalling the inevitable. The character continues to make tests, but the interval is now measured in minutes rather than hours. Furthermore, regardless of the successes achieve, the character starts to suffer the attribute loss described above at each interval.

A character whose attribute, either constitution or psyche, is dropped to zero from lack of sleep immediately falls unconscious no longer able to stay awake. Such a character will sleep for the minimum required (see the table again) plus 30 minutes for each successful test made previously as the mind and body struggle to undo the damage done.

For example, Benoni is working on a role-playing supplement at 3 in the morning. He has been up since 3 AM the previous morning. He's not a "perfect physical specimen by any stretch of the imagination. With a constitution of 2, he requires 8 hours of sleep each day. Even though his constitution is considered "low average" for a human, he has a high psyche (4). So he rolls 4 dice verses a target number of 5 and gets 3 successes. He is able to remain awake and does not need to make another check for 3 hours.

He continues working on the supplement for the next three hours and makes another check. This time his target number is 6, and he only gets 2 successes. Two hours later, he rolls again verses a 6 and does not get any successes. His constitution drops by one. If he fails another test, he'll pass out sitting in front of the computer.

On his next test he scores a single 7 allowing him one more hour. Once that hour is up, his interval is measured in minutes and his target number continues to increase.

He fails the next rolls and passes out from exhaustion. He'll remain unconscious for the next 10 hours (8 minimum plus 30 minutes for each of the four tests he rolled).

Sleeping characters have the target number of any awareness checks increased by 8 while sleeping. Furthermore, if an event does occur that requires an initiative roll, sleeping characters have their action pools cut in half for the first full round of combat. This includes the initial initiative test.

In a normal situation, these only apply to the first round after combat. However, certain things, such as the effects of a particular toxin, poison, or magical effect, may increase that amount of time. If this is the case, such things will be noted in the description of the substance or effect.

- **Sleepless Characters**

Some characters, such as elves, are "sleepless." These characters still require rest; however, they do not sleep… at least not in the same manner than humans and other races do. The human mind needs to dream, but, for these beings, dreaming is a novelty. While humans spend their nights enacting vivid hallucinations of being the one red-shirted crewman to survive being beamed to the planet, elves spend their nights in quiet contemplation of the previous day's events. They enter a trance-like, meditative state. In this state, the character is still aware of his or her surroundings.

They cannot perform active tasks, but may still fulfill more passive activities.

A sleepless character can, for example, stand watch, observe the activities on a roadway, listen for a tel-com call, or watch a vid-caster. They could not, however, drive a wagon, ride a horse, or even sit in a tavern and guzzle dwarven spirits.

In games terms, the sleepless character must still "sleep," but they suffers no penalties to any attribute or skill checks because they are "sleeping."

Magic

Magic is a pervasive force on the Lady's Rock. There are few people whose lives are not touched by magic in some way, shape, or form. Though not every person on the Lady's Rock practices magic, it is believed that all people have in them the ability to harness this strange energy. Like a lot of things people believe, that is not technically correct, accurate, right, or true. Only a select few have the natural ability to harness magic.

Laws of Magic

Of course, while players think in terms of attributes, skills, and dice, characters have no idea what any of these things are… well, they might know what the words mean, but not in the context of the game… Despite that minor inconvenience, characters are aware of their limitations. These game mechanics are embodied in the Laws of Magic.

Some of these laws are the basis for the above mechanics. Others are things that the director will deal with behind the scenes. All magic on the Lady's Rock is governed by them and most people, even non-spell-casters, are at least vaguely aware of them.

Law of Equivalent Exchange

Quite simply, science is correct. Energy, including magical energy, can neither be created nor destroyed; it can only change form. As such, any mage attempting to manipulate magical energy needs to offer something of equal value. Often this is the mages own essence, though it is not unheard of for some mages to offer the essence of others in exchange for their mystical might.

Law of Reciprocal Resistance

Every time a spell is cast on a particular person, the magical energies used to cast that spell linger. Because of this, it is more difficult to cast a spell on someone who has already resisted that same spell cast by the same caster that same day.

Law of Knowledge

It almost goes without saying that understanding brings control. The more you know about magical theory, the better you will be at casting spells. The old adage that knowledge is power is never truer than when it applies to magic.

Rule of Threes

This rule states that whatever energies you send into the world return to you three fold.

Rule of Self

This rule simply means that the best way to learn magic is to know the self. Introspective meditation is an important tool for developing one's arcane power.

Rule of Synchronicity

This rule states that events happening near each other are some how related to each other.

Rule of Contagion

This rule states that you will gain attributes of things you come in contact with. If you have an evil item in your possession, you will become evil. If you come in contact with a cursed item, you will become cursed.

Rule of Association

This rule states that once objects come in contact with each other they continue to affect each other after separation. This is the reason some mages sneak into the bathrooms of their enemies and steal toenail clippings.

Rule of Attraction

This rule is actually composed of several seeming contradictions. First, the Rule of Attraction says that opposites attract. It also claims that like attracts like.

Rule of Balance

This is the notion that all things in life must be balanced… good and evil… right and wrong… hot and cold…

Rule of Names

The idea that knowing something's name somehow gives you power over it is a notion as old as magic itself. This rule states that creatures you summon must obey you if you know that creature's true name.

Rule of Personification

This is the rule that states that any phenomenon can be treated as having a personality and dealt with as one would deal with a person. Every thing on the Lady's Rock has a spirit. Those who know how can communicate with that spirit.

Rules of Invocation and Evocation

These two separate yet equal rules state that there are non-human entities in the multiverse with which you can communicate. That communication will occur either as if the entity is inside your body or as if it is outside your body.

Rule of Identification

This rule is simply the idea that by maximizing association with something you can become that thing and share its knowledge and power.

Rule of Perversity

This rule is not nearly as fun as its name would lead you to believe. Instead this is the fancy way mages have of referring to that old adage, *anything that can go wrong, will go wrong.*

Types of Casters

There are three types of spell-casters found on the Lady's Rock. Each type of caster fills a different role in society. Each also has its own benefits and drawbacks providing a unique game experience for each.

Hedge Wizards & Witches

Hedge wizards/witches are self-taught casters. They have the advantage of not being bound to an elemental aspect like mages, nor are they bound to a deity like clerics. It is not necessary to spend build points on an advantage in order to become a hedge wizard/witch. This makes them the most common form of caster found on the Lady's Rock. They are, however, the least powerful.

The down side of being a hedge wizard/witch is that you lack any and all formal training in the arcane arts. You do not have a casting skill or a summoning skill. Furthermore, you cannot gain the casting or summoning skill no matter how hard you try. You simply lack the connection necessary to make full use of arcane energy. Instead the hedge wizard/witch defaults on all casting rolls.

Hedge wizards/witches learn and caster spells like any other caster. And, with the noted exception of possessing the proper skills, all rules for casting spells apply to them normally.

Mages

Mages are trained in the arcane arts. They may have learned their craft through formal schools, such as the Suidae Verruca School of Wiz-craft and Witchery, or by apprenticing to another mage.

What truly separates magi from other spell-casters is their aspect to one of the elemental forces of the Lady's Rock. Each mage is more in tune with one of the five elements that make up all of existence – Boom, Sweet, Pungent, Orange, or Prickle-Prickle. This aspect makes some of the spells they cast more potent than others. The mage's personality is often reflective of their aspect, making this part of lives difficult to hide (see elemental aspects on page XXXX).

Clerics

While every member of a churches hierarchy is technically a cleric, when we use the term we are referring to those members of the clergy with such a profound connection with their deity that the connection allows them to manipulate the arcane energies of the universe. Depending on which deity the cleric worships, he or she may be better at casting certain spell and less adept at others. In this regard, the choice of deity is much like a mage's elemental aspect.

Clerics, however, have a distinct disadvantage that the mage does not have. Because the cleric's power stems from their connection with the divine, the cleric loses the ability to cast spells or perform summon spirits if that connection is severed. This is why it costs less build points to be a cleric than it does to be a mage.

- **Severing the Divine Connection**

The divine connection between the cleric and their chosen deity can be severed in several ways. Before we can explain how the connection is severed, we must first discuss what the connection is and, just as importantly, what it is not.

The connection between the cleric and his or her chosen deity is part belief in the deity, part adherence to the deity's ethos, and the divine favor of the deity. Should the cleric falter in belief, fail to upon hold his or her deity's ethos, or lose the deity's favor, the cleric loses his or her ability to cast spells.

This connection is not merely paying lip-service to the deity. It isn't simply praying at a particular time of day. It isn't tithing to the deity's church. These are all outward signs of the connection. They are not the connection itself. In fact, some of these things may not be appropriate to a particular deity.

A god of thieves, for example, would hardly expect his followers to meet and pray at dusk or dawn. At dusk is when the thieves should be plying their trade, and dawn is when they should be hiding from the authorities. Forcing a ritual at these times would be counter-productive. Such a deity may, however, require considerable tithes.

Meanwhile, a deity of war might require a brief prayer before entering combat. He might require an elaborate ritual prior to going to war or to commemorate an important victory. Requiring a ritual every third day of the week would serve no purpose, however. In truth, it would encourage followers to pay lip-service to the deity because the rituals would be done out of habit rather than genuine devotion.

- **Deities, Belief, and Spell Power**

Spells with a power of 1 to 3 gain their power from the cleric's belief in the deity. Even if the cleric loses the favor if his or her deity and fails to follow the deity's ethos, these spells still function normally as long as the character believes in the deity and that he or she is doing the deity's work. If the cleric no longer believes in the deity, no spells function.

Spells with a power of 4 to 6 gain their power from following the deity's ethos. Even if the cleric looses the deity's favor, these spells continue to function normally as long as the cleric adheres to the deity's ethos. Should the cleric fail to follow said ethos, then spells with a power of 4 or greater no longer function properly.

Spells with a power of 7 or more come directly from the deity. Such spells can only be cast if the cleric has the favor of his or her chosen deity. If the cleric loses the favor of their deity, no spells with a power of 7 of higher function properly.

If a cleric attempts to cast a spell with a power he or she is no longer able to access because of a severed or impaired connection to the divine, the spell instead functions as if it had a power equal to the highest level available to the cleric.

For example, Tamas is trying to cast a spell with a power of 8. He is a devoted follower who adheres to his deity's ethos, but he recently anger the deity and no longer has its favor. He cannot access spells of this magnitude. However, since he does follow the deity's ethos, he can cast spells with a power of 6. The spell functions as if it was cast with a power of 6 rather than 8.

- **Restoring the Divine Connection**

If the divine connection is broken, the cleric can only restore it by atoning for his or her misdeeds. For small infractions this atonement may be as simply as performing a ritual of purification. For larger infractions, it may require the cleric to go on a quest or perform some other duty for the deity or church in question.

Clerics who make a habit of damaging and restoring their divine connection, and those who commit egregious acts against their deity or church may find themselves having to do more to regain their connection to the divine. These clerics may be forced to perform an obeisance in order to regain their lost glory. This obeisance varies from deity to deity and cleric to cleric. It usually serves as a reminder of the cleric's "crimes" and reminds the cleric of their devotion to their deity. The obeisance is a punishment and should be an inconvenience to the cleric at best and should have an effect on play.

NOTE: An obeisance cannot provide any additional benefit to the character. For example, a character whose obeisance is to pray before casting a spell cannot use that prayer as a verbal component when casting the spell.

Sample Obeisance:

- Praying at a particular (or multiple) times each day
- Not eating a certain food
- Never cutting one's hair
- Always wearing a particular item
- Only using a particular weapon
- Performing a particular ritual at a particular time
- Only killing in self-defense and even then only if there is no other option
- Not consuming alcohol

Elemental Aspects

A mage's elemental aspect isn't just what spells he is more adept at casting and which he is less adept at casting. His aspect is a gateway to his soul. It doesn't shape his personality; it is his personality. It doesn't guide his life; it is his life.

Just as there are five elements that make up the whole of existence, there are five different aspects for mages. Once a child demonstrates some magical aptitude, that child is tested to determine his or her aspect. Children that are born aspected to Boom, Sweet, Orange, or Pungent live normal lives. Those few unfortunate children that are born aspected to Prickle-Prickle are taken away and never heard from again. Luckily, no such children have been born in over 100 years.

Boom

Boom, as the name suggests, is an explosive aspect. Passion drives the mages that are aspected to the element of Boom. They are an ambitious lot who thirst for power. Boom-aspected mages are quick to love and quick to anger. A fire burns inside them. They pour their hearts into everything that they do. The hottest fires burn brightly, but they quickly burn themselves out.

Advantages: +2 dice to casting Divination Spells and summoning Boom Elementals, +3 dice to casting Evocation Spells

Disadvantages: -1 dice to casting Illusion and Transmutation Spells, -2 dice to casting Enchantment, -3 dice to casting Conjuration Spells

Sweet

Sweet, as you may have guessed, is a pleasant aspect. Mages with this aspect are easy-going. They travel with the currents of life rather than fighting them like others are often called to do. Though they are not overly cheerful, they can be nauseatingly pleasant…and "sickeningly sweet" has been used to describe more than one of these mages.

Advantages: +3 dice to Abjuration and Biomancy Spells, +2 to summoning Sweet Elementals

Disadvantages: -2 dice to Divination, Enchantment, Illusion, and Transmutation Spells

Pungent

Mages that are aspected to Pungent are as harsh and abrasive as their namesake. They are intellectuals who pride themselves on their mastery of logic and reason. It is not that these mages lack emotions; they just refuse to allow themselves to be governed by them. Because pungent-aspected mage's rely on reason and are seldom swayed by emotions, others often think those with pungent aspect to be arrogant and condescending. The others are often correct. Pungent-aspected mages often *do* think themselves superior to others.

Advantages: +2 dice to casting Divination and Illusion Spells and summoning Pungent Elementals, +3 dice to casting Enchantment Spells

Disadvantages: -1 die to casting Transmutation Spells, -2 dice to casting Abjuration and Evocation Spells, -4 dice to casting Biomancy Spells

Orange

Orange is a strange element. It is a color as well as an element and that color brings forth images of warmth and comfort. Orange-aspected mages are warm as well. They are caring and charitable. Those aspected to Orange are slow to anger and quick to forgive.

Advantages: +2 dice to casting Conjuration Spells and summoning Orange Elementals, +3 dice to casting Transmutation Spells

Disadvantages: -2 dice to casting Abjuration and Evocation Spells, -3 dice to casting Divination Spells

Religions & Deities

As is often the case when dealing with an empire that spans the whole of the known world, the pantheon on the Lady's Rock has changed significantly over the years. Deities that were once worshipped strictly by a single race or tribe find new adherents and grow in power. Other deities find their influence waning as former worshippers begin to revere more potent entities.

The supreme deity of the Lady's Rock is Eris, the goddess of chaos and discord. It is only fitting that there are 23 deities who make up the pantheon she rules.

Ahbendon
The Whispering Shade

Honesty and honor are not the natural state of affairs for the living. Each day we make a conscious effort to be truthful to those around us despite that little voice in the back of our heads that tells us how easy things would be if we only told a little lie. Ahbendon is that little voice.

Ahbendon was once a powerful deity worshipped by armies of goblins and kobolds. As the empire pushed these races to the fringes of civilization, Ahbendon's power began to wane. He seemed destined for obscurity. Unfortunately, appearances were deceiving.

The empire's war against goblinoid creatures had not destroyed Ahbendon's power base; it had expanded it. Human generals had learned about this god of deception. When their military careers came to an end, they sought new conquests in the arenas of imperial politics. They turned to Ahbendon for aid, and they got it.

Symbol: Ahbendon's symbol is the silhouette of a stylized kobold's head. The horns and fangs of this head have been enlarged to unreal proportions and it is missing its lower jaw. A forked tongue darts out from between its fangs.

Advantages: +2 dice to casting Divination Spells, +3 dice to casting Enchantment and Illusion Spells

Disadvantages: -1 dice to summoning Orange and Sweet Elementals

Drawbacks: A cleric of Ahbendon must succeed on a psyche test with a target number of 9 in order to reveal information that he might be able to use to his advantage later.

Aren
The Lord of War

Aren was the deity worshipped by the hordes of orcish barbarians that plagued the fledgling empire. In his name, countless humans were send to the world beyond. Once humans saw the ferocity that Aren granted the orcs, it was just a matter of time before shrines to the Lord of war found their way into human military camps.

With the god granting his favor to both sides in the conflict, the field of battle quickly changed. The orcs had great numbers, but they lacked the training, discipline, and equipment of the imperial legions. Without their god's exclusive favor, the orcs were lost.

Of course, Aren was not the same deity to the humans that he had been to the orcs. Humans did not want to worship a green-skinned barbarian with protruding tusks. To the humans, Aren was a blond-haired soldier from the northernmost reaches of the empire. He still wielded his bipennis, but it was no longer the crude instrument of death the orcs had imagined.

Symbol: A bipennis (double-headed battleaxe) emblazoned on a tower shield.

Advantages: +1 die to summoning Boom Elementals, +3 dice to casting Abjuration and Evocation Spells

Disadvantages: -2 to casting Biomancy Spells

Drawback: A cleric of Aren must succeed on a psyche test with a target number of 9 in order to resist a challenge of arms.

181

Barak

The Storm Lord

Barak was originally a human deity of rain and fertility. Along with Chuck (the god of biscuits) and Durian (the goddess of agriculture), Barak watched over the humans as they tended their crops and turned them into food. All that changed when the inhuman savages began to prey on human settlements.

The walled cities of the human lands proved too formidable for the inhuman hordes. The rural lands, however, were less fortified and made for easier prey. They were farmers, not warriors, so they turned to their gods for deliverance.

The god of agriculture was a creator and a builder, not a soldier. Barak, as the god of storms, commanded not only the life giving rains, but the destructive lightning. It was in this aspect that the people turned to Barak.

These events in the world of men had a profound effect on the deity. Barak became less benevolent, and became a deity of war. While he was powerful, he was chaotic by nature and not the most dependable. He would later be divested of his warlike attributes as more soldierly deities made themselves known to humanity.

Symbol: The rune for a volcano superimposed over a bolt of lightning.

Advantages: +2 dice to summoning Boom Elementals, +3 dice to casting Evocation Spells

Disadvantages: None

Drawback: Clerics of Barak are quick to anger and prone to violence. A cleric of Barak must succeed on a psyche test with a target number of 12 to not repay even the most unintentional slight and to show mercy to a fallen foe.

Cetari

The Queen of Ice, The Cold Lady

Cetari is a holdover from a time when frost giants ruled the northern reaches of the empire. Cetari was their queen. She declared herself a deity made flesh, and her religion was the only one allowed by law. The humans that had been enslaved by the frost giants were forced to pay homage to this frigid ruler.

Eventually Cetari, who was not yet truly a deity, died. In death, he worship continued. Her kingdom, however, did not. Without the Queen of Ice to lead them, the frost giant kingdom fell into chaos. Seeing this weakness, it was only a matter of time before the slaves revolted. When they did, the frost giant kingdom fell, never to recover. By the time this happened, it was many generations removed from the Cold Lady that had once ruled them.

Sometimes people do irrational things just because their parents did them. When their parents only did those irrational things because their parents did them, you have the recipe for a tradition. The humans had grown so accustomed to paying homage to Cetari, not for love, but to appease the brutal matriarch. Eris, the supreme deity of the Lady's Rock, saw the humans revering this dead ruler. Assuming that they were doing it be cause they wanted to rather than the ridiculous truth of "we're doing it because the people who gave birth to me did it," Eris raised the dead frost giant queen and granted her ascension.

Symbol: A snowflake

Advantages: +1 to summoning Sweet and Pungent Elementals, +2 to Abjuration and Evocation Spells

Disadvantages: -2 to casting Biomancy Spells and summoning Boom and Orange Elementals

Drawback: None

Chalysse

The Mother of All Life, The Crone of Death

Chalysse has been a human deity for as long as humans have recorded history. She is the deity of the cycle of life and death presiding over both the birth of her children and their ultimate demise.

She is always pictured as a beautiful woman wearing a tattered cloak whose eyes are both menacing and comforting at the same time. In battle she is depicted wearing armor made from the bones of fallen foes, wielding a great sickle-sword, and surrounded by an army of the dead. These are not undead creatures. Chalysse hates those who would violate the natural cycle of life. Instead, they are the great heroes of old waiting to once again save the Lady's Rock.

Symbol: A chalice holding the flames of life.

Advantages: +1 die to casting Evocation Spells, +2 dice to casting Abjuration and Biomancy Spells

Disadvantages: -2 dice to summoning ancestor spirits

Drawbacks: Clerics of Chalysse must uphold the natural order. They must succeed on a psyche test with a target number of 15 or destroy any undead that they come upon.

Furthermore, they cannot heal or cure any creature whose time has come. If they do, the cleric takes one point of mind damage for each point of physical damage that they heal. This damage can be resisted with psyche and willpower using a power equal to that of the original attack.

For example, if a cleric of Chalysse attempts to heal a friend who suffered a fatal 16 points of damage from a battleaxe, the cleric would have to resist 16 points of mind damage with a target number equal to the power of the original attack (strength score of the wield plus the weapon rating of the battleaxe).

Chuck

The Lord of Biscuits

Chuck was originally the god of baking and a close friend of Barak and Durian. Together the three deities watched over the people who fed the fledgling human lands. Like Barak, Chuck had a darker side. Unlike Barak, it had nothing to do with his Advantages. Chuck is a lecherous being.

While Chuck's lusts are insatiable, he is not a sensual creature. Instead, he is brutal and demanding; he is a baker, after all. Breads, Cakes, and cookies do not need to be seduced. You simple force the ingredients together in a bowl, take what you want, and throw it in the oven. In fact, Chuck is so brutal that his more violent followers rival those of Kyerhan, something that makes the Master of Murder less than happy.

Symbol: A traditional chef's hat.

Advantages: +1 die to casting Transmutation Spells and summoning Boom Elementals, +2 dice to casting Illusion Spells, +3 dice to casting Enchantment Spells

Disadvantages: -2 dice to casting Biomancy Spells

Drawback: Like their deity, clerics of Chuck are lecherous swine. The cleric must succeed on a psyche test with a target number of 9 in order to avoid pleasures of the flesh when available.

Dumathan
The Silent One

Dumathan is often erroneously believed to be a dwarven deity simply because today he is often venerated by the more stoic members of that species. The Silent One is actually an elven deity. More than that, he was once an elf himself, a dark elf.

In life Dumathan was a drow wizard who obsessed over learning the secrets that others had deemed to dangerous for others to learn. While his quest did make him powerful, it was the knowledge Dumathan sought, not the power it carried. He died knowing the secrets of lichdom, but never becoming a lich. Chalysse, the goddess of life and death beseeched Eris to grant him divinity so that he might help her guard these secrets from those who would abuse them. Eris complied.

Symbol: An ancient glyph meaning silence

Advantages: +1 die to summoning ancestor spirits, +2 dice to casting Divination, Enchantment, and Illusion Spells

Disadvantages: -1 die to casting Biomancy and Evocation Spells

Drawback: Clerics of Dumathan must succeed at a psyche test with a target number of 9 in order to reveal a secret that the cleric knows.

Durian
The Queen of the Fruit

Durian is the deity of agriculture, plants, and the gifts of the earth. She is the patron of farmers, brewers, distillers, and other people who work the land providing for the needs of the people.

Durian was once Barak's lover & a close ally of Chuck. When Barak began to embrace his more violent side their relationship changed. His rains were no longer the gentle, life-giving caresses of a lover. Instead they were brutal and violent affairs. His worshippers fed his new found rage. It was just a matter of time before Durian became caught in the crossfire. When it finally happened, the goddess left her long time lover. They have not spoken since.

The lecherous Chuck hoped to take advantage of her fragile state. He had long desired the Queen of the Fruit, and now he had a chance to make her his. She rebuked his advances, but Chuck would not take no for an answer. It was the first time Durian allowed herself to become violent. She unleashed the fury of nature on the celestial baker. The two have not spoken since.

Symbol: A cluster of grapes

Advantages: +1 die to summoning Orange Elementals, +2 dice to casting Biomancy and Conjuration Spells

Disadvantages: None

Drawback: Durian's clerics suffer a +2 to all magical target numbers if they have not partaken of the fruits of the earth (vegetables, fruits, or products made from them) within the past 24 hours.

Dynah

The Sustainer of Order

Dynah is the goddess of law, discipline, social order, and nobility. Her followers include members of the nobility, law enforcement, military, and others whose lives depend on a strict order. Her blessing is sought before people are ennobled and her priests preside over the crowning of a new emperor should the current emperor die. This would give them almost unrivaled power if they were not so slavishly devoted to the law.

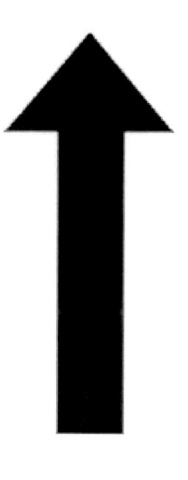

Symbol: A single arrow pointed upwards.

Advantages: +2 dice to casting Abjuration Spells, +3 dice to casting Divination Spells

Disadvantages: None

Drawback: Clerics of Dynah must succeed on a psyche test with a target number of 15 in order to violate the rule of law. They must also succeed a psyche test with a target number of 9 in order to not behave civilly and respectfully to duly appointed representatives of the law.

Eris

The Blessed Mother of Man, Queen of Chaos, Daughter of Discord, Sister of Strife, Concubine of Confusion, Mistress of Mayhem, Princess of Parties, and the Exquisite Lady

While other religions are tolerated, worship of Eris (by her Orthodox church) is the state religion of the empire. Though they technically apply to all deities, the grievances of the first plait were written specifically to protect the clergy of Eris.

She is the supreme deity on the Lady's Rock. She is the being grants ascension to others and those beings serve at her whim. In fact, some theorize that all deities on the Lady's Rock are simply Eris in disguise.

Eris created the Lady's Rock (see History of the World - Part 1, on page XXXX) out of boredom before she had any worshippers in ancient Greece or Rome. Before she abandoned our world, she shared some of the more impressive accomplishments of these cultures with her followers on the Lady's Rock. This is why things on the Lady's Rock are measured in miles and how they know what the word "geometry" means.

Eris (being the goddess of discord, chaos, confusion, madness, mayhem, strife, wild parties, and similar things) is a fickle deity. Some people worship her to gain her favor. Others pay homage to her in order to divert her attention from them. Regardless of why she is worshipped, the net result is the same. Eris has more worshippers than any other deity on the Lady's Rock.

Symbol: A stylized (warped) eight-rayed star of chaos

Advantages: (Orthodox) +1 die to casting Enchantment and Illusion Spells and summoning Boom Elementals, +2 dice to casting Evocation Spells
(Erisian) +1 Die to casting Evocation and Illusion Spells and summoning Boom Elementals, +2 to casting Enchantment Spells

Disadvantages: None

Drawback: Eris personally selects a unique Drawback for each member of her clergy… for some strange and confusing reason. (The director will assign a drawback using others in this list as examples.)

Jhaemaryl

The Lady of Blood and Lust, Mistress of Pleasure and Pain

Jhaemaryl is a unique fiend. Legends say that she is the offspring of a powerful Devil Lord and a Demon Princess. She served as a mercenary in the war between the two fiendish races for centuries. Then, one day, she grew tired of waging war against her brothers and sister. She left the field of battle taking her mercenary legions with her.

Jhaemaryl began to question why the fiendish races waged war amongst themselves rather than battling the more unified forces of the upper plane. Younger demons and devils, not wishing to die, flocked to her legions swelling their ranks. Then Jhaemaryl vanished leaving her followers to fend for themselves.

Her vast legions were reabsorbed into the forces of their respective races. The death toll of the great fiendish war continued to rise. A growing number of demons and devils began to pray that Jhaemaryl for an end to the fighting. Soon, she reappeared as the patron deity of the war that she had hated so much. This did not please the powerful fiendish deity.

When she felt she had sufficient worshippers Jhaemaryl made her move. Not only did she demand an end to the fighting, but she turned her forces against those demonic and devilish lords who had waged the war. Any who would not embrace her imposed peace were deposed, and Jhaemaryl became the undisputed ruler of the lower planes.

Symbol: An eye crying three tears of blood

Advantages: +1 die to summoning Boom Elementals, +2 dice to casting Illusion Spells, +3 dice to casting Evocation and Enchantment Spells

Disadvantages: -1 die to casting Biomancy Spells, -3 dice to casting Abjuration Spells

Drawback: Jhaemaryl's clerics revel in the flesh… both in pleasure and in pain. To them pleasure and pain are one and the same. They do not suffer penalties for taking physical damage, but, because they do not feel pain, they do not know how much damage they have taken. (in game terms, the director keeps track of damage for a cleric of Jhaemaryl.)

Kyerhan
The Lord of Murder

In life, Kyerhan was one of Jhaemaryl's lieutenants. When she ascended to divinity, he followed as her enforcer and assassin. Kyerhan is sent to deal with those who earn Jhaemaryl's ire.

As the exploits of this deity became more well-known, people began to worship Kyerhan as a separate entity rather than just the agent of Jhaemaryl. This has caused some concern in the halls of the Orthodox Church of Eris who see the ascendance of a deity of murder as a bad thing. Professional killers, however, see this as a sign legitimizing a profession that is arguably the second oldest on the Lady's Rock.

Symbol: The skull of a human merged with than of a demon.

Advantages: +1 die to casting Conjuration, Divination, Enchantment, Evocation, and Illusion Spells.

Disadvantages: None

Drawback: Clerics of must succeed on a psyche test with a target number of 9 in order to not take the life of a foe.

Laeroth
The Wise One, The Learned Hermit

Even before Laeroth ascended he appeared older than his elven heritage should have allowed. Legend holds that he was one of the first elves created by Eris.

In his younger days, the elven scholar traveled across the Lady's Rock gathering every tidbit of information and painstakingly recording it in one of the many tomes that he always carried with them. Once filled, Laeroth stored these in a small building nestled in a tree deep in the wooded hills of Aerondale that he was ancient even when Laeroth walked the Lady's Rock. This library has come to be known as the *Tree of Knowledge*. As the collection grew, so did the building creating a hodge-podge of wood and stone that appears more like the aftermath of a tornado than the most comprehensive library in the mortal world.

The library still exists. The high priest of Laeroth's church serves as the head librarian administrating the collection and overseeing a myriad of lesser priests who have pledged to preserve this knowledge. A cadre of specially trained warriors ensures that the library will remain for generations to come.

For his labor of passion, Laeroth was rewarded with immortality. Eris granted the venerable elf a new life and charged him with continuing his life's work. Today he sits in a small room in the otherworldly version of his earthly library chronicling all that the people have learned… and all that they will learn.

Symbol: A stylized representation of the tree of knowledge.

Advantages: +1 die to Abjuration and Enchantment Spells, +3 to Divination Spells

Disadvantages: None

Drawback: Laeroth's clerics must act to preserve all knowledge. They must make a psyche test with a target number of 16 in order to even allow someone else to destroy a tome or scroll.

Makath

The Pestilent Lord

Disease attacks people seemingly without rhyme or reason. This chaotic force of nature is governed by an equally chaotic being. Makath appears to be a rotting human corpse. Legends say that he was once a wizard of immense power. Despite his vast knowledge, Makath had one fatal flaw – he feared death.

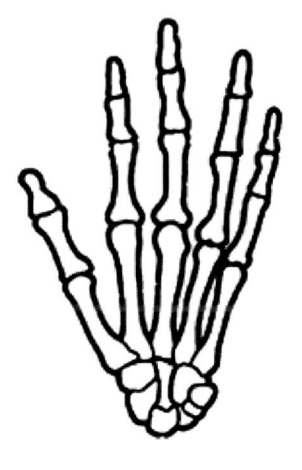

He wanted to become a lich. Unfortunately, he failed. Chalysse, the goddess of life and death, cursed him for his arrogance plaguing him with countless diseases while he lived. Eris took this punishment one step further and granted him the unlife he desired.

Symbol: A skeletal human hand

Advantages: +2 dice to casting Evocation Spells and summoning Boom Elementals, +3 dice to casting Conjuration Spells

Disadvantages: -2 dice to casting Biomancy Spells and summoning Sweet Elementals

Drawback: Clerics of Makath must make a psyche test with a target number of 9 in order to cure someone who has contracted a disease.

Manak

The Lord of Water

Manak is the master of lakes, rivers, and streams. Once he held a position of great power in the pantheon of the Lady's Rock. As the empire expanded, however, Manak's power waned. Inland waters are important to the people who live on the Lady's Rock, but their importance pales in comparison to that of the aether. The advent of aether-ships and inter continere travel, Manak became less and less influential eventually loosing control over commerce.

Symbol: An ancient alchemical rune meaning water.

Advantages: +1 die to casting Evocation Spells, +2 dice to casting Biomancy Spells and summoning Sweet Elementals

Disadvantages: None

Drawback: Like the water their deity governs, clerics of Manak sre fickle creatures. They must make a psyche test with a target number of 9 or they must repay any slight in kind.

Myra
The Mistress of the Heart

This fickle deity governs affairs of the heart. She does not concern herself with pure lust. That is the province of Jhaemaryl. Instead, Myra focuses on love and relationships between lovers. She watches over lovers and married couples. And, while the act of love is important, it is the feelings behind those acts that Myra finds more important.

When she appears to mortals, Myra takes the form of a perfect specimen of whatever race sees her. Humans see her as human. Elves see her as an elf. Dwarves see her as a dwarf. And orcs see her as an orc. Whatever form she takes, Myra does not inspire lust or longing. Instead those who see her are filled with the calm serenity one would find in the arms of a lover.

Symbol: A stylized knot

Advantages: +2 dice to casting Illusion Spells and summoning Boom and Orange Elementals, +3 dice to casting Enchantment Spells

Disadvantages: -4 dice to casting Evocation Spells

Drawback: Myrah's clerics are as beautiful as their deity. Clerics of Myrah must have a charisma of 6 or higher.

Narsin
The Great Hero

Narsin is a hero's hero, or at least that's how he appears to his followers. He wears gleaming platemail crafted of mithril and covered with gilded runes. Narsin wields an enchanted great sword forged from adamantine. He embodies all that is heroic and good. Bards tell tales of how Narsin slew dragons, vanquished demons, and saved countless damsels in distress.

The truth behind Narsin is a vastly different tale. While he often did perform many of the deeds attributed to him, Narsin rarely quested alone. Unfortunately, time seems to have robbed us of the names of these allies. This is probably because few, if any of them, survived their heroic trials. Narsin, however, did not perish because Narsin is not a hero; he is a coward.

Despite what the average denizen of the Lady's Rock believes, Narsin was not granted ascension to reward him for his heroism. Everyday Narsin hears the heroes of the Lady's Rock asking for his aid in doing things that Narsin himself would never be able to accomplish. He knows that Eris is punishing him for his cowardice.

Symbol: A Great Sword

Advantages: +1 die to casting Transmutation Spells, +2 dice to casting Abjuration and Evocation Spells

Disadvantages: None

Drawback: Clerics of Narsin must make a psyche test with a target number of 9 in order to resist a heroic quest.

Semis
The Grand Artifice, The Great Architect

Semis started out as the dwarven god of the forge. He is said to have crafted the sentient races in his divinely workshop. Of course, racial deities do not tend to remain exclusive to their race of origin. Once other species learned of Semis's ethos, it was just a matter of time before they too began to pay homage to the Grand Artificer.

Semis's area of influence then grew to include not only those who worked with metals and gems, but those who wrested these precious elements from the ground as well. His close association to the earth brought masons to the worship of Semis. Architects soon followed. Semis's ethos of hard work and dedication to your craft appealed to other craftsmen as well. Today, all artificers, Artisans, & Craftsmen pay homage to the master forger.

Symbol: A crossed hammer and tongs

Advantages: +1 die to summoning Orange Elementals, +2 dice to casting Conjuration and Transmutation Spells

Disadvantages: None

Drawbacks: When they encounter a new item, a cleric of Semis must make a psyche test with a target number of 7 or spend 5 turns (minus 1 per success) examining it.

Solvarus
The Lord of the Forest

Solvarus is seen as an elven archer clothed in green & brown leathers. He moves as quietly as a deer, can see as well as an eagle, and never misses when he looses an arrow from his mighty bow.

Solvarus is a nature deity, the lord of the forests. He is worshipped by hunters, woodsmen, trappers and furriers. He is the patron of ranger, including the super secret Yusidree Rangers, and many orders of druid.

Symbol: A cluster of oak leaves

Advantages: No woodland creature will attack a cleric of Solvarus unless they are attacked by the cleric or compelled to do so by magic.

Disadvantages: None

Drawback: None

Steve
The Noble Auditor

How Steve became a deity is unknown. He seems to have began his divine career simply as the god of cosmetology. Why Eris thought the world needed a deity of hair dressing, no one knows, but Steve's role in society has increased since then. Now Steve governs social status and the signs of that status. In a strange twist, Steve also became the deity of charities and charitable giving.

Symbol: A pair of sheers

Advantages: +1 die to casting Abjuration, Biomancy, and Illusion Spells, +2 dice to casting Enchantment Spells and summoning Sweet Elementals

Disadvantages: -2 dice to casting Evocation Spells

Drawback: Clerics of Steve suffer a +1 penalty to all magical target numbers when they are unkempt or less than stylish.

Tchoren
The Supreme Sorcerer

Tchoren is deity whom Eris has entrusted with governing the use & misuse of magic. He is not a deity of magical knowledge or understanding. Instead, Tchoren is the deity of magical power. He is the patron of sorcerers and mystics. Tchoren is a selfish deity. He is concerned with his own status and power. His followers are likewise obsessed with personal power. They specialize in spells that are flashy or destructive. They are not known for their subtlety. Scholars wonder why Eris tolerates the treacherous deity. Eris's clergy just shrugs.

Symbol: A flaming skull without a jawbone

Advantages: +3 dice to casting Conjuration and Transmutation Spells

Disadvantages: -1 die to casting Abjuration Spells

Drawback: Clerics of Tchoren must make a psyche check with a target number of 9 in order to share magical power… including magical items and spells… with anyone… or for any price.

Valderon
The Lord of the Five Virtues

Valderon is the patron of paladins regardless of what deity they may serve. When the Empire of Eristonia was merely a fledgling kingdom, Valderon was a soldier in service to a barbarian warlord. As Eristonia grew in power, it came into conflict with the barbarian horde. Valderon met the forces of the Eristocracy on the field of battle and sent many of them to meet their deity. Eris saw this noble warrior and was intrigued by his sense of honor and integrity. When the battle was over, the King of Eristonia had the leaders of the barbarian army execute, including Valderon. Even in the face of certain death, the warrior exhibited his unique sense of honor. Legend has it that Eris Herself appeared at the execution and took Valderon into the heavens.

Worship of Valderon is based around the five pillars of existence – Honor, Duty, Glory, Combat, & Victory. Each person is measured against these pillars. Honor represents how one deals with other people. It is honesty & integrity. Duty may be different for each worshipper. Fulfilling one's duties and obligations is important to followers of Valderon. Glory simply means increasing the greater glory of Valderon. Combat represents not only strength of arms, but also nobility and honor on the field of blood. Victory is the most misunderstood of the pillars. It is not simply winning, but represents the obligations that the winner of a conflict has to the vanquished. Valderon believes that behavior in victory is a window directly to the soul.

It is worth noting that the head of Valderon's church is Lady Shyressa of Goram, a beautiful human woman who has proven herself on the field of battle numerous times. She leads the church from the Cathedral of Valor in the City of Goram.

Symbol: An elaborate coat of arms containing five columns, one for each of Valderon's five pillars.

Advantages: +2 dice to casting Biomancy Spells, +3 dice to casting Evocation Spells, +4 dice to casting Abjuration Spells

Disadvantages: -2 dice to casting to Enchantment and Illusion Spells

Drawback: Clerics of Valderon must make a psyche test with a target number of 18 in order to act dishonorably. They must also make a psyche test with a target number of 9 or they must avenge any slight to their honor.

Vastra
The Aethereal Maiden

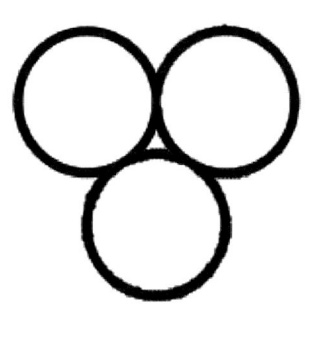

Vastra is the deity who governs the aether, the great seas of heavy air on which the land masses of the Lady's Rock float. With the invention of aethereal ships and the advent of inter-continere trade, Vastra has grown in power and influence. She is the patron of aethereal sailors and those who depend upon them for their livelihood.

Symbol: Three circles arranged in a triangle

Advantages: +2 dice to casting Conjuration Spells, +3 dice to casting Transmutation Spells

Disadvantages: None

Drawback: Clerics of Vastra suffer a +2 penalty to all magical target numbers when not within sight of the aether.

Spells

Defining Spells

In order to understand the mechanics behind magic in the game, you must first understand something about the world of the Lady's Rock. The world in which the character's live considers of two coexistent planes. Actually, it consists of several plane, some of which are coexistent, but that isn't really important to this particular discussion (see cosmology on page XXXX).

Obviously, the characters exist in physical space, called the material plane. The material plane contains all physical reality. If you can touch it, taste it, see it, smell it, or hear it, it exists on the material plane.

Physical reality is only part of existence though. The material plane in not the only reality we exist in. Human beings, like other sentient creatures, are more than just the bodies that they occupy. In fact, the body is merely a vessel for something more important – the soul. Souls exist on a dimension of reality known as the ethereal plane. The ethereal coexists with the material. They occupy the same space at the same time. Every living thing exists on both plans while they remain alive.

The ethereal plane is also the source of the magical energy that mages and clergy manipulate. The ethereal energy permeates every magical spell and every magic item on the planet. Spells retain the imprint of the person who cast it. This imprint signature remains until the energy of the spell dissipates… but more on that later.

To put things simply, magic is an energy that the spell-caster channels through themselves and shapes through the force of their will. In order to represent the spell in the fictitious relam of the Lady's Rock, they are assigned several characteristics – Power, Difficulty, and Enervation.

Power: The power of a spell determines its effects on the game. It is both the target number for the target to resist the spell and the target number for the caster to resist enervation. Furthermore, it is the maximum number of successes that can be applied to the variable effects of the spell. (Successes beyond the power of the spell still count for the purposes of dodging, resisting, and dispelling.) The maximum power at which the character can cast the spell is determined when he or she learns it.

Difficulty: Some spells are more difficult to cast than others. The difficulty of a spell is the target number for the caster to actually cast the spell. The difficulty is determined by the desired effect of the spell.

Enervation: Casting a spell is a grueling process that takes its toll on the caster. The enervation of the spell is the amount of damage that the caster takes *per two successes* achieved on the casting test (limited by the power of the spell). This damage is normally mind damage, but can be body damage… or even soul damage… depending on the power of the spell. Regardless of the type of damage, Enervation is always gaffed using psyche and willpower dice at a rate of ½ the character's psyche.

Note: Regardless of modifiers, the base enervation of a spell cannot be reduced below 1. This will make more sense once you get to the modifiers for the different schools.

Casting Spells

To cast a spell, the character selects the power level he or she wishes to cast the spell at up to the maximum power level at which he learned the spell. The character then rolls a number of dice equal to his or her casting skill with additional dice from his or her action pool if desired against the difficulty of casting the spell. The variable effects of the spell are multiplied by the number of successes achieved (up to a maximum of the power at which the spell was cast). These effects are applied to the target of the spell. The target may attempt to dodge or resist the spell.

Next, the enervation is applied to the caster. Multiply the number of successes achieved (again, up to a maximum of the power of the spell) by the enervation of the spell and apply the damage to the caster as outlined in the next paragraph.

If the power of the spell is less than or equal to the psyche of the caster, the damage is applied as stun damage. If it is more than the caster's psyche, but less than twice his psyche, it is applied as body damage. If the power of the spell is greater than twice the character's psyche, the damage is applied as soul damage.

The caster may resist this damage normally using his or her psyche with additional dice from his or her willpower pool if desired. Enervation cannot be dodged.

Defending Against Spells

There are two types of defense tests you can roll if you are targeted by a spell. Depending on the type of spell cast, you can either dodge the spell or resist its effects.

A character can only dodge spells that require the caster to touch the target. Other spells manifest at their target, so there is nothing to dodge. If a spell has an area of effect, character other than the target who are trapped in the spell's area may attempt to dodge the effect. However, in order to dodge an area of effect, the character must be able to move from his location to the area outside of the spell's effect.

Resisting a spell is different. Spells are resisted with either psyche or constitution augmented by willpower and vigor respectively. To determine which attribute applies, simply look at the effect of the spell. Spells with a physical descriptor, those that affect things that do not exist on the physical plane, and those that deal physical damage are resisted with constitution and vigor. All other spells are resited with psyche and willpower. A character can always choose not to resist a spell cast on them; which is why you don't have to roll resistance to healing spells.

NOTE: When casting a spell, the number of successes that is applied to the spell's variable effects is limited by the power of the spell. This does not, however, limit the number of successes needed to defend against a spell. Each success achieved by the defender still counters one of the caster's successes, but the defender must negate all of the casters successes, including those in excess of the spell's power, in order to defend against the full effects of the spell.

Dispelling

If you have an available action and have a higher initiative, you can attempt to dispel a spell cast by someone else. In order to do this, the character attempting to dispel the magic must roll his or her spell casting dice against a target number equal to the power of the spell to be dispelled.

The dispelling test is either a success or a failure. If the person attempting to dispel the magic does not achieve more successes than the person casting the spell, the spell takes effect normally as if no dispelling attempt occurred. The person attempting the dispelling test still loses an action, the one used to attempt to dispel.

Spell Signatures

Just as no two spell-casters are exactly alike, no two spells are identical. Even if two casters learn the exact same spell, there will be subtle differences visible to the trained eye. Every time a caster casts a spell, that spell is imprinted with the casters own unique signature making each spell unique.

When a spell is cast, this signature remains on the area and objects affected by the spell for one hour per power level of the spell in question. This signature can be used to by those who know what to look for as a means of identifying the person who had cast a particular spell.

Rumors persist that there are those who have learned to erase this signature, but they remain rumors. If such knowledge exists, those who possess it guard it jealously.

Sustained Spells

Certain spells require the caster to continually feed magical energy into the spell in order for the spell to continue to function. The caster must devote a portion of his attention to nourishing the spell with magical energy. This causes the caster to suffer a +2 penalty to all target numbers for each spell he or she is sustaining for as long as he or she chooses to sustain them.

Additionally, the caster must resist enervation each round that the spell is active equal to the base enervation of the spell… or equal to the enervation for getting one success on a casting test. Somatic components can be used to lower the target number ot resist this enervation just as they could during casting… provided the caster wants to devote the time to performing them. Material components can also be used to offset the amount of enervation, but these are also consumed… just as they were during casting.

Despite this, some spells will only function properly if they are sustained. Spells such as those that magically enhance attributes are useless if their duration is instantaneous, for example. Other spells, such as evocation magics, cannot be sustained even if the caster desires to do so. Exactly why this happens as it does is anyone's guess. Some say that it's the will of Eris… others think some other mysterious entity just did it to keep everything balanced…

Spell Ranges

In the d10 system, spells can have three different ranges depending on how the caster designs the spell. Depnding on the spell, you can make design it so that it only affects the caster giving it a range of "self." Also depending on the spell, you can desing a spell that requires that the caster touches his or her intended target giving it a range of "touch." Lastly, a spell that is neither "touch" nor "self" has a range of "Line of Sight." That's right… if you can see it, you can hit it. It is that simple.

Schools of Magic

There are nine schools of magic. Of these, only eight are practiced by the people of the Lady's Rock. The ninth schools, that of Necromancy, has been strictly forbidden and practicing spells of this school is the most egregious of crimes, punishable by summary execution without appeal or even a trial.

The remaining eight schools of magic are as follows:

Abjuration: The school of Abjuration contains defensive magics. This school is home to all of the shield, barrier, and wall spells that you might find use for while adventuring.

Biomancy: Spells that affect the life and health of living creatures are the province of the school of Biomancy. This school contains all of the healing spells that you may have a use for as well as those spells that augment attributes.

Conjuration: Creating things out of thin air is the province of the school of Conjuration. Creating food, light, changing temperature, and creating temporary weapons fall into this category. This school also deals with teleportation magics.

Divination: Spells from the school of divination reveal information about objects and people that you would not ordinarily gain simply by looking at them. These spells are also useful for masking that same information from others.

Enchantment: This school of magic contains those spells that charm, beguile, and magically compel a target to do things that they might otherwise no do. This school is extremely handy when asking your boss for a raise.

Evocation: Evocation is the powerhouse of the schools of magic. Fireballs, lightning bolts, and other direct damage spells come from this school making it very popular among adventurers.

Illusion: The school of Illusion deals with phantasms and figments. It allows you to make people see & hear things that are not really there.

Transmutation: The school of transmutation allows you to change something into something else. It is also used to change the properties of an item or person… causing them to levitate, for example.

Necromancy: This feared school of magic deals with death, undeath, and all the unsavory things that fall in between. This school of magic allows the caster to give a horrid semblance of life to corpses and skeletons. It allows them to rob the vitality from other living beings. And it allows them to cheat death and live forever.

Necromancy, giving new life to the dead, is considered the most heinous of crimes and is outlawed throughout the empire. Though most alive today are too young to remember when Vandal Nefar used the dark art to raise an army of the undead and seized control of the empire, all have heard the tales. They know the stories of fallen soldier rising to slay their comrades. The evil of these yarns is so ingrained into imperial culture than no one questions the summary execution of a suspected necromancer. Even in the most just imperial courts you are guilty as charged unless you can prove otherwise… and you only have as much time as it takes for the headman's axe to fall.

Creating Spells

Creating a spell is a three-step process.

1. Determine the desired effects of the spell
2. Design the spell
3. Learn the spell

This section will go through each of the steps so that you can create custom spells for your characters.

Determining the Effects of the Spells

First, you need to have some idea of what you'd like this spell to accomplish. Once you know what you want your spell to do, the design process is fairly simple.

Select the school that best fits your desired effects. It will be very easy to determine the proper school for some spells. Defensive spells, for example, belong to the school of Abjuration. The flashy offensive spells that we all know and love belong to the school of evocation. If you are unsure which school your spell fits in look at the different options available for each school. If no school allows you to create the spell you desire, chances are the spell you desire is beyond the scope of modern magic… maybe your spell will be possible in the future. Email us and we'll see if our crack staff of arcane researchers can't decipher the proper formula.

Once you have determined what school of magic best fits your spell, the next step is to select the variables that apply to your spell. Some variables affect the enervation of the spell others affect the difficulty of casting. Record each variable separately.

The total enervation modifier becomes the enervation for the spell. This is the amount of damage that your character will take for each success on the casting check.

The total difficulty modifier is added to a base of 5 and this is the difficulty for the spell. This is the target number of your character's spell-casting roll to actually cast the spell.

If these numbers are too high for your character, there is still hope. You can select component modifiers – verbal, material, or somatic components – in order to make the spell easier to cast.

Designing the Spell

Once you know what you want the spell to do and you've selected all the modifiers, its time to see if your character is capable of creating and learning the spell you've envisioned.

In order to create a spell, your character needs two things. The first is a place to research the spell. The second is the skill to do it.

Mages require a library of arcane tomes and a working knowledge of arcane theory… hence the arcane theory skill.

A cleric, on the other had, needs a shrine to their deity and a working knowledge of their religion.

As long as the character has access to these things, he or she can attempt to design the spell. Simply roll the applicable spell design skill against as target number equal to the difficulty of the spell, ignoring any component modifiers. The number of successes that the character achieves on this test represents the power at which the character can learn the spell.

Researching and designing a spell takes a number of hours equal to the power level of the spell. If your character rolls 8 successes it means that they spent 8 hours researching and designing (or meditating and praying on) a spell and it will function at a power of 8. If someone teaches a spell to the chatacter, the amount of time is half of the power rating that the character rolls. The mechanics are unchanged, however.

Keep in mind that this is strenuous activity and the mage or cleric will be fatigued as per the fatigue rules on page XXXX.

Learning Spells

Once you've designed a spell, the character must see if they can learn the spell that they have designed. This is process is not easy. It taxes the caster's mind and body. Even though the spell will not actually be cast during this process, the caster is affected as if he or she had casted the spell.

First the character makes a channeling test. The character rolls his or her spell-casting dice against the difficulty of the spell. The spell's difficulty can be modified by Verbal Components; however, if verbal components are used, the caster must use that component whenever he or she casts the spell.

Multiply the number of successes that the caster achieved on the channeling test by the enervation code for the spell. This is the amount of damage that the caster may potentially take if he or she does not succeed at harnessing all the energy channeled. Remember, if the power of the spell exceeds the caster's psyche, this is physical damage and is recorded under Body Damage on the character sheet. If power does not exceed the character's psyche, this is mental damage and is recorded under Mind Damage on the character sheet.

Once the caster has channeled the energy, he or she must harness the spell's power. To do this, the character makes a harnessing test rolling their psyche dice, plus any dice from willpower they might desire) against a target number equal to the spell's power. The power of the spell can be reduced (for this purpose only) by using a somatic component; however, if the caster uses a somatic component, they must then use this same component each time they cast the spell. Each success reduces the damage that the character will suffer by ½ of the character's psyche.

The caster can further reduce enervation damage by using a material component. The material components are consumed by the magical energy and mage receives automatic successes to resist enervation based on the purity of the component used.

If the caster fails to negate the enervation from the spell, he fails to learn the spell. If the caster does manage to negate all the enervation, he or she has managed to learn the spell. If the character learns the spell, he must spend one point of Mana per power level of the spell in order to bind that spell to the character. If he or she does not, knowledge of the spell vanishes after it is cast and the caster must relearn the spell in order to cast it again. The relearning process take 15 minutes per power level of the spell.

For example, Sven is trying to learn an armor spell. The base difficulty of this spell is 5, so Sven rolls his arcane theory dice against a target number of 5 and gets 6 successes. Sven has figured out how to cast an armor spell at a power of 6.

Sven hasn't been adventuring that long, but he's in fairly descent shape. He has a constitution score of 3, so he requires 15 minutes of rest for every hour of strenuous activity. Since he's been working on this spell for 6 hours, Sven needs to rest for an hour and a half and suffers 6 points of mental damage because of it. He opts to rest for the hour and a half to eliminate this damage, and the modifiers it will place on his next roll, before continuing.

Sven understands that spells achieving more successes is better for him. In the cast of his armor spell, the spell lasts one round per success. Since this is going to be his primary defense during combat, Sven wants this spell to last a while. Sven decides to use a single-word component to reduce the difficulty to 4.

Sven rolls his channeling test. He rolls his spell-casting dice and scores 8 successes. Because Sven is only able to learn the spell at a power of 6, only 6 of these successes count for enervation. These 6 successes are multiplied by the enervation code of Sven's armor spell, which is 4. Sven is risking taking 24 points of damage from channeling the energy from this spell. That's quite a bit of potential damage, and, because the power of the spell (6) exceeds Sven's Psyche score (4), the damage will be physical (recorded on Sven's Body Damage Monitor).

Sven decides that 24 points is too much to risk and he really wants to learn this spell so he uses a complex somatic component to reduce the power of the spell from 6 to 4 for his harnessing test. Each success he rolls will negate 2 points of damage (1/2 his psyche) He has 10 dice (4 from psyche and 6 from Willpower) The most he can hope to negate is 20 points, so Sven decides to add a material component to negate the remaining 4 points of enervation. This will require two automatic successes, so Steven decides to use a fixed essence (see refining essences on page XXXX). The fixed essence will give him two bonus successes against enervation.

If Sven succeeds in negating the damage, he learned the spell and must spend 6 points of Mana in order to make the spell his own otherwise it vanishes from his memory after it is cast.

If he fails to negate all the damage, he suffers whatever damage he could not negate and must begin the process again if he wants to learn the spell. This includes going back to the library and researching the spell again looking for the thing that he missed the first time.

Magic in the Making

Each school of magic has its own unique aspects that define its school and effects. In addition to these factors, there are several component factors that can be applied to any spell to easy the stress of casting. These factors must be determined at the time of spell creation. Once selected, they become integral to the spell and cannot be changed.

Verbal Components

Verbal Components help the mage or cleric focus during spell casting. Components cannot reduce a target number to less than one. These modifiers are applied to the difficulty of casting the spell making it easier for the mage or cleric to cast.

Single Word	-1
Incantation	-2
Complex Incantation	-3

A single word component is something that can be done while the caster is casting. It does not require an additional action.

An incantation is lengthier and takes up part of an action. It can be done in the same action as other things that take up part of an action, but must be done on a separate action that immediately precedes the actual casting.

A complex incantation requires an action all its own. This action must precede either the action in which the spell is cast or an action devoted to another component.

Somatic Components

When a caster uses a somatic component he either creates an arcane symbol with his hand or traces such a sigil in the air. These symbols force the magic to manifest in a particular fashion making it easier for the caster to resist the effects of channeling the magical energy. Somatic components reduce the power of the spell for the purposes of resisting drain only. The target of the spell still needs to resist the effects of the spell at its full power. As with verbal components, somatic components cannot reduce the target number to less than one.

One-hand Gesture	-1
Simple Gesture	-2
Complex Gesture	-3

A one-hand gesture is something that can be done while the caster is casting. A one-hand gesture does not require at additional action.

A simple gesture is lengthier and takes up part of an action. It can be done in the same action as other things which only need part of an action, such as an incantation. However, a somatic component must be done as a separate action from the spell and must immediately precede the action in which the spell is cast or an action devoted to another component.

Material Components

The Law of Equivalent Exchange is the reason for enervation. The caster gives up part of his or her life force in exchange for magical energy. Material components provide something else that the caster can exchange. It acts as armor against drain reducing the total amount of drain by the value of the material component. As many as two material components can be applied to any spell.

Variable Essences	1 Success
Fixed Essences	2 Successes
True Essences	3 Successes

Variable Essences: A variable essence can be applied to spells related to 3 elements potentially granting a bonus success to spells from six out of eight schools of magic. It grants one bonus success to resist enervation.

Fixed Essences: Fixed essences function provide two successes, but only for schools of magic associated with a two of the elements.

True Essences: True essences provide three bonus successes to resist enervation, but they only apply only to the schools of magic associated with a particular element.

Unlike other components, a spell-caster can choose whether or not to use material component at the time of casting. Using a material component to learn a spell does not mean that the caster must use them to cast the spell.

Once a material component is used to resist enervation that component is consumed by the magic of the spell.

To learn more about these essences, see refining essences on page XXXX.

Abjuration

Defensive magic is fairly straight forward. There are two variable parts to the spell. The first is the protection provided by the spell. The second is the enervation of the spell. The ratio of protection to enervation is one to one. For each point of armor value that the spell provides, it does one point of enervation per success.

The difficulty of casting any armor spell is always 5. The range is always touch. The duration of the spell is equal to the number of successes achieved on the casting test.

An area of effect abjuration spell creates a hemisphere shaped shield centered on where the caster was standing when it was cast. The shield originates at the caster and radiates outward as the spell is cast. Those caught in the path of the shield are either pushed back to the edge of the spell's radius, or they take damage equal to the armor value of the shield. This damage cannot be gaffed (because the character is choosing to take the damage), but may be absorbed by armor.

Note: People inside the shield can attack and damage each other normally as can two combatants outside the shield. Only attacks that pass through the shield are affected by it. I know that might sound like common sense, but, if I don't say it specifically, some player some where will try to use it to their advantage.

Also, since the shield is centered on the position where the caster was standing and not the caster, an area of effect abjuration spell is not mobile. It does not move when the caster does... and the caster is subject to damage for crossing through the shield just like everyone else.

Armor Value	Enervation
1	1
2	2
3	3
4	4
5	5
Etc…	

Armor value for an abjuration spell functions exactly like regular armor except that the abjuration spell does not have a vulnerability to any particular type of attack. Furthermore, because it is not light, medium, or heavy armor, it provides full protection against any attack, even those that would otherwise ignore armor.

Enervation Modifiers

+1 Area of Effect (5 feet per point of psyche)
+2 Extended Area (10 feet per point of psyche)
+3 Extended Area (15 feet per point of psyche)
+4 Extended Area (20 feet per point of psyche)
Etc…

Biomancy

Biomancy, as I've explained, is the opposite side of the necromancy coin. It entails using energy to heal damage to living things and enhancing their natural attributes.

Healing Spells

For each success on the casting test, the spell heals a number of points equal its healing factor. The caster must resist enervation equal to the enervation multiplied by the number of successes.

The base difficulty for healing spells is 5, though this can be modified by the factors listed below. The range on all biomancy spells is touch. The duration for healing magic is instantaneous. Once the spell is casted, the target immediately heals the damage indicated by the results of the roll… regardless of the outcome of the enervation test.

Healing Factor	Enervation
1	1
2	2
3	3
4	4
5	5
Etc…	

Difficulty Modifiers

-1 Restricted to a specific subspecies

Enervation Modifiers

-1 Requires a voluntary target
-1 Affects only a specific individual (such as "heal self")
-3 Provides only temporary healing (lasting for one round per success on the casting check)

Body Modification Spells

These spells increase the character's attributes. Powerful spells can even increase them beyond the target's racial maximums.

The base enervation for these spells is 2 per additional attribute point. This enervation is modified by the factors listed below.

The difficulty is, as always, 5 plus any modifiers selected from the list below. Though, as mentioned earlier, these spells are fairly useless if they are not sustained.

Difficulty Modifiers

-1 Restrict to a specific subspecies

+1 Affects physical attributes
+1 Sustained

Enervation Modifiers

-1	Requires a voluntary target
-1	Affects only a specific individual
+1	Affects the character's action pool (i.e. modifies CRD, QCK, RSN, or INT)

Conjuration

The school of conjuration encompasses two separate and distinct magical processes. The first is transporting something from one point on the Lady's Rock to another. These spells are known as conjurations. The second is creation something out of nothing for a limited duration. Spells of this nature are known as creation spells.

Regardless of the type of spells cast, items brought into existence cannot appear in a space occupied by something else. If the caster tries to make something appear in a space occupied by something else, the item appears in the closest adjacent unoccupied area.

The difficulty of casting these spells is 5, like other spells, and modified as per the factors listed. The duration of these spells is always 1 round per success achieved on the casting test. The items continue to exist regardless of the outcome of the enervation check.

The enervation level of conjuration spells is determined by the complexity of the item conjured or created and the other factors chosen from the list below. Since the complexities are consistent through both types of spells, we'll define them now before we get into the details of the spells themselves. The amount of any given item that can be created it also a factor of its complexity, so this will also be covered here.

Simple: Simple conjurations and creations are things that have no "real" substance... such as light or darkness. While they can have a profound effect on play, they cannot directly harm... or help... anyone. You can raise or lower the temperature, but not enough to cause damage or stop damage from being done. These spells circular area centered on either the caster or something the caster is touching at the time of casting and extending to a radius of 5 ft per level of the spell's power.

Minor: Minor conjurations and creations are able to call into existence non-living vegetative matter. Dead chunks of wood, edible vegetables and cotton are examples of things that can come into existence. The amount of the item that appears cannot exceed 1 ft^3 per level of the spell's power.

Major: Major conjurations and creations are capable of producing mineral matter. Gold, silver, and gem stones are the most common uses of these spells. The amount of the item that appears cannot exceed 1 ft^3 per level of the spell's power.

Complex: Complex conjurations and creations call into existence an amount of non-living animal matter. This is edible and free of disease, fungus, and other impurities. The amount of the item that appears cannot exceed 1 ft^3 per level of the spell's power.

Massive: Massive conjurations and creations produces an amount of animal matter much like "massive" spells. The difference is that the animal matter brought into existence by these spells is alive. Creatures created are of animal intelligence at best. Moreover, animals so created cannot have a number of total attribute points exceeding 1 per level of the spell's power making all but the smallest (weakest and dumbest) animals out of reach of all but the most powerful casters.

Divine: Divine conjurations and creations are capable of bring living, fully sentient animals into existence. The animals so created cannot have a number of total attribute points exceeding 3 per level of the spell's power. This makes it possible for casters to create even members of other player races.

Spells of the conjuration school also have a required success threshold based on the caster's knowledge of the subject. The more familiar the caster is with the subject of the spell, the more likely it is to succeed. If the caster fails to achieve the requisite number of successes, he or she has still attempted to call upon the power of the spell and must still resist enervation.

Familiarity	Successes Needed
Very Familiar	2
Studied Carefully	4
Seen Casually	6
Viewed Once	8
Unknown	10

Conjurations

Conjuration spells do not create anything... that's the province of creation spells. Instead, they take something that exists somewhere else and transport it into the presence of the caster. Conjuration spells bring the closest example of the desired item or creature to the caster and it appears in the closest unoccupied space.

This may cause unintended consequences for the caster and his allies. The gold coins the caster tried to conjure might come from the treasury of a local lord.

Complexity Factor	Enervation
Simple	1
Minor	2
Major	3
Complex	4
Massive	5
Divine	6

Creations

Creation spells actually create the desired item, object, or creature desired from the primal chaos that Eris used to create the universe. Objects so created do not last for an extended period of time, but they do last long enough for the caster to spend them at a merchant's shop… burn them in a fire… or consume them for nourishment.

Complexity Factor	Enervation
Simple	2
Minor	4
Major	6
Complex	8
Massive	10
Divine	12

Difficulty Modifiers

-1   Restricted to a specific type of item (such as coins, weapons, etc.)

Enervation Modifiers

-1   Restricted to a specific item (such as daggers, brigs, etc.)
-1   The spell only affects voluntary targets (in order to take this stricture, the target must be capable of volunteering.)
-1   Spell requires the caster to touch the target (normally impossible since the caster doesn't know where the target is before it appears or is creating it out of primal chaos and it doesn't exist to be touched)

Teleportation

While conjuration magics call things to the caster, the same magic can be used to send creature and objects from the caster's location to some other location. This is a relatively new application of conjuration magic, so it is not as fine tuned as other spells available to magi.

The target number for teleportation spells is 5. This can be lowered to 4 by only affecting living creatures and not the objects they wear or carry. It can be raised by one to be used on non-living, unattended objects. The difficulty can also be modified by selecting verbal components.

The enervation is also 5. It can only be modified by requiring the caster to touch the person or object to be transported and any material components the caster may have chosen to use.

Teleportation spells are subject to success thresholds, but the threshold is based on the caster's familiarity with the target location rather than the target of the spell. The power level of the spell must meet or exceed the total constitution scores of all the creatures to be transported plus the power levels of any magic items held by those creatures.

If the caster fails to achieve the requisite number of successes, the spell does not function properly. It may not function at all leaving the caster where he stood when he or she cast the spell. Or, it may send them to a random (read: chosen by the director) location between the point of origin and the intended destination. Regardless, the cast must still resist enervation.

Furthermore, in order to be completely successful, the spell must have enough power to transport all of the targets. The power must equal or exceed the total the constitution scores of the targets, excluding the caster.

Next, compare the powers of each unbonded magic item targeted to the power level of the spell. Any magic item that has a power level greater than that of the spell counts as a person in its own right with an effective constitution score equal to the difference.

The spell transports the magical items in the caster's possession first. This teleportation is so quick that it can be considered instantaneous for all intents and purposes.

The spell then begins transporting other targets in order of their constitution scores from least to greatest. Unbonded magic items are transported immediately after the person in possession of them. Once the spell has reached the limits of its power (the total constitution score transported meets the power level of the spell) the spell ceases to transport any remaining targets.

It is possible for the spell to "run out of power" while transporting magic items, including those of the caster. If this happens, any magic items that would have caused the spell to exceed its power level remain at the point of origin and are considered unattended.

Alternately, instead of having the spell fail, the caster can opt to take the difference between the constitution points he can transport and the amount the caster is attempting to transport in enervation. This enervation can not be gaffed. Furthermore, it becomes one category greater than it would normally be… mind damage become body damage… body damage become souls damage…

Dimensional Travel

Just as mages have discovered how to use magic from this school to transport items and creatures across the Lady's Rock it can also be used to open a portal to other planes of existence. Such travel is dangerous because the traveler and his or her companions must move bodily into the other dimension, making death a very real and permanent possibility. Rumors exist that mages of old were able to separate their spirits from their bodies, but such magics have been lost to time.

The difficulty of casting these spells is 5 modified by any difficulty modifiers selected during the design process.

The enervation for these spells depends on the plane that the caster wishes to travel to. It begins at a base of 5 with modifiers for different dimensions.

Like teleportation magics, the power of the spell must exceed the total attribute of the creatures to be transported. However, unlike teleportation which always uses the targets' constitution scores as a litmus test, which attribute are relevant depends upon the plane that the caster is attempting to travel to. Magic items whose power exceeds the power level of the spell have an effective attribute equal to the difference.

Plane	Attribute
Ethereal	Psyche
Shadow	Charisma
Material	Constitution

Furthermore, certain other dimensions can only be accessed from one of the other planes. For example, the realms of the deities can only be reached from the plane of shadows. It has also been suggested that other alien planes might be accessible for the ethereal plane, but none who have attempted this have returned to report their findings.

Dimensional travel spells open a portal to another plane large enough for the caster to enter. Creatures up to two size categories larger than the caster can use the portal but must crouch or crawl in order to do so. These portals remain open and usable by anyone who might happen upon them for a number of rounds equal to the number of successes on the caster's casting check.

It is also important to note that a separate spell is needed to return the caster to his native (the material) plane.

These spells can be modified by verbal, somatic, and material components like any other spell.

Plane	Enervation
Material	5
Ethereal	6
Shadow	7
Elysion*	8
Asphodel*	9
Tartarus*	9

*Caster must be on the plane of shadow in order to cast a spell opening a portal to these realms.

Of course, once you reach the plane in question, you still have to deal with the denizens of that plane… and angry deities are not to be trifled with.

Difficulty modifiers

-1 Traveling to the caster's patron deity's home plane
-1 Travel between layers of a plane the caster currently occupies

Enervation Modifiers

-1 for each size category small than the caster that the portal is.

+1 for each size category larger than the caster that the portal is.

Divination

The school of divination contains those spells that enhance the caster's perception… and those that mask the character from the divinations of others.

The difficulty of divination spells is, as always, a 5 modified by the difficulty modifiers listed below (surprise… surprise…)

The caster can use divination magics to detect people, places, and things. Such a spell will reveal the location of one such object per success if the spell has an area of effect and the things being detected is within the area of the spell's effect. Without an area of effect, the spell simply reveals whether or not the objects the caster is looking for are present and the number of these objects up to a maximum of the spell's power.

Divination magic can also be used to analyze an person, place, or thing. Such spells reveal one quality of the target for each success on the casting test. The spell begins with the most significant quality and continues into minutiae until it has revealed one detail per success. The details revealed by the spell may include things that the caster already knows. However, the spell will exclude any details that must exist in order for the spell to function. Remember, if the target is a creature, any objects worn or held are considered to be part of the creature for the purposes of magic.

For example, if a mage were to cast a spell called "Analyze Corpse" on a minotaur that the party had just slain and scored 6 success on his or her casting check, the results might look something like this.

1. *The target is a minotaur*
2. *The target is male*
3. *The target has an enchanted short sword secured to its back.*
4. *The target has an enchanted axe in its left hand.*
5. *The ring wore on the left hand is enchanted.*
6. *The target is wearing chainmail armor*

The spell does not reveal that the minotaur is dead because the spell only analyzes corpses. If the minotaur was not dead, the spell would not have functioned. The spell does mention the creatures race and sex because they are not contingent upon the spell functioning. It then begins to catalogue the minotaur's possessions. It lists magic items first… being magical itself, the spell gives preferential treatment to other magic. Then it lists mundane items.

The caster can also improve a target's senses, adding an additional die to any awareness checks for each success.

New sense, such as low-light vision, darkvision, thermal vision, and ether vision, can also be added to the target.

The caster can also "borrow" the senses of another person or creature. Multiple senses can be borrowed but each sense must be borrowed separately.

Lastly, the caster can veil his or her presence from others using divination magics. Each success achieved on the casting check for one of these spells becomes a success threshold for those who might try to cast divinations against the caster (or someone protected by the caster's spell.

Divination Effect	Enervation
Detect (Living or Magical)	1
Detect (Non-living or Non-magical)	2
Analyze (Living or Magical)	3
Analyze (Non-living or Non-magical)	4
Improve Sense	5
Add a New Sense	7
Borrow a Sense	9
Veil	3

Difficulty Modifiers

-1 Restricted to a particular type of target (magical items, living creatures, undead)

+1 Sustained

Enervation Modifiers

-1 Caster must touch target
-1 The spell only affects a particular subspecies of living creature or a specific type of item (drow, magical swords, etc.)
-1 Requires the target to be voluntary

+1 Area of Effect (5 feet per point of psyche)
+2 Extended Area (10 feet per point of psyche)
+3 Extended Area (15 feet per point of psyche)
+4 Extended Area (20 feet per point of psyche)
Etc…

Enchantment

Enchantments include any spell that changes an opponent's attitude, demeanor, or memories. These spells can be extremely useful for negotiating with the city watch, haggling with merchants, or getting a date for your senior prom.

The base target number for casting enchantment spells is 5 plus or minus any difficulty modifiers selected by the caster when the spell was designed. Of course, by now you should have figured that much out all on your own.

The enervation of the spell varies depending on the type of spell you are planning to cast.

Enchantment spells have a success threshold based on how well you know the target of the spell. The better you know the target… and the more the target trusts you… the easier it is to enchant them.

Type of Relationship	Successes
Intimate	1
Friend	2
Ally	3
Positive Acquaintance	4
Just Met	5
Never Met	6
Negative Acquaintance	7
Enemy	8
Personal Foe	9
Nemesis	10

Furthermore, unlike other spells, the target of an enchantment spell can gain bonuses or penalties to their target number to resist based on the suggestion you implant.

If you make a suggestion that has a positive affect on the target, they suffer a penalty to resist the effects of the spell even if complying with the suggestion is not something they would normally do. Keep in mind that this is "positive" from the perspective of the target, and does not take into consideration the caster's desire or the spell that has been cast.

Likewise, if you make a suggestion that has a negative affect on the target, the target receives a bonus to resist the effects of the spell even if the suggestion is something that the target would normally agree to. Again, this is viewed from the perspective of the target, and does not take into consideration the caster's desire or the spell that has been cast.

Consequences	Resistance Modifier
Fantastic	+3
Favorable	+2
Agreeable	+1
Neutral	0
Unpredictable	-1
Unfavorable	-2
Horrific	-3

Again, the consequences must be viewed from the normal perspective of the spell's target. The director is the final arbitrator as to how the target would view the consequences. There maybe things going on behind the scenes that skew the character's perspective. An otherwise honest guard may be facing eviction sending his wife and her newborn child on the street. The danger to his family makes the prospect of helping the party escape jail in exchange for a sizable bribe become favorable even though the guard's reputation would indicate otherwise.

Level of Enchantment	Enervation
Influence	3
Compel	6
Alter Memories	9

Difficulty Modifiers

-1	Restricted to a particular subspecies
+1	Sustained

Enervation Modifiers

-1	Restricted to a particular individual
-1	The spell requires a voluntary target
-1	The spell requires the caster to touch the intended target.
+1	Area of Effect (5 feet per point of psyche)
+2	Extended Area (10 feet per point of psyche)
+3	Extended Area (15 feet per point of psyche)
+4	Extended Area (20 feet per point of psyche)
Etc…	

NOTE: Yes, I understand that some people might not fully comprehend all the uses of these spells and may find the idea of requiring a voluntary target for an enchantment spell completely ridiculous. I assure you that there are uses for such a spell. For example, what if you hide some horribly evil artifact in some musty tomb deep in the earth and want to erase the memory of the artifact's location in order to keep it hidden even from yourself? There are other examples, but I'll let you use your imagination to figure out what they might be.

Evocation

The school of evocation contains all the "big money spells." This school is the bread and butter of fantasy role-playing. It is home to fireball, lightning bolt, and all the other spells you've grown to love.

All evocation spells have a base casting difficulty of… can you guess? That's right, 5 plus or minus difficulty modifiers selected from the list below.

Enervation for evocation spells is based on the damage that the spell does… plus or minus any selected enervation modifiers.

By default, evocation spells do damage only to living creatures. Armor still affects the damage done by these spells.

The caster can choose, at the time of design, if the spell ignores a specific type of armor. This option can be selected multiple times to ignore different classes of armor.

If the caster chooses "primal effects" at the time of spell design, he or she must select the type of elemental effect from the list provided. The spell then gains all effects associated with the primal effect chosen. These spells must take the "does damage to non-living" modifier in order to affect non-living things. Furthermore, if the target gaffs all of the damage from the spell, this also negates any secondary effects from the chosen element.

Acid: Spells with this primal effect generate a plume of nauseous fumes. This is considered heavy smoke within the spells area of effect (the 5 feet immediately surrounding the target if it is not an area of effect spell). This plume billows out and is considered light smoke for an area around the spell equal to the area of effect for the initial spell. For example, if the spell has a 20 foot radius, it is considered heavy smoke in a 20 foot radius around the original target and light smoke for 20 feet beyond that original area. This cloud remains for one round per power of the spell.

Furthermore, any object struck by the spell is marred by the acid. The armor value or object barrier rating of the object struck is reduced by 1.

Concussion: Unattended objects with an object barrier rating less than the damage factor of the spell are shatters by the concussive blast of the spell.

Fire: Spells that evoke primal fire ignite flammable materials reducing their object barrier rating by 1. Furthermore, if a character's clothing (or fur) is ignited by the spell, the target takes damage equal to the original damage inflicted minus base damage of the spell each round. Resisting this damage requires a normal gaffing roll against physical damage using the spell's power as a target number. Each round, the spell continues to burn the target. The target number to resist this damage increases by 2, but the amount of damage done decreases by the base damage of the spell.

Cold: The ground in the area of these spells becomes covered with a coating of ice that lasts for one round per power level of the spell. Movement through this area is reduced by half.

Lightning: Lightning is a double edged sword. Characters who are not grounded (those that are levitating, for example) suffer no damage from a lightning attack. Characters that suffer even a single point of damage from one of these spells may be subject to a knockdown. Compare *twice* the power of the spell to the character's Vigor Pool. If the character's vigor pool exceeds twice the power of the spell, the character simply takes damage. If twice the power of the spell exceeds the character's vigor pool, the character suffers a knockdown.

Damage Factor	Enervation
1	1
2	2
3	3
4	4
5	5
Etc…	

Difficulty Modifiers

-1 Target restricted to a specific subspecies or class of inanimate object (vehicles, weapons, etc.)

+1 Spell does damage to non-living things
+1 per type of armor (light, medium, heavy) that the spell ignores.

Enervation Modifiers

-1 Target restricted to a specific individual or a specific type of item (swords, wagons, etc.)
-1 Caster must touch the target
-1 Spell does Stun (mind) Damage

+1 Primal Effect
+1 Area of Effect (5 feet per point of psyche)
+2 Extended Area (10 feet per point of psyche)
+3 Extended Area (15 feet per point of psyche)
+4 Extended Area (20 feet per point of psyche)
Etc…

Illusions

Illusion spells bring forth phantasms that affect the targets' senses. Illusions can have visual, auditory, olfactory, gustatory, and even tactile elements.

While sight and sound might make sense as elements of an illusion, the other three senses are often ignored. This is probably because people fail to understand how important these sense are to the over all experience… or how they might be included in an illusion.

Olfactory (smell) and gustatory (taste) almost go hand in hand. Imagine a thunderstorm without the telltale scent of ozone in the air. You'd realize something was amiss almost instantly. Likewise, smoke billowing in your face leaves a sooty taste in your mouth… without that taste, the smoke would seem odd.

Tactile is by far the most misunderstood sense when it comes to illusions. A tactile illusion is still an illusion. It has no real substance. All illusionary bridge will not help you to cross a river even if it includes a tactile element. However, the heat from a fire is a tactile sensation… as is the pain from being burned. The cold emanating from a large block of ice is also a tactile sensation.

Despite the fact that you may feel warm sitting next to an illusory fire with a tactile element, the fire provides no heat. You're still susceptible to things like hypothermia.

More importantly, pain is a tactile sensation. Illusions that mimic an item that would normally cause pain and include a tactile element can harm others… as long as they believe the illusion to be real. These illusions have a damage factor of 1 and such damage is always mind damage.

There are two types of illusions that a practitioner of the illusory arts can perform. Each type of illusion has its place both in and out of combat.

The first is the obvious illusion. Obvious illusions appear cartoony. From a distance, it might be hard for someone to tell the difference, but up close, there can be no mistaking it. Obvious illusions cause less enervation than their more realistic counterparts.

Mages often take advantage of this difference when realism isn't a necessity. An inky black cloud of impenetrable darkness is unnatural anywhere. There is not reason that it needs to be a realistic illusion.

Obvious illusions are also helpful when the caster is trying to convey something visually to his or her companions. Generating an animated depiction of an ancient myth before their very eyes really brings the myth to life.

The second type of illusion, as you may have guessed, is the realistic illusion. These illusions appear real… at least real to the senses that the caster included in the spell during the design process.

Illusions can be made responsive as well. If an illusion is not responsive, interaction with that illusion allows the person interacting an immediate psyche test (augmented by willpower dice if desired) to disbelieve the illusion. Obvious illusions allow the person to add his or her reason to this test as well.

Type of Illusion	Enervation
Obvious Illusions	1
Realistic Illusions	3

Difficulty Modifiers

+1   Sustained
+2   Responsive

Enervation Modifiers

-1   Requires a voluntary target

+1   Includes visual elements
+1   Includes auditory elements
+2   Includes Olfactory or Gustatory elements
+3   Includes tactile elements

+1   Area of Effect (5 feet per point of psyche)
+2   Extended Area (10 feet per point of psyche)
+3   Extended Area (15 feet per point of psyche)
+4   Extended Area (20 feet per point of psyche)
Etc…

Transmutation

The school of transmutation is one of the most versatile schools of magic known on the Lady's Rock. It allows the caster to manipulate the qualities of a creature or object and make it into something other than what it is. Unlike illusory magic, these changes are very real… though they are not permanent.

The base difficulty for transmutation is… anyone… Bueller… five… This difficulty can be modified by the factors listed here or by selecting verbal components for the spell. The enervation caused by the spell depends on the complexity of the change taking place. The more complex the transmutation, the more it taxes the caster.

Simple: Simple transmutations are minor cosmetic changes such as hair, eye, and skin color. A simple transmutation cannot alter your appearance beyond the normal characteristics for your race. A common elven mage could not, for example, change his skin to coal black in the hopes of passing for a drow. Common elves do not have coal black skin.

Minor: Minor transmutations are also cosmetic changes, but they are no longer limited to the base characteristics for your subspecies. The common elven mage in our previous example could turn his skin coal black with a minor transmutation. These changes are still cosmetic, however. They do not change the character's attributes or abilities in anyway.

Major: Major transmutations actually allow you to become a member of another subspecies of your race. A common elf can actually become a grey elf or even a drow. The target of this spell loses all his normal racial abilities and gains those of the new subspecies. If the target has any attributes that exceed the racial maximums for the new subspecies, these attributes become the new racial maximums for the duration of the spell.

Complex: Complex transmutations allow you to change your race completely. In all other ways they function identically to "major transmutations."

Massive: Massive transmutations include completely changing the properties of a creature. The creature can be rendered insubstantial allowing it to pass through walls. It can be rendered weightless allowing it to float through the air. Any variables, such as altitude for levitation, are determined by the number of successes in increments of 5…such as 5 feet per success.

Divine: Divine transmutations include things such as changing the make up of a landscape. Raising a mountain from a plain, making a barren field fertile again, and lowering a verdant hill are examples of divine transmutations. Divine transmutations all have an area of effect equal to the number of successes achieved on the casting roll plus the psyche of the caster times 5 cubic feet.

NOTE: Transmutation spells can also affect objects, if the caster selects the proper options when designing the spell. Use the examples given for living creatures to determine which classification best explains what you are trying to accomplish when designing a spell to affect non-living things.

Also remember that attended object (those wore or held by a sentient creature) are considered part of the creature and not "non-living object" even though they are not alive.

Changes made to creatures by transmutation cannot raise or lower attributes by more points than the power of the spell.

Complexity Factor	Enervation
Simple	2
Minor	3
Major	4
Complex	5
Massive	6
Divine	7

Difficulty Modifiers

-1   The spell only affects a certain subspecies of creature or a particular class of object (vehicles, weapons, etc.)

+1   The spell affects non-living things
+1   Sustained

Enervation Modifiers

-1   The spell requires a voluntary target
-1   The spell only affects a specific creature or particular type of object (wagons, swords, etc.)
-1   Requires the caster to touch the target for the spell to take effect.
-1   Specific effects of the spell are assigned during design (a complex transmutation that only changes the target into a dwarf, for example.)

Refining Essences

Refining the essence of an element is not an easy process. The mage must refine the essence personally in order for it to work with his or her magic. The process of refining essences takes 8 hours. The refining ritual must not be interrupted otherwise all the work is lost. The caster must gather new raw materials And begin the process again.

Gathering Raw Materials

The good thing about finding raw materials is that everything in existence is composed of the five basic elements.

To determine what elemental essences can be distilled from an object, look at the table below and determine which of these categories is most applicable.

Material Properties

Hot	Boom & Pungent
Cold	Orange & Sweet
Dry	Boom & Orange
Wet	Pungent & Sweet

Every substance in existence is either hot or cold and either wet or dry. These properties can vary based on a number of factors. For the purposes of refining essences, the properties of the materials at the time of harvest are what matters. Desert sand, for example, is dry and hot if collected during the day, but that same sand would be cold and dry if harvested in the dead of night.

The only notable exception to this rule is the so called regal metals, copper, silver, electrum, gold, and platinum. These items carry all four (actually all five) elements to a varying degree. When a coin is refined, each coin produces a material component that has an effect based upon the amount of the element in the coin. The refined coin is treated as a true essence for the element that it is primarily composed of. It acts as a fixed essence for the secondary component of the coin and as a variable essence for the coin. Consult the table below to determine which elements are primary, secondary, and tertiary for each coin.

For example, a character who has refined a platinum coin would receive 3 successes if it was used as a material component for a boom related school, 2 successes for an ornage related school, and a single success if you were a vile outlaw hunted by every law-abiding creature in the empire for practicing necromancy.

Refining the Material

Refining the material takes eight hours. At the end of the 8 hours, the spell-caster makes an alchemy test with a target number equal to the number of units he or she is attempting to refine.

If the caster scores 3 successes on this test, he has created a variable essence. This component grants a single bonus success to resist enervation for the three schools associate with it (based on the two properties of the material used). Something that is cold and dry, for example, would grant this bonus success to Boom, Orange, & Sweet related schools.

If the caster scores 6 successes, he can choose to make a fixed essence instead. These grant two bonus successes to resist enervation, but only to the schools associated with two of the three schools. These schools must both have the same material property. For example, in the example above, the component could affect either Orange & Sweet or Boom & Orange. It could not, however, apply to both Boom & Sweet because these elements do not share a material property.

If the caster scores 9 successes, they can choose to create a true essence. True essences grant 3 bonus successes to resist enervation, but only to the schools associate with one element.

Schools and Elements

Boom	Divination & Evocation
Orange	Conjuration & Transmutation
Pungent	Enchantment & Illusion
Sweet	Abjuration & Biomancy

	Platinum	Gold	Electrum	Silver	Copper
Primary	Boom	Orange	Pungent	Sweet	Prickle-prickle
Secondary	Orange	Prickle-prickle	Sweet	Boom	Pungent
Tertiary	Prickle-prickle	Pungent	Boom	Orange	Sweet

Ritual Magic

In addition to casting spells, those capable of casting magic can also join together in a ritual casting. Casting as part of a ritual amplifies the abilities of the casters allowing them to harness more power than they could possibly hope to individually.

Requirements

At least two casters are required in order for a casting to be considered a ritual. One serves as the primary caster. Another participant (or a summoned spirit) serves as the spotter.

All casters involved in the casting must know a version of the same spell. Specifically, all of the variable effects of the spell, the difficulty modifiers, and the enervation modifiers must be the same.

At least one of the participants must know a divination spell to allow the primary caster to borrow the spotter's senses.

All of the required material components must be present and available for use.

Step 1

The ritual team must select a primary caster. This person will roll the casting check for the ritual team.

Step 2

The spotter is selected. This member of the team will be responsible for finding and "spotting" the target of the spell that the team will be casting.

Step 3

A magical circle surrounded by glyphs and runes must be drawn on the floor of the ritual chamber. This circle will link the members of the ritual team. It must be done in the presence of all members of the team, no of which can leave the chamber until the ritual is complete.

All materials for the spell are placed in the center of this circle and will be consumed (as normal) when the spell is cast.

Step 4

The ritual action & willpower pools must be determined. This is done by adding together the respective pools of all members of the ritual team.

Step 5

The ritual potential of the spells to be cast is determined. Do this by multiply the number of members of the ritual team (not including any spirits present) by the power that the caster of a spell knows that spell.

For example, if the person casting the spell linking the spotter to the primary caster knows said spell at a power of 6 and 6 people are participating in the ritual, the potential of the spell is 36.

If the same ritual's purpose is to cast a fireball at the target destroying him or her and the primary caster knows this spell at a power of 8, then the potential of the fireball is is 48.

Normally the number of successes that apply to a spell's variable effects are limited by the power of the spell. In a ritual casting, the number of successes is limited by the potential of the spell.

Step 6

One member of the ritual team must cast a divination spell allowing the primary caster to borrow the vision of the spotter. This spell must be sustained until the ritual is complete. If the caster of the spell cannot sustain it personally (such as when he or she must sleep), then the spell must be sustained by a spirit or spirits summoned by the caster.

Step 7

The spotter must find the target of the spell. Though the spotter leaves the confines of the ritual chamber, their departure does not disrupt the ritual… In fact, it is an essential part of it. The spotter becomes the agent of the ritual team.

All ranges for the ritual spell will be determined by the spotter. If a spell has a range of "line of sight," it is the spotter that must spy the target. If it has a range of touch, the spotter must touch the intended target.

If the connection between the spotter and the primary caster is disrupted, the ritual fails.

Step 8

Once the spotter has found the target, the ritual itself begins. The members of the ritual team begin chanting and the primary caster casts the ritual spell.

The primary caster rolls his or her spell-casting dice against the difficulty of the spell. They may choose to add dice from the ritual action pool to augment this roll. The maximum number of successes that may be applied to the variable effects of the spell is limited to the ritual potential of the spell.

Step 9

The effects of the spell are determined as they normally would be taking into consideration the increased potential of the spell.

Step 10

The target attempts to defend against the spell if desired. The target number for these tests is the power at which the primary caster knows the spell.

Step 11

The primary caster rolls against the enervation of the spell. Remember that the additional successes granted by dice from the ritual action pool and the ritual potential also increase the enervation caused by the spell. He or she may use as many dice from the ritual willpower pool to augment this roll as they desire.

Any enervation damage that is not gaffed by this enervation test is divided equally among the members of the ritual team with any remaining amount being suffered equally by both the primary caster and the spotter. The members of the ritual team do not receive another attempt to gaff this damage.

To determine whether this is mind or body damage, compare the power at which the primary caster knows the spell to the psyche score of each individual participant in the ritual. If the power is greater than the psyche of the individual member, that member suffers body damage. If it is less than or equal to their psyche score, that member takes mind damage.

For example, if the primary caster in our above example scores 30 successes on the ritual fireball and the enervation for the fireball is 3, then the ritual team risks 90 points of enervation. The primary caster rolls his or her psyche against the power of the spell that he or she knows using as many dice from the ritual willpower pool as he or she desires. Each success will gaff a number of points equal to ½ his or her psyche score.

If the primary caster has a psyche of 6 and rolls 23 successes on his or her test to gaff enervation, 69 points of enervation damage have been gaffed. The remaining 21 points are divided among equally among the members of the team, so each takes 3 points of damage from enervation. The remaining 3 points (21-18=3) are applied to both the spotter and the primary caster, so they each take 6 total points of enervation damage.

Summoning Spirits

Summoning spirits is always dangerous business. Spirits are mystical and magical creatures who are not easy to command. Calling a spirit, however, is the least of the summoner's problems. The spirit must be bound. A mage of cleric can only bind one spirit per point of his or her charisma attribute at one time.

Before one can learn how to summon spirits, one must first learn what kinds of spirits roam the Lady's Rock.

Types of Spirits

Elementals: Five different elementals exist on the Lady's Rock – Boom, Sweet, Orange, l;lsPungent, and Prickle-prickle. Of these, knowledge remains only to summon four. Knowledge of how to summon elementals of prickle-prickle (called necromentals by some) was systematically removed from the face of the world along with the other secrets of necromancy.

Every spell-caster who has the summoning skill can attempt to summon elementals. Depending on the summoner's aspect (if a mage) or patron deity (if a cleric) some elementals are easier to summon than others.

Ancestor Spirits: These spirits belong to the dearly departed. Only clerics may summon the spirits of the dead. Rousing a spirit of the dead from the realm of its patron deity is not a task to be taken lightly. Members of the clergy do so only when they must… or are certain that their deity will approve of the decision.

Familiar Spirits: These spirits become the boon companions to mages everywhere. A mage may only summon a single familiar at a time. Unlike other spirits, familiars are bound more completely to their summoners and are not limited to a set number of tasks.

Summoning a Spirit

Summoning a spirit requires a ritual. Mages must prepare a ritual chamber much like the one required for other rituals. A cleric needs only to have a shrine consecrated to their patron deity. Setting the stage for the summoning is just part of the preparation needed.

In order to summon a spirit, the summoner must make an offering. Clerics make an offering to their deity while mages make an offering to the spirits themselves. The value of this offering must equal or exceed 100 brigs times the power of the spirit to be conjured.

Summoning Components

Much like casting magical spells, summoners can use components to aid them in their endeavors. Verbal components lessen the target number to summon the spirit just as they lessen the difficulty to cast spells. Somatic components lessen the target number to resist enervation. Material components, beyond the offering made to the deity or spirit, can be used as armor against enervation, just as it is for spells.

Once the place, the offering, and the components have been gathered, it is time to summon the spirit desired. The summoner begins by selecting the power level of the spirit he or she wishes to summon. This will be the target number for the summoning check. Each success achieved on this test is a service that the spirit owes to the summoner.

The power of the spirit is also the target number for the enervation test. The enervation for summoning depends on the power of the spirit compared to the charisma of the summoner.

Ratio	Enervation
Power of the spirit is less than ½ the Charisma of the summoner	1
Power of the spirit is less than the Charisma of the summoner	2
Power of the spirit is greater than or equal to the charisma of the summoner	3
Power of the spirit is greater than twice the charisma of the summoner	4

Furthermore, if the power of the spirit exceeds the summoner's psyche, the enervation is physical in nature and is subtracted from body damage.

If the enervation from the summoning knocks the summoner unconscious or kills the summoner, the spirit makes a test to attain freedom from its bounds. The spirit rolls a number of dice equal to its power against a target number equal to the charisma of its summoner. Each success removes an owed service. If the spirit is able to negate all the services that bind it, the spirit is free.

A similar test is repeated whenever the summoner loses consciousness… though not when the summoner is sleeping. A spirit remains with its summoner, though not necessarily on the material plane, until its tasks have been completed. A summoner can bind one spirit per point of charisma. A mage's familiar does not count toward this limit.

For more information on spirits, see the section detailing them on page XXXX.

Services

For each success the mage or cleric achieves on his or her summoning test, the spirit summoned owes the summoner one service. As mentioned previously, this does not apply to familiar spirits.

Normally, these services must be performed in the presence of the summoner. For the purposes of this game, the spirit must remain within the line of sight of its summoner. Should the spirit leave this area, it is considered to be one an errand.

Errands: The summoner can command the spirit to perform a duty outside of the summoner's presence. Being away from its summoner weakens the spirit's link to our world and it burns one point of its power each day. This point it burned either at sunrise or sunset, whichever happens first, and continues each day at the same time until the spirit completes its assigned task and returns to its summoner or vanishes due to power loss. These power levels do not return to the spirit.

Ancestor spirits cannot be made to perform errands outside of their final resting place. Should a summoner demand such an action, the summoner loses one service and the spirit is able to make a test to liberate itself from the summoner's control as if the summoner has become unconscious.

Magical Aid: The spirit summoned can aid the caster to either cast or learn a spell. Only one spirit can be used to aid in learning or casting a spell. If the spirit is an elemental, the spell to be learned or cast must be from a school related to the element in question. The spirit provides an additional dice pool equal to its power level that can be used at any point during either the learning or casting process. This pool can even be used to aid in resisting enervation.

Requiring the spirit to perform this task burns away the spirit's essence permanently lessening its power by one point each time. If the spirit reaches a power of zero, it vanishes.

Nourish a Spell: A spirit can be called upon to sustain a spell that was cast by the spirit's summoner, feeding it with its own energy. Every turn (10 rounds), or fraction thereof, that the spirit sustains the spell burns away one of the spirit's power permanently reducing the power of the spirit by one. If the spirit's power reaches zero, the spirit vanishes.

Because spirit's use their power to sustain the spell, they suffer no penalties to dice rolls for sustaining a spell.

Physical Service: A summoner can require the spirit to manifest on the material plane and utilize its power on behalf of its summoner. Manifesting on the material plane causes the spirit to be subject to physical attacks, so this is not something they often enjoy.

Recharge a Magical Item: Some magic items have a set number of charges before their magic is expended. A spirit can be ordered to recharge a magical item. Each charge replaced costs the spirit one of its power ratings. If it reaches zero, it is destroyed. If not, these powers return at a rate of one per hour.

Binding a Spirit

A spirit is bound to its summoner upon summoning requiring the spirit to perform a number of services for its summoner. However, another person capable of summoning a type of spirit can attempt to wrest control of that type of spirit from the person who actually summoned it.

To accomplish this task, both summoners roll their summoning dice against a target number equal to the spirit's force. The person who actually summoned the spirit receives bonus dice equal to its charisma score and any bonus dice from aspect, patron deity, or advantages apply. The person that generates the most successes gains control of the spirit. However, this summoner must immediately resist enervation as if he or she had just summoned the spirit.

Banishing a Spirit

Banishing a spirit dissipates the magical energy that the spirit is composed of utterly destroying that spirit. To banish a spirit, a summoner rolls his summoning dice against the power of the spirit. If this summoner is the one that originally summoned the spirit, he or she receives bonus dice equal to their charisma score. The spirit rolls a number of dice equal to its power against a target number equal to the summoner's psyche score.

If the summoner scores more successes than the spirit, the spirit's power is reduced by one for each additional success the summoner rolled. If the spirit's power is reduced to zero or less, the spirit dissipates into the universe and that spirit is destroyed.

This process is not without risk to the summoner, however. If the spirit scores more successes, the summoner's psyche is reduced by one for each additional success scored by the spirit. If the summoner's psyche is reduced to zero, the spirit is free (see free spirits on page XXXX). If the summoner's psyche is reduced below zero, he or she becomes bound to the spirit in a reversal of the "natural order" and owes the spirit a one service per negative point of psyche.

If neither the spirit nor the summoner are defeated in a single round, the winner of the contest decides whether or not the contest continues. If the spirit is the victor, the number fo services owed are reduced by its net successes. If both are tied, the contest automatically continues regardless of the desires of the contestants.

Power and psyche lost during s banishing contest are regained at a rate of one per hour. Until a point is regained, the summoner and / or the spirit function at a reduced capacity. The spirit's special abilities are less powerful and the summoner may suffer physical enervation from spells that normally did mental damage due to the loss of psyche.
Releasing a Spirit

A summoner can release a spirit from service at any time without making a banishing test. A spirit so released automatically becomes a free spirit (see page XXXX). Most spirits do not like being summoned and are eager to return from whence it came. However, if the spirit was treated poorly, it very well may attack its summoner upon release. Depending on the spirit, how long it spent among men, and what it experienced while among them, the spirit may decide to remain in the world and explore its wonders.

Cosmology

The Cosmology of the Lady's Rock has been a point of contention among scholars for countless generations. It is not easy for those of us rooted on the material plane to understand. What follows represents a lifetime of work from the brightest minds on the Lady's Rock.

Some of this information is undeniably true. Some of it is little more than an educated guess. And some of it is nothing more than drunken speculation. Unfortunately, I am not sure which parts are what. You'll just have to learn the truth for yourselves.

Current thinking claims that reality as we know it consists of three planes that coexist in the same space and time. The first of these, the material plane, is the world that we see around us. It is our home. It is where we live, grow old, and eventually die. The second is the ethereal, a veil that separates the physical world from the spiritual world. The third is the plane of shadows, home to the souls of the living and the recently dead.

These scholars believe that our physical forms are merely a vessel in which our souls are anchored while we learn the lessons that we need to in order to achieve true enlightenment. They argue that our souls chose a life for us to lead in order for us to grow spiritually and that we cannot achieve our eternal rest until we've reached a state of spiritual oneness with the whole of existence.

If they are right, someone remind me to punch my soul square in the mouth when I die for not choosing a life filled with super models, private yachts, and expensive cars that move way too fast.

- **Ethereal**

The ethereal plane is a curtain that separates the real world from the realm of spirits, ghosts, and deities. It appears like the material plane, but the colors are muted and shapes lack definition... as if you're watching a movie through a fish tank. Spirits that wish to interact with the material world... and living creatures that wish to interact with spirits... spend a lot of time on the ethereal plane.

While you remain alive, your soul dwells on the ethereal plane trapped there by the bond between body and soul. Once this bond is broken the soul moves on to the plane of shadows (Erebus). Spirits & elementals dwell on the ethereal plane until they materialize. Even manifesting spirits, though visible on the material plane, remain on the ethereal.

Ether versus Aether

While the ethereal plane in the source of magic and home to the souls of the living, the aether is the vast sea of energy that covers the Lady's Rock.

The similarity in names may cause some confusion. Unfortunately, this is a by-product of a bygone age. Originally people on the Lady's Rock believed that the aethereal sea was a physical manifestation of the ethereal plane and that the aether was the dwelling place of departed souls. Even though their knowledge of the planes is much more advanced today, the original names remain... much like "tube" is still slang for television even though tubes have not been used in their construction for quite some time.

- **Erebus**

Also known as the Plane of Shadows, Erebus is home to the souls of those awaiting their final judgment... and those who are trying to avoid the same. It is an exact duplicate of the material plane but everything is dreary and dark. The shades of dead men and women roam the Erebus waiting to be sent to their final reward... or eternal punishment.

- *Trivium*

The Trivium. It exists in the exact center of the formless plane of shadow.

The Trivium is the court where all souls are judged. The lives of each soul are examined along with their inner most thoughts and desires. The tribunal then determines which plane the soul will go to spend eternity.

This divine court is composed of three judges, one appointed by the deities who rule each of the outer planes.

Aeacus

The member of the tribunal representing the forces of goodness, righteousness, and justice., Aeacus is a paladin who served Valderon in life. He was appointed to his present post by Myra, the Goddess of Love and Ruler of Elysion. His job is to make sure that the good souls are sent to their reward in Elysion.

Minos

The member of the tribunal representing the deities of Asphodel, Minos was a powerful wizard and king in the mortal realm. He was renowned for his understanding of human nature and his almost perfect sense of justice. Had

Aeacus been on the tribunal at the time, Minos may have ended up on the 6th sphere of Elysion. Of course, he wasn't.

Chalysse, the Goddess of the Cycle of Life & Death and ruler of Asphodel, asked Minos to serve her interests on the tribunal. Minos serves as a balancing force, not so much concerned with gathering souls as he is with ensuring that his brethren on the court treat each soul fairly and without bias.

Rhadamanthys

The member of the tribunal representing the interests of the lower planes, Rhadamanthys was unknown in the mortal world. This isn't because he was not a great or powerful member of society. It is because a truly great assassin and thief is not known to the world at large, and that is what Rhadamanthys was.

Upon his death, Rhadamanthys was ordered by Jhaemaryl, the Goddess of Lust & Blood and ruler of Tartarus, to serve her interests on the tribunal. There Rhadamanthys works to ensure that the ranks of Tartarus swell with those who will be willing to heed the Lady's call when it comes.

The Court

The Court is unique among all places in that it is part of the plane of shadow yet it is also permanent gateway to each of the outer planes. In fact, it is the gateway through which the dead must pass.

The Trivium has slightly different traits than the rest of the plane of shadow. Time does not pass here allowing the tribunal to judge each soul in its own turn without experiencing a huge backlog… especially during times of war. No magic, other than that of the tribunal and the various deities, function in the court. This is to stop the souls of the dead from attempting to influence the tribunal through magic.

In addition to the Court Chamber, the Trivium also houses records of every soul that passes through its gate. Three main halls house these records, one for each of the three outer planes. These volumes contain the details of a soul's life, any discussion the tribunal may have had about the soul, and the final decision about the soul's final destination.

No mortal has access to these records. In fact, they are only used if a deity wishes to appeal a decision of the tribunal. This rarely occurs because Eris Herself must hear the appeal. The deities do not like to involve the over-deity unless they absolutely have to.

The Outer Planes

The outer planes are the abode of the gods. They are also where souls go when they die. The outer planes have changed form several times since Eris first created the ladies rock. At one time there were 17 outer planes in the shape of a ring or wheel. Today there are only four.

Jhaemaryl was the first deity to leave her mark on the outer planes. By ending the bloody war between demons and devils and uniting all of the fiends, she forced the lower plans to merge into a single layered plan known as Tartarus.

Fearing a fiendish offensive, the forces of goodness quickly followed suit and consolidated their own power base. The seven upper planes merged to form the plane of Elysion so that they could present a united front in the war they were sure was to come.

The deities that had not taken sides in this conflict did nothing to coordinate their own defenses. On the outer planes, however, belief becomes reality. When the denizens of the material plane learned of the joining of the lower planes and the subsequent merging of the upper planes, they assumed that the unaligned planes had undergone a similar transformation. Because they believed it to be true, it became true and the plane of Asphodel was formed.

The fourth outer plane is known as the Empyrean. This plane is home to Eris herself. It was from this realm that Eris created the Lady's Rock. It was from this realm that she created the myriad of other realities, though even the most knowledgeable sage are unaware of this fact and mistakenly attribute creation to native deities. No one in the mortal realm knows anything about the Empyrean other than its name and the fact that Eris makes her home there. Mortals do not enter the Empyrean. This is where deities go when they die. Here Eris rules over the whole of existence tended by the shades of deities long forgotten… and some more recently vanquished.

On rare occasions, Eris *invites* the other deities to the Empyrean to address something that affects all of existence. Only one deity in the history of existence has declined Eris's *invitation*. That deity has been so completely erased from all of existence that no one, not even the other gods, can remember its name, what it was deity of, or where it made its home.

- ***Elysion***

Elysion is place where good people go after they die. At least that's what people on the Lady's Rock believe.

The plane consists of a mountain so large it defies description. In truth, the mountain is infinitely large. This mountain is home to magnificent creatures, spiritual entities, and deities who fancy themselves the "good guys."

Nine gleaming sphere of scintillating color orbits the mountain serving as its suns. These 9 sphere are home to the souls of good creatures that have passed away.

Elysion is unique among the outer planes in that the good-aligned dead do not go to rest in the realms of their patron deities. Instead, the deities that call this realm home have decreed that the eternal rest of their faithful servitors should be a reward and not affected by divine politics. These souls are sent to one of the spheres where they spend the rest of time in peace their goodness shining down on the mountain as a reminder to the deities and their celestial followers why they continue to fight the good fight.

Layers

- *The Mountain*

The mountain is divided into seven separate heavens. Mortals like to envision it as a series of mountain slopes. In reality, each heaven is a plane onto itself. The layers are each infinitely large and one can only access them by using existing portals or spells that allow travel between the layers of a pane.

Few of the deceased live on the mountain itself. That honor is reserved for deities, spiritual beings, and mortals of such great importance that a deity took a persona interest in the mortal's life.

Shamayin (the 1st Heaven): This heaven appears to be a verdant plain. It is home to Steve, the Noble Auditor. The God of Status holds court here. He greets all the souls that arrive on the plane and, based on their lives, assigns them to one of the nine spheres.

Raqua (the 2nd Heaven): This heaven is nothing but a desolate plain of white sand called the Plain of Heroes. Narsin rules over this bleak realm. Here the forces of goodness prepare for the coming war with the fiends. Celestial armies drill constantly waiting for the call to battle.

Sagun (the 3rd Heaven): This heaven is home to Valderon. The Lord of the Five Pillars, along with his most powerful servants & followers, stands watch over a spur of the burning river Phlegethon that passes through the only portal in Elysion that leads directly to Tartarus.

Machanon (the 4th Heaven): This forested mountain is home to Solvarus, the God of Forests & Hunting. Here the god stalks celestial versions of animals and hones his hunting skills. The animals, of course, are resurrected when the spheres crest the horizon.

Mathey (the 5th Heaven): Rows of cultivated, terraced fields climb the sides of this mountain. It is the home to Durian, the Queen of Fruit. Celestial beings gladly work the fields and vineyards of this layer. Durian's realm provides food for every creature in Elysion.

Zebul (the 6th Heaven): This heaven, once home to Barak, is wracked by terrible storms. No deity makes his or her home on this windswept peak. Former followers of Barak remain behind hopeful that their deity may one day return to Elysion.

Durian sometimes wanders this layer mourning for her lost lover. When she does, every other creature on the plane gives her a wide berth. The only creature brave enough to approach the goddess when she is lost in her memories is Myra, the goddess of love who dwells on the 7th Heaven.

Araboth (the 7th Heaven): This layer resembles a giant garden. All manner of flower can be found here. Their fragrances stir on the wind giving the layer an almost intoxicating nature. Araboth is home to Myra, the Goddess of Love.

- *The Spheres*

The spheres are home to the good souls who have passed on to the next world. These souls live in a paradise commensurate with the lives that they led on the Lady's Rock. Each sphere in infinitely large and consists of a idyllic realm where the souls live. Most planes have some semblance of government, but that government is determined by the souls who reside on that sphere. The goodly deities only take an interest in the affairs of these spheres when something goes awry.

1st Sphere: This sphere is home to good souls who, though good, abandoned sacred vows. Fallen paladins, those who continued to fight the good fight, and other creatures that led good, though decidedly flawed, lives.

2nd Sphere: This sphere is home to those who did good deeds only because they desired fame. Many supposedly good adventurers end up on the 2nd sphere after death.

3rd Sphere: This sphere is the abode of those who did good deeds out of love. Evil beings that reform in order to prove themselves to the ones they love end up here when they die, provided that their reformation is genuine.

4th Sphere: This sphere is the asylum of those who were both good and wise. People famed for their wisdom, including learned members of the clergy and wise nobility, live in this paradise.

5th Sphere: This sphere is dwelling place of those warriors who gave their lives for a good cause. In reward for their sacrifice, these soldiers spend their lives in peaceful bliss.

6th Sphere: The sphere is the abode of those who personified justice while alive. This is the most orderly of the spheres because the vast majority of those who embody justice also favor fair laws and swift punishment.

7th Sphere: This sphere is home to those who spent their lives in contemplation of goodly things. Hermits, Monks, and scholars can be found here.

8th Sphere: This sphere is home to the blessed. This is the eternal paradise where those who were sainted in life spend their deaths.

9th Sphere: This sphere is reserved for outsiders (the children of celestials and fiends, for example) who served the cause of goodness in their lives.

- **Asphodel**

This plane is home to both the "unaligned" deities and the people who served them in life. It appears to be a vast step pyramid with a garden planted on each step. Each step is a separate layer, and each layer is infinite in size.

Layers

Each terrace of Asphodel is home to those who served neither good nor evil while alive. The plane divides these creatures based upon the personality trait or traits that separated them from goodness.

That may seem odd to some people. Why would the unaligned after-life concern itself with what it would have taken the soul to be good? It doesn't make much sense. That is to say, it doesn't make much sense until you realize that punishment is part of human nature. We want to see those who do not meet our standards of goodness punished for their misdeeds. It was this desire that shaped Asphodel.

Of course, the deities who rule these realms do not concern themselves with what it would have taken for their followers to have led good lives, so punishment is rarely part of the afterlife.

1st Terrace: This terrace is home to those souls who who allowed their pride to get in the way of being good people.

Dina, the Goddess of Law & Order, resides on this terrace. She rules the terrace with velvet gloved iron fist.

2nd Terrace: This terrace contains those who allowed their envy of others to get in the way of leading a good life.

The god Dumathan, the Keeper of Secrets, makes his home here. His citadel is said to house every secret that ever was… and many that have yet to be. Dumathan hoards his secrets like a dragon hoards its gold. The only exception to this is Laeroth, the God of Knowledge. Dumathan sometimes finds himself needing to share his precious secrets in order to gain a more valuable secret.

3rd Terrace: On this terrace reside those souls who were quick to anger, their wrathful natures separating them from what is good.

Two warlike deities share this terrace. Every morning Aren & Barak march their armies onto the field of battle. They do this to cull the weak and hone the strong.

4th Terrace: This terrace is home to people who were not evil, but were too lazy to do good deeds.

In a strange twist of fate, Semis, the god of industry rules over this terrace. He forces the slothful to work his forges until they have worked their sins from their bones.

5th Terrace: Those who allowed their greed and desire for personal gain find themselves on this terrace when they die.

Laeroth's Library, *the Font of Knowledge*, dominates this terrace. Here the souls of the greedy satiate their avarice by helping the venerate elf collect the knowledge of all who live.

6th Terrace: Those who over-indulged themselves while others went without spend eternity on this terrace. The river Eunoe runs through this terrace. Those who drink from this river have their good natures enhanced erasing the guilt of their misdeed and granting them a second chance to earn paradise.

Vastra (the Goddess of Aether) & Manak (the God of Rivers, Lakes, & Streams) make their homes on this terrace. There realm looks like a series of grottos. This layer is unique in that it is the only place in the outer planes that has a direct connection to the ethereal plane, courtesy of Vastra.

7th Terrace: This terrace is the eternal resting place of those who gave into their carnal desires rather than lead a good life. A spur of the river Lethe runs through this terrace forming two pools. The first, the Lethe Pool, erases memories of the dead. While the second, the Pool of Mnemosyne (fed by the river of the same name), restores those memories.

This terrace is home to Chalysse, the goddess of the cycle of life and death. She is the most powerful deity on this plane and rules over the other deities who reside here. Because she is the deity of the cycle of life, Chalysse does not choose sides, both good and evil are a part of the web of life. Chalysse often uses the River Lethe to travel to Tartarus to meet with its fiendish lord.

- **Tartarus**

The plane known as Tartarus was once seven distinct planes, each devoted to an particular brand of evil. These planes were enveloped by a great war that was as old as time itself. Hordes of demons faced off against armies of devilish warriors leaving in their wake fields soaked in blood.

Those fiends who were not waging war spent their time torturing the souls of the evil dead. Each of the seven planes housed a different torment for those who failed to lead good and just lives.

That all changed centuries ago when a fiendish mercenary made a startling discovery. She led a small force of elite warriors on a desperate mission to intercept a shipment of weapons. They succeeded, but learned that the weapons had been furnished by power agents from the upper planes.

While her superiors saw this as the forces of goodness meddling in the affairs of the evil planes, she saw it for what it really was. The celestials wanted the fiends to fight amongst each other. It was a brilliant strategy… you have to give kudos where they are due… but the young officer could not sit idly by while her brethren were manipulated from without as well as within.

She withdrew from the war taking with her the mercenary legions she commanded. For several years no one heard from the young officer or her forces. Then, as suddenly as she had disappeared, she surfaced again. She advocated an end to the seemingly endless battles. Those who refused to lay down their arms were put to the sword.

In a relatively short period of time, lesser demons and devils were afraid to fight each other lest the mercenary company rain death down upon them. With the lesser fiends cowed, the officer turned her attention to the fiendish hierarchy. Demonic princes and diabolic lords both tried to kill the officer and suppress her calls for unity among fiends. The seed had already been planted. Despite their best efforts, the young warrior survived.

After centuries of rebellion, she emerged victorious. The princes and lords of the fiends, including her own parents, were put to death with all the pageantry of a royal coronation. Their remains were entombed in a manner befitting their former station.

With the forces of the underworld united for the first time, the planes they inhabited began to change as well. First the four "fringe" planes that had embodied the subtle shades of evil vanished, absorbed by the planes representing the more base forms of evil. Over time those three planes too merged until only one, Tartarus, remained.

Today, the young officer, now a god, rules over Tartarus and the forces of evil. She has done much to change the face of evil on the Lady's Rock. For starters, Tartarus is not the place of torture and torment that it once was. Instead of being punished for their sinful lives, the damned souls embrace their natures.

Layers

Scholars like to envision Tartarus as a vast pit. They depict it as a series of rings each deeper than the one preceding it. Like other planes, each layer of Tartarus is infinite, almost a plane onto itself. These layers are home not only to the souls of the damned, but also to the deities who reign over them.

Like the plane of Asphodel, souls on this plane are sorted by the way these souls lived their lives. Unlike previous incarnations of the lower planes, however, Tartarus is no longer concerned with punishing evil souls.

Previous lords of the lower planes promised their followers and eternity of torment when they died. Some of their followers were delusional enough to believe that they could escape this fate, but those deluded beings quickly learn the error of this belief. Jhaemaryl, the goddess who now rules Tartarus, has (correctly) determined that promising eternal punishment isn't much of an enticement for people to promote her agenda and pay homage to her and her underlings.

Despite this change in attitude, the belief in eternal torments still affects the way souls are distributed upon death. People like to be slaves to their long held beliefs… no matter how incorrect they may be.

1st Circle: This layer once served to punish those who refused to acknowledge the power of the deities. Today the souls of those who shun the divine still reside on the first circle, known as Limbo, but it is no longer a place of torture. Instead these souls reside in relative comfort. It is as close to paradise as many of them will ever come.

The great river Acheron, the river of sorrows, encircles the plane. The river once served to keep the souls in Tartarus. Today it is used as a defensive structure to keep out invaders that never come.

2nd Circle: The lustful were once tortured on this circle; now they revel in the pleasures of the flesh. This circle is a garden of pleasure and delights. The river Ameles (carelessness) runs through this circle divesting those who reside here from their inhibitions.

The Plains of Lethe, a vast prairie fed by the river for which the plain is named, provides those who dwell here with a chance to erase the memories of unpleasant experiences.

The presence of the Lethe and the Ameles provide the lustful with new opportunities. When you can remove your inhibitions and erase even the most traumatic memories, there is little you will not try.

3rd Circle: In days long since past, gluttons learned the error of their ways in this circle. Even the most shameless glutton can only consume so much, so this plane has become more subdued over the centuries. Now this layer serves as the agricultural center of Tartarus.

Chuck, the God of Bakers, makes his home on this layer overseeing the many farms and vineyards. Chuck longs to move his realm to the 2nd Circle, but Jhaemaryl has strictly forbid him to do this. In fact, she has told Chuck in no uncertain terms that stepping foot on that circle will spell his final death. After all, the lustful deserve to indulge themselves freely, and that cannot happen if Chuck is preying upon them.

4th Circle: This circle, known as Pluton, is the industrial center of Tartarus. Here precious ores are wrested from the bedrock of the plane. The River Eridanus is the life's blood of this layer. It powers great mills and allows for efficient transportation of raw materials.

Cetari, the Goddess of Cold, resides here in a palace crafted from black ice. She ensures that things run smoothly on this layer and punishes those who would disrupt the important business of Pluton.

5th Circle: This vast Stygian Marsh is fed by the River Styx. The river is rumored to be a gateway not only to the material plane, but other realities… in some of which the Great War has not yet ended.

Manak, the God of Disease, lives in this festering swamp. In his foul labyrinth he devises new diseases with which to plague the mortal realms.

The stygian marsh also serves as the last line of defense for the great City of Dis, whose wall can be seen at the center of this plane. Because the Stygian Marsh is infinitely large, the walls of Dis always seem to stand on the horizon. The city can only be entered by walking along a roadway paved with the skulls of those who did evil deeds with the best of intentions.

6th Circle: This circle and all subsequent circles lie inside the walls of the City of Dis.

This circle was once home to heretics. While heretics do still end up on this layer of the plane, it is also home to many other sinners that find there way to the City of Dis.

7th Circle: The seventh circle is the abode of those who indulged in violent behavior while alive. The circle itself is divided into three rings.

- The Outer Ring is home to those who commit violence against property. Vandals, arsonists, and other people who destroy property spend eternity here. Today these souls serve as the public works department for the City of Dis. They demolish old buildings and remove obstructions. The River Phlegethon, the river of boiling blood, flows through this ring of this circle. This river also flows through Sagun, the 3rd heaven, creating a link, the only direct link, between the upper and lower planes.

- The Middle Ring is a verdant forest, which seems out of place inside a city, but it is there nonetheless. Each tree is a soul that committed suicide. These souls are cursed to become the building materials for the city. Worse, these animated trees are also the construction crews that do the building.

- The Inner Ring is home to those who are violent against the gods (blasphemers), nature (bestiality), and the arts (Michael Bey films).

Kyerhan, the Lord of Murder, makes his home on this layer of Tartarus. He rules over those with violent tendencies and hones their skills should the Lady of Lust and Blood call for them.

8th Circle: This circle, known as Malbolge, contains those souls that committed fraud in life. Malbolge is divided into 10 separate ditches called "Bolgia" from which the layer takes its name. Each bolgia contains the souls of those who engaged in a particular type of fraud.

- The 1st Bolgia is home to panderers and seducers.
- The 2nd Bolgia is home to flatterers.
- The 3rd Bolgia is the final dwelling of those who practiced simony, the selling of offices or positions in a church hierarchy or selling other spiritual things.
- The 4th Bolgia is home to evil spellcasters and false prophets. It is also the home of Tchoren, the God of Magical Power and Obsession.
- The 5th Bolgia is home to corrupt politicians, making it a very popular part of the plane as a whole.
- The 6th Bolgia is the final resting place of hypocrites.
- The 7th Bolgia is a den of thieves. It is home to the Thieves' Guild of Dis, who rob from the rich and give to themselves with the blessing of the Lady.
- The 8th Bolgia is filled with the souls of advisors who misled those who trusted them for advice. Corrupt viziers, aides, and counselors all end up here.
- The 9th Bolgia is home to those who sow Discord. As such, this is a very holy place for followers of Eris, and it is the one place in Tartarus where Jhaemaryl does not have supreme authority. Instead she watches over the Bolgia holding it in trust for the Over-Deity. Those souls dedicated to Eris end up here when they die.
- The 10th Bolgia is the demesne of counterfeiters, alchemists, perjurers, and people who sell useless products to uneducated people.

Ahbendon, the God of Deceit, can be found in his palace at the center of the Bolgia. It is from this layer that he directs the espionage operations for the forces of the lower planes.

9th Circle: The 9th Circle is the "deepest" part of the Tartarian pits, if you accept the common visualization of this plane. It is officially divided into four zones in which the betrayers of the world are said to be punished.

Unlike other layers of Tartarus, those sentenced to the 9th Circle *are* punished. The powers that rule this plane cannot afford to let people believe betrayal is acceptable. The fiendish forces can tolerate all sorts of terrible behavior, but betrayal will undermine anything they hope to accomplish.

- Zone 1 (Caina): Traitors to kin are sent to this zone of the layer. It is governed by an ancient vampire who gfoes by the name of Kayne.
- Zone 2 (Antenora): Traitors to political entities can be found on this zone of the layer.
- Zone 3 (Ptolomaea): This zone of the layer is home to those who betray their guests or others under their protection.
- Zone 4 (Judecca): Those who betray their lords and benefactors can be found in this zone of the layer.

The Cocytus (the River of Lament) flows around and through this layer. The Cocytus is a river of molten ice. Some have heard this description and assume that this river is made of water, being the liquid form of ice. Those who have encountered this river know how untrue that statement is. The Cocytus is a river of primal cold created by the goddess Cetari as a gift to Jhaemaryl. It is liquid ice so cold it robs the warmth from anything that comes in contact with it. Even standing on its shores fills any creature with a bone-wrenching chill.

The river flows into a lake at the very center of this layer. The lake is perpetually frozen and shares its name with the river that feeds it. Jhaemaryl, the goddess who rules the fiends, governs the whole of Tartarus from her monolithic fortress, called Epithymia, in the center of this lake on this layer of the plane.

- **Empyrean**

As mentioned earlier, no mortal has seen the Empyrean. It is the home of Eris, the Goddess of Chaos, Discord, Mayhem, Strife, and other things.

Legends tell that this realm is pure and ever-changing chaos. The landscape undulates and morphs at the whims of the goddess who rules it. A grove of golden apples, each imprinted with the word "kallisti," is said to grow somewhere in the Empyrean, but no one knows for certain.

The Empyrean is the one place in the multiverse that most deities fear. This is because deities travel to the Empyrean for only two reasons. One is an audience with the Concubine of Confusion, something that rarely turns out well for the deity. The other is when they die.

While other deities are served by celestials or fiends and the souls of their followers, Eris is served by the essences of the deities that have died. All of the deities worshipped by ancient earthlings (Greco-Roman, Norse, Egyptian, Celtic, Aztec, Maya, Chinese, and others) now toil in the halls of Eris's realm. (The Hindu deities, who still have a large following in the Information Technologies sector, are said to visit them from time to time with Eris's blessing.)

The realms of these fallen pantheons can be found somewhere in the Empyrean. Mount Olympus, for example, can be seen cresting the horizon as you roam the Empyrean, and the walled compound of Asgard rests comfortably in its shadow. Violent storms wrack the summit of Mount Olympus as the mighty Zeus laments being laid so low. Meanwhile, Heimdall continues to stand vigil at the foot of the Bifrost bridge even though it no longer connects to Midgard… or anything else for that matter.

The former Greek goddesses, Hera, Athena, & Aphrodite serve as the personal maidservants of the Daughter of Discord in restitution for the "original snub," an affront that occurred at the wedding of Peleus and Thetis. Demeter tends the many gardens of the Empyrean while Dionysis makes the most heavenly wine you could ever drink.

A myriad of suns shine in the morning sky as the fallen sun deities take to the skies to fulfill their eternal duties. At night, the many moon goddesses replace than just as they did when they enjoyed the worship of humans and the influx of human belief.

The gods of the underworld from these pantheons linger in the shadowy corners of the realm refusing to accept their obsolescence and continually plotting to wrest control from the Mistress of Mayhem. Without the belief of their former followers, however, each is little more than a pale shadow of its former self and stands no change of ever usurping a deity that other deities fear… and created all of everything.

Periodically, humans pay homage to one of these deities. Under normal circumstances, this trickle of belief might have been enough to resurrect the deity. These new followers, however, do not have anything resembling pure belief. Theirs is a belief born of frustration and rebellion against the prevalent religions of their day.

From time to time, a new deity is born from human belief. The Empyrean houses realms for these contemporary deities as well. Eris knows it is just a matter of time before they too die… probably after they allow their followers to kill one another in the ideological wars that have waged since the beginning of recorded history.

All of this makes the Empyrean a terribly sad place. It is a monument, not only to the power of Eris, but to the failings of humanity and the deities they have worshipped throughout history.

Spirits

Spirits do not truly exist in any way we would recognize. They are nothing more than a disembodied consciousness given form and function by raw magical energy shaped by the will of a skilled summoner. While spirits are sentient, many of them, such as elementals and familiars, lack any real personality at the time of their summoning. Like people, these spirits develop personalities as they come into contact with others. Elemental, however, are predisposed to having a personality congruent with the element from which they are formed. You would be very hard pressed to find a docile Boom elemental or a blood-thirsty Sweet elemental, for example.

The largest single influence on the personalities of these spirits is the personality of the summoner. A cruel and vile summoner who delights in causing pain to others will create an elemental or familiar with similar interests. However, if the summoner is in the presence of other creatures who treat the summoned spirit well, it may grow to despise its summoner and actively search for a means of escape from its mystical bonds.

While a spirit is bound to serve its master and obey the master's commands, the spirit remains free to interpret those commands. Many spirits who chafe under the command of a cruel master obey the letter of the master's orders doing only what they must while secretly plotting their master's untimely demise.

Spirits do not have souls. As such, they do not have a "soul damage" category like living creatures. Spirits that suffer all of their points of "mind damage" lose one point of their power rating. Losing a power rating in this matter restores the spirit's miond condition monitor to zero.

Spirits that lose all of their points of "body damage" are forced from the material plane and must remain on the ethereal plane for 24 hours minus one hour per power rating of the spirit.

In the following descriptions, the letter P appears in several equations. The "P" is used to represent the power rating of the spirit summoned.

Spirits that materialize can engage in melee combat with sentient creatures. Some of these spirits may attack with their "hands" while others, such as ancestor spirits, might use the same weapon that they wielded in life. Regardless of the form this attack takes, it has a damage rating equal to one-half the power of the spirit in question.

Spirits all have both regular color vision and ether vision allowing them to watch the ebb and flow life energies through the world.

Ancestor Spirits

Ancestor Spirits are the consciousnesses of those who have died given a semblance of life by magical energies. Ancestor spirits can only be summoned by clerics. These spirits can only be summoned near their final resting place. The ancestor's consciousness appears to be an idealized version of what the spirit looked like when alive.

Once summoned, an ancestor spirit cannot leave its final resting place. This is not to say that they must remain in the spot where they were summoned, but they must remain on the ancient battle field, within the walls of the mausoleum, or on the grounds of the long forgotten cemetery.

Despite the fact that ancestor spirits have no real substance, the consciousness that holds them together is still beholden to the ideas that living creatures have. These spirits still walk to travel. They still believe they need to eat and drink. Even in death they still enjoy wine, song, and pleasurable company.

Ancestor spirits may appear to use different weapons or wear different types of armor. This is just the way that the consciousness chooses to manifest. The spirit's appearance does not change its abilities in any way.

Attribute Scores

Strength:	P+1	Reason:	P
Coordination:	P+1	Insight:	P
Quickness:	P+1	Psyche:	P
Constitution:	P+2	Charisma:	P

Dice Pools

Action Pool:	2P
Vigor Pool:	(4P+3)/2
Willpower Pool:	2P

Damage Rating for Physical Attacks: P/2

Skills: Ancestor spirit's have any skills that the director deems applicable to the spirit's past life at a rating equal to the attribute that normally governs that skill.

Special Powers:

Befuddle: The spirit can cause intense confusion in a single creature that it can see. Creatures targeted by the spirit's befuddle power have all target numbers increased by the power rating of the spirit.

If an action does not have a target number, the target makes a psyche test against a target number equal to the spirit's power rating. Each success is one round that the character can spend performing the action. The target still suffers the target number penalty to any tect or check.

Find: Ancestor spirits can find a person, place, or thing hidden within their final resting place.

If the spirit is searching for a person, the spirit rolls its power rating against the reason if the person searched for. The target of the search rolls his or her hide skill against a target number equal to the spirit's power. If the spirit achieves more successes, it locates the person. If the person scores more successes, it remains hidden.

If the target is a place or thing, the spirit rolls its power rating against a target number of 5. Each success reveals something about the location of the place or thing sought after.

Manifest: This ability allows the spirit to become visible on the material plane. Manifesting spirits can be seen by those on the material plane. They can use their powers and abilities against living or magical targets. They cannot, however, interact with any inanimate objects. Furthermore, they cannot attack unless the spirit has another special power or spell-like ability that allows them to do so.

Because they cannot interact with inanimate object, manifested spirits do not take damage from attacks from weapons unless they are magical. A living creature can attack the spirit unarmed & barehanded, however.

Materialization: The spirit takes physical form on the material plane. A materialized spirit can interact with any person, place, or thing on the material plane as if it were a physical entity. Materialized spirits do not age, they are immune to diseases, toxins, and poisons. Such spirits can make physical attacks. In addition, the spirit gains armor with an armor value equal to the spirit's power rating.

Spirits do not like to materialize. Taking physical form makes them subject to physical attacks. A materialized spirit that suffers all its points of body damage is banished from the material plane.

While materialized, the ancestor spirit may appear to use whatever weapon it wielded in life. This may be a frying pan for the spirit of a cook or a great sword for the spirit of a mighty general. Regardless of the form the weapon takes, it has a damage rating equal to ½ the force of the spirit.

Mishap: A spirit can use its control over its final resting place to cause apparently normal accidents to hinder those traveling through its domain. These mishaps are not dangerous in themselves, and the exact nature of the mishap will vary based on the target's surroundings.

To use this power, the spirit rolls a number of dice equal to its power rating against a target number of the target's reason or quickness (whichever is lower). Each success removes one of the target's actions for that round as a result of a mishap.

Protection: The spirit can use this power to protect creatures from the mishap power of other spirits. This is most often used when two opposing spirits share a final resting place, such as the scene of an ancient battle.

When the spirit invokes this power, any spirit using the mishap power must add the power rating of the protecting spirit to its target number to invoke the mishap power.

Shroud: A spirit's shroud power allows it to conceal things within its final resting place. The spirit's power rating it added to any target number to find the shrouded person, place, or thing. This power is effective against both mundane and magical abilities to find the target… including divination spells, search $ awareness tests, and the find power of other spirits.

Soothsaying: Spirits can tap into the magical currents of the universe and answer a question on behalf of its summoner. The spirit rolls a number of dice equal to its power rating against a target number of 5. Each success is a single "yes or no" question that the spirit can answer for the summoner.

The question must be related to the spirit in some way. If the question is not something related to the spirit, the soothsaying automatically fails. The director is the final arbitrator as to whether a particular question is something related to a particular spirit.

The questions can return an answer of yes, no, possibly, both yes & no, or neither yes nor no.

Elementals

Elementals are spirits that can be summoned by either mages or clerics. They are the embodiment of the elements that make up the whole of existence. Each type of elemental has its own powers and traits that make it better suited to some purposes than others.

In addition, though elementals of the same type have similar dominant personality traits, each elemental has its own unique personality.

Common Elemental Powers

Some powers are common to all elementals regardless of what element they represent. Theses powers are listed below for your convenience.

Envelop: The spirit is composed wholly of magical energy. It has no mass and occupies no real space on the material plane even when materialized. The spirit can use these qualities to its advantage. Any creature that occupies the same space as the spirit takes damage equal to ½ the spirit's power each round that he or she does so. The power of this attack is equal to the power of the spirit in question.

Should a creature not be foolish enough to become enveloped on its own, the spirit can attempt to "grab" its target and engulf it. This requires the spirit to make an attack roll with dice equal to its power and a difficulty of 5. The victim of the attack can dodge normally. If the victim fails to dodge the attack, he or she is enveloped by the spirit and takes damage each round.

The victim's only hope is escape requiring a strength check against the spirit's strength. The spirit can attempt to hold the victim rolling its strength against that of the victim. Whoever scores more successes is the victor.

Manifest: This ability allows the spirit to become visible on the material plane. Manifesting spirits can be seen by those on the material plane. They can use their powers and abilities against living or magical targets. They cannot, however, interact with any inanimate objects. Furthermore, they cannot attack unless the spirit has another special power or spell-like ability that allows them to do so.

Because they cannot interact with inanimate object, manifested spirits do not take damage from attacks from weapons unless they are magical. A living creature can attack the spirit unarmed & barehanded, however.

Materialization: The spirit takes physical form on the material plane. A materialized spirit can interact with any person, place, or thing on the material plane as if it were a physical entity. Materialized spirits do not age; they are immune to diseases, toxins, and poisons. Such spirits can make physical attacks. In addition, the spirit gains armor with an armor value equal to the spirit's power rating.

Spirits do not like to materialize. Taking physical form makes them subject to physical attacks. A materialized spirit that suffers all its points of body damage is banished from the material plane.

Materialized spirits can chose to forego using their powers and engage their opponents in melee combat. The spirit may "craft" various "weapons" from their bodies or may chose to use their fists, feet, tentacles, etc. Whatever form this attack takes it has a damage rating equal to ½ the power rating of the spirit using it. .

Movement: Elementals are not bound by the same laws that bind other creatures. For them, gravity is merely a suggestion. They can choose it ignore it when it suits their purposes.

Furthermore, a manifested spirit can ignore non-living barriers. It can pass through walls and meld into the earth.

A materialized spirit, however, must honor these barriers. Whether this is because the spirit is physically unable to pass through them, or it is simply rude to do so is a point of conjecture among scholars.

In addition, the spirit can use its own enhanced movement to augment the movement of its summoner or someone designated by the summoner. This counts as one of the spirit's tasks, so it is rarely done lightly.

When a creature's movement is enhanced by a spirit, its quickness is increased by the power level of the spirit for the purposes of determining how far the creature can travel in a single action.

Moreover, the creature can choose to forego its normal means of movement and use only to spirit's power allowing it to ignore gravity just as the spirit can.

For example, Herberthallan, an eleven mage, summons an elemental and uses one of its services to aid his movement. The elemental has a power rating of 4 and Herberthallan has a quickness of 5. Herberthallan's new movement rate is 45 feet per action (5 feet per point of quickness). If Herberthallan wanted to levitate, he could, but his movement rate would be based on the spirit's power, not his quickness giving him a movement rate of 20 feet per action.

Boom Elementals

Boom elementals are spirits formed from the element of boom. They are as temperamental and volatile as the mages aspected to this element.

Boom elementals don't mind being summoned as long as they get to kill someone or destroy something. Summoning a boom elemental to guard a room hidden by a gauntlet of traps and secret doors and the like which no one could ever hope to conquer is a good way to earn the spirit's ire.

Manifested boom elementals look like a cloud billowing smoke with flashes of brilliant color at their core. When they materialize, boom elementals often take humanoid shapes. Magical fire licks the skin of a manifested boom elemental… just touching them is enough to cause harm to most creatures.

Attribute Scores

Strength:	P-2	Reason:	P
Coordination:	P+1	Insight:	P
Quickness:	P+2	Psyche:	P
Constitution:	P+1	Charisma:	P

Dice Pools

Action Pool:	(4P+3)/2
Vigor Pool:	(4P+1)/2
Willpower Pool:	2P

Skills: Boom elementals have a fairly narrow skill set. They are focused on one thing and one thing only… blowing things up. They use their power rating as their skill level for any skill that the director desires them to have.

Special Powers:

Bolt of Boom: The boom elemental can unleash a bolt of magical energy at any creature or item it can see. The spirit rolls its power rating against a target number of five. This bolt of energy does damage (mind if manifesting; body if materialized) equal to one-half the spirit's power per success. The power rating of this ability is equal to the power rating of the spirit. It is gaffed with psyche if the spirit is manifesting and constitution if it is materialized.

As a creature of pure magic, the spirit can use this spell-like ability once per combat round without suffering any ill-effects, including enervation. The spirit can choose to utilize this power more often, but doing so requires the spirit to spend some of its own power reducing the power level of the spirit by one. Power levels spent in this manner return at a rate of 1 per hour.

Boom Wave: This ability is an area effect version of the *Bolt of Boom* power. This power creates an explosion of magical energy originating at the spirit and radiating out in all directions for 5 feet per power rating of the spirit. All creatures caught within the globe of destruction thus created take damage as per the *Bolt of Boom* above. The spirit cannot choose which creatures in the globe are unaffected making this power potentially dangerous to allies as well as foes.

Like the *Bolt of Boom*, *Boom Wave* can only be used once each round unless the spirit chooses to spend some of its own power. Use of one power does not count as a use of the other, so the spirit can use each in a single round without having to tap its own energies.

Spirit Armor: Not only are elementals creatures of magic, they are composed of the same primordial chaos that was used to create the universe. Because of this unique connection to all of creation, elementals receive a spiritual armor with an armor value equal to their power even while manifested. This is the same armor that the elemental would normally have when materialized. The elemental does not benefit from the same armor twice. This means that the elemental reduces all damage from any attack by its power level.

Orange Elementals

Orange elementals are the embodiment of the element of orange. They are patient, determined, & slow to anger. While orange is a color that invokes feelings of warmth, it can also invoke feelings of hunger, and orange elementals are hungry.

Orange elementals really don't care about the affairs of men… or women. They come when called and do what they are told. If they are treated fairly, orange elementals can even befriend their summoners, though this is rare.

Manifested orange elementals appear to be a cloud of orange-hued vapor that is vaguely humanoid in shape. When materialized, these elementals appear to be orange-skinned humanoids whose flesh undulates and writhes as they move. Bits of acidic orange flesh slough off from the elemental pocking and pitting the ground as it moves.

Attribute Scores

Strength:	P+4	Reason:	P
Coordination:	P-2	Insight:	P
Quickness:	P-2	Psyche:	P
Constitution:	P+4	Charisma:	P

Dice Pools

Action Pool:	2P-2
Vigor Pool:	2P+3
Willpower Pool:	2P

Skills: Orange elementals have a wide variety of skills, usually those necessary to create as well as those used to destroy. Orange elementals are some of the greatest chefs on the Lady's Rock. They also have a reputation for poisoning those they cook for. They use their power rating as their skill level for any skill that the director desires them to have.

Special Powers:

Acidic Touch: The touch of an orange elemental causes some of its acidic "flesh" to come in contact with whatever it touched. Objects, such as armor, touched by an orange elemental degrade as if they had been hit with an acid effect spell losing one point of armor value per successful attack (*NOT* success on an attack roll).

Corrosive Globules: The orange elemental can also hurl globules of its corrosive flesh at targets. The difficulty of this attack is 5 and its range increment is equal to the power of the elemental. This attack does damage equal to ½ the elemental's power per success and degrades armor as above.

Wave of Hunger: An orange elemental can send out a wave of intense hunger once each round. This wave originates at the elemental and radiates out in all directions for a number of feet equal to 20 multiplied by the power of the elemental.

The elemental rolls a number of dice equal to its power against a target number of 5. Each success does a single point of mind damage to all creatures within the ability's area of effect. Creatures targeted by this ability can attempt to resist its effects by rolling their psyche dice against a target number equal to the elemental's power rating. Each success reduces the damage by one.

The elemental can choose to utilize this power more often, but doing so requires the spirit to spend some of its own power reducing the power level of the spirit by one. Power levels spent in this manner return at a rate of 1 per hour.

Pungent Elemental

Pungent elementals embody the essence of the element of pungent. While many creatures of magic believe themselves to be powerful masters of the universe, the pungent elemental *knows* this to be true. They are harsh, abrasive, and condescending to even the most powerful of masters in a way that only a creature of pure magic can be. The only way that a summoner can hope to have an amicable relationship to a pungent elemental is to acknowledge the elemental's superiority and admit that the summoner is unworthy of the elemental's attention.

A manifesting pungent elemental appears are a amorphous cloud of pale, sickly greens and blues. When manifesting, they appear almost human, though their skin is tinged green or blue and their hair is usually the opposite color. Regardless, the manifestation or materialization of is almost always accompanied by an acerbic odor. The elemental sees no reason to hide its presence from inferior beings.

Attribute Scores			
Strength:	P-3	Reason:	P
Coordination:	P+2	Insight:	P
Quickness:	P+3	Psyche:	P
Constitution:	P-2	Charisma:	P
Dice Pools			
Action Pool:		(4P+5)/2	
Vigor Pool:		2P-1	
Willpower Pool:		2P	

Skills: Pungent elementals fancy themselves as intellectuals. They possess a wide variety of knowledge skills. They also have some combat skills, but they tend to rely on finesse rather than brute strength. They use their power rating as their skill level for any skill that the director desires them to have.

Special Powers:

Dreadful Howl: A pungent elemental can unleash a horrendous and bone chilling howl that causes even the most fearless warrior to freeze in their tracks. The elemental roll dice equal to its power against a target number of 5. Any creature that can hear the howl must roll their psyche score against the power of the spirit. If the potential victims do not score more successes on their psyche test than the elemental scored on its test, the victims have their physical attributes reduced by the the power of the elemental.

Pungent Breath: The elemental can release a cloud of noxious air from its being that is 10 times the spirit's power in radius. Targets caught within the cloud must gaff a number of points of damage equal to the spirit's power rating each round they are inside the cloud. The power of this attack is equal to the spirit's power rating. Armor, even magical armor, does not prevent this damage.

Shroud: A spirit's shroud power allows it to conceal things or people. Anything (or anyone) concealed by the spirit's power must be within line of sight for the spirit. The spirit's power rating it added to any target number to find the shrouded person, place, or thing. This power is effective against both mundane and magical abilities to find the target… including divination spells, search $ awareness tests, and the find power of other spirits.

Sweet Elementals

Sweet elementals are the embodiment of all that is wholesome, cute, and fluffy… in short, they are all things sweet. In fact, sweet elementals are nauseatingly sweet. They are pleasant, kind, and courteous. They consider it an honor to be called upon by mages and clerics alike.

Sweet elementals truly enjoy being summoned. They love helping others and doing good deeds. A selfish, or evil, summoner who chooses a sweet elemental must be careful about what services he demands. While the elemental must obey the summoner's commands, it can chose to obey the letter of the command rather than the spirit of it.

A sweet elemental manifests itself as a swirling mass of translucent cherry blossoms held aloft by an unseen breeze. When they materialize, a sweet elemental takes the shape of a young human girl with rosy cheeks and large, round eyes... usually holding a lollipop... I told you they were nauseatingly sweet.

Attribute Scores

Strength:	P	Reason:	P
Coordination:	P+1	Insight:	P
Quickness:	P	Psyche:	P
Constitution:	P+2	Charisma:	P

Dice Pools

Action Pool:	(4P+1)/2
Vigor Pool:	(4P+3)/2
Willpower Pool:	2P

Skills: Sweet elementals almost always have skills focused on helping others. All sweet elementals possess the treat injury skill. Sweet elementals rarely have specific combat skills, instead relying on their natural attacks and abilities. They use their power rating as their skill level for any skill that the director desires them to have.

Special Powers:

Aura of Calm: A sweet elemental can invoke an aura of calm that originates at the spirit and radiates out to a range of 10 feet per point of the spirit's power. The spirit rolls its power dice against a target number of five and records the number of successes. Creatures trapped in this aura must roll a psyche test against the spirit's power and achieve more successes than the spirit achieved. If they do not, they are unable to take any hostile action. This effect lasts for a number of rounds equal to the spirit's power even after the creature has left the area of effect.

Breath of Life: The sweet elemental is in tune with the energy of life on the Lady's Rock. The spirit rolls its power rating against a target number of five. This special ability heals a number of points of damage (mind if manifesting; body if materialized) equal to one-half the spirit's power per success.

As a creature of pure magic, the spirit can use this spell-like ability once per combat round without suffering any ill-effects, including enervation. The spirit can choose to utilize this power more often, but doing so requires the spirit to spend some of its own power reducing the power level of the spirit by one. Power levels spent in this manner return at a rate of 1 per hour.

Mystic Guardian: The elemental can defend its summoner and his or her allies from magical attacks. It does this by providing a dice pool equal to its power rating to a number of creatures equal to its power rating. This pool can only be used to resist the effects of magic and refreshes at the beginning of each initiative round just like other dice pools.

Sweet Perfume: A sweet smelling perfume permeates the air around the sweet elemental in a radius equal to 5 feet per power rating of the spirit. Anyone trapped in this area adds the spirit's power rating to any target numbers to perform hostile actions. This power can affects those within the aura of calm as well making hostility in this area very difficult.

Familiar Spirits

Familiar spirits are both more and less powerful than other spirits. A familiar spirit, often just called a familiar, can be a mage's most staunch ally if it is treated fairly. If it is mistreated, however, it can become a mage's worst nightmare.

Summoning a Familiar Spirit

Summoning a familiar spirit uses the same rules as summoning any other spirit with a few additions.

First, the mage must prepare a proper vessel for the familiar spirit to inhabit. This vessel is usually the body of a small animal chosen by the mage. Larger animals can be used, but it is impractical because the larger size of the creature limits its utility. Additionally, the vessel chosen cannot have a psyche score higher than the force of the familiar spirit summoned or the summoning fails.

Second, summoning a familiar spirit cost the mage mana (see "Improving a Character" on page XXXX). This is because of the unique nature and abilities granted by a familiar. The mage must spend a number of points of mana in order to bind the spirit to the vessel and more mana to bond the spirit to him or her self.

Bonding the familiar spirit to the vessel costs 5 times the spirit's power rating. Binding it to the mage costs a number of points equal to 6 plus the mage's psyche multiplied by 3.

For the mathematically inclined that's…

Mana cost to bond with vessel = Power x 5

Mana cost to bind with mage = (6+Mage's Psyche) x 3

For example, summoning a familiar spirit with a power of 5 would cost 25 mana points to bond it with the chosen vessel. A mage with a psyche of 4 attempting this feat would spend 30 more points of mana to bind the familiar to himself.

The mage must spend the mana to bind the spirit to himself before he begins the summoning ritual. If the ritual fails, these points are still lost.

Third, summoning a familiar spirit take a number of days equal to one plus the power rating of the spirit. (Rituals to summon other spirits take a number of hours rather than days.) The number of successes achieved on the summoning test can reduce this number. Subtract one day from the required time per success to a minimum of one.

The mage spends the entire day engaged in the ritual and must resist enervation at the end of each ritual day. The power of this enervation is equal to the power of the spirit plus the number of days spent in the ritual. The enervation each day is the same as it would be for any other spirit (see summoning spirits on Page XXXX).

The mage neither eats nor sleeps during this ritual. While the ritual is taking place, the magical energies of the ritual allow the mage to continue without dying of hunger or succumbing to fatigue.

If the enervation knocks the mage unconscious (or kills him) the ritual fails. If the mage survives and rolled at least one success on his summoning test, the familiar spirit appears and inhabits the vessel.

Having finally completed the grueling ritual and successfully summoned his familiar, the mage will collapse from pure exhaustion. The new familiar's first act on the material plane is to watch over its master while he recovers. The mage falls unconscious for a number of hours equal to the minimum sleep he requires each day (see page XXXX) multiplied by the number of days he was engaged in the ritual plus one hour per power rating of the familiar spirit.

For example, our mage from before is attempting to summon a power 5 familiar spirit. He rolls his summoning dice and gets 3 successes. The mage has a charisma of 4. Because the spirit's power exceeds the mage's charisma, the mage is going to take 3 points of enervation per success, Because the power of the spirit also exceeds the mage's psyche (4 from our previous example), the enervation damage is physical rather than mental.

The ritual to summon the familiar spirit would normally take 6 days, but the three successes on the summoning test reduce this to 3 days. At the end of each day, the mage must resist 9 points of physical damage. On the first day the target number to resist the enervation is 6. On the second day the target number is 7. On the third and final day, the target number is 8. If the mage successfully gaffs the damage each day, the familiar spirit merges with the vessel.

Our mage has a constitution of 3 requiring him to get 6 hours of sleep each day. Once the ritual is complete, he will sleep for 18 hours to make up this lost sleep plus 5 hours (for the power of the familiar spirit Twenty-three hours later, our mage is awake, alive, and meeting his familiar for the first time.

Lastly, unlike other spirits, a mage can only have one familiar at a time. The familiar does not count toward the number of spirits a mage can hove bound to him at one time.

Attributes:

The familiar spirit has physical attributes equal to the spirit's power plus the physical attributes of the vessel the familiar inhabits (see common vessels on page XXXX). The familiar has mental attributes equal to its power. Its dice pools are calculated normally.

Special Powers:

Familiar spirits can be called upon to perform any of the tasks that elementals and ancestor spirits can perform for their summoners. However, when the spirit loses power rating as a consequence of performing a task, this loss is temporary. The familiar spirit regains power at a rate of one point per hour.

If the familiar spirit loses all of its power due to services, it disappears from the material plane and it unable to manifest, materialize, or use any other power until it has regained at least one point of power.

Increased Potential: The mage gains a new attribute called "Potency." The mage's potency is equal to his or her psyche score plus the power rating of the spirit. Use the potency rating to determine whether a caster suffers physical or mental damage from casting a spell instead of the caster's psyche.

Sense Link: The mage can use the senses of its familiar seeing what the familiar sees, hearing what it hears, smelling what it smells, feeling what it feels, and tasting what it tastes. As long as the mage and his or her familiar remain on nthe same plane, this power remains in effect until the mage chooses to cancel the power.

While so engaged, the mage is oblivious to anything happening around his or her body unless the familiar is close enough to sense it. Because the mage feels what the familiar feels any physical damage that the familiar suffers, the mage takes as mental damage. Furthermore, the mage is unaware of any physical damage that his or her own body suffers.

Telepathic Link: As long as the mage and familiar remain on the same plane, they can communicate telepathically.

Common Vessels

Creature	STR	CRD	QCK	CON	RSN	INS	PSY	CHA	Action	Vigor	Willpower
Bat	1	7	5	1	1	5	1	1	9	4	4
Cat, House	1	7	4	1	2	4	2	3	9	4	6
Cat, Wild	2	7	4	2	2	4	2	2	9	5	5
Raven	1	6	6	2	3	4	3	2	10	6	6
Dog, Large	3	5	4	3	2	4	2	3	8	6	6
Dog, Small	1	5	4	1	2	4	2	3	8	4	6
Eagle	3	6	5	3	2	4	3	4	9	7	7
Fox	1	6	4	2	2	4	2	4	8	5	6
Goat	2	4	4	2	2	3	2	1	7	5	4
Hawk	1	9	7	1	4	8	4	5	14	7	11
Kite (bird)	1	6	5	1	1	4	2	1	8	5	4
Mongoose	1	8	7	1	2	5	3	5	11	6	8
Owl	1	8	5	2	3	6	3	4	11	6	8
Rat	1	6	5	1	1	4	1	2	8	4	4
Spider	2	4	4	3	1	3	3	2	6	6	5
Toad	1	4	1	2	1	3	2	1	5	3	4

Improving Your Character

At the end of each gaming session, or at the beginning of the next session, the director will award mana based on your performance. You can spend this manna to learn new skills, improve existing skills and increase attributes.

Improving Attributes

Attributes represent your character's natural aptitudes and talents. Increasing your aptitude and talent isn't easy. It takes time, energy, and dedication. Think of it in terms of the really real world. Raising your strength requires hours in a gym lifting weights. It requires eating the right foods in the right amounts.

It is equally difficult for your character… Actually, it might be more difficult because there aren't many gyms around to lift weights at… Despite this your character can raise any attribute one point at a time by spending an amount of mana equal to the desired attribute rating squared. For example, raising your quickness from 3 to 4 would cost 16 mana points.

An attribute an only be raised one point at a time and *cannot* be raised above the maximum for the character's race using mana points.

Learning a New Skill

Your character is free to learn new skills between gaming sessions. It costs 10 mana points to learn a new skill. Developing a new skill takes time. It is recommended that the director only allows each character to learn one new skill between sessions.

If the character has a skill at a minimum of 3, he or she can choose to have a new specialization. A character can only have one specialization per skill. Having more specializations defeats the purpose of specialization. Gaining a new specialization cost 3 mana points.

Improving Skills

Improving your character's skills is easier to do than raising your attributes. Just compare the current skill rating to the attribute that governs the skill. Consult the table for improving base skills and find the applicable modifier. Multiply the desired skill level by the modifier and raise your skill to the desired level.

Specializations are less expensive to raise than base skills. When improving a specialization consult the table for improving specializations and use the applicable modifier. A specialization *must* remain at least one rating higher than the base skill it is derived from. If the base skill ever equals the specialization, the specialization is no longer applicable and the character loses it (along with all the points spent on it).

Training

Finding someone to teach a skill to a character makes it easier for the character to improve the skill. It does nothing to help the character learn a new skill.

In order to train someone in the use of s skill the "instructor: must meet the following requirements:

- The instructor must have a rating of at least 3 in the skill to be trained.

- The instructor must speak a language that the student understands or have some other means (such as magic) of communicating with the student.

- The instructor must have the skill at a higher rating than the student.

If the instructor meets these requirements, he or she can train someone in a skill upto the instructor's skill level. It is not possible for the instructor to teach the student beyond his own skill level.

Training reduces the amount of mana needed to improve the skill. Rather than multiply the desired skill level by the multiplier listed on the improvement tables, training allows the student to apply the multiplier to his or her *current* skill level.

For example, a character with a coordination of 4 is raising his edged weapons skill from 3 to 4. It will cost the character 6 points to improve the skill on his own or 4 points with training.

Multipliers for Improving Base Skills			Multipliers for Improving Specializations		
The current skill rating is…	Active Skills	Knowledge Skills	The current specialization rating is…	Active Skills	Knowledge Skills
Less than the Attribute:	1.5	1	Less than the Attribute:	1	.5
Less than or equal to (2 x Attribute):	2	1.5	Less than or equal to (2 x Attribute):	1.5	1
Greater than (2 x Attribute):	2.5	2	Greater than (2 x Attribute):	2	1.5

The Director's Cut

Warning: *Reading this section of this book could greatly diminish your enjoyment of this game and / or campaign setting. Players are strongly advised and encouraged not to read beyond this page.*

Unless, of course, you aren't playing the game in order to have fun. Then, by all means, read on. After all, you, or someone you know, paid for this book...

Unless you're reading a pirated copy, in which case we'll have to hunt you down mercilessly like the dog that you are...

The job of being a director is not easy. As the Game Operations Director, it is your responsibility to dictate the actions of every man, woman, child, and creature that *is not* a player character. This is something that many people in your position forget.

You are not the master of the game... or even the dungeon. You aren't telling a story or refereeing the game. You aren't an administrator... or even an administrative assistant. All of these titles carry with them more responsibility than being the director of this game... and you have enough on your plate already.

While you do have quite a bit on your plate, your job is fairly easy to define.

"It is the purpose of the Game Operations Director to tell the player how the world reacts to the actions of their characters."

That's it... As director you will set the scene, and the players will do the rest. Here is a short list of things to keep in mind & help you while doing your job. If you have questions, thoughts, or concerns, let us know. We'll be happy to help out... and by that I mean, I'll help you until I've mad enough money that I can assign that task to some mid-level functionary with a bad comb-over.

- **Create a timeline of what the villains will do if the players do not interfere.** It will be easier to keep the game fluid if you're changing the villain's existing plan rather than making it up as you go. Remember, the villain wasn't planning on being foiled when he came up with the plan.
- **Plan encounters, not adventures.** Adventures are rigid and inflexible. Players rarely, if ever, do what they are supposed to in order to complete an adventure. They are happy, however, to move from encounter to encounter... just not always in the order you expect.
- **Do not plan around your players.** I don't know how many times I've read that you should tailor adventurers to your players. Stop for a minute and think about how utterly ridiculous that is. Why would a maniac bend on world domination intentionally build an impenetrable fortress with a flaw designed to be exploited by his or her archenemies? They wouldn't. (Building a thermal exhaust port that leads directly to your reactor system is just asinine, even if it is just the size of a womp rat.) Don't hand your player's victory; let them earn it. It'll mean more to them.
- **Don't force your players to play average <insert race of choice here>.** Look, we all play "average humans" in our everyday lives. I, for one, certainly don't want to do it in my free time. Besides, if the characters were merely "average" examples of their species, they'd be doing what average members of their species do. They would be blacksmiths and barmaids... not heroes who save the world.

- **Make their actions have consequences.** All too often players swoop into a small town, spend more gold than the inhabitants earn in a life time, foil the bad guy, and leave without a second thought. They never consider that they just ruined the economy of the small town. They don't give a second thought to the newfound power their money grants the inn keeper.
- **Remember that not all consequences are bad.** As I will discuss in the section about rewarding players, their actions in a town, even when not directly related to the "plot," can be important and rewarding. The inn keeper they overpaid might use that wealth to become mayor of the city. He may look favorably on the players should their characters return.
- **Keep your adventurers on the right scale.** Yes, we all want to become epic heroes and save the world, but try to be realistic. Don't involve your players in things where they have no real effect on the outcome. It might be fun to play an epic battle from time to time, but being a cog in a larger machine mitigates the importance of the player's actions. Let them do things that will have some effect. If they aren't powerful enough to influence kings and world leaders, keep them local until they are.
- **Keep the plot moving.** This doesn't mean force your characters to follow the plot line. What it does mean is that things happen if the players do not act. This isn't a computer game where the evil sheriff doesn't start killing townspeople until after the player arrives in town. If the players chose not to accept your plot hook, let them. Then show them what happened because of their inaction.
- **Your players aren't the only game in town.** Players often think that their party is the only group of people rummaging through dusty tombs and beating up evil wizards. That simply isn't the case. If the players can chose not to be blacksmiths like their fathers... and their father... and their fathers... so can other people. And sometimes those other people will adventure to get things that your players already have.
- **Base important non-player characters after characters from books, characters from movies, and people you know.** It is going to be much easier for you to decide how your best friend from high school would react in a given situation than "important city watchman # 3." The things you watch, the books you read, and the people you know have given you a veritable library of human behavior. Use it. Nothing makes NPCs more realistic than basing their personalities on those of real people.
- **Keep a folder of maps.** Eventually, your players are going to do something you haven't prepared for. Following the advice here will help you deal with that, but there is always the problem of

places. Players like to delve through detailed places. Have some places on hand just in case. If you don't have a map handy, use some place you are familiar with as a basis. Grandma's old farmhouse doubles as a wonderful home for a merchant in a small town. Your buddy's cabin up north makes an excellent home for a retired knight of the realm. You just need to modify them a little… and modification is easier when you're working without a net than fresh invention. It'll keep your locations consistent, realistic, and believable.

- **Don't be afraid to let your players have things.** I've played some games where the best equipment we ever had access to was what we purchased when we first made our characters. It sucks. Yes, it can be fun to be in a resource crunch once in a while. I'm all for it. But don't make it the status quo. Most of us spend out real lives in a resource crunch. Those that don't are either had ancestors who were… or are in for a rude awakening when they finally move out of their parent's house. Role-playing is about an escape from the daily grind, not living our real lives in a world without running water and flush toilets.
- **Don't let the rules get in the way of the game.** You're playing a game in order to have fun with friends, so have fun. Don't let the rules hamper having a good time. It's more important that you enjoy yourselves and play a fun game than to be sure you resolve any one situation according to the rules. Trust me. I know the guys who wrote "the rules" and I'm fairly certain that they would agree with me.

Assigning Target Numbers

One of the most daunting tasks that the director faces is assigning target numbers to various activities. The target number is the difficulty for a trained person to perform a give activity under normal conditions. Penalties for circumstances take the form of being able to roll less dice, not an increase in target number.

Try looking at it like this. A few years ago, I had a problem with my computer. I tried and trtied to resolve the issue, but I just couldn't get it. Finally, I called my brother, who happens to be a computer engineer. It took him several seconds to tell me how to fix the problem.

Now, did the problem spontaneously become easier for him to solve than it was for me? No, the problem remained the same. What differed was our skill level at solvfing the problem. In other words, he had more ranks in the computer operation skill than I did and was able to roll more dice.

Target Number	Chance of Success
1	90%
2	80%
3	70%
4	60%
5	50%
6	40%
7	30%
8	20%
9	10%
10	9%
11	8%
12	7%
13	6%
14	5%
15	4%
16	3%
17	2%
18	1%
19	0.9%
20	0.8%
21	0.7%
22	0.6%
23	0.5%
24	0.4%
25	0.3%
26	0.2%
27	0.1%
28	0.09%
29	0.08%
30	0.07%
31	0.06%
32	0.05%
33	0.04%
34	0.03%
35	0.02%
36	0.01%

Now, if the problem had to do with the video drivers for the computer and we were trying to fix it without a functioning monitor, then the problem would have become more difficult. Our respective skill levels would not have changed, but my brother would still have a greater chance of success because he has more dice to roll.

Let's use some examples that experienced players might be more familiar with – called shots & aiming.

If I am aiming at a target, the difficulty to hit that target somewhere is X. Deciding I am going to hit that target between the eyes is decidedly more difficult. This warrants a raise in target number.

In many games, taking time to aim a ranged weapon reduces the target number needed to hit your target. Does the target miraculously become easier to hit because I spend a few minutes lining up my shot, or do I just have a more chance to succeed? Nope, I just get more dice to roll because I'm increasing my chances of hitting, not making the target less difficult to hit. This may seem like semantics. In some games it is. This, however, is not one of them.

So, when assigning a target number, try not to think about the player, the character, or the situation. Start with a base target number of 5. Decide whether this task is more or less difficult than 50% under normal circumstances. Then determine if there are any circumstances that make the task itself more or less difficult. If there are, raise or lower the target number accordingly. Remember, no target number can be lower than one. Once you've determined how hard the task is, determine if there are any circumstances that limit or increase the number of dice the player can roll and assign that penalty or bonus…

And, if all else fails, just make it up.

Rewarding the Characters

Rewards to player actually take many forms. Sometimes those rewards are monetary in nature, sometime they take the form of items, and other times they are merely the gratitude of the non-player characters. Of course, earning mana to use to improve your character doesn't hurt either.

Treasure

Loot is an important part of the role-playing experience. Other than poor people (like me), most people carry some money on them at all times. Players who vanquish a foe and loot the body can and should receive this treasure... as well as any items the foe had on them.

A dragon traditionally has a horde of gems, coins, art, and other priceless artifacts. Player defeating a dragon will expect to find this treasure trove. Players who kill a dragon outside of his lair might quest to find the dragon's lair. There is nothing wrong with this expectation. In fact, if you ignore the players' expectations too often, they may decide to ignore your gaming night.

Social Rewards

Keep in mind that the gratitude of non-player characters can be a very important reward, especially if you are playing a campaign in which the party will encounter those NPCs again at some later point in time.

A grateful noble might show up to defend the party against the charges levied against them by a member of the lesser nobility. A grateful farmer may provide them with mounts at no cost to the party. An inn keeper might pass along vital information. Any of these things can be more valuable than all the gold in the world.

Issuing Mana Points

Some RPGs make experience a function of how many kills the character's score. Others have rejected this idea in favor of a "threat" system. While all of these methods provide a nice means of gauging experience, they tend to put emphasis on one particular aspect of the game. Players naturally want to see their characters advance, so they do the things that bring in experience.

So how to you issue experience in a way that keeps the game interesting, but doesn't focus too much on any one aspect of it? Like many things, the answer is so simple it might amaze you. You issue experience based on story and to reinforce behaviors you want players to continue.

Showing Up to Play: Every player who shows up to play deserves to earn some experience, give it to them. Just showing up to play earns the characters a point of mana.

Advancing the Story: Advancing the plot is important. After all, if the story doesn't advance, the game doesn't go anywhere. Issue some experience to everyone if the party manages to move the story forward. If a particular character does something important that significantly advances the story, issue that player extra experience unless that character did something that was completely out of character. A "stupid" barbarian that can barely speak has no business solving a complex alchemical riddle. If this happens, the barbarian should not be rewarded for bad role-playing even if he advanced the plot.

Role-playing: Since this is a role-playing game, role-playing should be a determining factor in issuing experience. Unfortunately, as I said earlier, it tends to be forgotten in most campaigns. To reward role-playing, anyone who puts forth *any* effort in this regard should earn some experience. Additional experience should be issued if they are able to role-play consistently. Issue more to anyone whose character acts "in character" despite the fact that the player knows that the behavior is not in the best interests of the character or that some other course of action might lead to better results.

Keep in mind that not all role-playing is social in nature. I once played in a group with a player whose character was a mute & illiterate barbarian. Anytime the player communicated with members of the party or NPCs he drew pictures on a sketch pad to convey his message. This was superb role-playing. Unfortunately, the person running the game, for reasons I cannot fathom, thought that not being able to speak was a "cop out" and refused to issue any "role-playing" experience points to the character. The player eventually quit playing in that game because of this lack of experience.

Surviving: Any character that lives through a role-playing session should earn something simply for not dying. Characters that face a significant threat to their lives and well-being and survive may be issued more for surviving that particular threat. However, you should avoid issuing extra experience for each and every combat that the party participates in. If experience starts to become "kill based" your game becomes no different than countless console RPGs available. Players can play console games whenever they feel like it. They aren't likely to set aside one night each week or month to show up and accomplish the same thing at your house that they could in their own.

Mana Awards Table

General Awards	
Showing Up to Play	1
Surviving to Play Another Night (or Day)	1
Plot Related Awards	
Moving the Main Story Along	1
Moving a Personal Story Line Along	1
Role-Playing Awards	
Good Role-Playing	1
Staying In Character	1
Good Role-Playing at a Detriment to the Character	2
Showing Bravery	1
Being Down Right Heroic	2
Demonstrating Intelligence	1
Avoiding Unnecessary Violence	1
Clever Idea that proves futile	1
Clever Idea that proves useful	2
Clever Idea that Saves the Party	3
Clever Idea that Saves Numerous People	4
Clever Idea that Saves the Country, Empire, or World	5
Quick Thinking	1
Making the Other Players Laugh or Cry	1
Making the Director Laugh or Cry	2
Threat Awards	
Defeating a Minor Threat	1
Defeating a Major Threat	2
Defeating a Great Threat	3

Magical Items

On a world where magic is so pervasive, it only stands to reason that powerful magic-users would harness the magic to aid spell-casters and non-spell-casters alike.

Below is a list of some of the magic items your players might encounter during their adventures. The number in parentheses after the name of the item is the item's power. This number is important to gauge the relative strength of the item and for attuning and / or bonding to the item (see attuning and bondin on page XXXX). If the items bears an enchantment beyond those listed in the description, be sure to add this enchantment to the power.

Mystical Substances

There are a wide variety of mystical substances that people on the Lady's Rock turn into weapons, armor, and other useful items.

Mystic Woods

Carbonis Wood: Carbonis wood is very resistant to fire. This property is the reason many cooking utensils are made from this dark & distant relative of the mighty oak.

Ghost Wood: The wood of the Ghost Wood tree has several unique properties that people have learned to exploit. First and foremost, the bark of this tree absorbs light. It is used in the creation of Dark Cells (D-Cells) used to power Dark-Suckers. Second, the fact that wood is semi intangible makes it valuable in the creation of a variety of traps and other objects.

Mystic Metals

Adamantine: This metal is black in color it can be polished to a glossy finish, but this is rare. Adamantine is the hardest metal known to exist. Weapons made from this metal are able to slice through even the toughest armor. In game terms, the armor value of non-adamantine armor is halved when hit with an adamantine weapon.

Armor made from this metal naturally has an armor value 3 points higher than its mundane counterpart. Adamantine armor is very heavy, however, and this increase in armor value also applies when determining if a character suffers a penalty for wearing the armor.

Mithril: Also known as "true silver," mithril is a rare metal that weighs half as much as a similar quantity of conventional metals. Weapons made of mithril are lighter than normal, but provide no additional bonuses. Consider the armor value of mithril armor to be half that of its mundane counterpart for purposes of determining the penalty, if any, the wearer suffers.

Orichalcum: This reddish-gold metal is semi-transparent and, when alloyed with steel, nearly indestructible. Only adamantine is stronger. Because of their magical properties, Orichalcum weapons can be used to parry magical attacks.

Orichalcum armor weighs the same as other armor of the same design and size. However, if the armor is enchanted, in addition to the added protection the orichalcum grants one die to magical resistance for each magical bonus.

Magic Armors

Most magical armor is enchanted to provide additional protection to the wearer. The armor usually bears an enchantment between 1 and 3… though enchantments as high as 5 have been known to exist. Each level of enchantment adds to the armor value of the enchanted armor… and to the power of the item.

Armor of Acid Resistance (1): Magical acid attacks are one of the most detrimental attacks that a warrior can suffer. It degrades the protective value of the armor. One of the earliest enchantments to armor was to make it resistant to the effects of acid. Armor of Acid Resistance doesn't necessarily provide any benefit to the wearer, but the armor itself is immune to the degrading effects of acidic attacks.

Armor of Command (9): This highly ornate plate armor is etched with symbols of royalty and nobility. It is often gilded and gem encrusted. This armor provides 3 additional dice to any social skill test made by the wearer. In addition, any enchantment spells cast by the wearer have the target number to resist the spell's effects increased by 3.

Armor of the Raider (1): This breastplate is veined as if it was made from a fleshless body. It provides the same protection as a normal breastplate. Its magical properties only become apparent if the wearer falls into the aether. The enchantments works into the armor cause the wearer to float, bobbing around like a cork until they are rescued or swim to safety.

Armor of the Ram (3): Armor of the Ram is half-plate armor with ram horns emblazoned on the pauldrons. The armor is enchanted so that the armor value of the armor is added to the damage rating of the any weapon the wearer wields for the purposes of deciding whether or not the opponent suffers a knockdown.

Dragon Scale Armor (2): Dragon scale armor is made from the scales of some large reptile, though it is rarely, if ever, made from the hide of an actual dragon. Dragon scale armor is hide armor that provides the same protection as scale armor. In essence, the wearer uses the armor value of hide armor (3) to determine whether ot not they suffer any penalties to wearing the armor and the armor value of scale armor (7) for defense.

Dwarven Pale Armor (3): Finding dwarven plate armor that is sized for anything other than a dwarf is extremely rare. The armor is crafted from adamantine. It provides an armor value of 12, but its special craftsmanship reduces the penalty to dwarven characters by half. Small non-dwarven characters can wear the armor, but they must consider the full armor value and will probably suffer serious penalties.

Elven Chainmail (5): This suit of chainmail is crafted from a delicate mesh of fine interlinked chain. The armor is weightless, but provides the same protective value as normal chainmail. The secret of crafting this armor is a closely guarded elven secret.

Magical Helms

Magical headgear has been around as long as magical armor. Magical helms can take many shapes, from the bucket helms of crusaders to the spangenhelms of norse raiders.

Fiendhelm (13): This magical helm appears to be crafted from the skull of a demon. It confers darkvision on its wearer. It also hardens their skin making it more like that of a fiend. This hardened skin has a leathery appearance and reduces the total damage inflicted in a single attack by three points.

Fiery-plumes Bucket Helm (27): This bucket helm is topped with a plume of fire. This fire does not generate heat, so it does not ignite flammable objects. It does, however, give off light equivalent to a torch.

The warrior wearing this helm uses twice his charisma to determine how much soul damage he can take before dying. More impressively, when the warrior reaches this enhanced threshold, he is instantly healed of all damage.

This magical healing is not without cost, however. Each time the warrior "dies" and is reborn, his or her charisma drops by one point. When his or her charisma reaches zero, they no longer have a soul. Their next death will be their last.

Characters with no charisma cannot use any social skills. They are uncouth, lacking all forms of etiquette or social grace whatsoever.

A character who removes this helm does not regain points lost to the helm's power.

Helm of Battle (8): This helm confers 2 extra dice to all initiative checks.

Helm of Bone (19): This metal helm is pitted and pocked from ages of abuse, neglect, and bloodshed. A ridge of bones crests this ancient helm like a spine and smaller ribs jut out from this spine to grip the helm like the talons of some foul beast. A leering skull sits atop the front of this helm menacing those who would attack the wearer.

The wearer of this helm can generate fear in those who can see him. This fear paralyzes its victims making them unable to act for 10 rounds (1 minute). Victims can make a psyche test against a target number equal to 3 plus the wearer's psyche. Each success reduces the duration by 1 round.

Helm of Brilliance (12): The enchantment on this helm grants the person wearing this helm has their reason attribute and all knowledge skills increased by 3.

Helm of Heroes (18): This helm grants the wearer one additional attack each round. This attack occurs at the end of the round and must be used to attack or it is lost.

Helm of the Hunter (18): Stag horns adorn this Corinthian-style helm crafted from a single piece of pounded metal. The wearer of the Helm of the Hunter gains low-light vision if they do not already possess it. They also receive 3 additional dice to hide and sneak test and 5 additional dice to awareness and tracking tests.

Magical Weapons

Like magical armor, magical weapons often bear an enchantment between 1 and 3. The level of enchantment divided between the weapon's difficulty, damage rating and damage bonus. No weapon can have a difficulty reduced to less than one for any reason.

For example, a Dagger +3 could have a new difficulty of 2 instead of the standard 3 and a damage bonus of +2 instead of the standard +1.

Arrows of Slaying (5): These powerful magical items can be fired from either a short or long bow. Each arrow is enchanted to kill a particular subspecies of creature. These arrows are so deadly because they inflict soul damage rather than physical damage upon their target. The damage is still resisted with constitution and fortitude as normal.

Against any foe other than the specified subspecies, these arrows act just like normal arrows. Once they have been fired, their magic is expended. Even if the arrows are recovered, they have lost their enchantment.

Club of Fangs (2): This club is studded with the fangs of different animals. At its wielder's discretion, these fangs can dislodge and stick in the target on a successful hit. The victim can make a constitution test with a target number of 8 in order to reject the fang. If this test fails, the fang imbeds in the victim's skin granting the club's wielder an additional success on his or her next attack against that target. The club has 12 fangs when it is first found. Once these twelve fangs have been used, the club becomes a normal club for that wielder. If another person attunes to the club, the fangs return.

Dagger of Venom +3 (4): This dagger has a difficulty of 2, a damage rating of 1, and bonus damage of +3. While this makes the dagger a formidable weapon, this is not the reason that the dagger is sought after. Three times per day, if a target fails to dodge an attack by this weapon, the attacker can opt to inject a paralytic poison into the victim's system. The poison takes effect even if the victim manages to gaff all the damage from the attack.

The poison paralyzes the victim, reducing his or her quickness. The attacker rolls a single d10; the result of this roll is the amount the victim's quickness is reduced. The victim can roll his or her constitution (plus vigor dice if desired) against a target number of 7. Each success reduces the penalty to quickness by one.

It takes 6 hours for the poison to work its way through the victim's system. Of course, most victims of this deadly weapon aren't wround 6 hours later to know that.

Dancing Sword (6): A dancing sword is a short sword of superb craftsmanship and made from gleaming mithril. Being made of mithril, the dancing sword is extremely light giving it a difficulty of only 3. Though it does the same damage as any other short sword, the dancing sword has another unique ability that makes it a much sought after weapon.

After the wielder of a dancing sword has fought with it for at least one round, he or she can release the weapon into the air. Rather than dropping to the ground, the blade remains in the air held aloft by magic. Moreover, the blade continues to fight as if its wielder still held it.

The blade attacks with the same skill as its wielder and has an action pool equal to that of its wielder. The blade rolls initiative separately from its "wielder" and uses its own attacks as the wielder desires. The blade does not gain any strength bonus on its attacks because no one is holding it.

Dwarven Hammer of Throwing (5): This weapon functions as a normal warhammer. However, this hammer is specially weighted to be used as a thrown weapon. This warhammer has a range increment of 10 feet. More importantly, it returns to the wielder at the beginning of the wielder's next initiative phase.

Flame Tongue (4): A flame tongue is a magical long sword with a leather–wrapped handle made of carbonis wood. On command its blade is wreathed in fire. On a successful attack, the flame tongue does an additional 6 points of fire damage. These 6 points are added to the total damage from the attack after the damage bonus is added. They are gaffed normally.

Frostbrand (7): This great axe has a difficulty of 6, a damage rating of 6 rating, and its bonus damage is 1. The enchantment on this axe absorbs the fire 10 points of fire damage dealt to the wielder.

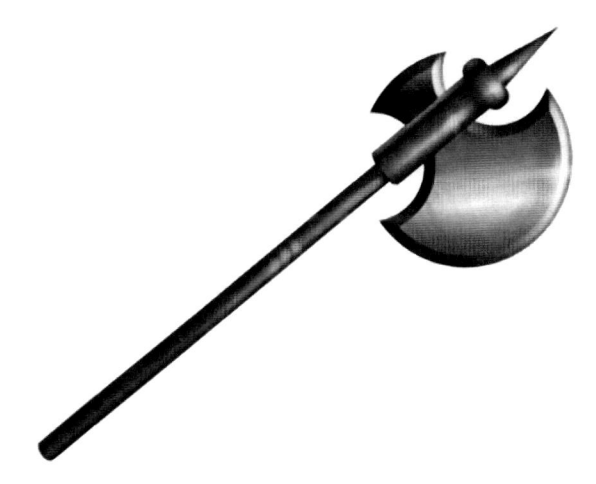

In addition to this impressive defensive measure, the frostbrand has an offensive ability as well. Each point of fire damage do absorbed can be redirected at the next person struck by the frostbrand. Despite being generated by fire damage, the extra damage inflicted by the frostbrand is cold damage.

Holy Avenger (5): This bastard sword has been blessed by the the high priest of a particular deity. These sacred weapons are then provided to holy warriors (paladins) who use them to do the will of their deity. Each holy avenger is dedicated to a specific deity. The blade will only work for those who have sworn themselves in service to that deity's clergy.

Holy avengers have a difficulty of 5 like other bastard swords. They inflict 6 points of damage per success and do bonus damage equal to the insight of their wielder.

Mace of Smiting (4): A mace of smiting has a head made of ghost wood making it a fairly useless weapon… unless you're using it against its intended target. The weapon does not damage to living being (aside from the eburnae). Against members of the undead, however, this enchanted heavy mace packs quite a punch. It has a difficulty of 4 and a damage rating of 3, and a bonus damage of 3. In addition, the wielder's psyche score is added to the total damage… this is in addition to the wielder's strength.

Sword of Justice (3): The sword of justice was created by the imperial ministry of justice to aid its agents in the field. When an official indictment is read allowed in the presence of the sword, its blade glows with a faint blue light. This light increases in intensity as the sword's wielder nears the criminal named in the indictment aiding the agent to track his prey.

In addition, when the weapons is used against person or persons named in the indictment, its difficulty is reduced by one while its damage rating and damage bonus both increase by 1.

Vorpal Blade (9): A vorpal blade is an extremely sharp weapon said to be able to cut through anything. The blade is crafted from a unique alloy of adamantine, mithril and orichalcum. It halves the protective value of any armor worn by its intended target. The statistics for the weapon do not change from its mundane counterparts, but the vorpal weapon does soul damage rather than physical making it one of the most deadly weapons on the Lady's Rock.

Magical Rings

Magical rings take many forms. They are generally circles of some precious metal and may have one or more gems set into them. The rings themselves are usually scribed with arcane runes and glyphs. The more discrete magical rings have these markings hidden on the inside of the band. The most dangerous of the magical rings have writing that can only be revealed by casting the ring into a fire.

The number of magical rings that a person can wear is limited to the number of fingers that person possesses. In most cases, this is ten, but the horrors of war might reduce this number… And, if you happen to have six fingers on your right hand, you'd be able to wear 11 rings at once. Of course, then you have to worry about that kid you left alive as a witness to your murder of his father. Revenge probably drove him to dedicate his life to the study of fencing so that, when he meets you again, he will not fail.

Regardless of the number of fingers that you have, you can only activate two rings at any one time. Rings that have a continuous effect number be continuously active and will limit the usability of other rings.

Ring of Arcane Might (9): This ring adds one to the potency of the spell-caster or grants them a potency if they did not previously have one (see *Increased Potential* under the description of familiar spirit's special powers on page XXXX).

In addition, this ring increased the amount of enervation resisted per success by 1.

Ring of Darkvision (1): This magical ring grants darkvision to its wearer. This vision functions in all regards as if the wearer had darkvision as one of his or her racial features.

Ring of Elemental Control (8): There are five different versions of this magical ring, one for each of the five elements.

The bands of these rings are made from interwoven strands of the three mystical metals – adamantine, mithril, and orichalcum. Each is set with a single stone that reveals the element that is grants control over.

Boom	Red
Orange	Orange
Prickle-prickle	Black
Pungent	Blue
Sweet	White

These rings provide three bonus dice to cast magical effects associated with an element and to resist those same effects. In addition, the ring grants five extra dice for the purposes of summoning an elemental or wresting control of an elemental from another summoner. Of course, these bonuses only apply to a particular elemental as determined by the color of the stone set into the ring.

Ring of Ether Vision (1): This magical ring confers ether vision to its wearer as if ether vision was a racial trait.

Ring of Invisibility (4): This ring confers invisibility on its wearer for a today of 1 hour each day. This can be broken up between several uses, but the total time in a rolling 24 hour period cannot exceed 1 hour.

While the wearer is invisible to normal vision, low-light, thermal, and darkvision, he or she remains visible to ether vision. In fact, they become even more visible to people using ether vision. Reduce all target numbers to see the ring bearer by 4.

Ring of Levitation (4): This ring confers limited flight to the wearer. This ability functions identically to the teg's racial trait of the same name. Even though the wearer does not have wings, the magic of the ring allows him or her to behave as if he or she did.

Ring of Nourishment (2): A ring of nourishment magically nourishes the body of the person wearing it. This is a continuous effect, so this ring is always active if the wearer wishes to benefit from this effect.

Because the wearer's body is magically nourished, he or she does not produce any waste… unless they choose to consume food or drink.

Ring of Regeneration (9): This ring greatly enhancing the healing abilities of its wearer. The character heals damage at an accelerated rate. Every Time the character fills their condition monitor, roll a single d10. If the result is 1 or higher (anything other than a zero), the character wearing this ring is completely healed of that type of damage.

If results from a silver, magic spell, magic weapon, or massive tissue damage (such as fire, acid, lightning, etc), then the roll must be 2 or higher (anything other than a zero or one).

This ring must be continuously active for the power of the ring to benefit the wearer.

Ring of Spell Storing (8): This ring can store a number of spells whose collective power rating does not exceed 10. The caster simply casts the spell as normal targeting the ring. The spell-caster records the number of successes he or she rolled on the casting test and the power of the spell. He or she then resists enervation normally.

When the wearer of the ring, who does not need to be the original caster, wishes to recall one of the spells contained in the ring, he or she simply issues a mental command. This can be done once per action and does not cost the wearer any actions.

Upon attuning or bonding to the ring, the wearer instantly knows the names and power ratings of any spells that might be contained within.

Ring of Spell Turning (8): Three times per day, this ring reflects upon 9 power levels of spell back at the caster who must resist the spell's effects as if it was targeted at him or her. If the wearer attempts to reflect a spell with a power rating of higher than 9, the turning fails and that use of the ring's power is exhausted.

Ring of Sustenance (varies): This ring sustains spells on behalf of the wearer. These rings have a power rating ranging from 1 to 9. Each round that the ring sustains a spell it burns away one of its power levels. When the ring reaches zero, the spell ceases to function. Power ratings burned away in this manner return at a rate of one per hour.

Ring of Truth (3): This ring alerts the wearer whenever a lie is told in the wearer's presence. The wearer must be able to hear the lie in order for the ring's power to take effect.

Ring of Wizardry (varies): This magical ring is found in 4 different varieties, unimaginatively called "Rings of Wizardry I – IV" (apparently the use of roman numerals makes these terrible names somehow more acceptable). The ring of wizardry has a power equal to 3 times the number of the ring giving them a power of 3-12.

Rings of wizardry provide a spell-caster with a special defense against enervation. Multiply the number of the ring by the wearer's psyche. This is the number of points of enervation that the ring absorbs per day.

This ring must be worn and active continuously in order for the power to take effect, but the wearer chooses which enervation is aborbed.

Magical Staves

Staves have been a mainstay of spell-slingers for as long as they have been slinging spells. These items contain 50 charges of magical energy when created. Roll 5 10-sided dice and add the results to determine how many charges a staff possesses when found.

Staff of Abjuration (Remaining charges/10): This staff contains a number of charges, each charge can be expended to receive an automatic success to either cast an abjuration spell or resist enervation from an abjuration spell.

Staff of Biomancy (Remaining charges/10): This staff contains a number of charges, each charge can be expended to receive an automatic success to either cast a biomancy spell or resist enervation from the same.

Staff of Conjuration (Remaining charges/10): This staff contains a number of charges, each charge can be expended to receive an automatic success to either cast a conjuration spell or resist enervation from the same.

Staff of Divination (Remaining charges/10): This staff contains a number of charges, each charge can be expended to receive an automatic success to either cast a Divination spell or resist enervation from the same.

Staff of Enchantment (Remaining charges/10): This staff contains a number of charges, each charge can be expended to receive an automatic success to either cast an enchantment spell or resist enervation from the same.

Staff of Evocation (Remaining charges/10): This staff contains a number of charges, each charge can be expended to receive an automatic success to either cast an evocation spell or resist enervation from the same.

Staff of Illusion (Remaining charges/10): This staff contains a number of charges, each charge can be expended to receive an automatic success to either cast an illusion spell or resist enervation from the same.

Staff of Transmutation (Remaining charges/10): This staff contains a number of charges, each charge can be expended to receive an automatic success to either cast a transmutation spell or resist enervation from the same.

Staff of Power (remaining charges/3): This staff contains a number of charges, each charge can be expended to receive an automatic success to either cast any spell or resist enervation.

Magical Medallions

Medallions are magical pendants that confer certain power upon the person wearing it.

Medallion of Aries (4): The medallion of Aries makes its wearer immune to surprise. Normally when a character is surprised, they only receive ½ of their action pool dice to roll initiative. Characters wearing the medallion of Aries retain their full action pool even when surprised.

Medallion of Taurus (4): Once per day, the wearer of a medallion of Taurus may activate its power and become immune to the effects of enchantment spells for 1 minute.

Medallion of Gemini (7): The wearer of a medallion of Gemini can cause a single target to act contrary to their normal behavior. The wearer must be able to see the target. The duration of the effect is normally one hour. The target rolls his or her psyche dice (and any dice from willpower if desired) against a target number equal to 3 plus the psyche of the wearer. Each success reduces the duration by 5 minutes.

Medallion of Cancer (3): The wearer of this medallion gains an eidetic memory. He or she remembers everything he sees or hears to the point where they could accurately reconstruct a map, picture, or page of text or relay an overheard conversation verbatim. This power lasts until the wearer repeats the information… draws the picture / map, rewrites the page of text, or repeats the conversation.

Medallion of Leo (2): The wearer of this medallion gains 5 additional dice to resist any fear effects.

Medallion of Virgo (6): Once per day, the wearer of this medallion can neutralize any poison or heal 8 points of physical or mental damage that the target is suffering.

Medallion of Libra (7): This medallion can be activated once per day, and its power lasts for 1 minute. During that period of time, any physical damage inflicted on the wearer in melee combat is suffered by the attacker as well. The wearer still takes damage, but any damage that the wearer is unable to dodge or gaff is inflicted upon attacker. The attacker can attempt to gaff this damage normally.

This medallion has no affect on ranged or magical attacks.

Medallion of Scorpio (5): The wearer of this medallion can instill the base feelings of greed, lust, or fury in a chosen target. The wearer must be able to see the target. The duration of the effect is normally one hour. The target rolls his or her psyche dice (and any dice from willpower if desired) against a target number equal to 3 plus the psyche of the wearer. Each success reduces the duration by 5 minutes.

Medallion of Sagittarius (3): The wearer of this medallion can compel another to speak truthfully. The wearer rolls a psyche test against the target's psyche. The target rolls his psyche test against 3 plus the psyche of the wearer. If the wearer gets more successes, the target must answer one question truthfully. This medallion functions once per day per point of psyche of the wearer.

Medallion of Capricorn (4): The wearer of this medallion can invoke the powerful curative influence of Capricorn. Once per day, the wearer can heal himself or one target touched of insanity, ability damage, or loss of one of his or her senses.

Medallion of Aquarius (5): Once per day, for a duration of 1 minute, the wearer of this medallion can pass through physical barriers of up to 10 feet in thickness. The barrier cannot be inherently dangerous (i.e. touching the barrier cannot cause damage to the wearer).

Medallion of Pisces (15): Once per day, the wearer of this potent magical item can cure all mind, body, and soul, damage that a character has suffered. This medallion's magic is so potent that it can even restore someone who has lost all of their soul points provided they have been truly dead for no more than 1 hour.

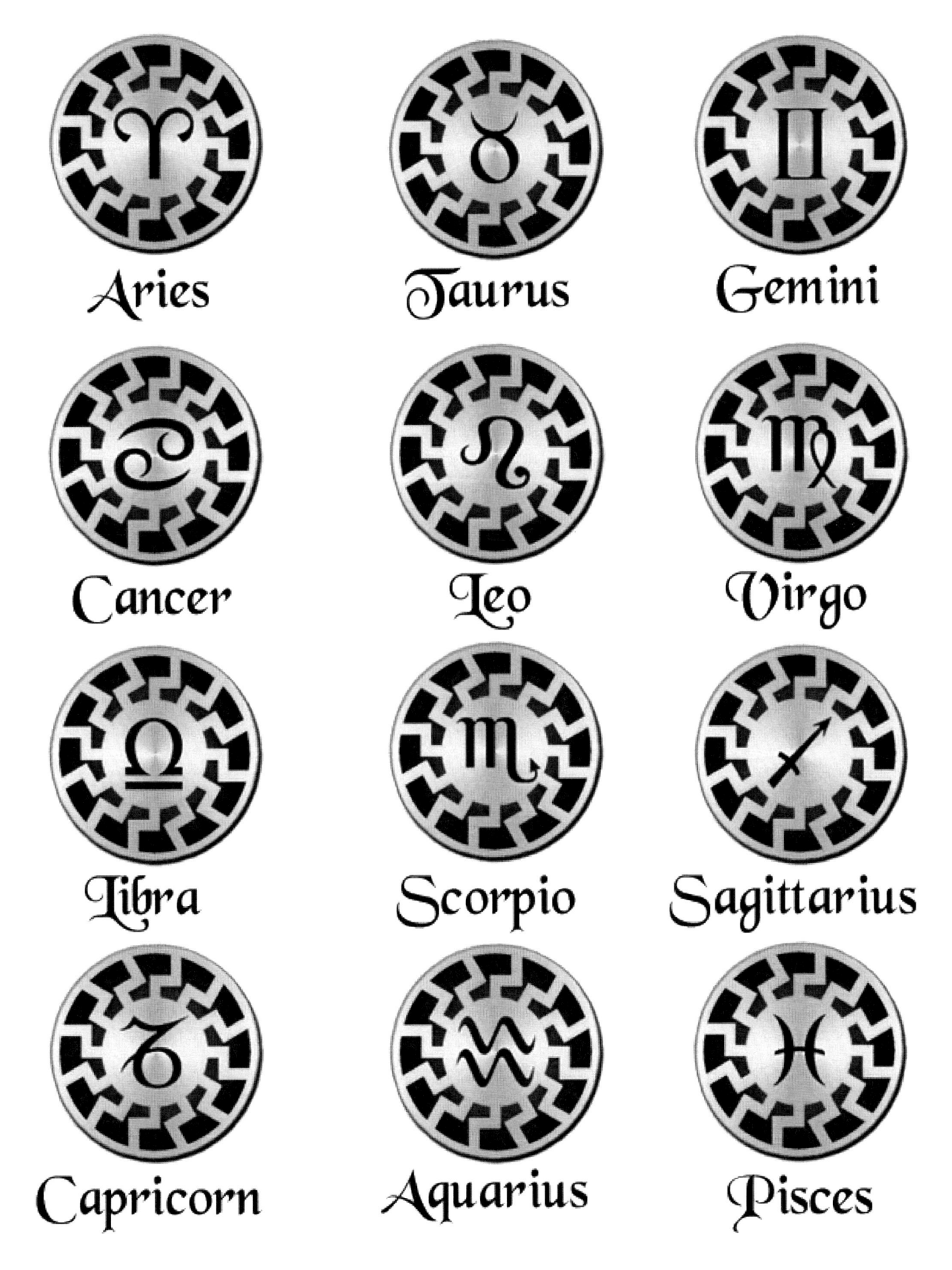

Aries	Taurus	Gemini
Cancer	Leo	Virgo
Libra	Scorpio	Sagittarius
Capricorn	Aquarius	Pisces

Medallion of Malaclypse, the Younger (2): The wearer of this medallion can conjure light in a radius of 20 feet. The light conjured by this medallion is even and clean, like the noon time sun. For 20 feet beyond the circle of clean light is an area of partial light. For 20 feet beyond that is a circle of minimal light.

Medallion of Malaclypse, the Elder (4): The wearer of this medallion can become invisible and undetectable by magical means for a total of 1 minute per day.

Medallion of Laeroth (3): The wearer of this medallion is able to communicate with any creature that speaks a language in its native tongue. It effectively grants the wearer the ability to speak any language.

Medallion of Myra (10): The wearer of this medallion can cause can invoke feelings of love, hostility, or ambivalence toward any one individual named when the wearer touches the target. The effects of this power last for one day per point of psyche of the wearer. The target can roll a psyche test against a target number equal to 3 plus the wearer's psyche. Each success on this test reduces the duration of the effect by 6 hours.

Each time this medallion is used against a target, the target number of resist the medallion's affects *decreases* by one.

Medallion of Durian (3): The wearer of this medallion is immune to any poison or toxin derived from plants. This includes alcohol, wine, and other fermented fruits of the earth.

Medallion of Aren (10): The wearer of a medallion of Aren becomes a force to be reckoned with on the field of battle. They gain skill in all melee weapons equal to their corrodination. If the wearer already has skill in a weapon greater than his or her coordination, this power of the medallion has no effect.

In addition, the wearer receives 2 additional dice for attack rolls and receives a bonus of +2 to the total damage dealt by any melee attack.

Medallion of Tchoren (4): This medallion grants its wearer the ability to use both their psyche and charisma to banish spirits. The character adds these two attributes together to determine the spirit's target number ot resist banishing and the number of dice the character rolls to banish the spirit. Furthermore, attribute damage caused by the spirit is taken alternately from psyche and charisma.

Medallion of Valderon (8): Once per day, the wearer of this medallion can generate an impenetrable field of divine energy centered on the medallion. This field covers the five feet immediately surrounding the caster and five feet beyond that. (If you are using a tactical map, the field is 9 five foot squares centered on the wearer of this medallion.) This field lasts for one minute. No damage can cross through this barrier (magical or otherwise). Those in the barrier cannot attack those on the outside and vice versa.

Medallion of Chalysse (8): this medallion is instilled with the power of the goddess of the circle of life. No creature, living or otherwise, can attack the wielder unless it is attacked first, without succeeding on a psyche test with a target number of 9.

Medallion of Manak (3): The wearer of this medallion is able to breathe water as if he or she had gills. They are, obviously, immune to the effects of drowning.

Medallion of Semis (2): The person wearing this medallion instantly knows the value of any crafted item or work of art.

Magical Amulets

Magical amulets protect the person wearing them from certain effects. Each amulet grants a number of bonus dice to resisting a particular effect of type of damage. The power rating of the amulet is equal to the number listed plus the number of dice granted.

Minor Mundane Effects (1+1 per 2 available dice): These amulets protect against mundane effects that are debilitating more than harmful. An example of this might be an amulet of proof against drunkenness.

Major Mundane Effects (2+1 per 2 available dice): These amulets protect against more substantial mundane effects. An example of these amulets might be an amulet of proof against poisoning.

Great Mundane Effects (3+1 per 2 available dice): These amulets protect against mundane situations that cause harm or death. An example of these amulets might be an amulet of proof against slashing weapons.

Minor Magical Effects (2+1 per 2 available dice): These amulets protect against a single spell. An example of this type of amulet might be an amulet of proof against fireball.

Major Magical Effects (3+1 per 2 available dice): These amulets protect against the magics from a single school. This might be an amulet of proof against divination, for example.

Great Magical Effects (4+1 per 2 available dice): These amulets provide protection against all spells associated with a particular element. An amulet of proof against pungent, would be an example of this type of amulet and would provide extra dice to resisting enchantment and illusionary magics.

	Malaclypse, the Younger	Malaclypse, the Elder
Laeroth	Myra	Durian
Aren	Tchoren	Valderon
Chalysse	Manak	Semis

243

Magical Apparel

There are many different kinds of magical clothing. Almost anything that can be worn can be enchanted. The only limitation what enchantments clothing can be imbued with is that the enchantment must have some correlation to the article of clothing. For example, enchanting boots to enhance your movement rate works just fine, but enhancing boots to boost your intelligence fails every time.

- **Magical Footwear**

Boots of Elvenkind (3): These boots allow the wearer to move almost silently through even the most obstructed natural terrain. They grant 5 extra dice to sneak tests when outdoors.

Boots of the North (2): These fur-lined boots grant their wearer sure footing on ice and snow. In addition, the wearer is able to walk across the tops of even the deepest snow drifts without sinking.

Boots of Speed (6): These finely crafted leather boots triple the wearer's quickness for the purpose of determining movement rate. Quickness remains at its original level for all other purposes.

Boots of Springing and Striding (6): These boots double the characters quickness for the purpose of determining his or her movement rate. Furthermore, these boots add 5 dice to any jump skill test that the wearer needs to make.

Boots of Weightlessness (6): These boots render the character weightless. The character does not trigger any traps that are activated by pressure plates. Furthermore, the character is able to walk on water and other liquids without breaking their surface.

Weightlessness has a drawback though. The character is only able to use ½ his or her strength score when checking to see if he or she is knocked down by the force of an attack.

Boots of Woodland Striding (5): This primitive looking footwear allows the wearer to transverse even the densest underbrush unhindered. Furthermore, when travelling through woodlands, the person wearing these boots leaves no footprints.

Slippers of the Spider (8): These silk slippers are woven from delicate strands of the finest silk. Looking closely at them reveals an intricate web-like pattern to the weave and they are slightly tacky to the touch. These slippers grant the wearer the ability to walk on walls or ceilings as a spider might.

- **Magical Outerwear**

Cloaks are another mainstay of enchanters everywhere. In fact, few articles of clothing are home to as many enchanted varieties as the simple cloak.

Cloak of Blending (7): A cloak of blending allows the character to blend in with their surroundings much like a chameleon does. The cloak grants 9 extra dice to hide checks and even allows the wearer to hide in plain sight by using only half of their hide skill when making the test.

Cloak of Darkness (4): The wearer of this cloak is able to generate globes of impenetrable darkness 30 feet in diameter. Only one such globe can be made each hour and the wearer of the cloak is able to see normally when inside the globe.

Cloak of Displacement (9): On command this cloak causes its wearer to move out of phase with the material plane. This displacing effect adds 3 to the difficulty of using any weapon against the cloak's wearer. This displacing effect functions for 15 minutes each day.

Cloak of Invisibility (5): Drawing up the hood of this cloak and drawing it tightly around oneself causes the wearer to become invisible. He or she can still see and here the world around them, but leaving the protection of the cloak, such as to attack, causes the wearer to become visible again.

Cloak of Non-Detection (3): This cloak shields the wearer from divination spells granting 5 automatic successes to resist the effects of these magics.

Cloak of Shadows (3): This mottles gray cloak allows its wearer to hide more successfully in shadows and darkness. The cloak grants an additional 6 dice to hide checks in darkness or shadows.

- **Magical Clothing**

Magical clothing covers a variety of seemingly normal items that have been enchanted, but not in such great numbers that they warrant their own category.

Belt of Giant Strength (STR modifier): Belts of giant strength come in 6 different types, one for each type of giant. Buckling a belt of giant strength around your waist immediately increases your strength score by a set amount depending on the type of giant the belt represents.

These macabre items are crafted from the tanned hides of the giants they represent. Owning one marks the wearer as an enemy of giants everywhere. They will attack the owner of such an item on sight.

Belts of giant strength are powerful and potent magical items. They are rarely sold unless the owner fails to understand the wondrous thing in his possession.

1. Hill: +6 STR
2. Stone: +9 STR
3. Frost: +12 STR
4. Fire: +15 STR
5. Cloud: +18 STR
6. Storm: +21 STR

Eye Patch of the Privateer (3): This eye patch appears to be a normal eye patch, the kind you would except to find a pirate wearing. The inside of the eye patch hides two small glyphs. When it is worn it provides the wearer with ether vision (left eye) and darkvision (right eye), depending on which eye is covered. The wearer simply switches eyes in order to switch vision.

Gauntlets of Ogre Power (3): These oversized chainmail gauntlets increase the strength of their wearer by 3 points.

Gloves of Dexterity (3): These tight-fitting, fingerless leather gloves increase the coordination of the wearer by 3.

Gloves of Arming (2): These gloves can take any shape or size. On close inspection ghostly runes, barely visible, can be seen. These runes form a complex glyph that opens a gateway to an extra-dimensional space. The wearer of the gloves can use this space to store weapons. The gloves are able to store two one-hand weapons or a single two-hand weapon. This weapon can be recalled from the extra-dimensional space at the mental command of the wearer. Recalling the weapons does not take an action.

Maniple of the Martyrs (4): This magic item only functions for clerics of the deity to whom it was blessed making their use rather limited. However, in the right hands, this simple stripe of cloth can be a powerful weapon.

A maniple of the martyrs is a strip of ornately embroidered cloth approximately 3 feet long. It is worn on the outside of a priest's robe across his shoulders.

A maniple of the martyrs doubles all magical bonuses for a cleric of the proper faith. It also doubles all penalties and doubles the target number associated with the cleric's drawback.

Mitre of the Faithful (3): This tall, pointed hat is often worn as a symbol of ecclesiastic authority. The front of the mitre is usually emblazoned with the symbol of the deity to which the mitre was dedicated. It cannot be used by members of another faith.

This holy vestment does two things. First, it identifies the wearer as a ranking member of the deity's clergy. Second, it identifies members of the faithful to the cleric. These may seem like miniscule powers, but, in times of uncertainty such as these, it is an invaluable tool.

Ribbon of Disguise (7): The ribbon of disguise is a silken ribbon that can be of almost any size or color. In truth, it can be any size or color. In fact, it can be any color or no color… any size or no size.

The ribbon of disguise allows the wearer to alter the shape, size, and color of his possessions and himself. He can assume the shape of any creature one size larger or smaller than he is. The disguise is not an illusion, but it does not change any of the character's attributes, abilities, or skills.

The same holds true for the items in his possession. His sword can take the shape of a dagger. It will have the size, shape, and weight of a dagger, but it is still a sword. It still has the same difficulty, damage rating, and bonus damage that it had when it looked and felt like a sword.

Changing shapes takes a single action and happens at the mental command of the wearer.

The ribbon is versatile, but it is very brittle. It cannot be used as a weapon or a restraint no matter what shape the wearer wills it into.

Males are often loath to wear a hair ribbon, so they often use this ribbon as a decorative band on a hat. This tendency has led to the belief that hats are enspelled to disguise their wearers.

Ribbon of Invention (2): Anyone who uses this ribbon to tie up their hair gains 3 addition dice to any build, craft, or repair skills as well as any knowledge skill related to building, crafting, and repairing.

Robe of Eyes (5): This robe is decorated with images of eyes. Wearing it confers a 360 degree field of vision and allows the wearer access to low-light, darkvision, and thermal vision as desired.

Miscellaneous Magical Items

This category of items contains those wondrous things that you don't wear and can't use to kill someone… at least not directly. Most miscellaneous items are what you might call "one-shot" items. As such, most people forego the bonding process and just attune to the item when they need to use it. (see attuning and bonding to magic items on page XXXX.)

Alchahest (5): This strange alchemical mixture is composed of bits and pieces of every substance known to man… and it can dissolve them all, save one. One ingredient is left out of the concoction during its creation so that a vessel of that substance can be used to transport it. Other than that one thing, alchahest can dissolve anything leading to its more common name – the universal solvent.

Alchahest can dissolve inanimate material at a rate of 1 cubic foot each second. A splash of this potent chemical does 10 points of damage against living things.

Bag of Holding (6): A bag of holding is an opening to an extra-dimensional space not unlike the gloves of arming. Unlike the gloves of arming, however, a bag of holding can hold more than just a weapon or two… a lot more. The only limitation to how much a bag of holding can hold, it seems, is that the inner fabric of the bag is very delicate and inserting any sharp object into the bag, whether it has an edge or a point, will tear the bag opening a rift in the very fabric of the universe. If this occurs, the contents of the bag, the person holding it, and everything within 100 feet of them disappears… sent to a random dimension or plane by the magic of the bag. The bag, of course, is destroyed.

Dust of Blindness (3): A single dose of this dust robs its target of sight for 1 hour.

Dust of Evaporation (3): A single dose of this alchemical dust covers a 10 cubic foot area instantly evaporating all water in that area. Living things in the area take 10 points of damage. This damage can be gaffed normally with constitution. The target number for the gaffing test is 7.

Dust of Illusion (2): This dust does not create illusions, it reveals them. A single dose of dust covers a 10 cubic feet causing all illusions in that area to glow with an eerie blue light.

Elixir of Charisma (3): Imbibing this magical liquid raises the character's charisma by 3 points for 10 minutes.

Elixir of Heroism (6): Imbibing this magical liquid grants the drinker the maximum strength and psyche for his species for 10 minutes.

Elixir of Magic Resistance (3): Drinking this magical liquid grants two bonus dice to resist magical effects for 10 minutes.

Philter of Love (2): Consuming this magical pink liquid causes the drinker to fall hopelessly in love with the first person whose name he or she hears spoken. The effect lasts for 20 minutes, but this time limit doesn't begin until the character actually sees the object of his or her new found affection. This philter does not function unless the mana cost is paid.

Potion of Heroism (9): After drinking this potion, a character gains the maximum strength and psyche for his or her species for 1 hour.

Potion of Magical Resistance (5): This magical liquid grants its drinker 3 additional dice to resist magical effects. These dice last for one hour.

Potion of Rage (3): The drinker of this potion enters into a berserk rage attacking every living thing he or she come in contact with for the next hour… or until he or she is killed.

Vitrol (5): Vitrol is an extremely effective bonding agent. It can be used to bond stone, metal, flesh, and anything else to anything else in any combination imaginable. One dose of vitrol covers up to 10 square feet and the only way to separate thing bonded by vitrol is with alchahest, giving rise to its colloquial name – sovereign glue.

Attunement and Bonding

When a mage or cleric casts a spell, magic demands that the caster makes an exchange for the power it provides. This exchange is the reasons that mages and clerics suffer enervation. Magical items are no different. They demand that the perspective wielder or wearer sacrifices something in order to utilize their power. Unlike spells which take from the caster regardless of his or her desires, magical items just require a bit of the character's essence in order to activate them.

There are two ways in which a character can activate a magical item – bonding or attunement.

Bonding to a magical item creates a nigh-unbreakable link between the item and its owner. The character can sense the location of the bonded item. If they are on the same plane, the bonded character always knows the relative direction of the item his or her distance from it.

Furthermore, the item is useless to a would-be thief until they have performed a cleansing ritual and a bonding ritual of their own. A magical sword will still function as a sword, but the thief will not be able to access any of the weapon's powers.

Bonding Ritual

In order to bond with an item, a character must spend 1 hour meditating on the item for each point of the item's power. Each hour, the character must spend 3 points of mana as he forges the mystical bonds between himself and the magical item. Once the ritual is complete, the item is bound to the character.

Unlike mundane items, magical items have a presence on the ethereal plane. When viewed from the ethereal, the item bears the magical signature of its owner, must like a spell retains its casters mystic signature. Furthermore, a thin silver cord links the owner to the item on the ethereal.

Because of this silver cord, bonded items can be used in ritual magic. The spotter need only be in possession of the magical item in order to "spot" the target for ritual magic (see ritual magic on page XXXX).

Cleansing Ritual

If the owner of an item dies, the bond between the owner and the item dies with them. Sometimes, however, people do not want to wait for the owner of an item to die before taking possession of it. Some plot the demise of the owner to speed up this process. Others simply cleanse the item of its previous bond.

A cleansing ritual takes a number of days equal to the power of the item. A circle is drawn on the ground to shield the item from outside influences. This circle serves to weaken the bond between the item and its rightful owner.

While the item is inside the circle, its owner must make an insight test with a target number of 5 and must score one success for each day the ritual has been taking place in order to learn the item's direction and distance from its owner.

For eight hours each day, the item must be attended. No one other than the person performing the cleansing ritual can enter the circle or the power of the ritual is broken. At the end of the final day, the person cleansing the item must make a psyche test (augmented by willpower if desired) against the power of the item. Then he or she must spend ten mana points minus one for each success achieved on the psyche test in order to sever the bond between the item and its owner.

Once the mana has been spent, the link is severed. Even if the item's previous owner were to find it, he or she would need to bond to the item again.

The owner of an item may cleanse an item may perform a cleansing ritual on him or her self in order to sever this bond. It occurs identically to the above described above.

Attunement

Sometimes bonding to an item is impractical. Spending the better part of a day meditating isn't a very welcome prospect if you're skulking through a dungeon being hunted by a band of goblins. In these situations, the character can simply attune themselves to the item.

Attuning to a magic item takes 1 minute per power rating of the item. At the end of this brief period, the perspective user spends mana equal to the power of the item. He or she then has access to the item's powers for 24 hours or, in the case of single use items like potions, until it has been expended. Once the 24 hour period has expired, the attunement vanishes as if it had never existed.

The user does not gain the power to sense the items distance from him or her or the direction to the item. In addition, should the item be lost or stolen, there is no need for anyone to perform a cleansing ritual on order to attune or bond to the item.

Many times the creator of a single use item will pay the attunement cost at the time of creation. Because of this, attuning to a single use item is not always necessary.

Artifacts & Relics

People often misuse the terms artifacts and relics. On the Lady's Rock, artifacts are immensely powerful and unique magic items. If there is more than one of them, no matter how cool it might be, it is not an artifact.

A magical item may be something really cool. A relic might be extremely powerful. An artifact need not be either of these things. What does truly separate an artifact from lesser items is a story… a legend… one told by bards and sung by minstrels.

Finding or destroying an artifact is often the objectives of an entire campaign… This is especially true if your uncle disappears on his eleventy-first birthday and leaves you a magical ring that he stole from a deformed, bipedal frog and leaves the fate of the known world in your hands. Of course, then you'll have to trek across to drop the ring in the cauldron of an active volcano even though you are good friends with a "powerful" wizard who can speak with giant owls.

Like all magical items, artifacts that are well described seem to hold the players attention more. Another trick to making good artifacts is to not have them all be good… Like Uncle Ben says, "With great power comes great responsibility."

Relics are also extremely powerful items. They are not, however, unique. There may only be one of them now, but, at one time, there were more. Many relics have religious connotations and some even require a character to adhere to a specific religious ideology in order to use them.

Armor of the Warrior Queen (Artifact)

The Legend: In centuries long since past, warring tribes of nomads roamed the great plain that would one day become the imperial heartlands. Tiyet was born to one of the wives of a tribal chieftain.

During a skirmish with a rival tribe, the chieftain was slain. The victorious tribe installed one of their own as chieftain and forced the warriors to take a blood oath of loyalty to their new masters.

The young Tiyet was taken by this new chieftain as a concubine herself. Her life as a concubine was difficult to say the least. After 5 years of brutal treatment, Tiyet had had enough. She secreted into the new chieftain's tent, quietly slid his great sword from its sheath, and separated his head from the rest of his body.

Holding the head of her tormentor high in the air, she triumphantly exited the tent. The dead chieftain's most loyal warriors protested, but the most experienced warriors in the tribe had fought for Tiyet's father and quickly answered their concerns.

With the heads of her enemies resting on pikes outside her tent, Tiyet held her first council of war. Her first order of business was bringing vengeance to those who had brought her once-mighty tribe low.

The following night, as the moon reached its zenith, Tiyet's tribe robe for the camp of their oppressors. This first battle clearly demonstrated Tiyet's ability to wage war effectively leaving no doubts in the minds of her people that she was fit to lead.

Tiyet ordered her mounted archers to ride circles around the enemy encampment raining death down on them. Arrows fell from the night sky driving their steely barbs through tents, finding tender flesh. Before the camp could be roused by the guard to mount a proper defense, majority of its warriors were pinned to their cots, impaled on feathered stakes.

With the first wave of attack complete, Tiyet sent in footmen with torches to burn the camp to the ground… not one living thing was spared. Men, women, children, hunting dogs, and riding horses were put to the sword. As the last of the flames dwindled to the faint glow of ember, Tiyet and her men drank heartily to their victory.

Word of Tiyet and her daring midnight raid spread throughout the plains. Members of other oppressed tribes flocked to her camp. Tribal chieftains everywhere feared that she would come for them next. Soon she had assembled the largest fighting force the world had seen up until that time and it focused its eyes on the remaining chiefs.

One by one Tiyet and her horde sent chief and loyal warrior to commune with their deities until the land surrounding Tiyet's camp was a forest of limbless trees with human faces.

With the persistent skirmishes and tribal wars finally at an end, the nomads of the plains began to erect permanent settlements and the foundations for civilization were laid. Tiyet selected a pastoral basin where the plains abutted the churning aethereal seas for her capital. Her followers erected a mighty fortress of stone to serve as her seat of power.

It was this period of growth and prosperity that brought the fledgling human kingdom to the attention of the elves and dwarves. These two ancient enemies met in secret council to discuss the threat of men. Man's wars with other men had kept them in check… too busy to killing themselves to bother anyone else. Now that men were no longer killing each other, it was decided that men posed too great a threat to the world to be allowed to remain at large. For the first time in history, the elves and dwarves set aside their differences and joined forces to destroy their common enemy – men.

The first casualty of this war was a small town at the edge of an elven wood. As the townsfolk enter the forest to harvest trees to support the fledgling kingdom's rapid growth, pointed-eared assassins fell upon them leaving none alive. By the time word of this attack reached Tiyet's fortress, the second town, a fishing village nestled at the foot of an ancient mountain, had fallen to the dwarves.

Faced with attack from two fronts, Tiyet sounded the call to arms and brought her military machine back to life. Every man, woman, and child who could heft a blade or draw a bow was pressed into service. The hordes that had roamed the plain had been the largest army ever assembled, yet it paled in comparison to the one Tiyet unleashed on her elven and dwarven foes.

Soothsayers looked to the heaven for portents of the future. Priest prayed to their deities beseeching them for aid. And small cabal of powerful spell-casters, calling themselves the Gadbians, met for the first time.

The enemies of men had no idea what horrible forces they had release upon the world.

The elves were used to fighting hit-and-run skirmishes. They would attack and retreat to the safety of their forest homes. Men would chase them to their forests and then burn the forest to the ground.

The dwarves built their mountain fortresses to be impregnable. It was of little comfort when men collapsed the entrances trapping them in the bowels of the earth.

It was during the time of burning trees and falling mountains that the dark plot was hatched. The dark elves, the true children of Eris, conspired with the dwarves to strike a mighty blow against the humans. While Tiyet and her armies harried the elven forces on the surface, the drow and dwarves dug deep into the earth tunneling beneath the human capital.

As Tiyet and her forces returned to their home having driven back the elves and dwarves, the Lady's Rock trembled. The weight of a legion of fully armed and armored humans marching in perfect cadence was too much for the earth to withstand. When the ground finally stopped moving, the capital and the basin in which it was built fell into the aether. It was merely by the blessings of the goddess that Tiyet and her army survived.

This latest act of treachery at the hands of the dwarves, she was unaware of drow involvement at the time, could not go unanswered. Tiyet was not longer content to leave the dwarves trapped in their earthen cities. She wanted them dead.

She gathered her generals and formulated their plan. She would lead her armies to the doors of the dwarves' largest citadel. Her mages would rend open the mountain side and her troops would not rest until the remaining elves lived in a forest capped with dwarven skulls.

In secret, at Tiyet's behest, the Gadbians began performing an arcane ritual lasting a lunar month. When the ritual was completed, they presented Tiyet with a magnificent suit of plate armor to wear in the titanic battle to come. It was the first suit of plate armor in recorded history. All made since have been but pale shadows of this masterpiece.

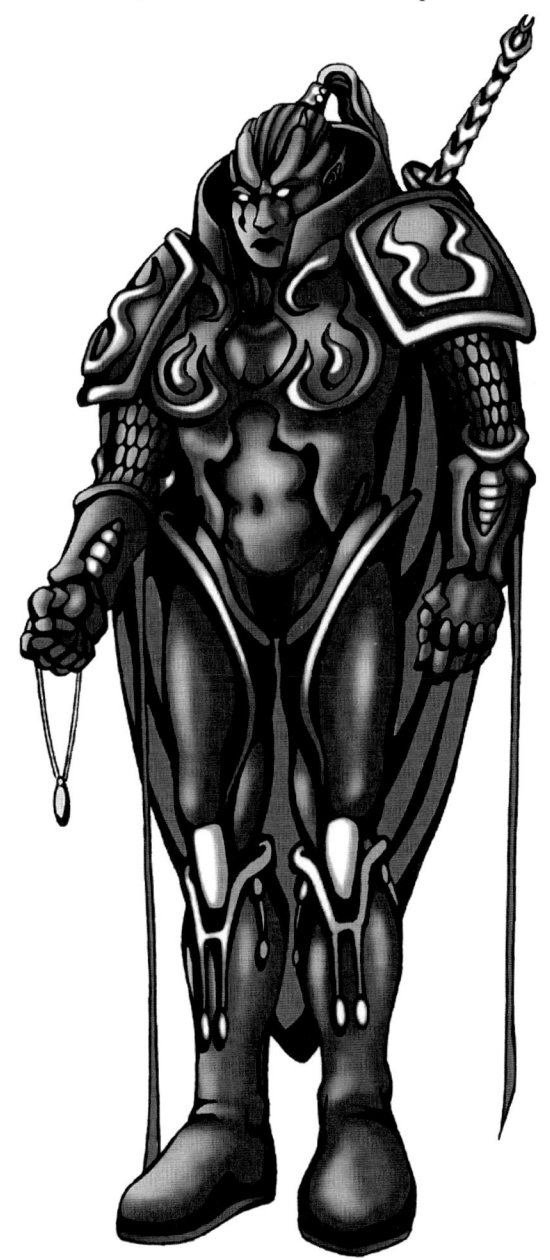

The epic battle took place on the plains bordering the dwarven lands. Heavy dwarven infantry with cover from skilled elven archers met human mounted archers & blood-thirsty warriors. Tiyet proudly rode at the vanguard.

In the end, it was neither elf nor dwarf that felled this mighty warrior. Realizing that Tiyet's single-minded hatred of the dwarves clouded her judgment, a human warrior from a noble clan tried to reason with her, but the enraged queen would hear nothing. A battle ensued. Blinded by her anger, the great warrior woman fell consumed by her wrath and ire.

The noble warrior immediately pressed for peace, a single united empire, in a desperate effort to save his ill-fated species from certain annihilation. The leaders of the dwarves and elves recognized the young man's wisdom and supported his call for a cease fire… and so the Empire of Eristonia was born.

Newly crowned Emperor Trennan De Veci had Tiyet's corpse taken and buried in a tomb befitting her regal status. He entombed her in the ground and set a standing stone atop the barrow. He also ordered a temple of Eris built on the spot to protect her body from those who would defile it.

The Armor: The breastplate and pauldrons of this suit of plate armor are made from adamantine with orichalcum inlays. Scales of mithril cover the wearer's arms. It grants an armor value of 12 to its wearer, but its unique design allows it to weigh as much as scale armor (Use the armor value of scale armor to determine any penalties the wearer may suffer.)

The Truth: Unlike many legends surrounding ancient artifacts, this one is fairly accurate… except for the part about Trennan being a noble warrior…

In reality, Trennan De Veci was the last living relative of the tribal chieftain that had first conquered Tiyet's people. He had clandestinely met with the leaders of both the elves and dwarves promising peace after he assassinated Tiyet if they promised they supported his claim to the throne.

Trennan did order Tiyet buried, along with anything that might have served as symbol to those who would have opposed his rule, in a non-descript valley deep in dwarven lands. Her body lies in a dark, trap-filled tomb deep beneath the earth… along with the bodies of any warriors who chose to remain loyal to Tiyet.

He also ordered the construct of a vast temple to Chalysse on the site, that much is true. It can also be said that he did so to protect it from those who did not respect the sanctity of death, provided that includes necromancers who may have returned the dead leader to life. The church of Chalysse sees the undead as an abomination and destroys them on sight. Who better to stand watch over an enemy you do not wish to see reborn? Trennan even went so far as to order the construction of false tombs to stop would be tomb robbers, and loyal follower, from finding Tiyet's resting place.

Because the tomb was built in an out of the way valley deep in the dwarven mountains, the temple quickly fell into obsolescence. There was no community to minister to and the vile deeds that the temple served to hide left the surrounding valley barren. After Trennan's death, the church of Chalysse recalled many of the priests serving in the temple leaving only a skeletal band of priests remained, tasked with guarding a treasure they were told nothing of.

The lack of use and small number of clergy sentenced the once magnificent edifice to neglect and disrepair. Unused dormitories became home to carrion bird, the only creatures that lived in the valley. Roofs collapsed and walls crumbled. By the time the church abandoned it completely, during Vandal's War, much of the complex had been unused for more than a millennia. The seven centuries since the building was abandoned were not kind to the once glorious cathedral either. Now this gargantuan monument is little more than ruins itself.

The Maiden's Kiss (Artifact)

The Legend: Long ago in a lonely tower their lived a powerful wizard. Like most wizards, he was mad with power. And even though he was immensely powerful, he craved more power… more … always more…

This wizard was experimenting with dark and dangerous magics in his quest for more knowledge and an ever increasing grasp of things arcane. As is often the case, he needed an assistant… someone who could do the really dangerous stuff so that the wizard didn't have to risk his own neck. After all, what's the point in having phenomenal power if it leaves you lying in a persistent vegetative state? So the wizard took on an apprentice, a young woman. If you happen to be a decrepit old man and need an assistant, why wouldn't you select a young woman?

The two worked side by side unearthing secrets that are better left forgotten. Over time, the young woman began to have feelings for the wizard. He did not share these feelings, but he was not above using them to his own advantage. So he toyed with the young woman's affections.

All was well until one fateful night. The pair had just summoned up a powerful demon. The demon offered the wizard immortality in exchange for something very precious – the young woman. The young woman was terrified at the prospect, but the wizard, being who and what he was, agreed.

The demon waved his clawed hand, muttered some arcane phrases, and then vanished with the girl. The wizard began to revel in his new found power. He would live forever! Now nothing would stop him in his quest for arcane might.

But making a deal with a demon is seldom a good idea, no matter how good it may sound. In fact, the better it sounds, often the worse of an idea it is. This was the case with the wizard.

Yes, he was immortal. He would never die. But the demon never said that he would not age nor did he say that the wizard would never feel pain. Though his mind remained as sharp and alert as it was the day he first enter the Suidae Verruca school of Wiz-craft and Witchery, his body was not so lucky… He wasn't dying, of course, the demon had promised that he wouldn't. But the wizard faced the grim prospect of spending eternity in a body that was rotting away. Soon he would be a sentient pile of dust.

The demon had had the last laugh, or so it seemed. The wizard's thoughts changed from his quest for power to a new quest – life… his very existance… and, when the prospects for a new life seemed slim, for vengeance.

The demon sensed his turmoil and began to plague his nightmares, sending him visions of the horrendous tortures that the young woman was made to endure while in the demon's care. The mage, already consumed by desperation, could not take it any longer. Again he went to the summoning chamber and called the demon's name.

The demon sensed that something was amiss, but the power of the magic compelled huim to heed the call. The demon laughed as he appeared before the aging wizard. The wizard demanded that the demon release him from his curse and return the girl. The demon refused. The wizard threatened the demon with destruction if he did not comply, but the demon scoffed at his omnious words.

The contract was binding. Only through sacrifice could the wizard hope to defeat him, and there was no way that such a self man could make such a sacrifice. After all, he had condemned the woman who loved him to eternal torment in order to reach his own goals. No, the wizard would fail and he deserved to suffer.,

The wizard began to chant the words of power as he made the proper gestures. The demon chuckled at the wizard's attempt to harm him. The demon knew that someone so blackhearted could never make the sacrifice necessary to free the woman.

But his mirth turned to fear when the wizard pulled out an extremely rare material component – the eyes of a man who cannot die.

The resulting release of magic tore the demons flesh from his very bones. He screamed in agony, but the demon did not die. The wizard wasn't looking for justice, after all. He wanted vengeance, and he had gotten it.

The demon's torment was not finished. As I said, the demon did not die. He was not destroyed as the wizard had threatened. Instead his spirit was trapped in his shattered bones. The wizard had cursed the demon to share his own fate. To add insult to injury, the wizard took the demons bones and crafted a mighty weapon out of them…a weapon that would serve those who hunted demons and those who would conspire with them. He dubbed the weapon "The Maiden's Tears" in memory of young woman that he had sacrificed in his quest for power. The demon would spend eternity slaying his own kind. He would not die. He would never be free. As long as the wizard suffered, the demon would as well.

No one knows what happened to the undying wizard. Some say that he still roams the Lady's Rock hoping that some day the weapon he created from the bones of that demon with find his own heart and give him peace. Regardless of his fate, the weapons surfaces from time to time. Those who wield it become great heroes and their legends live on… just like the wizard.

The Weapon: The Maiden's Tears appears to be a short bow crafted from the bones of one or more demons. The bones are held in place by a framework of pure adamantine and a string of mithril fires arrows straight and true.

Depite appearing to be a short bow, Maiden's Kiss has the range of a composite short bow. In all other ways it is a normal short bow, save one. At the wielder's discretion, he can take a point of soul damage to enchant the arrow fired by the bow. Enchanted arrows are wreathed in a black flame that radiates such intense cold that touching it sears your flesh. Opponents struck by this arrow have their souls burned away by this unholy fire. In other words, it does soul damage. All that remains is a pile of oily, black ash from which the creature can never be brought back to life.

The Truth: This story makes for an interesting tale. It is often told by bards as the tavern's hearth dwindles to embers. It would be better though if the story were true. Yes, the Maidens' Tear was created by a black-hearted mage. But it is not a weapon of retribution. Instead it is an elaborate test.

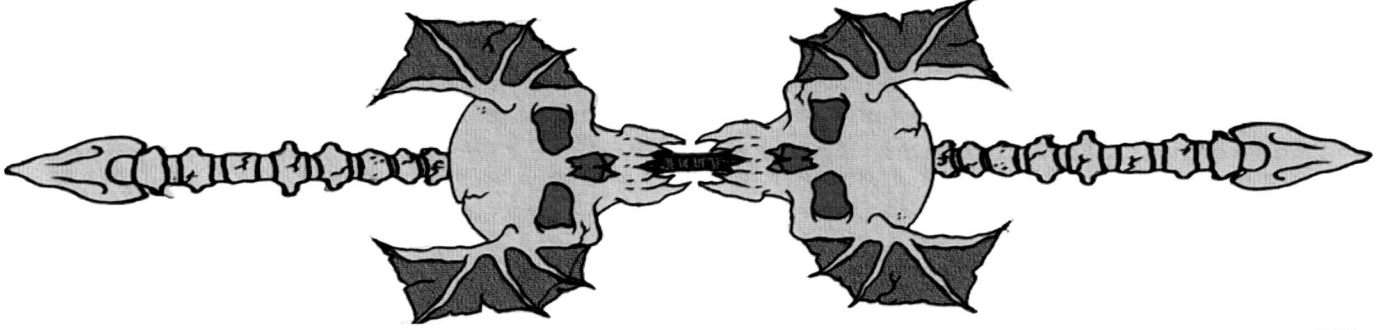

Every victim whose soul has been burned by the bow is banished to the realms of torment. Since those who wield the bow often use it to rid the world of the most dastardly

beings in existence, this realm is populated by some of the vilest people to ever live. The bow-wielder becomes a hero and his tales live on forever, but what about the bow-wielder. Why is it always in the hands of someone new when it resurfaces?

The answer is this. Eventually, the bow-wielder becomes corrupted. Drunk with fame, soon he craves the hero's life. And when he ceases doing goods for the sake of the world and starts doing it for his own sake, the bow fulfills its purpose and condemns the bow-wielder to the same fate that he condemned so many others to.

One day he draws back the flaming string and the fire burns him. Unbeknownst to the wilder, the point of soul damage used to activate the bow's special power never heals, though the wielder never suffers penalties for damage accumulated in this manner. When this damage finally kills the bow-wielder, Black fire erupts from the bow. It creeps up his arm and eventually engulfs his body, consuming its wielder as well. When this happens, the uppermost skull sheds a single blood red tear to mark the passing of another wielder. Then the bow waits for its next wielder.

The former hero finds himself trapped in a realm of pure evil. Once there he must lead an army of his victims against a similar army formed by one of the wielders that preceded him. The victor remains gaining control the remnant of both armies. Then they prepare for the death of the next bow-wielder. Eventually the wizard will summon his new general to lead an army of undead across the Lady's Rock. The wizard plans to subjugate the world. And why shouldn't he? After all, he did it once before. Such is the evil of Vandal Nefar.

The Shield of Rayuk, the Bold (Artifact)

The Legend: History tells the tale of Rayuk, the Bold, a brave dwarven knight swore to the service of Semis, the god of Artifice. Day and night Rayuk slaved over his forge trying to perfect an alloy that was light as mithril yet hard as adamantine.

One fateful night in the Aftermath of 2086 while the rest of the empire celebrated afflux, his dream was realized at long last. He took this new alloy and forged a shield of singular beauty and perfection. It was light enough for even the frailest halfling to heft effortlessly, yet strong enough to defend against even the mightiest of blows.

Rayuk took this shield and journeyed forth to the Capital of the Barony of Kargrave in hope of presenting the shield as a gift to his Thane. It was during the evening of the second day of his journey that Rayuk met with disaster.

That aftermath had brought with it particularly harsh storms. Deep mountains of drifting snow crawled across the landscape. Cruel winds blew out of the west robbing everything that moved of life-giving heat. Dark gray clouds obscured the evening sky shielding the planet from even the dim light of Malaclypse, the Elder. Facing starvation, a group of human brigands had set an ambush intending to trap fat merchant caravans that would certainly come to trade with the dwarves. Instead, they caught Rayuk in their net.

As Rayuk traveled down the woodland road, a hail of arrows launched from the trees pelting the unsuspecting craftsman. Reacting quickly, he ducked his head, clung to his warhorse, and urged the mighty beast on. The arrows struck the shield on his back with all the force they could muster, but it was not enough to pierce the new alloy.

Rayuk spurred his steed on hoping to reach the capital as quickly as possible and return with the Thane's army to vanquish these brigands. The brigands were not so easily dissuaded. Weeks of living on the brink of starvation makes men desperate, and desperate men do unwise things. Rather than allow the noble dwarf to escape, the brigands gave chase.

Rayuk waqs in unfamiliar territory, but they did not call him "the bold" for nothing. Fearlessly he charged ahead hoping to outrun his pursuers. Unfortunately, hunters often hunt in terrain they know extremely well. The brigands used this knowledge of the area to steer the unsuspecting dwarf into a narrow ravine where they could kill him and take his goods.

Rayuk lost his life in the ensuing battle, but not before he had slain seven of his assailants. The remaining brigands took his treasure, including the shield, and made for the mountains of the barony. The secret of the shield's alloy was lost when its creator perished in that cold ravine.

The Thane of Kargrave spared no expense hunting down Rayuk's killers and soon the shield was recovered. The Thane had the shield hung on the wall of his throne room in homage of the dwarven smith that had crafted the magnificent item. There is hung for many years until it was stolen one night by an unknown thief. The shield has never been seen again.

The Shield: The Shield of Rayuk is a heavy steel shield that acts like a tower shield. The light weight alloy from which the shield was constructed halves the penalty for fighting with two weapons… or negates it completely if the bearer has ambidexterity. *NOTE: This applies only to the use of the shield. The bearer still suffers any applicable penalties with his or her other weapon.*

In addition, the shield of Rayuk has one very unique property that allows it to change the field of battle provided the shield-bearer has not moved since the first blow of combat was struck. Once per engagement, the shield's bearer can select any ally within 20 feet of his position. Calling upon the power of the shield, the bearer and the chosen ally disappear, instantly reappearing next to each other in a location ten feet from where the shield-bearer first invoked this power. The shield-bearer and the ally now occupy adjacent areas (5ft squares if you are using a combat grid). The shield-bearer chooses their positions upon reappearing.

If the chosen area contains any combatant, friendly or otherwise, the power fails. It can be attempted later provided the shield-bearer has not changed his or her position.

If the ally wishes to resist the power of the shield, he or she rolls a number of dice equal to their psyche score against a target number equal to the psyche of the shield-bearer. The shield-bearer, in turn, rolls a number of dice equal to his or her psyche *and* charisma against a target number equal to the ally's psyche. If the shield-bearer achieves more successes, the power functions regardless of the ally's desires.

The Truth: Much of the tale of Rayuk, the Bold is untrue. In fact, more if it is untrue than is true. Such is the case with myths and legends.

For starters, Rayuk was not a dwarf; he was a gnome. The dwarven minstrels that first told this tale could not stand to sing the praises of a gnome, so they took poetic license with the story.

Second, he was far from bold. To say he was cowardly would be an insult to cowards everywhere. If truth be told, Rayuk made every gluttonous yet lanky teenager with bushy hair and a scraggly goatee that raced around the countryside with his talking Great Dane look down right brave. That's why this "noble dwarven knight" built a shield rather than a warhammer, battle axe, or other weapon.

Lastly, it was not some ragtag band of brigands who ambushed Rayuk. It was the baronial guard. The Thane of Kargrave could not stand the thought of gnome having

created such a wondrous item, so he sent his personal guard to collect the shield and eliminate its creator.

In the Thane's defense, however, he did spare not expense in finding Rayuk's killer. It didn't cost him a since lance to walk into the next room and hear his Captain of the Guard report his success.

Robe of the Arch-Magi (Relic)

The robe of the arch-magi is a relic much sought after by mages throughout the empire.

The robe appears like any other of exquisite craftsmanship until it is worn by a mage. Once it is donned the robe changes colors to reflect the personality of the mage wearing it. No matter which mage dons the robe, an intricate pattern of arcane glyphs and runes can be seen along the hem.

The Robe: The robe of the arch-magi has an armor value of 5 when worn by a mage. All target numbers to resist magic are halved for the wearer of the robe. In addition, the robes grant the mage 3 extra dice to resist magical effect including enervation. Finally, the power of any spell cast by the mage is considered to be two higher for the purposes of determining the maximum number of applicable successes and the target number for the target to resist the spell's effects.

Spagenhelm of Vulnerability (Relic)

Despite its name, these magical helmets are prized by military commanders throughout the empire.

253

The Spaganhelms of Vulnerability were first made by the dwarves during their first war with men. It was the magic of these helms that allowed the dwarves to tunnel beneath the human's capital city and drop it into the aether. Dwarven artillerists continued to use these helms in service to the empire until the rebellion of Vandal Nefar when the secret of making them was lost. Now they are treasured heirlooms passed down through the generations.

The Helm: A Spangenhelm of Vulnerability does not make its wearer more vulnerable, as you might suspect from its name. Instead, it allows the wearer to see the vulnerability in other people, places, and things. The power of any weapon wielded by a wearer of one of these helms is increased by one making it particularly brutal in combat. This increase also applies to siege weapons, both direct and in-direct fire, fired by the wearer.

In addition, the wearer receives 5 additional dice to detect secret doors, hidden compartment, and pressure plates that trigger traps as these things are often the weakest point in the objects containing them.

Staff of the Magi (Relic)

A staff of the magi is a quarterstaff usually crafted from some exotic wood and shod with mystical metal. The surface of the staff is covered with arcane sigils and runes.

The Staff: These staves only function for mages. A staff can shed either brilliant light or impenetrable darkness at a radius of 60 feet on command. The staff has a spirit with a power level of 9 trapped within it. This spirit has the powers of magical aid, nourish spell, and increase potential. When the use of these abilities costs the staff-bound spirit a power rating, the power returns at a rate of one per hour as if it were a familiar. It is not a familiar, of course, and a mage that wields one of these staves may also have a familiar.

<u>Bonding to an Artifact or Relic</u>

Once cannot attune to an artifact or relic. They are simply too powerful to be enslaved to the whims of men.

Bonding to a relic takes 24 hours consecutive hours of meditation with the relic. After that time, 25 points of mana are spent and the character is bonded to the relic.

Artifacts do not require any ritual in order to bond to them. Whether sentient or not, artifacts have a personality. Only those who are well suited for the artifact (a bold female warrior for the Armor of the Warrior Queen, for example) have any hope of bonding to them. Once a suitable candidate comes in contact with the artifact, it exacts a tribute of 25 points of mana. If the candidate does not have 25 points of mana, the item will not function.

If the perspective candidate lacks the mana, but retains possession of the artifact, the artifact will siphon ½ of the mana that the character earns until it has absorbed 30 points at which time it will function.

If a character who is *not* a suitable candidate to use the artifact retains possession of it, the artifact will siphon ½ the mana the character earns, but will not function.

Furthermore, the power of the artifact will attempt to change the character into a suitable candidate. This often begins subtly with the artifact influencing the character's actions… an opposed psyche test is required. Artifacts have an effective psyche of 9 or more (the director should set it to be appropriate to his or her campaign). If the artifact achieves more successes, the character acts as the artifact desires. If the character achieves more successes, he or she is free to act as they see fit. *NOTE: Some artifacts will use this power to try and kill the person holding them in order to make way for a new user.*

Artifacts may even go so far as to change the sex, species, or other aspect of the possessor if necessary. The director should make these changes as is appropriate for his or her campaign.

Artifacts are powerful items and should be dangerous to own, wield, wear, or even possess. Thieves will attempt to steal them. Other prospective wielders will attempt to kill current users in order to get the artifact for themselves. Not to mention the artifact's own stake in the matter.

Finding an artifact should be an epic quest. Keeping an artifact should make that quest pale in comparison. Making your dream a reality is the easy part… keeping it a reality is the real trick.

Minutiae

While the a good overall campaign idea may bring satisfaction to a director, the players want to campaign world that they can believe in. They want something that works. In role-playing, as in real life, the devil is in the details.

This section contains those out of the way rules that have a place in almost every role-playing game, but never seem to make it into the rule books...

Aging

What happens as your characters age? And, if adventuring doesn't kill them, how long will they live?

Honestly, most of these questions are irrelevant. People rarely play the same character long enough to make aging a factor. The only time these rules really come into play is when people want to play characters that are already past their prime. That being said, here are the answers to your questions.

Each race has an average life expectance. Once a character reaches that expectancy, roll a number of 10-sided dice equal to the character's constitution score and all them together. Add this result to the racial life expectancy and you'll know how long your character will live. Do not calculate the result until your character reaches his or her life expectancy number, however, as the character's attributes may change as they age.

Race	Life Expectancy
Ailure	75 years
Dwarves	450 years
Elves	750 years
Gnomes	500 years
Goblins	90 years
Halflings	200 years
Humans	100 years
Minotaurs	65 years
Orcs	70 years

Some races, such as the teg and mephisti, do not have natural life spans. These species do not age as we think of aging. Even though they get older, they remain unchanged by the passage of time.

Teg exist for 500 years and then all the teg but 5 dissipate back into the universe to create new teg. It is possible, though extremely unlikely, for one teg to have continually existed since the creation of the Lady's Rock.

Likewise mephisti were already alive, they died, and came back to life as something different. They don't age... they just stop existing once their internal conflict has been resolved. How that conflict is resolved is a matter for the player and director to decide... and by that I mean for the director to decide, but that he or she should at least pretend to listen to the player before making the decision.

Half-breeds have a lifespan equal to the averages between their two parent species. A quarterling, for example, would have a life expectancy of 150 years, the average between a human and a halfling. And a half-elf would have a life expectancy of 425 years, the average between elves and humans. Meanwhile, a Bapahan could only expect to live for 83 year (human – minotaur) and a half-orc could expect to see 85 year if he never left his home.

Tieflings & Crimbil are a special cases. Tieflings have a life expectancy of 383 years. Crimbil live for 500 years and then dissipate just like their teg parents. These races were not included on the table because no other half-breed was. Consistency... there is something to be said for consistency.

Once the character reaches 30, regardless of race, he or she needs to check for attribute loss. Trust me, once you hit 30, things start to slip unless you work to keep them (i.e. spend mana). To make this check roll a single 10-sided die for each attribute. Remember that zero counts for zero and to reroll and add the results if you roll a 9. If the roll is higher than your attribute, all is well. If the result is lowerr than your attribute, then your attribute is reduced by 1. Consult the "Loss Due To Aging" above table to see which attribute checks need to be made at what intervals.

If your character's attribute is reduced to zero, that means that your character loses that body function. A character with a quickness of zero cannot move. A character with a strength of zero cannot lift anything. A character with a reason of zero lacks the ability to think. You get the idea. When this happens, the character begins to die taking one point of soul damage each day until the process is complete. (see Death and Dying on page XXXX).

For races that live more than 200 years, check again every 25 years until the character dies.

Loss Due To Aging

Age	Attribute Checks
30	QCK
40	STR, CRD, & QCK
50	All Physical Attribute
60	All Physical Attribute plus INS
70	All Physical Attribute plus RSN & INS
80	All Physical Attribute plus RSN, INS, & PSY
90	All Attributes
100	All Attributes
125	All Attributes
150	All Attributes
175	All Attributes
200+	All Attributes

255

If you are creating a character that is older than 30 years, your receive 5 bonus build points for each interval listed on the table. Roll at each interval for attribute loss as appropriate. If you lose any attribute points, you receive 3 bonus build points for each attribute lost. These bonus points can only be spent on skills. Spending them on attributes would defeat the purpose of checking for attribute loss.

Drinking

Now I'm not advocating the use of alcohol, but those of us who have played role-playing games for a while know that many epic adventures find their beginning in a local tavern.

So, invariably, the question arises, is my character drunk? Here's how you find the answer…

First, you need to know what it is you are drinking. Then find the target number on the table below. Add one to the target number for each drink the character has beyond the first.

Now you need to find your drink threshold. Your character can consume one drink each hour for each point of constitution that the character has.

Roll your character's constitution dice against the target number. If you fail to score one success for each drink in excess of your drink threshold, your character starts feeling the effects of the alcohol. Once you start feeling the effects of alcohol, your target number is modified by your level of inebriation as well.

For example, a character with a constitution of 3 can drink 3 drinks each hour. He or she needs one success for every three drink he or she has had within the last hour. The target number is equal to the base target number for the type of alcohol plau the level of inebriation.

Type	Made From	Target Number
Beer	Cereals	1 - 2
Wine	Grapes & Other Fruits	1 - 3
Brandy	Fruit Juices	4 - 5
Whiskey	Cereals	4 - 6
Rum	Molasses / Sugars	4 - 6

Level One ("Smiley"): The character is drinking and their mood improves, but it has no notable effect on game play.

Level Two ("Friendly"): The character's attitude improves. He is considered to be on level better acquainted with anyone attempting to charm him or her either by magic or by skill. Consider any suggestion that isn't life threatening to be the equivalent of a charm spell and use the tables provided in the description of enchantment spells.

Level Three ("Charming"): At this level of drunkenness, not only does the character's attitude improve another step, but he or she *thinks* that everyone else's attitude has improved as well and acts accordingly.

Level Four ("Buzzed"): The character loses one dice from any coordination & quickness based skills he or she tries to use.

Level Five ("Feeling Good"): The character is at the line between feeling good and being drunk. Coordination & quickness based skills are reduced by another die (2 dice total). In addition, the character's psyche is reduced by one.

Level Six ("Drunk"): Now the alcohol is starting to have a serious impact on the character's actions. Coordination and quickness skills are reduced by another die (3 total). Psyche is reduced by another point as well (2 total). In addition, the character's reason & charisma related skills are reduced by one as well making communication with other people who aren't equally inebriated difficult. Conversing requires a reason test with a target number of 6 in order to communicate anything other than the simplest concepts.

Level Seven ("Hammered"): The character's coordination, quickness, reason, & charisma skills are reduced yet again. Psyche is also reduced again. Communications is still difficult and the target number is increased to 7.

Level Eight (Bombed): Now the character is feeling very, very good. Unfortunately, it's all in his head… and his liver. Coordination, quickness, reason, & charisma skills decrease yet again. Psyche also drops as well. The communication difficulty increases to 8 for complex ideas. Moreover, even simple communications becomes more difficult requiring a language test. Even more dangerous, once the character reaches this level of inebriation alcohol has started to block his or her pain receptors. They continue to take damage normally, but they have no idea how much damage they've taken.

Level Nine ("Shitfaced"): By this point, the character isn't feeling much of anything. Again the character's coordination, quickness, reason, & charisma based skills are reduced by another die. The character's psyche is also reduced again.

Level Ten ("BlackOut"): The character suffers another decrease to coordination, quickness, reason, & charisma skills and loses another point of psyche. The character still can't feel a damn thing, it doesn't really matter. The character isn't going to remember anything about the night anyway.

The levels of inebriation continue beyond level ten. By now you should have a good idea what effects it has on the character.

When your character's psyche drops to zero… he or she passes out. He or she can make a constitution test with a target number equal to the level of inebriation that caused him or her to fall unconscious. The character remains unconscious for 1 hour minus 5 minutes per success achieved on this test.

If the character regains consciousness, he or she is still drunk and doesn't get to start over from the beginning. The only thing that will "reset" the character's "drunk counter" is sleep.

If no successes are scored, then the character is out for the night and will remain asleep until he or she has gotten twice the normal amount of sleep required for a night.

Even once the character awakens, he or she is still in trouble. They must still deal with the hangover… which is a treat in and of itself.

The character awakens suffering from the effects of a night out on the town. The character has an inability to concentrate on anything for any length of time. Noises cause the character's head to pound with pain. He or she can only use 50% of his or her psyche & charisma until the hangover has passed. Furthermore, all skills receive only half of their dice pool. The character is irritable, uncoordinated, and sluggish.

These penalties continue for one hour for each level of inebriation the character made it to before passing out or going to sleep.

Racial Beverages

Different races specialize in different types of alcohol.

Dwarves, for example, excel at making beers and whiskeys. (Why whiskey you ask? Because some one some where decided that dwarves were Scottish.) Elves make some of the most exquisite wines in all of existence. Halflings are masters at maxing brandy.

Falling Damage

A falling character takes 1 point of damage per cumulative 10 feet fallen (i.e. 1 point for the first ten feet, 2 more points for the next ten feet, 3 points for the next ten feet.) The power of this attack is 3 plus the number of feet divided by 10 (i.e 4 at 10 feet, 5 at 2 feet). Armor does not reduce the power of a fall.

Feats of Strength

In the d10 system, you will not find a chart explaining how high your strength must be in order to lift a certain amount of weight. That's what strength tests are for.

First look for the strength score of the character on the table below. Then determine the amount of weight that the character can lift per success. Then have the character make a strength test against a target number of 5. Each success allows the character to lift the amount of weight listed.

For example, a character with a strength score of 3 is able to lift 300 pounds for every success he or she achieves on a strength test with a target number of 5.

Strength	Weight per Success
1	50
2	150
3	300
4	500
5	750
6	1050
7	1400
8	1800
9	2250
10	2750
11	3300
12	3900
13	4550
14	5250
15	6000

Notice of Criminal Indictment

By the Power Vested in Me by the Magistracy of the Empire, Endorcesd by the Minister of Justice of the Holy Empire, This Notice of Criminal Indictment is Hearby Registered Against

_____

On the Charge(s) of _____

_____

A Grievance of the _____ Order

Willfully and Maliciously instigated by the Accused on the Following Date and Time at the Indicated Location:

Date of Crime: _____
Time of Crime: _____
Place of Crime: _____

The Accused is Required to Appear in the Courtroom of the Honorable Magistrate _____ Within ____ Day(s) of Receiving This Notice.

Signed: _____
Deputy of the Court
Date: _____

Waiver of Liability

I, _____, do hereby state that I am a jackass of unprecedented proportions. I believe, against all rational thought and scientific evidence, that it is possible for a human being to successfully dodge a bullet and / or arrow fired at them by a compitent person with a high degree of proficiency and expertise in the use of said impliments. My arrogance goes so far that I have decided, for the first time in my life to put my own ass on the line to prove the foolish statements I have made at the gaming table.

Therefore, I authorize Erisian Entertainment, or the authorized agent thereof, to fire upon my person with the afore mentioned weapon so that I can demonstrate a level of natural ability thus far only attributed to superheroes which are completely fictional.
I realize that, in all likelihood, I will die as a result of these actions. Realizing that I an such an ignorant ass that I would better serve the whole of humanity by decomposing and possibly fertilizing a weed or two, I agree to hold Erisian Entertainment free of any liability that may result from my death. I further instruct my family and friends not to persue and civil action against this company. After all, they were kind enough to provide me with the scientific evidence that I would not survive well in advance.

Freely signed on this _____ Day of _____
in the year _____

_____   _____
Signature   Witness

INDEX

Actions, **176**
Active Skills, 137
Advantages, 145
Aerondale, 27, 28, 47
Aether, 79
Ailure, 79, 88, 142
Architecture, 15, 140
Artisans, 16, 26, 27, 29, 30, 31, 32, 33, 34, 35, 37, 38, 39, 41, 43, 44, 45, 46, 47, 48, 49, 50, 51, 52, 53, 54, 55, 56, 57, 58, 59
Belaris, 26, 27
Blood Vine, 21
Calydon, 27, 47
Camaysar, 28, 48, 76, 77
Canya, 46, 47, 48, 66
Carbonis Tree, 21
Casting, 140
Chaparran, 30, 31, 73
Character
    Concept, 84
    Creation, 84
    Improvement, 143
Chasmali, 29, 30, 58
Combat, 140, 151, 156, 175
Continere, 79
Creatures, 232
Crime, 61, 62, 63
    Capital, 62
    Contraventions, 62, 63
    Indictable, 62
    Summary, 62
Critical Failure, 137
Critical Success, 137
Cutharne, 41
Damage Bonus, 156
Damage Bonuses, 156
Damage Rating, 156
Damage Ratings, 156
Damage Type
    Ballistic, 157
    Impact, 157
    Slashing, 157
    Stun, 157
Damage Type Piercing, 157
De Veci, 33, 41, 58, 71
Deimism, 74, 79
Deimist, 37, 70, 71, 74, 79
Devecia, 33, 65, 66, 71
Director, 242
Disadvantage, 145
Dizalakia, 57
Dodging, 176, 177
Dolus Meretricis, 75, 77

Doves, 33, 70, 71
Duidan, 27, 31, 32, 55
Dwarf, 8, 9, 16, 20, 26, 27, 29, 30, 31, 32, 33, 34, 35, 36, 37, 38, 39, 41, 43, 44, 45, 46, 47, 48, 49, 50, 51, 52, 53, 54, 55, 56, 57, 58, 59, 141, 142, 167
Eating, 22
Education, 13, 14, 17, 18, 59, 147
Elbanin, 34, 35, 37, 56, 57
Elements, 5
    Boom, 13
    Orange, 13, 14
    Prickle-Prickle, 13, 14
    Pungent, 13
    Sweet, 13
Elf, 20, 26, 27, 29, 30, 31, 32, 33, 34, 35, 37, 38, 39, 41, 43, 44, 45, 46, 47, 48, 49, 50, 51, 52, 53, 54, 55, 56, 57, 58, 59, 80, 167
Emperor, 1, 3, 13, 15, 16, 17, 18, 30, 31, 32, 33, 36, 37, 41, 43, 45, 49, 51, 52, 53, 54, 55, 56, 58, 59, 61, 62, 63, 65, 69, 71, 72, 73, 74, 75, 81, 139
Empire, 1, 11, 13, 14, 15, 16, 17, 18, 19, 20, 21, 23, 26, 27, 30, 31, 32, 33, 35, 36, 37, 38, 39, 41, 44, 45, 46, 47, 48, 49, 50, 52, 57, 58, 59, 60, 61, 62, 63, 65, 66, 67, 69, 70, 71, 72, 73, 74, 75, 77, 80, 88, 140, 142, 147, 151, 155, 156
Entertainment, 15, 20, 185
Equipment, 156, 167
    Techno-magical, 167
Eris, ii, 5, 6, 7, 8, 9, 10, 11, 12, 13, 14, 16, 17, 18, 22, 56, 61, 67, 68, 69, 79, 80, 137, 141
Eristocracy, 13, 16, 17, 18, 26, 30, 31, 38, 56, 59, 61, 62, 67, 79, 141
Exardonia, 53, 54
Experience Points, 246
    Improving your character, 143
Freemen, 15, 18, 26, 27, 29, 30, 31, 32, 33, 34, 35, 37, 38, 39, 41, 43, 44, 45, 46, 47, 48, 49, 50, 51, 52, 53, 54, 55, 56, 57, 58, 59
Gadbians, 71, 72, 77
Ghost Wood, 22
Grievance, 73
Halfling, 20, 26, 27, 29, 30, 31, 32, 33, 34, 35, 37, 38, 39, 41, 43, 44, 45, 46, 47, 48, 49, 50, 51, 52, 53, 54, 55, 56, 57, 58, 59, 80
Healing, 186, 187
Holidays, 14
Honblas, 35, 38
Human, 20
Humans, 26, 27, 29, 30, 31, 32, 33, 34, 35, 37, 38, 39, 41, 43, 44, 45, 46, 47, 48, 49, 50, 51, 52, 53, 54, 55, 56, 57, 58, 59
Imperial Military, 21, 65, 140
Improvement
    Character, 143
Initiative, 18, 59, 175

Kadoch, 36, 41
Kargrave, 36, 37, 41
Keroon, 36, 37
Khembryl, 35, 36, 38, 39, 41, 49, 56
Khymbria, 35, 39, 46, 47, 75, 140
Knights of the Temple of Eris, 67, 80
Knowledge Skills, 140
Kolopan, 46, 48, 51, 65
Lecabel, 42, 43
Lecabela, 43
Legions, 3, 65
Magic, 13, 19, 140, 148, 151, 154, 191, 248
    Casting, 140
    Laws, 191
Malaclypse, iii, 6, 9, 11, 12, 14, 80
Maldinach, 44
Malgrin, 43
Malinova, 29, 30, 58, 66
Markesh, 45, 47, 53
Markune, 44
MErelan, 45
Millikan, 47
Ministries, 13, 59, 71, 77
Molikroth, 47
Money, 18
Mytheria, 48
Mytherie, 48
Naergoth, 38, 50, 52, 65
Nasredin, 49, 59
Navy, 3, 65, 156
Nefar, 13, 16, 35, 36, 38, 41, 43, 49, 56, 61, 72, 75
Nerilka, 51
Nezathar, 52
Nobility, 16
Noble Peerage, 26, 80
Oberlan, 47
Orc, 80
Orders of Grievance, 61, 63, 73
Organization
    Dolus Meretricis, 75, 77
    Templars, 67, 80
    Watchful Order of Mages, 77
    Watchmen, 69
Organizations, 65
    Doves, 33, 70, 71
    Gadbians, 71, 72, 77
    Teksarian Rangers, 31, 33, 60, 73, 75
Orthodox Church of Eris, 13, 16, 17, 18, 22, 62, 67, 68, 69, 79, 80, 141
Parrying, 176, 177
Petiron, 50, 52
Pleroma, 58
Polyfather, 17, 38, 67, 68, 80
Province, 61, 143, 151, 155
Range Increments, 156
Restoria, 49
Royalty, 16
Rule of Five, 137
Rule of Nine, 137
Rule of Zero, 137
Saerlan, 48, 51
Skill Test
    Direct, 136

Skill Tests
    Open, 136
    Parallel, 136, 142
    Unskilled, 136
Skills
    Concentration, 137, 143
    Specialization, 143
Smoke Tree, 21, 22
Social Class
    Artisan, 16
    Artisans, 26, 27, 29, 30, 31, 32, 33, 34, 35, 37, 38, 39, 41, 43, 44, 45, 46, 47, 48, 49, 50, 51, 52, 53, 54, 55, 56, 57, 58, 59
    Freemen, 15, 18, 26, 27, 29, 30, 31, 32, 33, 34, 35, 37, 38, 39, 41, 43, 44, 45, 46, 47, 48, 49, 50, 51, 52, 53, 54, 55, 56, 57, 58, 59
    Thralls, 15, 17, 26, 27, 29, 30, 31, 32, 33, 34, 35, 37, 38, 39, 41, 43, 44, 45, 46, 47, 48, 49, 50, 51, 52, 53, 54, 55, 56, 57, 58, 59
Spells, 151
    Casting, 140
Spending Experience Points, 143
Sugar Stalk, 24
Suidae Verruca, 13, 20, 35, 38, 192
Summoning, 140
Syandar, 29, 48, 76
Sylaire, 38
Tax, 19
Taxes, 19
Teg, 79, 120, 128
Teksaria, 31, 69, 73
Teksarian Rangers, 31, 33, 60, 73, 75
Telantis, 54, 55, 57
Teldevar, 53
Templars, 67, 80
Tessadyl, 53, 54, 72
Thralls, 15, 17, 26, 27, 29, 30, 31, 32, 33, 34, 35, 37, 38, 39, 41, 43, 44, 45, 46, 47, 48, 49, 50, 51, 52, 53, 54, 55, 56, 57, 58, 59
Time, 12
    Days, 11, 14
Tributarial, 61, 80, 151, 155
Tserakhar, 56
Undead
    Lich, 41
Valermos, 55
Valindar, 56, 57
Valturis, 56
Vandal Nefar, 13, 16, 36, 38, 41, 43, 49, 50, 52, 56, 61, 72, 75
Vassago, 56
Vathek, 57
Von Rohm, 57, 58
Watchful Order of Mages, 77
Watchmen, 69
Weapon
    Damage, 156
Weapons
    Blunt, 157
    Edged, 138, 158
    Hand-to-Hand, 157
    Polearms, 159
    Qualities, 156
    Range – Ammunition, 161
    Ranged, 160
Zarthen, 52